Barbara CARTLAND

*Three Complete Novels of
Dukes and Their Ladies*

Barbara Cartland: 5 Complete Novels
Moon Over Eden
No Time for Love
The Incredible Honeymoon
Kiss the Moonlight
A Kiss in Rome

Barbara Cartland: 3 Complete Novels
A Night of Gaiety
A Duke in Danger
Secret Harbor

Barbara Cartland: 3 Complete Novels
Lights, Laughter and a Lady
Love in the Moon
Bride to the King

Barbara Cartland: 5 Complete Novels
of Dukes and Their Ladies
A Fugitive From Love
Lucifer and the Angel
The River of Love
The Wings of Ecstasy
A Shaft of Sunlight

Barbara Cartland: 3 Complete Novels
of Earls and Their Ladies
A Gentleman in Love
Gift of the Gods
Music From the Heart

Barbara Cartland: 3 Complete Novels
of Marquises and Their Ladies
Ola and the Sea Wolf
Looking for Love
The Call of the Highlands

Barbara Cartland: 3 Complete Novels
of Royalty and Romance
Song of Love
Revenge of the Heart
A Witch's Spell

Barbara CARTLAND

Three Complete Novels of
Dukes and Their Ladies

The Disgraceful Duke

Never Laugh at Love

A Touch of Love

WINGS BOOKS
New York • Avenel, New Jersey

This omnibus was originally published in separate volumes under the titles:

The Disgraceful Duke, copyright © 1976 by Barbara Cartland.
Never Laugh at Love, copyright © 1976 by Barbara Cartland.
A Touch of Love, copyright © 1978 by Barbara Cartland.

This edition contains the complete and unabridged texts of the original editions. They have been completely reset for this volume.

This 1996 edition is published by Wings Books,
a division of Random House Value Publishing, Inc.,
40 Engelhard Avenue, Avenel, New Jersey 07001,
by arrangement with the author.

Wings Books and colophon are registered trademarks of Random House Value Publishing, Inc.

Random House
New York ● Toronto ● London ● Sydney ● Auckland

Printed and bound in the United States of America

Library of Congress Cataloging-in-Publication Data

Cartland, Barbara, 1902–
    Three complete novels of dukes and their ladies / Barbara Cartland.
        p.   cm.
    Contents: The disgraceful duke—Never laugh at love—A touch of love.
    ISBN 0-517-15046-8 (pbk.)
    1. Man-woman relationships—Great Britain—Fiction. 2. Nobility—Great Britain—Fiction. 3. Historical fiction, English. 4. Love stories, English.   I. Title.
PR6005.A765A6   1996b
823′.912—dc20   95-47626
                                                            CIP

8   7   6   5   4   3   2   1

CONTENTS

THE DISGRACEFUL
DUKE

Author's Note

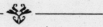

The Theatre Royal, Drury Lane, continued to be unlucky until 1809, when it was destroyed by fire—the
blaze lit all London.

Richard Brinsley Sheridan was faced with utter ruin
as the building was under-insured.

The theatre was rebuilt and opened in October
1811, and is the Drury Lane we know today. It is the
theatre of Edward Kean—the greatest Shylock of all
time—of Elliston, Macready, Dan Leno, Sir Johnstone
Forbes-Robertson and Sir Henry Irving.

From Nell Gwynne to Ivor Novello, Drury Lane
stands alone, no other city in the world has its rival.

It is part of our history and as long as London lasts
there will always be a part of it known as "The Theatre
Royal, Drury Lane."

CHAPTER ONE

1803

"*H*ow do you feel, Papa?"

"I will—be all—right," Beau Bardsley gasped.

But as he spoke he sank down on his chair in the dressing-room and stared at his face in the mirror with an expression almost of despair.

Shimona hovered behind him uncertain what she should do.

The fit of coughing which had racked her father in the passage after they had entered the Stage Door seemed to have sapped his strength to the point of exhaustion.

Without speaking, Joe Hewitt—Beau Bardsley's dresser—brought his master a glass of brandy mixed with water, and set it down on the dressing-table beside the grease-paint, the salves, the powder-puffs and the hare's foot.

To lift it to his lips Beau Bardsley had to employ both hands.

After a few sips the spirit seemed to revive him and in a very different voice he said to his daughter:

"You should not have come here with me."

"I do not intend to leave you, Papa," Shimona replied firmly. "You know as well as I do that you ought not to be performing to-day."

Beau Bardsley did not reply and they both knew the answer without having to put it into words.

He had to work.

Not only did he require his salary to keep them alive, but it was also only a question of a week or so before the management of the Theatre Royal, Drury Lane would consider he was due for a benefit.

Beau Bardsley drew his watch from his waistcoat pocket with a shaking hand.

"You've plenty of time, Mr. Bardsley," Joe Hewitt said in a soothing tone, as if he fancied his master was worrying about it.

Beau Bardsley gave a deep sigh.

They all knew that in his present state it would require considerable physical effort on his part to get into the clothes he wore as Hamlet.

There was one blessing, however, Shimona thought to herself.

Her father had played the part so often that it was no effort for him to remember his lines, and once he faced the footlights he would be inspired as he always was by the applause and adulation of his admirers.

At this moment the Theatre Royal Drury Lane was filling up with an audience who acclaimed Beau Bardsley as one of the finest actors "Old Drury" had ever known.

They came to see him even though at the moment the theatre itself had fallen on hard times.

Mrs. Sarah Siddons, who had reigned there as the undisputed Queen for twenty-one years, had left London to rest. When she returned, it was to the stage at Covent Garden.

There was an almost insurmountable difficulty in finding an actress capable of taking her place.

But as long as Beau Bardsley was billed, the audience flocked in. Unfortunately his health often prevented him from honouring his commitments.

He put out his hand now to pick up the grease-stick

and as he did so he could see Shimona reflected in the mirror.

"You should not have come here," he said again. "You know I do not allow you to be seen in the theatre."

"Joe can keep your visitors away," Shimona replied with a smile. "Besides, Papa, you must rest between acts and not make the effort to entertain anybody."

"I always promised your mother that you should have nothing to do with the theatre," Beau Bardsley said.

"And we will always do as Mama wished," Shimona replied, "but I know she would not have wanted me to leave you when you are as ill as you are now."

She looked at her father again and said in a low voice:

"Would you not be wiser to cancel the performance before it begins?"

There was every reason for her apprehension, for Beau Bardsley's handsome face was almost devoid of colour, his lips were bloodless and he seemed to have difficulty in lifting his eye-lids.

"I have to go on," he said almost savagely. "For God's sake, Joe, give me some more brandy!"

The dresser snatched up the empty glass and hurried to the side of the room where there was a grog-table loaded with bottles and a large number of glasses.

Shimona knew only too well how much of her father's money was expended on entertaining the social personalities who fawned on him.

But he also played host to members of the cast whom he felt were in need of a stimulant and to whom he was always ready to extend an overgenerous hand.

At least three quarters of Beau Bardsley's salary every week, his daughter reckoned, was given away to those who spun him a hard-luck story or who were genuinely in need.

There were many in the profession who blessed him

for saving them from the gutter, from starvation, or from prison.

Because he had once played with them on the stage, or because they had a common interest, Beau Bardsley would feed, clothe and pay the debts of any impoverished actor or actress who begged him for help.

Those who had suffered in consequence had of course been his own wife and daughter.

Despite all the years he had worked and commanded a high salary, he had no savings left. Every penny had been spent and the bulk of it on other actors.

Yet looking at him now Shimona knew that she would not have her father any different.

Even when he was ill, even when it was an effort for him even to speak, he still had a magic quality about him.

It was his glamour which kept the audiences spellbound, and his deep resonant voice had a quality which seemed to draw the very hearts of those who listened.

The second glass of brandy brought a faint flush to Beau Bardsley's cheeks, and as the dresser deftly removed his coat and waist-coat he began with a hand which gradually became more steady to apply the grease-paint to his handsome countenance.

The son of a curate at Bath Abbey, Beau Bardsley, who had been christened Beaugrave, ran away when he was sixteen to go on the stage.

He had been obsessed by the theatre, which in Bath had reached the heights of distinction when it was honoured by being the first theatre outside London to be granted the title "Royal."

The actors and actresses who made their reputations there had no more eager and enthusiastic admirer than the clergyman's son.

After some years of playing small parts in the London theatres, including Drury Lane, Beau Bardsley had returned to his native town.

His father had been appointed to a living in another part of the country, and the theatre was filled with young and enthusiastic actors who were to become some of the greatest in the land.

John Henderson, who after five years at Bath went to London as David Garrick's natural successor, became one of England's leading actors.

He in his turn had been much struck by a young actress whom he had seen performing in Birmingham, and he recommended her to the Directors of the Bath Theatre, who engaged her.

As she had recently been dismissed by Garrick after a few unsuccessful months at Drury Lane, she was glad to have the chance to get before a fashionable audience, and this time she was no failure.

Sarah Siddons' debut in Bath was a triumph!

She was a phenomenal success, particularly in tragic roles.

Being a woman and an extremely intelligent one, she looked around to find actors who would enhance her own performance and intensify the glamour she exuded whenever she appeared behind the footlights.

It was therefore not surprising that she looked very favorably on the compellingly handsome Beau Bardsley.

Sarah Siddons was to be the greatest tragic actress of the English stage.

She was beautiful and she had an excellent figure, but these attributes were unimportant beside the power she could exert over an audience.

Beau Bardsley had been with her when in 1782 she had returned to the scene of her failure—The Theatre Royal Drury Lane.

He had often told Shimona what happened.

"When Mrs. Siddons went on the stage at rehearsal she was in a state of panic," he related. "But gradually the play—*Isabelle, or The Fatal Marriage*—took hold of her and as it continued many of the company were in tears."

"She was so convincing in her death-bed scene," Beau Bardsley went on, "that her own eight-year-old son Henry, who was playing the part of her son in the play was actually deceived into believing that his mother had really died. He howled the place down until she finished the scene and comforted him."

"Tell me about the first night, Papa," Shimona would beg, even though she had heard the story over and over again.

Beau Bardsley would laugh.

"The audience were nearly drowned in tears," he replied, "and long before the final scene there was frenzied applause."

He smiled as he continued:

"I think we were all stunned by the ovation and Mrs. Siddons was too overcome to speak the Epilogue. She could only bow to a storm of cheers."

For the next one and twenty years Beau Bardsley had appeared in practically every important production in which Sarah Siddons played the lead.

But now she had gone and, although he could fill the theatre which had been re-built nine years earlier, he was at nearly fifty years of age almost too ill to carry on.

Shimona watched her father anxiously as, his make-up finished, he rose to his feet and went behind the brown linen curtain at the back of the room to change into his clothes for the First Act.

The new theatre had cost over £220,000 and had been designed by Holland, the architect of Carlton House. The dressing rooms were certainly a great improvement on the discomfort, dirt and darkness of the old one.

Old Drury had been in a shocking state, having stood for 117 years since 1674.

But Shimona used to love hearing tales of what it had been like when her father first played there.

Then it had been easy to imagine Nell Gwynne selling oranges at 6d a fruit to the Gallants; Samuel Pepys the diarist ogling the women; and Charles II and his mistresses filling the Royal Box.

The audience would wander all over the stage and behind the scenes. There were "Fobs" who preened themselves and "Vizards" who were ladies of the town disguised by black masks.

"Garrick drove the people from the stage," Beau Bardsley told his daughter, "but it was shove and push outside the pit entrance for hours before the doors opened."

"What happened then, Papa?" Shimona would ask.

"Men used their fists, the weakest were trampled underfoot, the pickpockets reaped a rich harvest!"

Beau Bardsley had performed in the last play at the old Theatre, called "The Country Girl" and he was in Macbeth with Mrs. Siddons when the new Playhouse was opened on 21st April 1794.

The house was packed on that occasion, but it had not proved a lucky building, and Richard Brinsley Sheridan was, everyone knew, deeply in debt.

Shimona later had much admired the new Playhouse from a box where her mother had taken her to watch her father perform although they were forbidden to enter the Stage Door.

Certainly it was spacious and lofty.

There were four tiers and the boxes were on the lines of an Opera House, but Holland had thought more of appearance than of the convenience of the audience.

It was found that the Gallery was too high and so far away that its occupants had difficulty in hearing the actors and the eight boxes on the stage itself and the eight on either side of the Pit were no use at all.

But the total capacity of the new Theatre Royal was 3,611 and in money £826.6s.Od.

It certainly had many modern requirements. There was even a fire-resistant curtain made of iron.

This, Beau Bardsley told Shimona, had been undoubtedly the star attraction of the opening nights and it aroused an already excited audience to a wild enthusiasm.

"Somebody struck it heavily with a large hammer," he told her, "to demonstrate its strength and solidity."

"What happened then, Papa?" Shimona would ask, though she knew the end of the story perfectly well.

"When it was raised," her father replied, "the audience was thrilled by the sight of a cascade of water rushing down from tanks in the roof and roaring into a huge basin where it splashed and rumbled over artificial rocks."

"It must have been exciting!"

"It was!" her father agreed, "and when a man appeared in a boat and rowed about, the audience could scarcely contain itself!"

It was only when she grew older that Shimona realised that what Sheridan had called his "Grand National Theatre" was unlucky from the very beginning, mostly owing to the disastrous condition of his finances.

From the highest to the lowest, payment of employees was spasmodic and there were constant strikes.

Good actors were sacked because they demanded their overdue wages and their places were filled by inferior players.

On Saturday mornings the actors would besiege Sheridan's room.

"For God's sake, Mr. Sheridan," they would cry, "pay us our salaries. Let us have something this week!"

If he was there, he would turn on his charm and faithfully promise that he would pay what he owed them, then vanish by another door.

Only Shimona and her mother knew how much Beau Bardsley gave away to the poorest actors and staff, and how they suffered in consequence.

They had to forgo the little luxuries and even the good food to which they should have been entitled through the success that Beau Bardsley had achieved with the London audiences.

That he never worried was no answer to the problem and yet, like those who watched him play his parts, they adored him, and his wife found it impossible even to grumble at the extravagant manner in which he helped others.

There was a sudden loud knock on the dressing-room door.

"Five minutes, Mr. Bardsley!" the call-boy shouted.

Then Shimona could hear him hurrying down the stone passage, hammering on every dressing-room door and repeating his parrot-cry.

Her father came from behind the curtain and she looked at him anxiously. But, as so often had happened, the atmosphere of the theatre was beginning to lift him out of himself.

Already he seemed to carry his shoulders straighter, his chin was higher and his eyes were alight with that irresistible magic which held the audience spell-bound.

His costume became him and his thinness, which at times was pitiably obvious in his ordinary clothes, made him, behind the footlights, look like the young boy he was portraying.

He walked to the dressing-table, applied a little more rouge to his face with the hare's foot and touched up the corners of his eyes.

"You look very handsome, Papa!"

It was something Shimona had said to him ever since she was a small child and he smiled at her with great tenderness before he replied:

"You will stay here while I am on the stage and Joe is not to open the door to anybody."

"I'll see she's all right, Sir," Joe Hewitt promised.

"Two minutes, Mr. Bardsley!"

The call-boy's shrill voice accompanied by his knock on the door seemed to lift the last remaining remnants of Beau Bardsley's exhaustion from him.

He gave a last glance at himself in the mirror, then turned toward the door.

"Good luck, Papa!"

13

He smiled at Shimona again, then he was gone and she heard him speaking in his deep voice to several people outside in the passage as they made their way towards the stage.

She wished she could be at the front of the house to see him performing one of his most memorable roles, which invariably had evoked paeans of praise from the critics.

One critic had written the previous week:

"I have run out of complimentary adjectives where Beau Bardsley is concerned."

And the *Morning Chronicle* had said:

"The man ceases to be human as soon as he appears, and he manages to transport himself and his audience to the foothills of Olympus!"

Shimona rose from the red plush sofa on which she had been sitting and automatically began to tidy her father's dressing-table.

There was a miniature of her mother which he carried with him always; painted by Richard Cosway, it was, Shimona thought, an almost perfect likeness.

She looked so beautiful, so young and happy, and it seemed impossible to think that she was dead and they would never see her again.

Cosway had made her large eyes shine with the adoring light that had always been in them when she looked at her husband, and her fair hair had strange shadows which were faithfully portrayed against the soft blue background.

Holding the miniature in her hand Shimona looked down at it with the pain in her heart that came whenever she thought of her mother.

How was it possible that she had died so suddenly and so quickly that they had not even realised she was ill until she was gone from them?

"We were always thinking of Papa," Shimona told herself now, "and we did not realise that Mama needed attention until it was too late!"

She felt an inescapable sense of loss stab her like a physical wound.

As she returned the miniature once again to its hook in the velvet case, she glanced at her own reflection in the mirror and saw how closely she resembled her mother in looks.

She had the same pale shadowy fair hair, the same large eyes, the same oval forehead, the same softly curved lips.

There was also something of her father's looks in Shimona's face.

His Grecian profile seemed somehow to give him a spirituality which was seldom seen upon the stage and it also made his daughter seem different from other young women of her age.

She was lovely, there was no doubt about that!

There was also something unique about her, which was one of the reasons why Beau Bardsley kept her away from the people who frequented his dressing-room at Drury Lane and who, although he called them his friends, he never invited to his home.

Beau had always kept his family life strictly private from the moment he had caused one of the greatest scandals that Bath had ever known.

Because of it he had been determined not to expose his wife to the familiarity and the free and easy morals of the theatre world.

It was when he was playing some of his last parts at Bath with Mrs. Siddons before they both went to London, that Beau Bardsley had noticed a girl in a stage-box.

It was not surprising that he became aware of her, for she was there day after day. She was usually accompanied in the afternoon by a maid or footman and in the evening by an elderly couple whom he learnt later were her father and mother.

There were plenty of people in Bath to tell him about Annabel Winslow.

Her beauty had taken the fashionable society which congregated in the Assembly Rooms by storm.

She was fêted and sought after by the Dandies and Bucks of eligible age and she was adulated by the elderly noblemen who found her manners as charming as her appearance.

All Bath appeared to be delighted when Annabel's engagement was announced to Lord Powell, a gentleman whose wealth and distinction had already impressed itself upon the pleasure-seeking visitors to the famous Spa.

He had come to Bath because he was suffering with rheumatism in his legs, but after one look at Annabel his rheumatism was forgotten and he lost his heart!

Lord Powell's was undoubtedly the most important offer of marriage Annabel had received and her father, Sir Harvey Winslow, lost no time in accepting on her behalf.

But no-one realised that, if Lord Powell had lost his heart, Annabel had also lost hers.

Her parents had not concerned themselves with her passion for the theatre. After all, it was good for her education to listen to Shakespeare's plays, and Mrs. Siddons as Lady MacBeth and Desdemona was the talk of the Pump Room.

Sir Harvey and Lady Winslow also thought her excellent in Garrick's version of Hamlet and they did not notice particularly the actor who played the name-part.

They were therefore stupefied with astonishment, as indeed was the rest of Bath, when Annabel ran away with Beau Bardsley. When Mrs. Siddons left for London and Drury Lane, Annabel and Beau followed her.

Sir Harvey cut his daughter off with the proverbial shilling and returned to his Estates in Dorset, saying that he never wished to hear of her again.

Annabel was, however, supremely and utterly happy with the man she had chosen for her husband, and when Shimona was born in 1785 she thought it would be difficult for any woman to be more blessed than she had been.

From the time they married there was never another breath of scandal where Beau Bardsley was concerned.

It was to be expected that he would be pursued by women of every sort and kind; but while he was always courteous and pleasant, they found him elusive and impossible to meet outside the theatre.

As soon as a performance was over he went back to the little house in Chelsea where he lived with Annabel and Shimona and craved no other company but theirs.

Perhaps it was the puritanical streak in him which he had inherited from his clergyman father, or maybe a sense of guilt at his own shortcomings towards his parents that made him ultra-strict with Shimona.

She had no idea that her life was different from that of other children or that she and her mother might have been living on a desert island for all the contact they had with other people.

From the moment Beau Bardsley left his home to the moment he returned there was always a feverish activity to get everything ready for him, to make his home-coming a perfect one.

From the time she was a tiny child Shimona was told "you must not bother your father," "you must not upset him," "you must not worry him," and her whole object in life therefore was to make him happy.

The only amusement that was permitted outside the ordinary round of her life at home was when she and her mother went to the theatre to see her father in each new role.

It was then he seemed to her to be a very different person from the man who held her on his knee to kiss and fondle her.

On the stage her father became a Knight like those of whom she read in story-books.

There was something inspiring and spiritual about him too, which made him seem almost like the angels in which she had believed ever since her mother had taught her to say her prayers.

If the audiences worshipped Beau Bardsley for his looks and the magical hours of pleasure he gave them, his daughter worshipped him because to her he was everything that was fine and noble personified in one man.

Beau Bardsley had, despite his father's poverty, been well educated.

He had been accepted in private schools at reduced rates because his father was a clergyman and the parts he played also gave him a command of the English language and a knowledge of history which he imparted to his daughter.

Although she never went to school and never competed with other children, Shimona was far better educated than was considered necessary for the average girl at that time.

In fact through her father's tuition she received to all intents and purposes a boy's education, while her mother imparted the accomplishments which were considered obligatory for a well-bred young woman.

When her mother died Shimona experienced a loneliness that she had never encountered before.

Now there were long days at home when there was nothing to do but talk to her old Nurse and await her father's return.

Because she was lonely and because time often hung heavy on her hands she started to read the newspapers and enjoy all the anecdotes and gossip that her father brought home in the evenings.

Whereas before her death, Beau Bardsley had talked with his wife about the problems and quarrels of the theatre and about those who visited his dressing-room with their scandal and gossip, he now talked to Shimona.

She had always been excluded in the past from anything that appertained to the outside world, but now, because his wife was no longer beside him, Beau allowed Shimona to take her place.

For almost the first time, Shimona at eighteen, began to realise that she was missing something.

She heard about Balls, Assemblies, Receptions, great parties at Carlton House, dinner at Almack's Club where one had to receive a voucher from one of the distinguished hostesses before being admitted.

"Will I ever be able to go to a Ball, Papa?" she asked Beau one evening.

He had returned from the theatre to tell Shimona how he had refused an invitation to a party at the Duke of Richmond's at which the Prince of Wales was to be present.

Beau Bardsley looked at his daughter as if he saw her for the first time.

She was very lovely in a muslin gown with its high waist outlining the soft curves of her breasts, and her skin was very white against the red velvet chair on which she was sitting.

In fact she looked so lovely that he drew in his breath as he remembered that his wife Annabel had looked almost exactly the same when they had first met.

"A Ball, my dearest?" he repeated, his thoughts elsewhere.

"Yes, Papa. Have you forgotten that I am eighteen? Mama told me about the Ball that was given for her when she made her début, and I would so love to go to one myself."

Beau Bardsley stared at her for a long time, then he said:

"It is impossible!"

"Why?" Shimona enquired.

He rose to his feet to walk across the room as if he was finding words in which to answer her and finally he said:

"You might as well face the truth. The *Beau Monde* invite me to their houses because I am a celebrity—a

celebrity but merely an actor. It amuses them to condescend to those who have reached the top of their profession."

His voice sharpened as he went on:

"But while they will accept me, their wives and
daughters would not accept my wife and daughter."

"Why not, Papa?"

"Because an actor can never be the social equal of
those of noble birth. Because I am what I have made
myself—you must suffer."

Shimona gazed at him wide-eyed before she said
hesitatingly:

"Although you are an actor, you are a . . . gentleman, Papa. Your father was a Canon before he died
. . . Mama told me so."

"My father was ashamed of me," Beau Bardsley replied. "He planned that I should enter the Church. He
envisaged me inspiring a congregation with my ora-
tory from the pulpit."

He smiled a little wryly.

"I doubt if my congregation would ever have filled
Drury Lane."

"And the Winslows were a County family and much
respected in Dorset," Shimona persisted.

"And how often have you been asked to stay with
your grandfather and grandmother?" Beau Bardsley
asked.

There was a long silence.

"I think . . . I understand."

"If I was meant to be punished for running away
with your mother and being given the greatest happiness any man could ever know on earth, it is now,"
Beau Bardsley said, "because, my dearest, I cannot
give you all the things I would wish to."

Shimona had run into his arms.

"You are not to think about it, Papa. I am happy,
terribly happy just to be with you. Do you think I
worry about Balls when I can watch you on the stage
and we can be together when you come home?"

Beau Bardsley had not replied. He merely bent his head and kissed his daughter on the cheek.

Then he said almost beneath his breath:

"The Bible is right. The sins of the father *are* visited upon the children."

Shimona had heard the pain in her father's voice, and never again had she mentioned the fashionable world or the irrepressible longing she felt at times to be part of it. But she listened even more intently to her father's stories.

Every evening when he returned home, while he ate his supper she would ask who had visited him in his dressing-room and who was in the principal Boxes in the theatre.

She also coaxed him into telling her stories about the social personalities of the *Beau Monde.*

It was not that she wished to listen to scandal; it was just that she was curious about the people who lived in the world outside the little house in Chelsea, who were very much less real to her than the characters of Shakespeare or those whom she loved in Sheridan's "School for Scandal."

Sir Peter Teazle, Sir Benjamin Backbite and Sir Harry Bumper all meant much more in her life than the Prince of Wales and the Bucks and Dandies who accompanied him when he occupied the Royal Box at Drury Lane.

When she visited the theatre, Shimona would look around her and try to identify some of the people about whom her father talked.

Now as she waited in the dressing-room she heard the applause beginning to roar out like distant thunder, and rising to her feet she opened the door so that it came to her in great waves of sound.

She knew that once again her father's magic had infected the audience to the point where they would be rising in their seats, clapping and cheering him as he took bow after bow.

She stood in the open doorway and looked down the

long passage which was dimly lit by candles in wooden sconces.

It was then Shimona remembered that the other actors also would be returning to their dressing-rooms and quickly shut the door.

Her father came in followed by Joe who had been waiting for him in the wings. Now his cheeks were flushed and there was a light in his eyes which was always there after a particularly successful performance.

"They loved you, Papa!"

"It went well," Beau Bardsley answered.

He turned toward his dressing-table and as he did so he was suddenly seized by a fit of coughing.

It was as if it had been held back for so long that now it was a paroxysm that racked his whole frame so that he coughed and coughed until it seemed that the very sound of it must tear him in pieces.

Joe and Shimona helped him to the chair, and when finally the spasm ceased the sweat was pouring down Beau Bardsley's forehead and his eyes were closed.

He was shaking and once again it was a glass of brandy and water that revived him.

This time Shimona knew that Joe had made it stronger even than it had been before.

It was an effort to get her father changed in time and an almost superhuman effort, she was well aware, for him to obey the call-boy's voice as he shouted imperiously:

"One minute, Mr. Bardsley!"

There was a note of rebuke because the leading actor was not already in the wings.

Joe went with his master to the stage, then came back.

"He's bad, Miss Shimona!" he said abruptly as he came into the dressing-room.

"I know, Joe, but he will not rest. I begged him not to come to-day."

"He'll kill himself, Miss Shimona. You mark my words!"

Shimona stifled a little cry which came to her lips.

"The Doctor said the same . . . thing, but he will not . . . listen and . . . and he has to work."

"I understands, Miss."

"You have been with him for so many years, Joe. You know as well as I do that he has never saved a penny."

"I knows, Miss, and on Saturday morning they'll be around him like hawks. I often thinks as how he never touches his wages himself. So many other fingers are digging at it."

"If he can keep going a little . . . longer he will get a . . . benefit," Shimona said.

"He's due for one, Lord knows!" Joe said, "but the theatre ain't doing well except when the master's playing, an' I has a feeling the management thinks that if he gets a benefit he might go off on a holiday."

"That is exactly what he ought to do," Shimona replied. "The Doctor said only yesterday that he should go to a warmer climate for the winter. It will be November soon and he will never stand the fogs and the cold winds."

They looked at each other anxiously and then, as if he could not bring himself to speak of it any more, Joe said:

"I'm taking a glass of brandy to the stage. If he has another coughing fit it's the only thing that'll enable him to carry on."

Shimona did not answer. She only sat down on the sofa again.

The future seemed bleak. She wondered what her mother would have done.

She looked across the small dressing-room at the miniature standing on the dressing-table.

"Oh, Mama," she whispered, "help us. How can Papa go on like this? Joe says he will kill himself and then what will happen to me? Please, Mama, please help us! You must know the trouble we are in."

She felt the tears come into her eyes as she spoke.

Then because she was afraid that her father might notice if she cried, she quickly wiped them away.

Shimona could never bear to remember how distraught he had been when her mother died. At times she thought he would go insane, and because she had to give him her strength she had never let herself cry in front of him.

Sometimes she thought it was all that sustained him, all that had prevented him from collapsing completely.

There was another long wait. Then at last she heard the applause break out and knew that the play had ended.

"I must get Papa home as quickly as possible," she told herself. "Joe can call us a carriage which will be waiting at the door and Nanna will have supper ready. Then he must go straight to bed."

She wondered if it would be wiser for him not to change but to go home as he was.

Her father was always very fastidious about his appearance, but there would be nobody to see him and his long grey cloak would conceal the velvet costume he wore as Hamlet.

"I am sure that would be wise," Shimona decided.

Now the noise in the distance was gradually subsiding and she heard the voices of the actors outside in the passage. Then she heard her father say:

"If you will just wait a moment, Your Grace, I will look and see if the dressing-room is tidy."

"My dear Bardsley, I have been in enough dressing-rooms not to worry whether they are tidy or not," came the reply.

Shimona knew immediately that her father was saying this to warn her that he had a visitor, and rising she quickly slipped behind the curtain as the door opened.

"As I might have expected," she heard an amused voice remark, "your dressing-room is a model of neatness, and certainly there are no suspicious petticoats about!"

"No, Your Grace,"

Beau Bardsley spoke abruptly as if he resented the insinuation.

"I know you want to get home, Bardsley," his visitor went on. "I am well aware how you hate to hang about after the performance is over, but I have to see you—I need your help."

Beau Bardsley gave a light laugh.

"My help? How can I possibly be of help to the Duke of Ravenstone?"

Shimona listening knew that her father was in his own fashion informing her who was present, and at the same time warning her that she must on no account reveal her presence.

She had heard him speak of the Duke of Ravenstone, and everything he had said about him came to her mind as she listened intently.

"Will you have a drink, Your Grace?"

"No, thank you."

Shimona realised without being able to see him that the Duke had seated himself on the sofa she had just vacated.

"I will come straight to the point," he said. "I need an actress . . ."

"Then you have come to the wrong man, Your Grace," Beau Bardsley interrupted sharply. "As you are well aware, I never effect introductions to the members of the cast in this or in any other theatre."

The Duke laughed.

"My dear Bardsley, you are barking up the wrong tree! If I wanted to meet an actress for my own needs I would have no difficulty in meeting her, and I certainly would not need you to introduce me!"

"Then how can I help you?" Beau Bardsley asked in a different tone.

"It is a long story, but I will be brief," the Duke replied. "My sister married a Scotsman by name of McCraig. He is now dead, but my nephew Alister

McCraig is very much alive and was married over a year ago to Kitty Varden. You remember Kitty?"

"Good Lord, of course I do!" Beau Bardsley exclaimed. "But I had no idea that McCraig was your nephew!"

"I do not trouble myself with relatives as a rule," the Duke continued. "In fact they bore me to distraction, but I knew Kitty when she was on the boards. Who did not?"

He paused as if waiting for confirmation of this and automatically Beau Bardsley answered:

"As Your Grace says—who did not?"

"Surprisingly she has made my nephew very happy, but Kitty is still Kitty! Though she may no longer be acting, she still looks very much the same as she did when she sang those bawdy songs which nearly took the roof off!"

"I remember them," Beau remarked dryly.

"Then you can imagine that with her red hair and her voluptuous bosom, which seems to have grown even more ample in the last two years, she is hardly likely to impress her husband's great Uncle—The McCraig of McCraig!"

"I seem to have heard of him," Beau Bardsley remarked.

"Some people call him the uncrowned King of Scotland, which is certainly true where his own Clan are concerned, and he is, incidentally, an extremely rich man."

Shimona felt her father move restlessly as if he was longing to reach the end of the story.

"I am sorry to bore you with this," the Duke remarked, "but the position quite simply is that for years my sister has been trying to make The McCraig take an interest in Alister, but he can leave his own money where he wishes."

Shimona thought that by this time her father would be as interested as she was.

"Go on," she heard him say.

"The McCraig, out of the blue, has notified his intention of coming to London. He wishes to see the Prime Minister on Scottish Affairs and he has informed my nephew Alister that he would like to meet his wife."

The Duke paused for a moment before he went on:

"There is no doubt that, if he approves of the marriage he will, as my sister has been trying to persuade him to do, make Alister his heir."

There was silence before Beau Bardsley said:

"Speaking frankly, Your Grace, it is hardly likely he will approve of Kitty."

"That is very obvious, not only to you and me, but also to Alister."

Again there was a pause before the Duke continued:

"That is why you are the only person who can help me, Bardsley."

"How can I do that?"

"You can find me an actress who will play the part of my nephew's wife for two days. That is all I require. Just two days for a woman to act the part of a lady sufficiently well to convince a dour old Scot that she is a suitable wife for his heir."

"Are you serious?" Beau Bardsley asked.

"Completely!" the Duke answered. "I have thought hard about this, and it is to my mind the only possible way that Alister can receive a large sum of money and inherit something like a million when The McCraig dies!"

"As much as that?"

"It might be more!"

"Do you really think he can be deceived by someone acting a part?"

"Good God, why not?" the Duke exclaimed. "You fellows create an illusion and make people believe anything you want them to. Half the women present in the audience to-night were crying when you died."

"It is different behind the footlights," Beau Bardsley murmured.

"An actor's job is to present an illusion and make it

seem real," the Duke remarked. "Whatever you say or do the audience believes it to be the truth. I am asking for a woman to make a man of eighty believe that she is a decent, respectable person. It should not be very hard."

"I find it almost impossible to think of anyone who could do that," Beau Bardsley said.

"I admit it might not be easy to find someone who looks and sounds right," the Duke conceded after a moment. "But, you are a gentleman, Bardsley, and that is why I came to you. I do not want the dross showing through the gold too quickly."

Beau Bardsley was silent for some seconds before he said:

"For the moment I cannot think of a single soul who could play such a part. There is Judith Page who rather specialises in Ladies of Quality, but she is too old. There is Sylvia Verity."

"Good God, not her!" the Duke ejaculated. "One drink and the polish comes off that refined accent!"

"I know," Beau Bardsley conceded.

"There must be someone—perhaps someone new in the theatre," the Duke persisted. "She does not have to do much, beyond keeping quiet, and I will teach her the few lines that are necessary."

Beau Bardsley must have looked at him for he said quickly:

"Nothing like that, Bardsley, I promise! This is strictly business and, if the girl is pure, then she will leave my house as pure as she came—that I promise you!"

"*Your* house?" Beau Bardsley questioned.

"My nephew is at present staying with me at Ravenstone House in Berkeley Square. I have invited The McCraig to be my guest for the two days he is in London. I will take every care to see that your protegée is not alone with him at any time. Either Alister or myself will be there to bridge any uncomfortable moment and to answer any difficult questions."

Beau Bardsley did not speak and the Duke went on:

"Perhaps I should have mentioned already that I consider a proper fee for this piece of exceptional acting would be 500 guineas!"

He laughed.

"You look surprised, Bardsley."

"It is a lot of money, Your Grace!"

"I am prepared to pay that and any more that is required to ensure that my nephew inherits his great-Uncle's money. As I have already told you, it is worth taking trouble for a million!"

"I suppose it might be possible to find someone suitable," Beau Bardsley conceded. "You know as well as I do, Your Grace, there are thousands who would jump at the chance of earning that sort of money! But they might let you down—it is not worth the risk!"

"I knew you would be the only person who would understand," the Duke said. "That is why I have forced myself on you when you made it obvious that you did not wish to talk to me."

"I must apologise if I seemed impolite."

"Not at all! We all know you return to your house in Chelsea to be with your family who must not be contaminated by people like myself."

The Duke spoke with laughter in his voice and he went on:

"Your obsession for privacy may cause resentment in some quarters, Bardsley, but as far as I am concerned, I admire you for it!"

"I thank Your Grace."

Shimona heard the Duke rise to his feet.

"If you fail me, Bardsley," he said, "then I swear I will put you at the top of my long list of enemies!"

"I only wish you would ask the assistance of somebody else," Beau Bardsley said.

"You know the answer to that," the Duke replied. "There is no-one else—no-one else who would understand what the hell I am talking about! I want a *Lady*,

Bardsley, and I do not believe there is any other actor in this theatre who would know one if they met one."

"You are very scathing, Your Grace."

"God knows, I do not intend to be. I suppose I have had more fun in the theatres of London than any other man alive," the Duke remarked. "Do you remember Perdita? And Rosa Lenin? And that attractive little creature who screamed the place down when I tried to be rid of her? What was her name?"

"Betty Wilson!"

"Yes, of course! Betty Wilson! She even hired men to break the windows of Ravenstone House. I cannot see any of them acting the part, can you? No, Bardsley, you and I know exactly what is required and, as I said before, only you are capable of finding her."

"I think it will prove impossible!" Beau Bardsley said slowly.

"Then I will tell you what I will do," the Duke said. "I will give the lady—and she had better look like one —500 guineas, and there will be another 500 guineas for you to squander on the rag, tag and bobtail who come to you with stories of their old mothers dying in cold garrets! £1,000 guineas, Bardsley! That should make it worth your while."

There was no answer, then the Duke added:

"Send your choice to me at Ravenstone House an hour before noon to-morrow. That should give my nephew and me time to instruct her in the fundamentals of the situation before the old boy arrives for luncheon."

The Duke opened the door.

"£1,000 guineas, my dear man! It is worth thinking about!"

CHAPTER TWO

Beau Bardsley sank back against the cushions of the hired carriage and shut his eyes.

His cloak was wrapped over the black velvet suit which he had worn in the last act of the play, but he had removed the make-up from his face and in the flickering lights from the linkmen's lanterns Shimona could see how pale he was.

They drove for some way in silence, before she said tentatively:

"Will you be . . . able to do what the Duke . . . asked?"

"I should imagine it would be quite impossible to find the sort of woman he requires at such a short notice."

Her father's voice did not sound too exhausted, and after a moment Shimona said:

"We need 500 guineas, Papa."

"I know that, but playing a part off the stage is very different from playing one on it."

"Why?"

"Because actors speak the lines they are given, and most of the women in the profession are uneducated and of a doubtful character."

There was silence, and then as if he knew what his daughter was thinking Beau Bardsley said quickly:

"Not Sarah Siddons: she indeed was different. But it

31

would be much easier to find an actor to look and behave like a gentleman than an actress to play a lady."

Again there was silence before Shimona said in a very small voice:

"We need 500 guineas, Papa, desperately! I . . . suppose I could not . . . play the . . . part for . . . you?"

Beau Bardsley was suddenly rigid and it seemed as if he was stunned into silence. Then he said:

"Are you crazy? Do you think for one moment that I would allow you to do such a thing or to go to the house of that man?"

"I have heard you . . . speak of the Duke, Papa."

"Then you know how disreputable he is and how much I despise him."

"But why, Papa? What has he done?"

"He stands for everything that is lecherous and debauched. Do you know what they call him behind his back?"

"No, Papa. How should I?"

"He is known as 'His Disgrace', and it is an apt designation."

"But Papa, what does he do?"

"I would not soil your ears with repeating the scandals in which he has been involved, or the menace he is to women, not only in his own world, but also in the theatre and the night-haunts of London."

"You mean that he . . . pursues women?"

"And they pursue him," Beau Bardsley answered. "He has more charm in his little finger than most men have in their whole body, and he uses it entirely to his own ends."

Her father spoke so violently that Shimona looked at him apprehensively in case it should bring on another fit of coughing.

"I have seen too many of the hearts that Ravenstone has broken," he went on, "the lives he has disrupted and ruined, the chaos he has caused in one way or another! If you want the truth, I loathe him!"

"You were polite to him, Papa."

"How could I be anything else?" Beau Bardsley asked. "A nobleman in his position could do me irreparable harm if I chose to make an enemy of him."

"How could he do that?" Shimona asked.

"There is no point in discussing it. I shall have to try to do as he wishes. I only hope to God I can think of some young woman who would be suitable."

There was silence, until Beau Bardsley said almost savagely:

"You would think he could find someone himself. He knows enough women, but of course they are not the sort who would deceive anyone."

Shimona said no more, but as they journeyed on she began to pray that her father would find the woman the Duke wanted and earn the 500 guineas.

With that much money he could go abroad as the Doctor wished.

In the sunshine of Italy she was sure that his cough would go, and he would put on weight and be again as strong as she remembered him when she was a child.

Always then he had seemed full of exciting and irrepressible vitality that made the tempo rise the moment he entered a room.

"Papa is back, Mama!"

She could hear her voice screaming with excitement as she ran helter-skelter down the stairs to open the front door before her father could raise his hand to the knocker.

"Papa! Papa!"

Her arms would go round his neck and he would lift her off her feet, swinging her around until she was giddy or tickling her until she laughed hysterically.

Then he had been very unlike the pale-faced man who now crept back to Chelsea every night, often too tired to eat the delicious suppers which Nanna cooked for him.

"He must rest! He must get away!" Shimona told herself.

33

Once again she was praying to her mother for help, feeling that wherever she was in the Heaven in which she so fervently believed, she would somehow contrive to be near the man she had loved with all her heart and soul.

"You must help us, Mama," Shimona said beneath her breath. "Papa will die if he goes on like this!"

Now the carriage had reached Sloane Square and was proceeding down King's Road.

"As soon as Papa has had something to eat," Shimona told herself, "he must go to bed. If he means to find the actress that the Duke requires, he will have to be up early to go in search of her."

The horses came to a standstill and Shimona put her hand on her father's arm.

"We are home, Papa!"

"Ho-me?"

It seemed for a moment as if Beau Bardsley was dazed and uncertain of what he was saying. Then with an effort he followed Shimona from the carriage, bending his head to do so.

It might have been that or the wind whistling round the corner which started him coughing.

He stood on the pavement doubled up with the paroxysm which shook him once again.

Nanna, who had been waiting for them, opened the door, and while he was still coughing they helped Beau Bardsley up the steps and into the small hall.

The rasping sound he was making seemed to echo round the walls.

"Let's get the Master upstairs," Nanna said to Shimona. "We'll try to persuade him to go straight to bed, but if he comes down again he'll wish to change."

Shimona put her arm around her father's waist, but the cabman who had followed them into the house intervened.

" 'ere, I'll 'elp 'is Nibs," he said. "An' proud to do it! Me an' the missus have waited many an hour to see 'im on the stage."

Beau Bardsley was not coughing so violently now but he was swaying with exhaustion and it seemed as if he might have fallen to the floor had not Nanna been holding him.

The cabman moved to his other side and he and Nanna almost literally carried him up the stairs to the front room.

It was Shimona's mother who had insisted that the best room in the house, which should have been her Drawing-Room, should be a bed-room.

"Papa is home so little," she had said to Shimona, "and we never entertain. It will be much better to make the bed-room into a place where he can not only rest but study."

The front room therefore, with its three long windows opening onto the tree-lined Square outside, was furnished with all the treasures which Shimona's mother had collected over the years.

There was also a sofa and some chairs, so that it was like a Sitting-Room, and usually Beau would lie in bed while her mother sat beside the fire and sewed.

Shimona, when she was a child, would sit cross-legged beside him reading him extracts from her fairy-stories.

Although she had not realised it, this had been a lesson in elocution, because her father would check her if she did not pronounce every word accurately with the intonation and timing for which he himself was famous.

Now when they reached the landing Shimona ran ahead to take the cover from the bed so that the cabman and Nanna could lift Beau Bardsley onto the top of the blankets and lay him back gently against the pillows.

"Thank you," Shimona said to the man as he turned toward the door. "How much do we owe you?"

"Oi'll take nothin' from th' Guv'nor," the Cabby answered. "It's payment enough, as ye might say, for the pleasure 'e's given me."

"Oh, thank you!" Shimona exclaimed.

It always touched her when people spoke in such a way about her father.

"Nah ye look arter 'im," the cabman admonished as he started down the stairs. "Oi don' loik the look of 'im, an' that's a fact! Ye'd best get the Doctor right away or The Lane'll lose the greatest actor it's ever 'ad."

"I will do that and thank you," Shimona said as she shut the front door behind him.

She ran up the stairs to find Nanna outside the bedroom looking apprehensively at the handkerchief which she held in her hand.

"What . . . is it?" Shimona asked in a whisper.

"We have to call the Doctor," Nanna said. "He's coughing blood, and it's not right—it's not right at all!"

"I will go!"

"At this time of night?" Nanna asked. "You'll do nothing of the sort. You'll find his warm milk ready on the stove. Persuade him to drink it and I'll get back as quickly as I can."

"Wait a moment!" Shimona cried. "I will ask the cabman to go for Doctor Lesley."

She ran down the stairs and managed to stop the hackney-carriage just as it was driving off.

The cabman heard Shimona calling him from the steps and pulled in his horse immediately.

"Wot is it, Missy?"

"Would you be kind enough to ask the Doctor to come to my father?" Shimona asked. "You are right. He is very ill. Very ill indeed!"

"Oi'll fetch 'im for yer. Where's 'e live, Miss?"

"Not far away in Eaton Square," Shimona answered. "At number 82 and his name is Doctor Lesley."

"Leave it to me!" the cabman said and, whipping up his horse, set off at a pace which told Shimona that he realised how urgent the matter was.

It was with great difficulty that she and Nanna managed to get her father undressed and into bed by the time Doctor Lesley arrived.

He was a blunt, good-natured man who had a great reputation amongst the top professionals of the Theatrical world. He had in fact, met Beau Bardsley through Richard Brinsley Sheridan, whom he had attended for many years.

He was, Shimona knew, not only her father's doctor, but also a friend and admirer of his talent, and her mother had trusted him implicitly.

He had been a tower of strength when Mrs. Bardsley had died, and Shimona often thought that if it had not been for Doctor Lesley her father would have had a nervous breakdown and made no effort to continue with his acting career.

When Shimona met him in the hall, Doctor Lesley smiled at her, which proclaimed his affection more effectively than any words.

"Oh, Doctor Lesley, I knew you would come when you got my message!" Shimona said breathlessly.

"It was fortunate that I was still at home," he replied. "I was just about to leave to visit an elderly Countess but she can wait! How bad is your father?"

"Very bad! He got through the performance tonight but it was only with the help of brandy, and now he seems to have collapsed. Nanna says he is coughing . . . blood!"

The Doctor's lips tightened.

"It is what I expected," he said. "I told you long ago that he should rest and that you must get him away to a warmer climate. These cold winds are murder to a man in his condition."

"I know," Shimona said miserably.

"I suppose there is no money in the kitty as usual?" Doctor Lesley remarked as he started to climb the stairs.

Shimona did not bother to answer.

Doctor Lesley knew as well as she did how every penny her father earned was given away with a generous hand.

The Doctor went into the bed-room, telling Shimona to wait.

She went downstairs to the small Sitting-Room at the back of the house which she and her mother had used when they were alone.

It always seemed to her to be redolent with her mother's presence.

It was here she had done her lessons; it was here they had sat and talked during the long afternoons and evenings when her father was at the theatre.

It was in this room that her mother had imparted to her daughter her own simple philosophy of life which Shimona had tried to make her own.

And everywhere there were portraits and mementos of her father.

The picture over the mantelpiece had been painted just before he had run away from Bath with the beautiful Annabel Winslow.

There was a miniature of him by Richard Cosway executed at the same time as he had commissioned the miniature of his wife.

There were sketches of him in his greatest roles, and caricatures which had been drawn by some of the most famous cartoonists in the land.

There were theatre posters and special tributes which Beau had received from time to time from the towns where he had played or from the company with whom he had acted.

"Mama loved him so much," Shimona thought to herself. "Why can she not help him now?"

Then insidiously, almost as if someone was saying it, the thought came to her of the 1,000 guineas which could be earned so easily if only her father would allow her to do so.

Then she remembered the anger in his voice when she suggested it and knew it would be impossible for her to persuade him.

The door opened and Doctor Lesley came in.

Shimona did not speak. She only looked at him and knew what he was going to say before his lips moved.

"Your father is very ill, my dear," he said after a moment.

"Do you mean . . . that he is going to . . . die?" Shimona asked in a voice he could hardly hear.

"Yes, unless we do something positive to prevent it," Doctor Lesley replied.

"What can we do?"

"First there is no question of his going on stage to-morrow or for a long time ahead," the Doctor said. "Secondly, we have to get him out of London and if possible to a warm climate."

He put his hand on Shimona's shoulder as he went on:

"I know the circumstances you are in, my dear, and I think the only thing I can do is to try to raise the money from your father's friends and admirers."

He gave a sigh.

"I have a feeling it is likely to be much easier for your father to give than to receive."

"That is true," Shimona answered. "And he would hate feeling that he was asking for charity."

"There is no alternative," Doctor Lesley said, "and I promise you, Shimona, I am not speaking lightly when I say that time is important. We have to get him away!"

Shimona clasped her hands together. Then she said:

"I have a chance, Doctor . . . of . . . earning 1,000 guineas. But could you keep Papa from being . . . aware of what I am . . . doing?"

She saw an expression in the Doctor's face which made her say quickly:

"It is nothing really wrong; but Papa, as you know, does not like me to do anything outside the house."

"Will you tell me what it is?" Doctor Lesley asked.

Shimona hesitated.

"It is a . . . secret, and it is not . . . mine. All I can say is that . . . someone asked Papa to-night to find a . . . woman who would act a . . . certain part for two days."

"And for that they are prepared to pay 1,000 guineas?" Doctor Lesley asked and she heard the suspicion in his voice.

"It is a difficult part," she explained, "and in fact could only be played by someone who is . . . well born."

"You are sure it will not involve you in anything—unsavoury?"

The Doctor hesitated before the last word.

"I promise you I will not be involved in anything which you or even Mama would think wrong or damaging to me personally."

She looked up at the Doctor pleadingly.

"It is only Papa who is prejudiced against my meeting anyone outside this house."

"Your father is almost fanatical on the subject."

"That is why he must not know what I am doing." Shimona said. "But I shall be able to earn 1,000 guineas, with which I can take him abroad and he can rest until he is really well again."

"It certainly seems a solution to the problem," Doctor Lesley said slowly. "At the same time I wish you could be a little more explicit."

Shimona did not answer.

She had the feeling that if she told the Doctor that the Duke was involved he would, like her father, refuse to allow her to go to Ravenstone House.

The Duke had promised that he would not interfere himself with anyone who was willing to play the part.

There had been, Shimona thought, an unmistakable note of sincerity in his voice when he said:

"This is strictly business, and if the girl is pure she will leave my house as pure as she came—that I promise!"

"It will be all right, I know it will be all right," she said to Doctor Lesley. "But in no circumstances must you let Papa know about it."

The Doctor stood staring into the fire for a few minutes before he said:

"God knows if I am doing the right thing, but it is actually a case of saving your father's life."

"Then why should you . . . hesitate?"

He turned his head to look at her.

"I am very fond of you, my child. I have known you since you were a little girl and I have watched you grow up into a very beautiful young woman. I would never forgive myself if you were harmed in any way."

"I am sure I will not be," Shimona said quickly.

"You know nothing of the world," Doctor Lesley said, "and to a young woman it can be a very dangerous place."

"If what I am doing at any time seems . . . dangerous," Shimona answered, "then I promise you I will come back straight away."

"You promise me that?"

"I promise!"

The Doctor parted his lips as if to say something else, then he changed his mind.

"Very well!" he said abruptly. "I will trust your judgement and I will keep your father from knowing what is happening."

"How will you do that?" Shimona enquired.

"He will sleep to-night after what I have given him to prevent him from coughing," the Doctor replied. "I will call early to-morrow morning and see that he sleeps through to-morrow and the following day."

Shimona put out her hands.

"Thank you, Doctor. I knew that you would not fail us. Mama always said you were the kindest man she had ever met."

"And because I admired your mother more than any woman I have ever known, I feel responsible for you," the Doctor said, "so for God's sake, my dear, take care of yourself!"

"I am quite confident I can do so," Shimona replied.

The Doctor turned towards the door.

"I shall be wondering all night whether it would have been better to collect the money from among your father's friends."

"I should be surprised if you managed to raise anything like 1,000 guineas!"

"And if I am honest, so should I!" the Doctor replied.

He picked up his cloak which he had left in the hall, set his hat on his head and opened the front door.

Outside his smart Brougham was waiting, and as soon as he stepped into it the coachman set off in the direction of the West End.

Slowly Shimona went upstairs.

She went into the bed-room where Nanna had blown out the candles, but by the light of the fire she could see that her father was asleep.

He looked more relaxed and therefore younger than when they left the theatre.

He was breathing evenly, and it was difficult to realise that unless she could do something about it he was under sentence of death.

"I must save Papa . . . I must!" Shimona told herself.

Then she thought that the fact that she could earn 1,000 guineas had been a direct answer to a prayer.

Perhaps her mother knew all about it and through some Divine power they could not understand, had sent them this life-line.

"If she can do that," Shimona asked, "why should there be any reason for me to be afraid?"

Her mother would protect her even in Ravenstone House.

The Duke walked into the Library and found his nephew, Alister McCraig, standing in front of the fire reading the *Morning Post*.

"Good-morning, Uncle Yvell," he said as the Duke entered.

"Good-morning, Alister, I hope I have solved your troubles for you."

Alister McCraig put down the newspaper and looked eagerly at the Duke.

He was a nice-looking man of twenty-five with a pleasant, but rather stupid face and fair hair with a touch of red in it.

It would have been difficult to mistake him for anything but a soldier: he had in fact served in a Regiment of the Brigade of Guards until, when he married an actress, he had been forced to resign his Commission.

"You have found someone to act the part?" Alister McCraig asked.

"Not yet, but Bardsley will find someone for me. I made sure of that!"

"How did you make sure of it?"

"I offered him so much money that it would be almost impossible for him to refuse to do as I wish," the Duke answered.

"That was very kind of you, Uncle Yvell. But you know I could never pay you back unless Great-Uncle Hector coughs up, as we hope he will."

"I am not asking you to pay me back," the Duke answered. "I am hoping you will get your fortune and then I need never bother about you again!"

"You have been damned kind over this, Uncle Yvell, and I shall never forget it," Alister McCraig said. "You are the only member of the family who has spoken to me since I married Kitty."

"You must admit it came as something of a shock to the majority of them," the Duke said in an amused voice. "It would have done the sanctimonious old hypocrites a lot of good, were it not that it was likely to leave you a pauper the rest of your life!"

"I am well aware of that!" Alister McCraig said.

There was a faint flush on his cheeks, and the Duke thought it was understandable how Kitty with her shrewd little brain and an eye for the main chance had thought it worth while to leave the stage for a husband who would be chivalrous and considerate to her for the rest of her life.

There was no doubt that Kitty had caught and enslaved Alister deliberately and, the Duke thought, with the sole object of becoming respectable.

She had enjoyed a long line of distinguished lovers before Alister had become infatuated with her.

Yet no-one had suspected for one moment that beneath her exuberant and rather disreputable career she had always longed for the security of a wedding-ring.

"Well, she has achieved her ambition," the Duke thought, "and there is nothing anyone can do about it."

At the same time he was determined if possible to save Alister from the worst consequences of his extremely ill-advised marriage.

A rich man would always be forgiven an offence for which a poor one would be ostracised indefinitely.

"I suppose your mother has never seen Kitty?" the Duke asked.

"As you know, for some years she has not been well enough to travel South from Northumberland, and I have made innumerable excuses not to take Kitty to see her."

"Quite right!" the Duke approved. "There is no point in upsetting her."

"None at all," Alister McCraig agreed, "but I had no idea that she was still trying to get Great-Uncle Hector interested in me."

"I wonder how she has managed to do it?" the Duke asked reflectively.

He seated himself in a wingback chair by the fireside and was looking at his nephew with critical eyes as he stood in front of him.

"I can tell you exactly," Alister McCraig said. "Mama is very transparent in all her intrigues."

He paused, and as the Duke did not speak, went on:

"She has told Great Uncle Hector that I shall doubt-less produce a long line of McCraigs, and they must be educated and brought up in the right way, so that they can be a credit to the Clan McCraig."

"Good Lord! So that is her angle!" the Duke laughed. "If nothing else, my sister is undoubedly a clever diplomat."

"She sent me a copy of the last letter she wrote to Great-Uncle Hector," Alister McCraig said, "and it is that which is bringing him hot-foot to London."

"I see . . ." the Duke remarked reflectively. "There are going to be difficulties if The McCraig wishes to take his place at the first Christening!"

"He cannot live for ever!" Alister McCraig said pee-vishly. "And as far as I am concerned, once he has settled some money on me he can die as quickly as possible!"

"Which is, of course, a most admirable sentiment!" the Duke said ironically.

"Oh, for God's sake, Uncle Yvell," Alister McCraig said in a tone which betrayed his nervousness, "I hope you are not going to start reproaching me."

The Duke did not speak and he went on:

"It has been drummed into me by my father, my mother and all my other relations, except you, ever since I was a child that I had to marry someone befit-ting my station in life; someone who was the right sort of wife for a Chieftain. The idea of it has always made me sick!"

The Duke thought that perhaps here was the answer to why Alister had given Kitty Varden, a Music-Hall Comedienne with a reputation for singing lewder songs than had ever before been heard on a stage, a wedding-ring.

It was, however, obvious that his nephew was on edge, and if he was to have a nervous actress to cope with too, the Duke decided to pour oil on waters that looked like being somewhat tempestuous.

"I am sure everything is going to be all right," he said soothingly. "Bardsley is a gentleman, the son of a clergyman as it happens, and he will find us exactly the right sort of wife that you should have had."

"I must say he looks as if he had good blood in him," Alister McCraig remarked. "He does not seem like the usual run of actors."

"He is not!" the Duke said briefly.

There was silence for a moment, then he said:

"I think it is absolutely essential that not a word of this arrangement should be spoken of outside this house. You are well aware, Alister, how a tit-bit of this sort could go round the Clubs like wildfire, and it would only be a question of time before The McCraig learnt of it."

"That is true," his nephew answered. "As a matter of fact I have not even told Kitty of your idea."

"You have not?" the Duke asked in surprise.

Alister McCraig looked uncomfortable.

"I had a feeling that if I did," he said, "she might insist on meeting Great-Uncle Hector herself. Now she is settled down she has almost forgotten her past and thinks everyone else has too."

The Duke threw back his head and laughed.

"My dear Alister, if you had not told me that I would not have believed it! If Kitty thinks anyone will ever forget those songs she used to sing, she must have lost what brains she had!"

"Kitty is perfectly content being married to me," Alister McCraig said truculently.

"You have only been married a year, my dear boy. Give it time!"

He saw his words offended his nephew and added quickly:

"You have been very sensible in not telling Kitty what we are doing. Never trust a woman with a secret if you can possibly help it. Besides, as I have already said, the fewer people know the better! It would be far too good a story not to repeat."

46

"That is what I thought, Uncle."

"Then keep your mouth shut, and the most important thing will be to persuade our little actress that unless she also is silent she will not be paid."

The Duke glanced at the clock over the mantelpiece and noted that the hands stood at one minute to twelve o'clock.

His nephew followed the direction of his eyes and said quickly:

"I think, Uncle Yvell, it would be best if you saw this woman alone first. You are much cleverer than I am getting people to do what you want, and I might mess it up."

Without waiting for his Uncle to agree Alister McCraig moved across the Library.

"I will be in the Morning-Room when you want me," he said as he reached the door, then he was gone.

There was a smile on the Duke's lips as he bent forward to pick up the *Morning Post*.

He had never had much opinion of his nephew and he thought it was typical of him to shirk the interview at the last moment and shift the responsibility onto his shoulders.

At the same time he was determined if possible to see that Alister was set up for life, and thus unlikely to be an encumbrance upon himself in his old age.

"Damn all relations!" he thought. "They are always an infernal nuisance!"

He glanced down at the paper, wondering as he did so if he had to be tied not only to his nephew but also to The McCraig of McCraig for the next forty-eight hours.

The idea appalled him as there was in fact a very amusing party being given that night at the house of Mrs. Mary Ann Clarke; who had once been his mistress but was now under the protection of the Commander-in-Chief of the Army.

It would be the sort of party the Duke reflected, which scandalised and shocked even the easy-going, pleasure-seeking society that centred round Carlton House.

The difficulty would be of course, to get away.

"Perhaps the old gentleman will retire early," he told himself. "Then I can escape."

He felt almost like a school-boy planning how to play truant but with a very different end in view!

There was a cynical twist of amusement on the Duke's lips as the door opened.

"Miss Wantage, Your Grace!"

The Duke rose to his feet.

There was a little pause before Shimona entered the room. Then as she came slowly towards him, holding herself proudly, she was aware of how frightened she was.

She had thought when she left home that it would be quite easy to arrive at Ravenstone House and tell the Duke she had been sent by Beau Bardsley.

She had everything planned in her mind and it was only when Nanna had found her a hackney-carriage and she set off alone that she began to feel nervous.

Nanna had been far more difficult to convince than the Doctor, and although once again Shimona had not revealed who had offered to pay 1,000 guineas, Nanna had been scandalised at the whole idea.

"What would your poor mother say? What would she think?" she kept repeating.

"Mama would wish us to save Papa's life," Shimona answered, "and there is no other way, Nanna."

"There must be! Surely Doctor Lesley can find the money somehow?"

"How could he possibly find 1,000 guineas?"

"It isn't right, Miss Shimona! It isn't right that you should leave the house and go off on your own. I've never heard of such a thing!"

"It will only be for two nights, Nanna."

"Nights?" Nanna snorted and made the word sound disreputable and ominous.

"I have promised Doctor Lesley," Shimona went on,

"that if anything seems wrong I will return home immediately. I shall not be very far away."

"You will give me the address or you don't leave this house," Nanna said firmly.

"Yes, of course," Shimona agreed.

Then she hesitated, for to say she would be staying at Ravenstone House would certainly reveal the fact that she was meeting the Duke of Ravenstone.

She did not think Nanna had ever heard of him, but she had remembered, when she was behind the curtain in the dressing-room, hearing her father speak of the Duke in the most disparaging manner to her mother.

"Ravenstone is after that pretty girl who is the *ingenue* in Act II," Shimona heard him say once when he thought she was not listening. "I have warned her, but the silly little fool is mesmerised by him like a rabbit by a snake!"

"She cannot know what His Grace is like," her mother had said in her soft voice.

"She knows and she still does not care!" Beau Bardsley replied. "There is something about that man which hypnotises women, and until he has left them they are not aware of the sort of devil with whom they have become entangled."

"Is he really as bad as that?" Mrs. Bardsley had asked.

"He is worse!" Beau Bardsley had replied. "He is a disgrace to his title, to his blood, to the stock from which he has sprung! I have no use, Annabel, for a man who betrays his own class."

When her father talked like that Shimona did not realise that he might have been in the pulpit for which he had been intended.

But she had always imagined that the Duke would indeed look like a devil, and once to amuse herself she had drawn a caricature of him with horns on his head and a tail showing beneath his coat.

She had not been able to draw his face since she had never seen him, but she had imagined him with slanting eyes and arched eye-brows, a long thin nose and pointed ears.

All she had listened to, all she had imagined came back to her mind as she drove through Hyde Park Corner and along Piccadilly towards Berkeley Square.

As the carriage turned up Berkeley Street she had an impulse to tell the cabman to stop and take her home to the safety of Nanna and her sleeping father.

For the first time she realised how little she knew about the world, how ignorant she was of social behaviour!

She had never been to dinner-parties, she had never even helped to entertain people in her own home with the exception of Doctor Lesley, the parson and some of the elderly ladies engaged in charitable work from the Church which she and her mother attended on Sundays.

Sunday to Beau was a day of rest and he never accompanied them.

But Shimona knew that she and her mother were an object of curiosity as they walked up the aisle to sit in an inconspicuous pew behind those which were marked with the names of those people who paid for them.

"I am saving Papa! I am saving Papa!"

Shimona repeated the words over and over to herself to give herself confidence.

She felt as if her legs were suddenly very weak, and she was conscious that her heart seemed to be fluttering inside her breast in an extraordinary manner as the carriage came to a standstill.

She looked out and saw a large and very impressive house on the north side of the Square.

It was in fact far bigger than Shimona had anticipated, and when she entered the marble Hall with its great carved staircase and alcoves in which stood Grecian statuary, she felt very small and insignificant.

The Butler had led her to a pair of double mahogany doors.

"May I have your name, Madam?"

Shimona had already decided to call herself Want-age. It happened to be a name in a book which she was reading, and she thought it sounded quiet and unimportant, which was what she wished to be.

She had dressed herself with great care.

She had few gowns to choose from and the muslin that had been made by Nanna was very plain, but the cloak which covered it was of a blue which matched her eyes and had been bought for her by her mother.

Her bonnet was high-crowned but not over-fashionable, and the blue ribbons which ornamented it were simple but in perfect taste.

The Butler opened the door.

"Miss Wantage, Your Grace!" he said in a manner which made Shimona feel as if he had blown a fanfare.

Then she remembered that for the first time she was to meet face to face the man she had thought of as a devil.

Almost instinctively, as if she was taking part in a play, she paused as the door shut behind her.

She looked across the room and she saw not the devil she had anticipated, but an extremely good-looking man, who was surprisingly young for his reputation.

He was by no means as handsome as her father, nor were his features in the least classical, and yet he was outstandingly distinguished-looking and had a natural grace and elegance which Shimona knew derived from his breeding.

He also stood looking at her, taking in the little pointed face under the plain bonnet, the slim figure in a muslin gown and the wide, dark blue eyes that looked at him questioningly.

He had expected that Beau Bardsley would send him someone attractive, but not a woman so exquisite or so beautiful.

In fact she was so inexpressibly lovely that, cynical and satiated though he was with all the delights that

51

the female sex could offer him, the Duke was for the moment speechless.

Slowly, very slowly, Shimona advanced towards him. Then almost as if he remembered his manners, he moved towards her.

"You come, I think, from Mr. Beau Bardsley?"

With an effort and in a voice which did not sound like her own Shimona managed to reply:

"Y . . . yes . . . Your Grace."

She curtsied and felt as she did so that it was a relief to be able to take her eyes from his.

The Duke bowed.

"I am very grateful to you, Miss Wantage. Will you not be seated?"

"Thank . . . you."

Shimona sat down on the edge of a chair beside the fire and looked at him with eyes in which to his surprise he could see an unmistakable expression of fear.

"You must not be frightened," he said in the voice which she had last heard from behind the curtain in her father's dressing-room. "I know this may be an unusual part for you to play, but I am quite certain you will do it most admirably!"

"Thank . . . you."

"Have you been on the stage long?" the Duke asked, seating himself. "I cannot remember ever having seen you in a play?"

He thought even as he spoke that it was an idiotic question.

If he had once seen this beautiful creature behind the footlights it would have been impossible for him not only to forget her, but to fail to try to make her acquaintance.

Shimona glanced at him for a moment, then she said:

"Will you . . . tell me . . . Your Grace . . . exactly what is . . . required of me?"

The Duke smiled.

"What you are really saying, Miss Wantage, is that you have no wish to answer questions about yourself."

"I did not . . . mean to be . . . impertinent . . . Your Grace."

"You are not. I do not think you could be," he replied.

There was an expression in his eyes which made Shimona look away from him.

She wished that her heart was not pounding so wildly, almost as if it would burst from her breast, and she was ashamed of the fact that her hands were still trembling.

"It is warm in here," the Duke said unexpectedly. "I think you would be wise to remove your cloak, and I am sure you would be more comfortable without your bonnet."

"Y . . . yes . . . of course."

Shimona rose to her feet like a child obedient to a command.

She unclasped her cloak at the neck and the Duke took it from her.

He came close to her to do so, and she had a strange feeling. It was not of panic, but something very like it which she could not explain to herself.

As the Duke laid her cloak on a chair against a wall, she undid the ribbons of her bonnet and he took that also.

"You have brought enough clothes with you for two nights?" he asked.

"Yes . . . Your Grace."

He came back to the fireside and resumed his seat.

Shimona sat opposite him.

The light from the flames shone on her fair hair, and yet it still held the mysterious shadows that Richard Cosway had painted so skilfully in the miniature of her mother.

Her eyes, the Duke thought, were the blue of a stormy sea and not the pale colour one would have expected with such a white skin. Her nose reminded

him of the statuary he had seen when he had last been
in Greece.

He realised she was waiting for him to speak and
after a moment he said:

"Beau Bardsley doubtless will have told you that my
nephew could inherit a very large sum of money if his
Great-Uncle, The McCraig of McCraig, likes his wife to
whom he has been married for a year."

Shimona was listening intently and he went on:

"He has in fact told his mother, who is a widow, and
his Great Uncle, very little about the woman he has
married, which makes it easy for you to play the part."

"Do they know her name?" Shimona asked.

"They have been told her real name, which is Katherine Webber," the Duke replied, "but not the one she
used professionally. You will of course be called Katherine while you are here."

Shimona acquiesced with a little inclination of her
head.

"What is your christian name, Miss Wantage?" the
Duke asked.

"Shimona!"

As she spoke she thought it might have been wiser to
call herself Mary or Jane.

"I have never before known anyone called
Shimona," he remarked.

"I must . . . remember to answer to . . . Katherine."

"Of course, and my nephew will tell you anything it
is necessary for you to know about his wife."

As he mentioned Alister McCraig, the Duke noticed
that Shimona glanced towards the door as if she expected someone over-powering or even menacing to
enter the room.

"You will not feel nervous with Alister," he said
soothingly. "He is an easy-going, charming young
man. In fact the only person of whom you need fear at
all will be The McCraig himself."

"Why is he called The McCraig of McCraig?"
Shimona asked.

"It is a title which some clans give their Chieftains
and of which they are very proud. It gives them the
standing of an Earl or perhaps a Marquess in this
country, and I am certain The McCraig would not
change it for any other title, however distinguished."

"I have read about the Clan McCraig in the history
of Scotland," Shimona said.

"You are interested in history?"

"I love it!" she answered.

"Why?" the Duke enquired.

Shimona thought for a moment. She was used to
answering her father's questions seriously, so she replied:

"I suppose because it shows us the evolution of
civilisation. I particularly enjoy the history of Greece."

"You look like a Greek goddess yourself," the Duke
remarked. "But I expect many men have told you
that."

To his astonishment his words brought the colour
flaming into Shimona's cheeks and her eyes dropped
before his.

It was in fact the first compliment she had ever been
paid by a man other than her father or the Doctor.

"We were . . . speaking of the . . . task which lies
ahead of . . . me, Your Grace," she managed to say
after a moment or two.

"Yes, of course," the Duke agreed.

Then as if he could not help himself he asked:

"Surely you are very young to be on the stage?
There must be something better you could do!"

Shimona looked at him with a worried expression in
her eyes, and he knew that she was not going to give
him a truthful answer.

CHAPTER THREE

The dinner was coming to an end and Shimona had been entranced with everything about it.

She had never imagined a Dining-Room could look so attractive or that a table could be literally groaning under gold ornaments and candelabra.

It was also tastefully decorated with flowers and, as she sampled dish after dish served on gold plates by powdered flunkeys, she felt as if she was acting a part on the stage.

"And that is exactly what I am doing!" she told herself.

At the same time she had had no idea, she thought, that the props and the scenery would be so magnificent!

The McCraig of McCraig had not in fact been as frightening as she had anticipated.

She knew that he was eighty years of age, but he certainly did not look it; for he held himself stiffly upright and there was an inescapable dignity about him which Shimona thought must win respect wherever he went.

He was, with his high-bridged nose, his white hair swept back from his square forehead, his shrewd eyes under bushy eye-brows, exactly how she thought a Chieftain should look.

As the evening progressed she could not help

wondering how Alister McCraig could have married a somewhat disreputable actress when he had so much history behind him and such distinguished forebears.

Both the Duke and Alister realised that The McCraig was agreeably impressed by Shimona from the moment he saw her.

It would in fact have been hard for him not to do so. As she curtsied to him, her grace had reminded the Duke of the swans on his lake at Ravenstone.

But while she bore herself proudly there was no mistaking the touch of fear in her eyes and the worried look in her lovely face, which, the Duke thought perceptively, pleased the old Scot.

After all, he told himself, The McCraig was expecting not only an ill-bred actress, which Kitty undoubtedly was, but also someone who might be pert and aggressive simply because she would think he was condescending to her.

But Shimona actually played no part except that of being herself, striking just the right note of respect without being obsequious.

Luncheon was announced soon after The McCraig had arrived, and he talked of his journey south to the Duke while at the same time, they all knew, watching Shimona from under his thick eye-brows.

"I have an appointment with the Prime Minister," he said as luncheon was ending, "at half after two."

"I will order a carriage for you," the Duke remarked.

"That will leave you two young people free for an hour or so," The McCraig said to his great-nephew and Shimona.

"What would you wish to do?" the Duke enquired.

He thought with a faint air of amusement that the answer was all too obvious.

What woman, especially from the world of the theatre, could resist such an opportunity to spend money? He waited with a mocking look in his eyes for Shimona's answer.

She was however looking across the table at The
McCraig.

"Would it be . . . possible, Sir," she enquired,
"If you are . . . visiting the Prime Minister, for me
to . . . see the House of Commons?"

"I am sure it could be arranged," The McCraig answered. "You are interested in politics?"

"I read the Parliamentary reports every day in *The
Times*," Shimona replied, "and I have been deeply distressed by the reports of the Highland evictions."

As she spoke she wondered if she had been indiscreet. The McCraig might be one of the landlords who
were prepared to evict their own people to make the
land nothing but a sheep-walk.

But fortunately she had struck the right note.

"I am glad you feel like that," The McCraig said. "It
is a gross injustice, a betrayal of our own flesh and
blood and those who perpetrate such atrocities should
be shot!"

He spoke with a violence which seemed to boom out
in the Dining-Room.

Then he talked for ten minutes of the sufferings of
the Highlanders who, uprooted from all that was familiar, had been transported to Canada and other
parts of the world, without even adequate provision
being made for them when they arrived.

"I do not expect," he said at length, "to find much
understanding and sympathy amongst the Sassenachs,
but I might have known that your husband, being a
McCraig, would have made you realise the iniquity of
what is happening in the north."

He beamed at his great-nephew as he spoke and
luncheon ended in an atmosphere of mellow good humour.

The Duke's carriage conveyed The McCraig with Alister and Shimona to the House of Commons, and arrangements were made on their arrival for them to be
shown to the Strangers' Gallery.

They sat there for over an hour until they were

notified that The McCraig had finished his business with the Prime Minister.

He was in somewhat of a bad temper when they joined him because the Hon. Henry Addington, who had replaced the brilliant William Pitt, was a weak man who found it hard to make a decision.

He was obviously not prepared to agree to implement the reforms which The McCraig advocated.

But as they drove back to Berkeley Square, Shimona managed to coax the old gentleman back into a good humour which continued until it was time to change for dinner.

The bed-room she was to use at Ravenstone House was, Shimona thought, almost as impressive as the rooms downstairs.

Her mother had taught her to appreciate beautiful furniture and she exclaimed with delight over the French commodes in her bed-room, just as she was longing, when she had time, to inspect the exquisitely carved Charles II gilt tables which ornamented the Salon.

There were two maids to wait on her and she enjoyed the hot bath prepared with jasmine which was set in front of the fire, and the lavender-scented towels with which she could dry herself.

She kept wishing she could tell her mother all about the house, then wondered if her mother, like her father, would be very angry at her being a guest of the Duke.

There was something about him which was definitely frightening, she thought, and yet at the same time she found it hard not to admire him.

It was not only because of his good looks, it was also the way he walked, as if he owned the whole world, and his air of distinction.

She found herself thinking continually that the house and its contents were a fitting background for him.

"Why does he shock people so much?" she asked

herself, "and why does Papa say that he behaves like a
devil?"

The Duke's manners were impeccable and she knew
that he was trying in every possible way to prevent her
from feeling embarrassed or anxious at any question
which The McCraig put to her.

She realised it was for his own ends, and yet it was
impossible, where she was concerned, not to think of
him as being kind and considerate.

When she went downstairs holding on to the bannis-
ter of the carved staircase, she felt an irrepressible little
thrill of excitement at the prospect of spending the
evening with the Duke.

She had glanced at her reflection in the mirror before she left her bed-room and thought that Alister
McCraig would not be ashamed to own her as his wife.

Because she thought it made her look older she was
wearing one of her mother's evening-gowns.

It was a deep blue which matched the eyes of both of
them, and there was a shimmer of silver beneath the
soft gauze with which it was made, and sprinkled in the
tulle which framed the bodice there were tiny dew-
drops of diamonds.

It was the sort of elaborate gown which could have
been worn to a Ball or a Reception, and yet no-one but
Beau Bardsley had ever seen it.

"Why do you buy such elaborate gowns, Mama,
when you never go out, but only dine at home with
Papa?" Shimona had asked.

Her mother had hesitated for a moment before she
replied:

"It is difficult to explain, dearest, but your father
meets many beautiful women, not only in the theatre,
but also when he is invited to the houses of the nobil-
ity."

She gave a little sigh.

"I am not included in the invitations, but I wish him
to see me looking my best, as I would if I could accompany him."

There was something pathetic in the words which made Shimona say quickly:

"You always look beautiful, Mama, whatever you wear. Papa has often said that to him you are the most beautiful woman in the whole world!"

"I want him always to think so," Mrs. Bardsley said softly, "and that is why I dress to please him."

Shimona had understood, but because there was often a shortage of money, the elaborate gowns were not as many as her mother would have wished.

Nevertheless, as they had been kept so carefully, there was, now that her mother was dead, quite a number for Shimona to choose from.

That her choice was a good one she knew as soon as she entered the Salon.

The three men were waiting for her by the fireplace, and as she moved towards them she found it impossible for her eyes not to seek the Duke's. There was an expression in his that she knew she had wanted to see.

The conversation at dinner proved even more interesting than it had been at luncheon.

The McCraig talked of the difficulties in the Highlands and the Duke talked of sport.

Because Shimona listened wide-eyed and with interest to everything that was said, they drew her into the conversation and explained to her all she did not understand.

Now as dinner finished she looked a little nervously at the Duke and asked:

"Should I . . . retire and leave you to your port?"

Her mother had told her that this was what happened at the end of a formal dinner and the Duke smiled as if she had done the right thing.

As they all rose to their feet he said:

"We will not be long."

Shimona went from the Dining-Room down the passage to the Salon.

A flunkey opened the door and as soon as she was

alone she started to examine the treasures which the room contained.

There was so much to see, so much to admire, that she was in fact quite surprised when the gentlemen joined her.

She turned as they entered holding in her hand a miniature of a lovely woman which had been lying on one of the tables amongst a collection of snuff-boxes.

The Duke came to her side.

"I see you are admiring one of my miniatures," he said. "I have a large collection in another room."

"I am sure this is by Richard Cosway."

"It is a portrait of my mother."

"Oh, how strange, he also painted mine!" Shimona exclaimed.

As she spoke she wondered if she had made a mistake, but The McCraig had walked to the fireplace and was talking to his great-nephew.

"That is another thing we have in common," the Duke said in a low voice.

"Another?" Shimona questioned.

"There are many—we both love beauty for one."

"Yes . . . yes, of course."

She did not know why, but she found it difficult to talk naturally when he was standing so near to her.

There was also a note in his voice which made her vibrate just as she and the audience would vibrate to her father's voice on the stage.

Because she felt shy she put down the miniature and walked towards the fireplace.

The McCraig looked at her from under his eyebrows and said:

"I have been thinking that you have been extremely kind in listening to an old man talking about his hobby-horses ever since I arrived. To-morrow you must tell me something about yourself."

"Everything you have said, Sir, has been so interesting," Shimona answered. "I feel that anything I could relate would pale into insignificance."

The McCraig smiled.

"You are too modest," he said. "But there has been enough talking for to-night. You will, I know, excuse me if I go to bed. I am used to early hours and I have travelled a long way."

"I am sure you must be weary, Sir," Alister said.

The McCraig turned to the Duke.

"Good-night, Ravenstone, I am enjoying your hospitality and thank you for it."

"It is a very great pleasure," the Duke replied.

The McCraig touched Shimona on the shoulder and smiled at her.

"I shall look forward to our talk to-morrow."

He walked across the Salon with his shoulders back and his head held high while Alister hurried after him to escort him to the foot of the staircase.

The Duke and Shimona were left alone.

"You have been very clever with him," the Duke said approvingly.

"I think he is a very charming old man," Shimona answered, "and so interesting."

"Were you really interested in his tales of Scotland? Or was that part of the act?"

"Of course I was interested!" Shimona replied indignantly. "Who could fail to be?"

"And you enjoyed visiting the House of Commons?"

"It was thrilling! I have imagined so often what it was like, but hearing the speeches and seeing the Members sitting on the benches was quite different from what I expected."

"Different?"

"They were so . . . casual about it," Shimona explained feeling for words. "Sprawling with their feet up, their hats tipped over their eyes and half the time no-one seemed to be listening!"

"That is the way we are governed," the Duke smiled.

"Perhaps that is how democracy should be," she said reflectively, "not regimented, but at ease until one is galvanised into fighting for something that is really worthwhile!"

The Duke looked at her in surprise, but before he could speak Alister joined them.

"God, but you were magnificent!" he exclaimed to Shimona. "You have the old man eating out of your hand. I would never have credited that a woman could be so clever!"

There was something about his enthusiasm which jarred on Shimona.

She turned to look at the fire feeling somehow as if he made her feel cheap and a fraud.

"What are the plans for to-morrow?" the Duke asked.

"There is a Military Parade which he wishes to attend in Hyde Park in the morning," Alister replied. "Apparently one of the Scottish Regiments is taking part. In the afternoon he proposes to visit Kew Gardens."

The Duke laughed.

"I can see you are in for a riot of fun and gaiety!"

"Am I to go with you?" Shimona asked.

"I am afraid you will have to," Alister replied.

"Oh, I am glad!" she cried. "It sounds so exciting, and I have never seen a Military Parade."

"I will make arrangements for you all to be at the saluting base," the Duke said.

"You will not be able to come with us?" Shimona asked. "How disappointing for you!"

"Indeed it is most regrettable, but I have a previous engagement," the Duke replied and his eyes were twinkling.

"Please come with us in the afternoon, Uncle Yvell," Alister pleaded. "You know a lot about gardens because of the fine ones at Ravenstone, but I can hardly tell one flower from another."

"Then I see I shall have to sacrifice myself," the Duke replied. "Would you like to tell Captain Graham of our intentions so that he can make arrangements regarding the carriages and of course the seats at the Military Parade?"

"I will tell him at once," Alister agreed. "He will not have gone to bed?"

"Captain Graham never goes to bed," the Duke answered and his nephew laughed.

"I am sure that is true. Who except a superman could be Comptroller of your household?"

He walked away and the Duke said in explanation to Shimona:

"Captain Graham is my secretary and general factotum. You will find he can procure everything you want, everything you need, and, if necessary, at a moment's notice, arrange a journey to the moon!"

"I have no wish to visit the moon," Shimona answered. "It always looks such a cold and empty place. One of the twinkling stars would be far more exciting!"

"That is what you have been the whole evening," the Duke replied. "A twinkling star. Do I have to tell you that you have been quite wonderful?"

Her eyes dropped before his and she said a little incoherently:

"I think . . . Your Grace . . . it is time for me to . . . retire to bed."

"So early?" the Duke questioned. "Would you not wish to dance, to seek some of the many amusements with which London abounds?"

"No, no, of course not," Shimona replied quickly, thinking how horrified her father would be. "Your Grace will understand that like The McCraig I also am . . . tired."

"You do not like to dance?"

Shimona was just about to say that she had never been to a dance. Then she remembered that would not be in keeping with the actress she was supposed to be.

"It is . . . sometimes very . . . pleasant," she said after a moment.

"But you do not wish to dance either with Alister or with me?" the Duke persisted.

There was a perceptible pause before Shimona replied:

"I think, Your Grace, it would be a mistake for me to be seen in . . . public with Mr. Craig, when many people must be . . . aware that he is . . . married."

The Duke smiled as if he realised she had thought up the excuse.

"You are a very strange person," he said slowly, "and I am being completely honest when I say quite unlike anyone I have ever met before."

She looked up at him to see if he was mocking her, then found it hard to look away.

"Tell me the truth. Are you really looking forward to seeing a Military Parade to-morrow and going to Kew Gardens?"

"I especially want to see Kew Gardens again," Shimona said in a low voice, "I have not been there since . . ."

She stopped.

She had been about to say that she had not been there since her mother's death. Then she wondered if it was a mistake to say too much about herself.

She did not realise how expressive her eyes were.

"You have not been there since you were with someone who mattered a great deal to you," the Duke said.

Shimona did not reply. She was thinking how unexpectedly perceptive he was.

"Who was that person?" he enquired and there was a note in his voice that she did not understand.

Because she felt compelled to answer him she said:

"My . . . mother."

"And she is dead?"

"Yes. She . . . died two years . . . ago."

"And you loved her very much?"

"More than I can ever say."

"But you have other members of your family?"

"Yes . . ."

Shimona felt embarrassed by his interrogation and

glanced towards the door. But there was no sign of Alister McCraig.

"May I . . . retire, Your Grace?"

"Are you running away from me or my questions?"

"Perhaps . . . both, Your Grace."

"But you are not so afraid of me as you were when you arrived?"

She looked at him in surprise. She had hoped he had not realised how frightened she had been.

Unexpectedly she smiled.

"I am still frightened . . . Your Grace, but now my legs will support me and my heart has stopped turning . . . somersaults."

He laughed.

"The question I would like to ask you," he said after a moment, "is whether you judge people by what you have heard about them, or by what you yourself feel?"

Shimona tried to find words with which to answer him. Then before she could do so Alister McCraig came back into the Salon.

"Everything is arranged," he said, "and now, if you will forgive me, Uncle Yvell, I am going back to Kitty.

"I told her I had to be with you to discuss financial matters with your Attorneys. She knew I would remain for dinner, but she will certainly not expect me to stay the night."

"Very well, Alister," the Duke replied, "but you had best be back in time to breakfast with your Great-Uncle."

"I will not be late, that I promise you," Alister answered. "I certainly do not wish to disrupt the excellent impression our brilliant little actress had made on him!"

Once again Shimona felt his words were slightly degrading.

She curtsied low to the Duke, but not so low to her supposed husband.

"Good-night, Your Grace. Good-night Mr. McCraig."

Then she went quickly from the Salon before they could escort her.

Driving towards the party which the Duke had expected he might have to miss that evening, he thought how simply and without a hitch everything had proceeded.

He had imagined that all sorts of difficulties might arise when The McCraig met his great-nephew's supposed wife, but there was no doubt that Shimona had swept away his opposition and any feeling of aggression he may have had, from the very first moment.

She was in fact, the Duke told himself, the most amazing actress he had ever encountered—if indeed she was acting.

He had asked Beau Bardsley for a lady and Beau had certainly provided him with one.

There was good breeding, the Duke thought, not only in Shimona's exquisite features, but also in her long fingers, her arched insteps, and in every word she spoke.

Hers was not the assumed accent of a "Lady of Quality" which he had heard so often on the stage, nor had she any need to pick and choose her words.

She was as natural as a flower, and that, he thought, was what she resembled: the purity of a lily, perhaps a rose still in bud, or again the syringa blossoms which scented the gardens at Ravenstone in the spring.

"Good God, I am becoming a sentimentalist!" he told himself and tried to concentrate on Mary Ann Clarke.

He had in fact, when he had grown bored, introduced her to His Royal Highness.

Mary Ann at twenty-seven was not only extremely attractive, she also loved life and bubbled over with a gaiety which was all her own.

"If anyone can make H.R.H. forget his frigid, ugly,

German wife, his Army duties and money difficulties, it is Mrs. Clarke," an Officer under his command had remarked.

Established by her Royal protector in a large mansion in Gloucester Place with twenty servants including three coachmen, and three Chefs, Mary Ann was making the most of her new position.

At her parties she supplied her guests, the Bucks and Blades of St. James's with beautiful girls of every colour and led her Royal protector into wild excesses.

It was of course expected that every Gentleman of Fashion should have a mistress, and despite the sanctimonious boredom of the Court at Buckingham House it was a robust, bawdy, promiscuous age.

The rowdy parties and the very undesirable friends the Prince of Wales collected around him came in for a lot of criticism, anything which happened at Carlton House was mild compared with the orgies that took place in other noblemen's houses.

A large number of His Royal Highness's closest friends were certain to be at Mary Ann's this evening.

They would include the two most notorious Dukes in England, Queensbury and Norfolk, both of them celebrated drunkards and the former a dedicated lecher.

Sir John Wade, an amazingly disreputable figure who derived a large fortune from a brewery, was sure to be another guest. His wife had numbered the Duke of York among her lovers.

Thinking of the fair charmers with whom he had spent many amusing hours before he tired of them, the Duke's mind lingered on Fanny Norton.

The daughter of a dressmaker in Southampton, after many protectors including Richard Brinsley Sheridan and the Duke himself, she had been sold by Colonel Harvey Aston, a leading light of the Quorn Hunt, when he was hard up for 500 guineas, to the Earl of Barrymore.

A doubtful exchange, as nicknamed 'Hellgate'

because of his violent temper, the Earl was one of the most debauched men in London.

The Duke remembered how Fanny had been led on a silken halter into Colonel Aston's Dining-Room where he was presiding over a stag-party which included "Hellgate."

She wore only a single garment, giving His Lordship every chance of seeing what he was getting for his money.

Buying a mistress had become quite a vogue.

When he was young the Duke of York had bought one of his first mistresses, the daughter of an hautboy player, for £1,500.

Lord Hervey's doxy was a tiny, doll-like creature called Vanelle Vane and the Prime Minister also fancied her. Lord Hervey made her over to him for a generous sum.

"Thank God I have never needed to buy a woman!" the Duke thought to himself as his carriage travelled towards Gloucester Place.

He could not blind himself to the fact that they rushed into his arms before he even signified any interest in them.

But he was, as they all knew, extremely generous to those whom he took under his protection, although unfortunately he was also known to tire of them very easily, and any pretty Cyprian he fancied soon found herself looking around for another banker.

Nevertheless, the Duke thought, these pretty, expendable "bits o' muslin" could be amusing if only for a short time.

The carriage was crossing Oxford Street and looking out through the window the Duke saw on the pavement a ragged man selling a publication which was greatly in demand by those who could not afford to set up their own establishments.

It was called *The Whoremongers Guide to London* and contained addresses of Houses of Pleasure and descriptions of those known as the "Covent Garden Nuns."

There were as usual a number of street-walkers standing near the lamps which illuminated quite effectively the more frequented thoroughfares. Some of them looked very young and were in fact little more than children.

Their eyes were painted, their lips reddened, and there was no mistaking the eagerness with which they tried to accost every male passer-by.

As the carriage drove on quite suddenly the Duke had no wish for the type of entertainment which he knew was waiting for him in Gloucester Place.

He unexpectedly felt bored at the thought of Mary Ann Clarke's exuberance and the simulated professional gaiety of the girls she would have chosen with such care.

He found himself thinking of two worried blue eyes and a soft voice which had a note of fear behind it.

The Duke bent forward and rapped with his gold-handled cane on the front of the carriage behind the coachman.

The horses were drawn to a standstill and the footman jumped down to open the door.

"White's Club!" the Duke ordered.

As the horses were turned round and started back the way they had come he said to himself in a tone of astonishment:

"Good God! I must be getting old!"

The afternoon was as sunny as it had been in the morning. The air was crisp but it was warm for late October, and Shimona had discarded her blue cloak and was quite warm enough in the jacket which covered her gown.

She had found the Military Parade in the morning as exciting as she had anticipated, and when the Scottish

Regiment marched past, led by the pipe band, her eyes
had been shining and she seemed so thrilled that The
McCraig had looked at her with approval.

"I never believed that men could appear so magnificent as they do in the kilt," she told The McCraig as
they drove back to Berkeley Square.

"You and your husband must come and stay at Castle Craig, then you can see and hear my own pipers,"
The McCraig replied.

The words made her feel as if doused with cold water.

With an effort Shimona remembered that she would
never be taken to stay at the Castle nor would she hear
The McCraig's pipers.

As if he sensed her sudden embarrassment, Alister
said quickly:

"I remember hearing your pipers when I was a small
boy, Great-Uncle. I used to creep out of bed when we
stayed at the Castle to hear them going round the table
at dinner and longed to be downstairs."

"Well, you are old enough to enjoy them now," The
McCraig replied, "and when you have a son of your
own you must teach him the history of the McCraigs
and how well they fought in battle, marching behind
their own pipers."

"I shall do that," Alister said and there was no doubt
of his sincerity.

The McCraig had looked at Shimona.

"I do not wish to make you blush," he said, "but I
would like to see my great-grand-nephew before I
die."

His words did make Shimona blush and she was
thankful when the carriage came to a standstill in
Berkeley Square.

Luncheon was a small meal compared to the large
dinner they had eaten the night before, and Shimona
wondered whether the Duke's slim, athletic figure was
due to the fact that he ate little and took a large
amount of exercise.

She had learnt from Alister that his appointment that morning had not been of a very serious nature, but that he always rode for several hours in the Park, schooling the horses which his grooms found too hard to handle.

As soon as luncheon was finished they set off for Kew Gardens, and now at the Duke's suggestion they travelled in two Phaetons, he tooling one and Alister the other.

Both Phaetons had a groom up behind, but Shimona found herself to all intents and purposes alone with the Duke.

She did not pretend to herself that it was not something that she wished for and enjoyed.

She had known last night, when she thought over what had happened during the day, that what she most notably remembered were her conversations with the Duke.

When he was present, she thought, it was difficult for her to notice anyone else or even attend to any conversation in which he did not take part.

She could not understand this, except that she realised he had the same kind of magnetism that her father had, a power to draw people to him and to hold them spellbound.

Never before, she thought as they drove along, had the sun seemed so golden or the day held a magic which it was difficult to put into words.

"You are warm enough?" the Duke asked as the horses moved more quickly when they were free of the heavy traffic in Piccadilly.

"I am very warm," Shimona replied. "It is such a lovely day!"

She looked up at the sky as she spoke and the Duke glanced at her perfect profile and the long line of her neck before his attention returned to his horses.

"One day," he said, "I must show you my garden in the country. It was laid out by my grand-father when

73

he made many alterations to the house and he employed the great gardeners of the time."

"Let me guess who they were," Shimona said. "Charles Bridgeman, William Kent and Capability Brown."

"You are very knowledgeable, Miss Wantage, and completely correct in your assumption."

"Have you any of the William Kent furniture?"

"Several pairs of tables," the Duke replied.

"Oh, I would love to see them!" Shimona exclaimed.

"I want to show them to you."

She was just about to ask more about them when she remembered that she would never have a chance of seeing the Duke's gardens or his furniture.

To-morrow morning she would disappear out of his life as unceremoniously as she had come into it.

Never, never must her father guess where she had been or what she had done!

She was already trying to concoct a story to explain how they now had enough money to go abroad.

Doctor Lesley would help her there, she hoped, and she would bully Nanna into never disclosing that she had been away from the house in Chelsea for two nights.

At least Nanna had not known where she had gone because, although she had insisted on having Shimona's address, it had in fact been placed in an envelope which Nanna had sworn she would not open except in an emergency.

"If Papa becomes dangerously ill and Doctor Lesley tells you to send for me, then open the envelope," Shimona instructed her.

"I don't like all this secrecy," Nanna said fiercely. "If your mother's looking down from Heaven at us—God rest her soul!—she would say the same!"

"Mama would want us to save Papa," Shimona repeated for the thousandth time.

But Nanna was still grumbling when she left the house.

"Nothing matters except that Papa should get well," Shimona told herself now.

At the same time she was conscious of something almost like a little ache in her heart at the thought that she would never see the Duke again—never again see his handsome face, or hear his voice with that particular note in it that always made her feel a little breathless.

She had been aware that he looked at her admiringly when she came into the Salon before luncheon, having removed the bonnet she had worn for the Military Parade, to find him having a glass of sherry with The McCraig.

It had been an effort to walk across the room towards him, and yet at the same time it was difficult to prevent herself from running to reach him.

"What are you thinking about?" he asked now, breaking in on her thoughts.

"I was thinking about your house in the country. Is it very large?"

"Very large, very impressive and I think very beautiful!" he replied laughingly.

"Then it must be," she answered, "because you have such good taste."

He turned to look at her fleetingly and she saw that his eye-brows were raised.

"Was that rude?" she asked quickly. "Should I not have said it?"

"It is a compliment which I accept with great pleasure!"

Shimona thought for a moment, then she said:

"But you are surprised that an . . . actress should recognise good taste."

"I did not say so."

"But that is what you thought."

"The truth is that I am afraid of your reading my thoughts so easily."

"As I . . . am when you read . . . mine."

"You have something to hide and you are in fact hiding it from me very successfully."

There was silence until, when they had driven further, the Duke said:

"I wish that you would trust me, even though there is little reason why you should do so."

Shimona sighed.

"I . . . want to trust you . . . and I hate having . . . secrets . . . it is very . . . difficult . . ."

"I have a feeling, although I may be mistaken, that you find it hard to lie."

"I have never lied!" Shimona said quickly, "except . . ."

"Except at this moment?"

Shimona made a gesture with her hands.

"Please . . ." she pleaded, "you are making it very . . . difficult and I am doing what you want."

"And doing it brilliantly," the Duke said in a low voice. "So much so that I am not only astonished and bewildered, but also intrigued and most curious!"

Shimona sat staring straight ahead of her.

The sun glinted on the silver of the horses' harness and it seemed to dazzle her eyes, or was it that she was dazzled by the man beside her?

They reached Kew Gardens and Alister, who had been following close behind, drew up his horses near to them.

It was obvious as soon as they began to walk around the gardens that The McCraig was very knowledgeable about plants and shrubs, especially about those that had recently been discovered.

Alister never said a word, and as the old man seemed content to talk to Shimona, the Duke also relapsed into silence.

"Discovering a new plant is just as exciting, if not more so, than discovering a new planet," The McCraig said.

"You are thinking of Uranus, Sir," Shimona smiled. "I have read how it was discovered by Sir William

Herschel, who was a musician before becoming an astronomer."

"That is right!" The McCraig said, obviously delighted at her knowledge. "And I expect you know that it was David Douglas who brought the Douglas Fir from the West Coast of America."

"I am afraid I am more interested in flowers, Sir," Shimona said, "which my mother loved. She told me how excited she was when she first saw the gold lily—*lycoris*—when she was a little girl."

"A beautiful bloom," The McCraig said. "But I prefer the Fuchsia which was introduced only a few years ago and which I can grow in Scotland."

"I can understand that," Shimona smiled.

They looked at the Chinese Pagoda and at the Chinese gardens around it which were of particular interest to The McCraig.

"Do you know anything about the Chinese?" he asked Shimona.

"I know they have ancient medicines which they have found efficacious over the centuries," she replied.

"Medicines?" he queried.

"All flowers and plants have medicinal qualities."

"I know there are herbs used by the gypsies and some country folk," the Duke interposed, "but are you telling me that ordinary flowers can be used medicinally?"

Shimona smiled at him.

"Of course they can! Roses for instance to help the heart and liver, and not only to prevent pain but also heal internal wounds."

"I never realised that before!" the Duke exclaimed.

"The lily-of-the-valley is particularly good for rheumatism and depression and also helps the brain."

"Then I can think of a number of acquaintances who need that," the Duke remarked dryly.

"Have you made a study of this?" The McCraig enquired.

"My mother was very interested in herbs and flowers

and she taught me quite a lot about them," Shimona replied simply.

"Your wife is far more talented and knowledgeable than I ever expected in anyone so young," The Mc-Craig said to Alister as they walked back through the Gardens to where their Phaetons were waiting.

"I am a very lucky man!" he said lightly.

"You are indeed! Very lucky!" The McCraig answered and there was no doubt that he meant it.

As they drove back in the Phaeton the Duke said:

"Once again you have given a performance that was not only faultless but would bring any audience to their feet!"

"It was not a . . . performance!"

"I realise that."

"We are lying to him about only one thing," Shimona said. "Surely therefore what we are doing cannot be so very . . . wrong?"

She was pleading with him almost like a child who wishes to be reassured, and after a moment the Duke said:

"I do not think that anyone would consider it wrong to make the old gentleman happy, which he obviously is in your company, and to allay his fears where his great-nephew is concerned."

"But if he ever finds out?" Shimona asked.

"That is something which must not happen! Alister made a monumental mistake in marrying this woman, but I do not wish him to be penalised for the rest of his life."

The Duke spoke almost harshly.

"Would you . . . feel that about any . . . actress he had married?" Shimona enquired.

"If he had married someone like you I should have been delighted, as obviously The McCraig is, that he had found anyone so exceptional."

"But at the same time you think that a man should not . . . marry out of his own . . . position in life."

There was a pause before the Duke answered:

"I will not insult your intelligence by denying that I think marriage should be between two people who are born equally."

"Then what you are saying is that it is what a man *is,* rather than what he *does,* which counts?" Shimona argued.

The Duke drove on a little way before he replied:

"You are pushing me into a corner from which I find it difficult to extricate myself. What you are really asking is this: if a gentleman, like Beau Bardsley, and a lady, such as you obviously are, are on the stage, is that of more importance than the class in which they were born?"

"Yes," Shimona said in a low voice. "That is what I am . . . trying to say."

"It depends on what they want of life," the Duke answered. "If they are content with the plaudits of the crowd, if they want professional success and fame, then the fact that they are not accepted as the equal of those who consider themselves of social importance cannot be of any consequence to them."

Shimona did not reply, then he said:

"I have a feeling, however, it would always be of consequence to a woman."

He turned to look at her before he added:

"I have already asked you if there is not something more worthwhile and more suitable you can do than to be an actress."

CHAPTER FOUR

*T*he gentlemen came into the Salon where Shimona was once again looking at the *objets d'art.*

She turned with a smile and The McCraig said:

"Come here, Katherine. I want to speak to you and Alister."

He spoke seriously and Shimona gave the Duke a little worried glance before obediently she followed the old man to the hearth-rug.

He stood with his back to the fire and as Shimona and Alister joined him he said:

"I understand that the Duke has been kind enough to accommodate you here in this house while you look for one of your own. I am sure you appreciate his generosity. At the same time I know that it is important for you both to have a home."

He paused and Shimona wondered what he was going to say.

"I have thought it over . . ." he continued, "and I realise that Alister cannot afford at the moment to buy a house which would be a proper back-ground for his wife, and in the future a family."

Shimona saw that Alister was listening intently and there was a faint smile on his lips as if he anticipated what was to come.

"I have therefore decided," The McCraig went on, "that when I return to Scotland I will settle a sum of money on my great-nephew which will enable him to live comfortably as befits his station in life, and when I die he will be my heir."

His voice ceased and for a moment there was a silence that seemed more impressive than words. Then Alister exclaimed:

"That is exceedingly generous of you, Sir. I am more grateful than I can possibly say."

"I do not mind telling you, my boy," The McCraig replied, "that when I came south I was somewhat anxious as to what sort of wife you had chosen. However although Katherine regrettably is connected with the stage she is everything I would have wished for the wife of the future Chieftain of the Clan."

He looked at Shimona as he spoke.

"Thank . . . you," she murmured.

She wished she did not feel so guilty and that they had not been obliged to deceive this fine old gentleman. She thought also how horrifying it would be if he ever found out the deception that had been practised upon him.

Because she felt guilty, Shimona moved forward impulsively and kissed The McCraig on the cheek.

"Thank you for making Alister happy," she said.

She knew The McCraig was pleased at her gesture. Then as if he suspected them of being over-emotional he said almost harshly:

"I am now going to say good-bye, Katherine, as I shall not expect to see you in the morning."

Shimona looked surprised and he explained:

"I am leaving very early as I have been invited to stay the first night of my journey north with the Earl of Glencairn near Leicester. He is an old friend of mine, and I have promised to be his guest."

He looked at the Duke as he said:

"I hope, Ravenstone, it will not be inconvenient for me to leave at seven o'clock?"

"It is not in the least inconvenient," the Duke

replied. "But are you certain it will not be too long a day for you?"

"I am used to rising early," The McCraig replied, "and as I wish to dine with the Earl, the sooner I am on the road the better!"

He held out his hand to Shimona.

"Good-bye, my dear. I hope it will not be too long before I may entertain you at Craig Castle, and that many relatives of your husband may have the pleasure of meeting you."

"I shall look forward to it," Shimona answered as she curtsied.

"I shall doubtless see you in the morning, Alister," The McCraig said to his great-nephew.

"Of course, Sir."

This time they all escorted The McCraig to the foot of the stairs. He walked up without the aid of the bannisters and Shimona thought it was easy to think of him as a King in the Highlands.

As soon as he was out of ear-shot Alister said:

"I must go back to Kitty. If I am to be back here by half-after-six to-morrow morning, the sooner I am asleep the better!"

The Duke did not reply and Shimona had the idea that he despised Alister for thinking it a hardship that he must rise early.

Although she felt that she also should say goodnight she moved back towards the Salon and when the Duke followed her the door was shut behind them.

She walked to the fireplace and he moved slowly across the room towards her, looking as he did so at her face bent towards the flames and the light from them shining on her fair hair.

"It is entirely due to you," he said, "that the campaign to improve Alister's finances has been overwhelmingly successful!"

There was a note in his voice which did not make it sound as complimentary as the actual words.

"I feel . . . ashamed," Shimona murmured. "The

McCraig is so magnificent and so honest and straight-forward that I am sure it is wrong of us to deceive him."

"We have discussed this already," the Duke replied. "There was no other way that he could be persuaded to make Alister his heir."

"Do you think when the time . . . comes that Mr. McCraig will make a good . . . Chieftain?" Shimona asked in a low voice.

"Does it really concern you one way or the other?" the Duke enquired.

Shimona was silent. Then she said:

"Perhaps it sounds impertinent, but because I have been involved I do mind. I would not want the members of the Clan to be disappointed or disillusioned."

"I have a feeling," the Duke said, "that Alister has learnt a lot from associating with you these last two days. He may in future insist on his wife behaving as she should do."

"A wise man once said that when a stone is thrown into a pond the disturbance from it goes on rippling out and one has no idea where the consequences will end," Shimona said in a low voice.

"That is true," the Duke replied. "But the consequences that you have evoked can only be good."

"How can you be sure of that?"

"I am sure because of your intrinsic goodness."

Shimona looked at the Duke in surprise.

Then as their eyes met she felt once again that strange magnetism that held her spellbound and made her feel almost as if he was drawing her towards him.

She made a little movement as if she would break the spell and the Duke said:

"I want to talk to you, Shimona. Sit down."

His voice was very serious. Her eyes widened and there was a questioning look in them before she obeyed him.

"First of all," he began. "I want to give you the

money that was promised to you and which you have
earned so brilliantly."

He took a sealed envelope from the table as he spoke
and held it out to her.

Shimona took it automatically, but as she did so she
wished she could refuse it.

Then she remembered that her father's life de-
pended upon it and with a little murmur of thanks she
laid it beside her on the sofa.

"I felt you would wish the money to be paid in
notes," the Duke said. "They are of a large denomina-
tion that can easily be changed."

Shimona did not speak and he went on:

"I would have preferred to pay it into a Bank for
you. It could be dangerous for you to carry so much
money about."

His words gave Shimona an idea.

"I have a message for Your Grace, from Mr. Bardsley."

"A message?" the Duke enquired.

"He asked," Shimona continued, "if you would pay
the money you owe him directly into his Bank."

The Duke smiled.

"That is extremely sensible. If I gave Beau Bardsley
notes, I am quite certain he would have given them all
away long before he left the theatre. Have you any idea
of the name of his Bank?"

"Yes . . . he told me it was Coutts."

"The money will be paid in to-morrow morning,"
the Duke said. "I gather you know Beau Bardsley
well?"

"Yes."

"Have you asked his advice about going on the
stage?"

"N . no."

"Then I am sure he would advise you against it as I
do," the Duke said.

There was a pause, before he went on:

"Tell me something, Shimona, and I want the truth. Have you as yet played a part in the theatre?"

She looked up at him and somehow it was impossible to lie.

"Not . . . yet."

"That is what I suspected," the Duke replied. "Now listen to me. Whatever you may feel about the glamour and lure of the theatre, you are wrong—completely and absolutely wrong!"

"Why should you say that?" Shimona asked.

"Because I know the theatrical world," the Duke answered, "and while some women, although very few, can reach the top of their profession simply through their talent, for the rest it is a very different story."

Shimona knew what he was trying to say, but because she was embarrassed, she could only look into the fire.

"I do not believe for a moment," the Duke went on, "that you could cope with the sordid intrigue which is necessary for an actress to obtain a part she wants, or even to get a hearing, without someone to fight her battles for her. Do you understand?"

"Y . yes . . . I understand," Shimona said in a low voice.

"Then give up this absurd idea," the Duke insisted.

Shimona rose to her feet.

"I think, Your Grace, there is nothing to be gained by discussing it."

"I have not finished all I wish to say."

Shimona looked irresolute.

Because she could not give the Duke the answers he wanted, she wished to run away.

On the other hand she did not want to leave him, knowing this was their last night together and after tomorrow she would never see him again.

"You will tell me nothing about yourself," he went on, "but I am sure that the reason you wish to go on the stage is because you need the money."

She knew that he was feeling for words before he went on:

"What I am about to suggest may sound strange, but I want to help. I want to do what is best for you."

"Please . . . Your Grace . . . do not say any more."

"I must," he answered. "I want to offer you, Shimona, enough money so that you can be independent."

Shimona drew her breath and now she was looking at him.

"I swear to you," the Duke said, "that I will ask nothing in return except what you wish to give me. There are no conditions attached to my offer—none whatsoever!"

He spoke impressively and even as the words of refusal came to Shimona's lips he said:

"I think you know there is a great deal more I could say to you—a great deal I want to say. But I promised Beau Bardsley when he sent you here that you would leave my house as pure as when you came into it."

Shimona's eyes flickered before his and the colour rose in her cheeks.

"I have kept my promise," the Duke said, "but you will never know how difficult it has been and how much I have wanted to make love to you, to tell you that you are the most beautiful person I have ever seen in my whole life!"

"It . . . it is . . . n . . . not . . . t . . . true," Shimona stammered a little incoherently.

"It is true, absolutely true!" the Duke said, "but I gave that promise and I will not break it. So there is only one thing I can ask you: when may I see you again?"

Shimona drew in her breath.

"Never! We shall never . . . meet again!"

"Do you really mean that?"

"It is . . . impossible . . . I cannot . . . explain . . . but it is impossible!"

"And you will not accept my offer of independence?"

Shimona shook her head.

"No, Your Grace. I know you mean it kindly, but you have given me everything I want."

"500 guineas?" the Duke queried. "My dear child, how long do you think that will last?"

"Long enough," Shimona answered.

She was thinking that with the 500 guineas her father was to receive they would be able to stay abroad for at least six months.

"Enough for what?" the Duke enquired.

Shimona did not reply and he exclaimed almost angrily:

"Why must you be so mysterious? Why must you perturb me by giving me no explanations—by leaving me knowing as little about you now as when you first came?"

She did not answer and he said:

"That is not quite true. I know a great deal about you—about your character, your personality, your sweetness, and indeed your purity."

He struck on the mantelpiece with his clenched fist as he said:

"Knowing what I feel, do you really think you can walk out of my life and that after to-morrow I shall never see you again? It is impossible! Completely impossible!"

"It is . . . something you have to . . . accept."

Shimona paused before she added:

"If it makes you . . . happier, I will . . . not go on the . . . stage."

"Then what will you do? Where will you be?"

"I am going . . . abroad."

"Abroad?" the Duke echoed. "To live? And do you think that wise when there is also the possibility of war breaking out with France again?"

"Italy may not be involved," Shimona said quickly.

"So you intend to go to Italy."

She realised she had made a slip and therefore did not answer him.

"I have a feeling that if you reach Italy this year, you may not be able to return."

He came a little nearer to her.

"Who are you going with? Is it a man who is taking you away from your own country and everything that is familiar? Are you marrying him?"

Shimona gave a deep sigh.

"I cannot answer any of those questions, Your Grace. I think it would be wise now for me to retire to bed."

"I think it would be wise," the Duke replied, "but I do not intend to let you go until you tell me the truth."

"I cannot . . . please . . . I cannot!"

"I have asked you to trust me."

"I . . . I want to . . . but it is impossible . . . I swear to you that it is . . . impossible . . . otherwise I would do so."

She was pleading with him and he reached out his hand to take her chin in his fingers and turn her face up to his.

"Could anyone look like you," he asked almost savagely, "and yet be ready to deceive me?"

"I am not . . . deceiving you."

It was difficult to speak because the touch of his fingers gave her a strange sensation.

He did not release her but looked deeper into her eyes and seemed to come closer.

"You are so beautiful!" he said. "So unbelievably, incredibly beautiful!"

Because the note in his voice made her breathless and because her throat seemed somehow to be constricted Shimona put up both her hands as if to ward him off.

"Please . . ." she begged, "please . . . you are frightening me."

The Duke took his fingers from her chin.

"I do not wish to do that, but you are driving me mad!"

There was a fire in his eyes which made her tremble but she managed to stammer:

"You . . . you will . . . forget me and thank you . . . Your Grace . . . for all your . . . kindness."

"Do you really mean that?" the Duke asked. "What can I say? How can I persuade you that you must not go?"

"I have to," Shimona answered. "There is nothing . . . more to be said . . . and it will only make . . . everything more . . . complicated."

"Why? Why?" the Duke asked. "Why can you not tell me the truth? What are these secrets you are hiding?"

Shimona turned to pick up the envelope from the sofa.

"Good-night . . . Your Grace."

"If you really mean never to see me again," the Duke said, "and if you do intend to go abroad where I cannot find you, then will you let me kiss you good-bye?"

She did not answer and he said with a twist to his lips:

"It is not much to ask, and may I say it is something I cannot remember having asked before in the whole of my life."

He looked down at her worried little face and he said very softly:

"You do not have to tell me that you have never been kissed, and I want more than my hope of Heaven to be the first."

Shimona told herself she should not listen to him, that she should leave the room immediately.

She tried to think of her father, but somehow everything seemed to be swept away from her but the Duke's pleading voice and the strange feeling she always had when he was near to her.

She looked up at him and was lost.

There was something in his eyes that was irresistible, something too which seemed to unite them in a manner which Shimona could not explain, and yet was a wonder she had never known before.

He came closer still and now very gently, as if he was afraid to frighten her, he put his arms around her and drew her to him.

Vaguely, far away at the back of her mind, she thought she ought to struggle, but it was impossible.

There was a rightness, something inevitable about what was happening that might have been planned since the beginning of time.

"You are so perfect!" the Duke murmured, then his lips touched hers.

It was a kiss so gentle, so tender, that Shimona was not afraid and she was conscious of feeling secure and protected because the Duke's arms were round her.

Then as his mouth took possession of her she felt as if everything beautiful she had ever heard and seen was concentrated into a feeling that was an ecstasy of wonder and of joy.

The room disappeared and there was no longer the warmth of the fire, the fragrance of the flowers or the light from the candles.

There was only a sky brilliant with stars and they were alone beneath it, a man and a woman who had found each other across eternity.

The Duke drew her closer still and now his lips became more insistent and more demanding. At the same time there was still a gentleness that precluded fear.

How long the kiss lasted Shimona had no idea.

She only knew when finally he raised his head that she felt dazed and bewildered as if she had fallen back to earth from the very heights of Heaven.

For one moment she looked up into his eyes.

Then with an inarticulate little murmur she turned and ran from the room leaving him standing, staring at the closed door long after she had left.

Shimona had to wait for a long time on the doorstep before, after repeated rat-tats on the knocker Nanna came to open it.

"My dearie!" she exclaimed when she saw who was standing there. "I'd no idea it'd be you, but you're so early. It's not yet six o'clock."

"I know," Shimona answered.

She walked into the house and the cabby who had brought her from Berkeley Square carried in her small trunk.

She paid him and when he had gone Nanna asked:

"What's happened? Why are you here at this hour?"

"It is all right," Shimona said soothingly. "I wanted to get away as soon as I could. I have the money, Nanna. We can leave for Italy as soon as Papa is able to travel."

Nanna did not answer and Shimona said quickly:

"Why do you look like that? How is Papa?"

"I don't like the look of him," Nanna replied. "The Doctor came yesterday and he's coming again this morning, but I won't lie to you, dearie, he seems to be sinking."

"I will go to him."

Shimona pulled off her cape, flung it on a chair and ran up the stairs.

Her father's room was in darkness.

She pulled open the curtains and let in the grey misty light of the early morning.

Now she could see him lying against his pillows and she knew that what Nanna had said was true.

There was something transparent about his face that had not been there before.

He had always been too thin, but now his cheeks were hollow, there were dark lines beneath his eyes and there was altogether an insubstantial look about him.

Shimona stood looking at him for a long time. Then as he still seemed to be asleep, she made up the fire and went from the room.

Nanna was carrying her trunk upstairs.

"Has he been coughing very much?" Shimona asked.

"Sometimes in his sleep," Nanna answered, "and very badly when he is awake. The Doctor's kept him drowsy and he hasn't realised you've not been here."

"We must try and persuade him to take some food," Shimona said.

It was however difficult and although she tried to coax her father into eating a little breakfast he would only drink a cup of coffee and shook his head to every other suggestion.

"You must get strong and well, Papa."

"I am—tired," he replied in a far-away voice. "Too tired to—think, too tired to—act."

As if the word "act" impinged upon him he said in a different tone:

"Act! Are they—expecting me at the—theatre?"

"Not to-day, Papa," Shimona answered. "To-day is Sunday."

It was not true, but she thought it would prove as an excuse for him to rest and she gave a sigh of relief as his head went back against the pillows.

"What am I—playing on—Monday?" he asked after a moment.

"Hamlet," Shimona replied. "You are playing Hamlet all next week and the theatre is sold out."

She felt sure that this was what he would want to hear.

There was a faint smile on his lips as Beau Bardsley said:

"That should mean—they will be able to—pay the staff."

"Yes, of course, Papa."

Nanna came in to tidy the room and when she had done so she said she would wash and shave "the

92

Master." She sent Shimona downstairs to prepare him an egg whipped up in milk.

"Add a little brandy to the glass," she said. "It'll give him strength if he won't eat anything."

When Shimona came upstairs again her father was coughing.

Perhaps it was because he had been moved while Nanna washed him, but whatever the reason he was coughing with a wrenching, rasping sound which seemed to shake his whole body.

He coughed and coughed, and now there was more blood on his handkerchief than there had ever been before and Shimona looked at Nanna with frightened eyes.

Finally Beau Bardsley lay back exhausted and Shimona was terrified by his pallor and by the difficulty he had in breathing.

It was then she heard a knock at the door and guessed that it was Doctor Lesley.

She sped down the stairs and when he saw her he exclaimed:

"I am glad you are back, my child! If you had not been I had intended to send for you."

He saw the question in Shimona's eyes before he drew her into the small Sitting-Room.

He did not speak and after a moment Shimona said:

"I have the money. If Papa is well enough I can take him abroad."

Doctor Lesley was still for a moment before he said very quietly:

"I think, Shimona, you would rather know the truth. It will be impossible for your father to travel anywhere. In fact, my dear, there is nothing I can do to save him!"

Shimona used to wonder later how she would ever have managed without Doctor Lesley.

When her father died, he had done everything and

in fact it was difficult for her to realise what was happening, except that she had an intolerable sense of loss.

She had somehow never imagined that he would die as her mother had, so quickly. One moment they were there and the next there was just an empty void which nothing could fill.

And yet his death had been beautiful, in a way he himself would have wished to die if he could have chosen it.

It was in the afternoon of the day that Shimona returned home. She was sitting alone by her father's bedside, striving to face the truth of what Doctor Lesley had told her and trying vainly to believe that a miracle might still save her father.

The light from the fire cast a glow upon his face and he did not look so pale and insubstantial as he had done early in the morning.

With his clear-cut features and square forehead he looked like a Greek statue, and Shimona wondered if any man could be more handsome or more compelling than her father.

But even while she thought about him, it was impossible not to remember the attraction of the Duke and the irresistible expression in his eyes which had held her spellbound.

She had only to think of him to feel a quiver go through her and to know again that strange rapturous sensation that she had felt when he kissed her.

She did not for a moment regret that she had let him hold her in his arms and that for the first time in her life a man's mouth had possessed hers.

"I will always have that to remember," she told herself, "even though I shall never see him again."

Even if her father died and she did not go abroad, their paths would never cross.

The Duke lived in one world and she in another, and she had done the only thing possible in running away so that after the wonder and perfection of his kiss they had not descended to the bathos of commonplace words.

In letting him kiss her and hold her in his arms she had brought down the curtain on what she knew would always be the most wonderful experience in her life.

Sitting by her father's bed-side she now admitted to herself that what she felt for the Duke was love, the same love that had made her mother run away from Bath, and from her rich and distinguished fiancé, with an actor.

But the love of Annabel Winslow, a Lady of Quality, for a distinguished young actor was different from the love of a daughter of an actor for a noble Duke.

Even if he wished it, which Shimona was sure he did not, they could never marry. It would be the same *mésalliance* that Alister McCraig had made in marrying Kitty Varden.

"I love him . . . but our love must never be spoilt or defamed," Shimona told herself.

Even in her innocence she knew that what he felt for her was different from what he had felt for other women.

It was not the licentious, debauched Devil of whom her father had spoken, who had offered her independence and promised at the same time that he would ask nothing in return.

She had known by the sincerity in his voice that he meant what he had said.

It might have been a difficult promise to keep. It might have proved quite impossible for them to be near each other and not succumb to the magnetism which drew them together.

But at least the offer had been made, although she thought no-one, certainly not her father, would have believed it.

"I believe the Duke," Shimona told herself and felt an irrepressible yearning to see him again and talk to him.

Never had she thought anything could be so fascinating as to see him sitting at the head of his table, distinguished and at his ease, driving beside her in his Phaeton, or at that last inevitable moment when he had put his arms round her and drawn her close against him.

"I love him, I love him!" she whispered.

Then she felt ashamed that she should be thinking of the Duke when her father was near to death.

But love was something which no-one could control. Her mother had said once:

"When I first loved your father, I realised that nothing else was of consequence in the whole world—not my family, my friends or the men who courted me. Everything seemed to vanish except for one man."

Shimona had not really understood at the time, but now she knew exactly what her mother had meant; for that was what had now happened to her.

It was what she had felt when the Duke kissed her and she was no longer in this world but in some enchanted place where they were alone, completely alone, save for the wonder of their love.

He had told her she was like a twinkling star, and she thought when he kissed her that the stars fell from the Heavens to lie at their feet.

"I love him! Oh, God, how much I love him!" she told herself, and knew that the future was dark and empty because it would not contain the Duke.

A coal fell in the fire and Shimona rose to pick it up with the tongs and put it back.

When she turned towards the bed she saw that her father's eyes were open.

"Annabel!"

She hardly heard the word, and yet it was spoken. She moved towards him.

"It is Shimona, Papa."

She put her hands on his and bent forward towards him, but he did not seem to see her.

"Annabel!" he said again. "Oh, Annabel—my darling!"

There was a sudden vibration in his voice, the same tone that vibrated through an audience and made them feel that everything he said touched their hearts.

Shimona felt the tears start in her eyes. Then still with that strange note thrilling through his voice, Beau Bardsley said:

"Annabel! It has been so long! My beloved, how I have missed you!"

It seemed to Shimona that for a moment there was a radiance in his face that seemed to tranform him and a light in his eyes that was indescribable.

Then his eyes closed but there was a smile on his lips, and Shimona knew that he was dead.

It was Doctor Lesley who decided that for Shimona's sake the funeral should take place very quietly before it was announced to the public that Beau Bardsley was dead.

He arranged everything and the only mourners who followed the coffin to the graveside were herself and Nanna.

It was a wet, blustery day and Nanna sobbed as the coffin was lowered into the grave and the earth was thrown upon it, but Shimona was dry-eyed.

She knew that her father and mother were together again.

His body was enclosed in the plain oak coffin which Doctor Lesley had ordered, but his spirit was happy with the radiance which had been in his face and the joy that had vibrated in his voice.

"I am the one who has been left behind," Shimona told herself forlornly.

She had driven back from the funeral in a hired carriage, with Nanna still wiping the uncontrollable tears away from her eyes.

It was impossible for them to talk that day and Nanna shut herself in the kitchen, as she always did when she wished to be alone. Shimona went to her mother's Sitting-Room to look at the portrait of her father over the mantelpiece.

She found it hard to realise that never again would she hear him come back to the house in the evening to tell her what had happened at the theatre or lie in the bed upstairs learning his lines ready for his next performance.

She knew that she had to plan what she and Nanna would do in the future.

Thanks to the Duke's concern for his nephew, they had enough money for it not to be an urgent matter. At the same time she knew it would not last for ever.

It was impossible for Shimona not to keep thinking of the Duke, remembering everything he said to her, going over and over again the moments when they had been together.

Sometimes she wondered whether she would have been happier if she had never gone to Ravenstone House. If she had not tried to earn the money which was to save her father's life, she would have saved herself from having a broken heart.

That was what she had.

She had always laughed at the phrase when she had heard it spoken in one of the plays.

Now she knew it could be a reality; for the pain in her own heart seemed to grow worse day by day, and she was never free of it.

However much she tried to tell herself sternly that it was a thing of the past and something to be forgotten, she longed for the Duke with an intensity which at times frightened her.

And almost insidiously the temptation came to her to do as he wished, to accept his terms, to tell him that after all she would agree to anything he suggested as long as she could sometimes see him.

Then she told herself that that was only the first step to destruction.

She was not so foolish nor so ignorant as not to be aware that the reason why her father did not wish her to be associated with the theatre was the loose morals which seemed inevitably involved in theatrical life.

It had been impossible for Shimona not to understand when it was said that the leading-lady was under the protection of some nobleman who had financed the production, or that the producer had pushed his current mistress into an important part simply because he found her attractive.

Even though her father was careful about what he said in front of her, the gossip of the theatre was part of his life.

Shimona was astute enough to piece disjointed sentences together and know the truth, even when her father and mother attempted to hide it from her.

It did not really shock her; she only thought that it was unpleasant or, as Doctor Lesley had said, "unsavoury," and she knew that as far as she was concerned such a life would be entirely and absolutely wrong and contrary to everything in which she believed.

"The love that Papa and Mama had for each other," she thought, "was a very beautiful, holy thing."

She was sure, although she had never come in contact with it, that illicit love was the opposite.

And yet it was hard to believe that her love for the Duke and his feelings for her were anything but right and good.

There had been something unmistakably spiritual in the feelings he had evoked in her.

She had felt when he took her up towards the stars that they were both a part of the Divine, and her love was in fact as holy as her prayers and the feelings of reverence she had in Church.

"How can that be wrong?" she asked.

But she knew the answer. There was nothing wrong

in what she had done so far, but she must go no further.

"What will become of us?" she asked Nanna two days after her father's funeral.

"I've been thinking about that," Nanna replied. "We've got to face the facts, Miss Shimona. We can't live here forever!"

"Papa owned the house."

"Yes, I know," Nanna agreed, "but there's rates to be paid, repairs to be done, and we have to eat."

Shimona looked at her wide-eyed as she went on:

"I've been thinking that if I went out to work we could perhaps keep going for at least a year or so."

"Do you really think I would sit here and let you work for me?" Shimona asked. "That is absurd, Nanna. If anyone works it should be me. I am young and strong."

"And as innocent as a new-born babe!" Nanna finished scornfully. "What do you think you could do?"

"I do not know," Shimona answered. "There must be something."

She gave a little sigh.

"Perhaps after all I could go on the stage."

"And have your father and mother turn in their graves?" Nanna asked furiously. "That's the last thing you'll do, Miss Shimona, and then over my dead body!"

"Well, what else is there?"

"We'll think of something."

Shimona knew they were the consoling words of a Nurse to a fretful child and that, despite the effort she made to deceive her, Nanna was really worried.

"Well, I've not got time to think about it now," Nanna went on in a brusque tone. "I want to get down to the shops. We're out of bread and I want to buy some eggs for supper. At least we've enough money not to starve for the next month or two."

"Shall I come with you?" Shimona asked.

Nanna looked towards the window.

"It's drizzling," she said. "You've been out once to-day. You keep by the fire and put the kettle on in about half-an-hour. If I see a muffin-man, I'll buy some muffins for tea."

"That will be nice," Shimona smiled.

She knew Nanna was trying to give her a treat. She had always loved muffins when she was a small girl and would listen for the muffin-man's bell as he came down the street carrying the tray on top of his head.

Nanna bustled away with an empty basket on her arm and Shimona sat down in front of the fire.

She wondered what the Duke was doing now.

Perhaps, she thought a little forlornly, he was with a beautiful woman, elegant and sophisticated, someone who amused him and talked the language of the world in which he lived.

They would have private jokes about the people they both knew. They would gossip about the famous personages she had read about in the newspapers.

Perhaps he would be going to dinner at Carlton House to be surrounded by more beauties like the Duchess of Devonshire, Lady Jersey and the fascinating Mrs. Fitzherbert, who had captivated the Prince for so many years.

"I am not part of the social world, I am not part of the theatrical world, I do not belong either in the city or in the country. In fact I belong to nowhere!" Shimona thought dismally. "I am just an 'odd one out.'"

It seemed strange that when the day before yesterday the newspapers had been full of reports of Beau Bardsley's death there was no mention of her.

They had all of them revived the story of how her father had run away from Bath with the beautiful Annabel Winslow.

But apparently they had forgotten, if they had ever known that the handsome actor and the beautiful Society girl had produced a child.

Doctor Lesley had brought Shimona all the newspapers so that she could read the glowing obituaries that had been written about her father.

There had been a long column in *"The Times"* and another in *"The Post"* besides a news report about the financial state of Drury Lane now that the actor who had brought in the audiences was no longer there.

One correspondent had written:

> *Something will have to be done, but it appears that no-one in the management had any idea what it should be.*

There were many sketches in the newspapers of Beau Bardsley in his leading roles, but even when she had read everything that was written about him Shimona felt that there was so much left unsaid.

The newspapers did not describe his generosity and his kindness to his fellow-actors, and none of them had understood how his whole life had centred round his home, his wife and daughter.

"I have protected you from the newspapers as I know your father would have wished me to do," Doctor Lesley said.

But because she was so anonymous to the extent that no-one had ever heard of her, Shimona could not help feeling that she had died too.

The house which had once held three happy people united by their love for each other, was now only a hollow shell.

Sitting in front of the fire she was just thinking that it was about time she put the kettle on when she heard a knock on the front door.

She thought perhaps Nanna had forgotten her key, and jumping to her feet she ran across the small hall and opened the door.

Then she gave a gasp, for it was not Nanna who stood there in her black cloak and bonnet, but the Duke.

He was even more resplendent than she

remembered, with his starched white cravat, the points of his collar high above his chin, and his high hat at an angle on his dark head.

As they stared at each other, it seemed to Shimona as if she had flown across the world to find the person who was waiting for her on the other side of it, and she felt an extraordinary sense of home-coming, security and protection.

"Shimona!" the Duke exclaimed.

She thought that her name had never sounded so attractive as it did spoken in his deep voice. Then slowly, as if he forced himself to remember his manners, he took his hat from his head.

"May I come in?" he asked. "There is a great deal I have to say to you."

She opened the door a little wider and he walked into the hall and seemed much too large for it.

Shimona shut the door behind him and without speaking led the way into the small Sitting-Room.

The Duke looked up at Beau Bardsley's portrait over the mantelpiece.

"Now I understand! You are Beau Bardsley's daughter, but I had no idea he had one!"

"Papa would never . . . allow me to have . . . anything to do with the . . . theatre," Shimona answered, wondering why her voice sounded so strange.

"I can understand that," the Duke said, "and yet he let you come to me to act the part I required."

"Papa was . . . unconscious and knew nothing about it. I came because I needed the money to take him abroad. I hoped it would . . . save his life."

There was a perceptible quiver in her voice and the Duke said:

"I asked you to trust me."

"I dared not do so," Shimona replied. "Papa would have been so . . . angry that I did not . . . intend to tell him anything about it . . . until he was well."

"I understand," the Duke said. "Shall we sit down? I have a lot to say to you, Shimona."

"Yes . . . of course," Shimona answered. "I apologise, Your Grace, for my bad manners. I was not expecting to see you."

"I know that," he answered. "How could you have done anything so cruel as to slip away from the house before anyone was awake? When they told me you had left I could hardly believe it!"

Shimona said nothing, and seeing the colour come into her cheeks and the flicker of her eyes he knew what she was thinking.

"I was determined to find you again," he said after a moment. "I went to the theatre to be told that Beau Bardsley was away ill. I thought it was only a temporary indisposition. I called the next day and the next, until I saw the newspapers and learnt he was dead."

"How did you manage to find this house?" Shimona enquired.

The Duke smiled.

"I was not going to be defeated," he answered, "and I remembered that you had asked me to pay the money I owed Beau Bardsley into Coutts Bank. They gave me his address."

"I never thought of that."

"I thought you could not have," the Duke replied, "and now I have found you, I will not allow you to hide from me again."

She did not answer and after a moment he said in a gentler tone:

"I am very sorry about your father. He will be deeply missed, as you well know. No-one could act as he could, or look so compellingly handsome."

His eyes went up to the portrait as he added:

"I can see now a faint resemblance between you. If I had had any sense I would have noticed it before."

He looked around the room.

"So this is the private part of Beau Bardsley's life upon which no-one was allowed to encroach. Having seen you I am not surprised that he was so protective. He was right in trying to keep you safe."

Shimona sat down in a chair opposite him, her fingers locked together and the Duke knew she was very tense.

"I would not do anything to distress you," he said quietly, "but once again, Shimona, I need your help."

"My help?" she questioned.

"I suppose we might have expected that our little charade could not really have such a conclusive and happy ending."

"Something has gone . . . wrong?"

"Not exactly wrong," the Duke answered, "but The McCraig, having reached safely the home of the Earl of Glencairn near Leicester, has been taken ill."

"Oh, no!" Shimona replied. "I am sorry."

"I understand it is not a dangerous illness," the Duke said, "and I think myself it is just exhaustion. For a man of eighty to travel so many miles must have taken its toll of his strength."

"Yes . . . of course," Shimona murmured.

"The McCraig has however, decided that before he returns to Scotland he will set his house in order. In other words, he will settle on Alister the sum of money he promised and will also make a new will. But before he does so, he wishes to see you both."

Shimona stiffened.

"To see . . . me?"

"It is quite understandable," the Duke smiled. "After all, a great deal of money is involved and I think he wishes to impress upon Alister exactly how it should be expended."

"But . . . why should he want . . . me to be present?" Shimona asked.

"That of course is entirely your fault," the Duke said with a smile. "You have captivated him, Shimona. He was delighted with you, and if he wants to see you again then who shall blame him? I am in exactly the same boat!"

Shimona looked away towards the fire.

"It is impossible!" she said after a moment.

"Why?" the Duke enquired.

She tried to find a reason but there did not seem to be a very valid one.

There was no longer her father to be kept in ignorance of her movements. There was in fact no-one.

Yet underneath the apprehension she felt at committing herself to acting a part and again deceiving The McCraig, there was an irresistible excitement because she would be able to go on seeing the Duke, at least for a little while.

"When I found you," the Duke went on, "hoping that perhaps someone in Beau Bardsley's household would have some idea of where you might be, I was going to suggest that you and I could drive to Leicester together and Alister could follow in his own Phaeton."

Shimona did not reply and he went on in a beguiling tone:

"Of course if you prefer to go in a closed carriage I shall understand, but personally that is something I abominate on such a long journey."

"Yes . . . of course . . . I should like to . . . drive with you," Shimona said in a small voice, "but . . ."

"What is worrying you?" the Duke asked.

"I do not know," Shimona replied. "It seems . . . wrong somehow to . . . go on with this . . . pretence."

"When I was small," the Duke said, "my Nurse used to say that one lie always leads to another."

Shimona smiled.

"I am sure your Nurse said the same thing," the Duke remarked.

"She often says it," Shimona replied. "But The McCraig is such a kind old man."

"He can be a hard, tough one, when it suits him," the Duke said. "He has needed a great deal of persuading before he could see that as the next Chief Alister was entitled to some consideration."

He paused before he said quietly:

"I am quite certain that, if you had not been you, he would not have been half so generous."

Shimona gave a little sigh.

"I wish you would tell him the truth."

"That is completely and absolutely impossible," the Duke said firmly. "He would feel defrauded and insulted, both of which are intolerable to a Scotsman!"

Shimona was silent for a moment. Then she said:

"Could you not do . . . without me?"

"I think it would be impossible," the Duke replied. "Will you tell me why you are so reluctant to do what I ask of you? Can it possibly be that you do not trust me to behave as you would wish me to?"

He saw the colour come into Shimona's cheeks and he added quickly:

"I promised your father that I would do nothing to hurt you, and I swear that the last thing I would want to do now would be to shock or frighten you."

He paused for a moment before he added very softly:

"Do you believe me?"

"I believe you!" Shimona answered.

"Then what worries you?" the Duke asked. "If you are not afraid of me, why are you afraid?"

"I . . . think of . . . myself," Shimona said in a low voice. "I thought I would . . . never see you again . . . I told myself I had to . . . forget everything that had . . . happened . . . and now you are here."

"Did you really think I would let you go?" the Duke asked. "I had every intention, Shimona, of seeing you again and finding you however cleverly you hid yourself away."

"But . . . but . . . why?"

"Because something happened between us that was different from anything that ever happened to me before," he answered. "Even now I cannot explain what you mean to me. I just know that I cannot lose you."

He gave a sigh before he said:

"It is like finding an incredible treasure. You know it is one, and yet there is so much you have to learn about it before you are aware not only of its true value, but also of its history and its very existence."

He bent towards her.

"That is what I feel about you, Shimona. You are unique! Someone who seems to have come to me from another world."

He was speaking with a note of sincerity and also passion in his voice. Then as their eyes met it seemed as if the words they were saying to each other were quite unnecessary.

"That . . . is what I . . . feel too," Shimona whispered.

"My precious! My darling!" the Duke exclaimed.

He put out his hands towards her as the door opened and Nanna came into the room.

CHAPTER FIVE

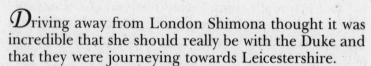

*D*riving away from London Shimona thought it was incredible that she should really be with the Duke and that they were journeying towards Leicestershire.

The whole entourage filled her with excitement she had never known before.

First, she was travelling with the Duke in his yellow and black Phaeton with a groom up behind wearing the Ravenstone livery, as were the four outriders with their white wigs and black velvet peaked caps.

Alister followed them in his own Phaeton, although his team of four horses was not of such magnificent horse-flesh as the Duke's.

Behind them again came the Duke's travelling chariot with Nanna, very straight-backed and disapproving, sitting inside.

It was Nanna who nearly made it impossible for Shimona to undertake the journey.

When she had returned to the house to stand in the Sitting-Room, her face rigid with disapproval, the Duke had risen to his feet.

"I will leave you now," he said to Shimona. "I have to tell Alister I have found you and make arrangements for tomorrow. I will return later this afternoon to tell you what is planned."

When he had gone Shimona faced a storm of protest.

She had hoped before she went to Ravenstone House that Nanna had never even heard of the Duke.

But her very first words as the door closed behind him told Shimona all too clearly that she had not only heard of him, but also knew a great deal about him.

"What's that wicked man doing here?" she enquired angrily. "He wouldn't have dared to cross the threshold when your father was alive."

"He is the Duke of Ravenstone, Nanna," Shimona answered.

"I know well enough who he is," Nanna said. "His groom told me whose Phaeton was waiting outside our door. You're not to speak to him again! D'you hear me, Miss Shimona? You're not to have anything to do with him."

"That is impossible, Nanna."

"Why should it be impossible?" Nanna enquired.

Hesitatingly, because Shimona was choosing her words with care, she told Nanna that it was the Duke who had paid her 500 guineas for pretending to be his nephew's wife and it was his money that had been paid into Beau Bardsley's account in Coutts Bank.

"You'll send it back immediately!" Nanna said. "His money's tainted and no decent person would lay a finger on it!"

"It will not be very decent for us if we starve!" Shimona answered.

"You can't touch pitch without being contaminated," Nanna retorted. "I couldn't eat a mouthful if I thought it was paid for by a Duke who is a disgrace to his name and his family!"

Shimona did not speak and she went on:

"I've heard your father often enough saying he's known in the theatrical profession as 'His Disgrace' and that's what he is—not a fit person for you to know about, let alone speak to."

"It is too late for all that now," Shimona said wearily. "I know him, Nanna, and I must help him."

"Over my dead body!" Nanna said firmly.

"His Grace has always been polite and considerate towards me."

"And what was he saying as I came into the room?" Nanna demanded. "He was speaking to you as no gentleman worthy of the name should speak to a lady who is unchaperoned, a girl who had no more idea of the wickedness of the world than a newly-born kitten."

Nanna ranted on and on, until finally she said:

"You're not going to Leicester with the Duke and that's that! What you're going to do is meet your grandparents."

"My grandparents?" Shimona exclaimed in surprise.

"I've been thinking it over," Nanna said, "and there's nothing for it but for you to go where you belong."

"Do you mean Mama's parents, or Papa's?"

"I believe Canon Bardsley is dead," Nanna replied, "but about two years ago your mother's father, Sir Harvey Winslow, was still alive. I saw his name in one of the newspapers."

"But he said he would never speak to Mama again, after she ran away with Papa. She told me so."

"Hot words are often spoken in anger," Nanna answered, "and unless Her Ladyship has changed a great deal in the years, she always loved her daughter and she'll love you."

"If they did not wish to know Mama, then they will have no wish to know me."

"They may not even know of your existence, and when they do, I'm as certain as I stand here that they will welcome a grandchild."

"It is no use talking about it, Nanna! I am not crawling to them on my knees!"

"I'm going to get in touch with them," Nanna said, "and nothing you can do or say'll stop me. I know it's the right thing. Anything would be better than being mixed up with that evil man and his goings on."

"What has the Duke done that has upset you so much" Shimona asked.

"I've been hearing bad things about him for years," Nanna answered. "I've heard your father denouncing him over and over again, and he and your mother told me of the way in which he behaved to that poor Miss Minnie Graham."

"That was a girl who was acting with Papa," Shimona said almost beneath her breath.

"Pretty little thing she was, but she was led astray like so many others and then there was no saving her."

"What happened to . . . her?" Shimona asked in a low voice.

"When the Duke was tired of her she found another gentleman to expend his money on her," Nanna answered scornfully. "Playing the lead, she was, at Birmingham when your father last spoke of her."

She gave a kind of snort which was a regular sound of hers when she was disgusted.

"The wages of sin are not always death in this evil world," she remarked tartly.

"Whatever the Duke has done or not done in the

past," Shimona said, "I have to go with him tomorrow. I cannot let him down and I cannot ruin Mr. McCraig's life or upset his Great-Uncle."

"You've no call to be getting into such a tangle, Miss Shimona," Nanna cried angrily. "Never have I heard of such a mess, and what your mother would say I don't know!"

"I have to go, Nanna."

"I'll speak to His Grace when he returns," Nanna said grimly, and that was all Shimona could get out of her.

But the Duke had his way.

Nanna asked him into the Dining-Room and they were in there a long time while Shimona waited in the Sitting-Room feeling apprehensive of the outcome.

What would the Duke think of being talked to severely by a servant?

If he was offended by it, he might walk out of the house without saying good-bye to her.

She felt she was being torn in pieces by the conflict that was taking place.

She could understand only too well what Nanna felt, and she knew that the condemnation in her voice was exactly the same as there had been in her father's when he spoke of the Duke.

But how could she make anyone understand how differently he had behaved to her?

How there existed something between them that seemed to contradict his reputation and the scathing manner in which people denounced him.

Then she told herself that perhaps she was being deceived.

What did she know about men—or any man—and especially anyone who was as important as the Duke?

Was there perhaps one law for the aristocrats and one for ordinary people? And had her father been more censorious than someone else might have been simply because of his upbringing?

It was so difficult for her to know the truth, difficult

to be fair. She had to admit that the Duke must have behaved disgracefully in some ways, otherwise his reputation would not have reached the ears of her mother and herself.

But whatever he had done, Shimona felt she was in honour bound to finish what the Duke had called their "charade" in which she had taken a part to help Alister McCraig.

If he was exposed now, if his great-Uncle realised that he was married to the sort of actress that he had supposed, then everything would be much worse than if he had told the truth from the very beginning.

"I am committed! I must help him!" Shimona told herself, and wondered how much longer the Duke and Nanna would be in the Dining-Room.

At last the door of the Sitting-Room opened and he came in.

Shimona realised that he did not shut the door behind him and that Nanna was waiting in the hall.

"Everything is arranged," he said, "and there is only one change in our plans."

"What is that?" Shimona asked nervously.

"As I do not exactly see eye to eye with the Earl of Glencairn, I have sent a groom to Leicester to ask The McCraig if he will honour me by being my guest at my own house. It is not far from where he is staying, not more than five miles, and I think it would be more comfortable for all of us if there were no strangers present."

"I can understand that," Shimona said, remembering that she must pretend to be Alister's wife.

"Then everything is arranged," the Duke said, "and I will call for you at half-after-nine, if you can be ready."

"I will be ready," Shimona promised, her eyes alight with relief because Nanna had not been able to prevent her from going with the Duke.

There had been no chance of a private conversation

between them, and only now when they were alone in the Phaeton did she ask:

"You are not . . . angry?"

"Angry?" he enquired. "Why should you expect me to be?"

"I thought perhaps Nanna was rude to you yesterday and you might be . . . incensed about it."

The Duke smiled.

"She was not rude," he answered. "She was only very firm, as Nurses always are. I rather felt I was back in the Nursery and being punished for some extremely reprehensible misdemeanour."

"I was afraid of that," Shimona said in a low voice.

"It was what I deserved," the Duke said, "and you should not have taken part in what your Nurse described as 'disgraceful goings on'."

"Nanna was very shocked. She has never allowed me to lie."

"And quite rightly so."

He was keeping something back from her, Shimona thought, and she looked at him a little apprehensively.

She felt as if some barrier had been erected between them, but she was not certain what it was and anyway it was impossible to put her feelings into words.

The Duke was charming, polite and somehow reserved, but when they had luncheon together in a private parlour at the Coaching Inn he looked at her with an expression in his eyes which made her feel shy.

Alister had gone ahead to meet a friend at Northampton and Shimona had been half-afraid that Nanna would insist on being with her. But without any argument Nanna and the valet lunched in the Travellers' Dining-Room.

They had driven very swiftly for a great number of miles and Shimona was hungry.

It also seemed for the first time since her father had died that the misery that had encompassed her like a fog was lifting and she was once again in the sunshine.

She had thought never again to see the Duke, and

yet she was now with him. She was hearing his voice, he was near her, and because he was there her sensation of wonder and joy was increasing every moment.

She had taken off her travelling-cloak with its fur-lined hood which had framed her face, and while they had their meal her hair was very fair against the dark oak panelling of the Inn.

When they finished and the servants left the room her eyes were very blue as she lifted them to the Duke's face.

"I . . . thought I would . . . never see you again," she said in a low voice.

"That was your decision—not mine."

"I knew how . . . angry Papa would be, but it was the only way that I could have taken him to . . . Italy."

She thought the Duke would want to talk to her about it and perhaps tell her again that he had minded the thought of losing her, but to her surprise he rose from the table to say:

"If you have finished, I think we should be on our way."

There was somehow a harsh note in his voice and something she did not understand in the way he looked away from her, his eyes seeming to avoid her face.

"What is . . . wrong?" she asked.

"Why should you think that anything is wrong?" he queried.

"Something has changed you. It must have been something Nanna said. Please . . . please do not listen to her. I have never . . . believed the things that she has been . . . told about you."

"You have—never—believed them?" the Duke repeated slowly. "What have you been told about me?"

Shimona made a little helpless gesture with her hands.

"Nothing very positive. Just that Papa did not

approve of some of the things . . . you have . . .
done."

The Duke walked towards the log-fire to stand with
his back to Shimona looking down into it.

"Your father was perfectly right," he said, "and I am
sure everything he heard about me was the truth.
Come, we still have a long way to go before it gets
dark."

There was nothing Shimona could do but put on her
cloak and follow him outside to where the Phaetons
were waiting.

There were fresh teams of horses belonging to the
Duke to convey them, which she learnt were always
kept ready on the road to Leicester in case at any time
the Duke should require them.

Nanna was also waiting to see her into the Phaeton.

"If it gets cold or begins to rain, Miss Shimona," she
said, "you're to travel with me. I've no wish for you to
get a chill."

"I am very warm, thank you, Nanna," Shimona replied, "and the Phaeton has a hood that can be raised if
we require it."

Nanna pursed her lips together and Shimona hurried away so that she could not argue any more.

She wished in some ways that Nanna had not come
with her, but she knew she must have insisted on it to
the Duke, and he in fact would think it only correct
that a lady should travel with her lady's-maid.

'But I am not a lady,' Shimona thought miserably. 'I
am only the daughter of an actor, acting a part, and
more unhappy than I have ever been in my whole life
because I am in love.'

She was unhappy at the moment because the Duke
was unpredictable and because she was becoming
more and more convinced that a barrier had been
erected between them.

Yet he had only to smile at her or to speak to her in
that deep voice for her heart to turn over in her breast

and for her to feel as if the larks were singing in the sky above them.

"I love him!" Shimona told herself as they journeyed on.

She thrilled every time her shoulder touched his arm and every time he turned his head to look at her and their eyes met.

It seemed then as if it did not matter what he said or how he behaved.

The feeling they had for each other was still there, and while he might exert a rigid control on every other part of him he could not control the expression in his eyes.

"How long are we going to stay at your house?" Shimona enquired.

She tried to speak normally and not to allow her anxiety to reveal itself in the tone in which she spoke.

"I have an idea that The McCraig will not wish to linger once he has made his will," the Duke said. "He is an old man and he wants to be with his Clan as much as possible before he dies."

"He is really ill?" Shimona enquired.

"No, I think it was just an indisposition caused by too much travelling," the Duke replied, "but it has certainly been to Alister's advantage."

"When will Mr. McCraig join us again?" Shimona asked.

"He said he would pick us up the other side of Northampton," the Duke replied.

Sure enough in another few miles they saw Alister McCraig in his Phaeton waiting for them at a crossroads.

They did not slacken speed but waved and he fell into line behind them.

"Do you always travel in such grandeur?" Shimona asked, looking at the out-riders and thinking how smart and impressive they looked.

"I like to be safe from Highwaymen and I like my comfort," the Duke replied. "If we were to break down and were forced to stay in some uncomfortable Inn, one of my servants is an excellent cook, and they can all look after me as well as my valet does."

"I suppose that is what one would expect of a Duke," Shimona replied, thinking a little wistfully how they had never been able to employ more than one maid to help Nanna in the house.

"There is no particular virtue in comfort," the Duke said, "but it is something which, like money, makes life very much easier. Thanks to you, Alister will now live in a comfort he never expected."

"It is nice that you should be so concerned about him."

"You must not find virtues in me which I do not possess," the Duke replied. "It is my fault entirely in the first place, that Alister was in danger of losing his inheritance."

"How could that be true?"

"I introduced him to Kitty Varden!"

"But you did not expect him to marry her?"

"Good Heavens—no!"

There was silence. Then in a very low voice Shimona said:

"Did you think he might . . . wish her to be his . . . mistress?"

For a moment there was another silence, until the Duke said angrily:

"Will you not talk in such a manner? It does not become you and there is no reason for you even to know of such things!"

Shimona looked at him in surprise and he went on:

"Your Nurse is right. What you are doing now can only have a corrupting influence, and the sooner it is all over the better!"

His mouth was set in a hard line when he finished speaking, and he used his whip for almost the first time since they left London as if he wished to hurry his horses on to their destination.

Shimona relapsed into silence. There seemed to her nothing she could say.

She only felt inexpressibly that she was alone.

They reached the Duke's house, which was called Melton Paddocks, as the afternoon was drawing to a close.

As they came down a straight drive it stood in front of them and was not, Shimona thought, a particularly attractive house.

The centre block was three storeys high with two wings of only two storeys reaching out on each side like two arms.

She thought they must have been a later addition to a Queen Anne building and she was to learn later that she was right.

She had the impression that the house did not welcome them, but it was quickly dispelled as the Phaeton was drawn to a standstill and servants in the Duke's livery came hurrying from the front door and she saw The McCraig waiting to greet them.

"I hope you have not been here long, Sir," the Duke said as he held out his hand to the old gentleman.

"No, indeed, I arrived only half-an-hour ago," The McCraig replied.

They went into a large room which was, Shimona thought, extremely masculine in the manner in which it was furnished.

There was a long leather sofa and arm-chairs and the walls were decorated with paintings of horses and dogs.

"I am glad to see you, my dear," The McCraig said to Shimona.

"I am sorry you have been ill, Sir."

"Not ill," he said sharply as if he resented the thought of a weakness. "Just a trifle tired and a little troubled with my heart."

"Your heart?" Shimona asked quickly.

"A passing twinge," The McCraig said lightly. "But I wanted to see you and Alister before I went north."

"And I am very pleased to see you again," Shimona smiled.

He patted her shoulder affectionately. Then she was introduced to the Duke's agent, a Mr. Reynolds, who was in charge of the house and the estate.

"I hope everything will be to Your Grace's satisfaction," Shimona heard him say. "We did not have much time to prepare for your visit."

"I have told you before, Reynolds," the Duke said sharply, "that I do not intend to give long notice, or indeed any notice, when I wish to stay in my own house."

A Housekeeper was waiting to take Shimona upstairs, an elderly grey-haired woman in rustling black, and when Shimona had been shown into her bedroom she found Nanna there.

"You are not too tired, Nanna, after such a long journey?"

"I've been worrying about you, sitting in an open carriage when you should have been inside with me in the warm."

"I am warm enough," Shimona answered, "and I like being in the fresh air."

But Nanna did not wish to talk.

She made Shimona lie down before dinner, and because she was in fact more tired than she would have admitted, she fell asleep.

When she awoke it was to find her clothes had been unpacked and there was a bath waiting for her, with one of her prettiest gowns laid out on the bed.

"I hope you had someone to help you, Nanna," she said, realising how much had been done while she was asleep.

"There's been help of a sort," Nanna sniffed disdainfully. "But this is not a happy house, Miss Shimona. I know that already."

"How can you be sure?"

"A bad master makes a bad servant!" Nanna snapped.

Shimona gave a little sigh. She felt she could not bear another argument over the Duke at this moment, and she was well aware that Nanna had come north determined to find fault with everything.

"I expect the servants resent us turning up at a moment's notice," she said. "You know yourself how difficult it is to have everything prepared so quickly."

"The Housekeeper's too old for her job if you ask me!" Nanna snapped.

She went on grumbling all the time Shimona was having her bath and getting dressed. But as she went downstairs she was too happy at the thought of seeing the Duke and being close to him to worry about Nanna or anyone else.

She had hoped to have a chance of talking to him alone before they were joined by the others, but Alister McCraig was already in the Sitting-Room with the Duke, and The McCraig joined them a few seconds later.

"I have arranged for Glencairn's Attorney to attend us after dinner, Ravenstone," he said. "I hope that will not be inconvenient?"

"No, of course not, Sir," the Duke replied.

"I sent him a draft of my intentions this morning which I asked him to translate into legal language. All I will have to do is to sign the documents. It would be a help if you would witness my signature."

"I am at your service," the Duke replied.

The McCraig looked at Shimona.

"I think, my dear," he said, "you will be pleased with my arrangements!"

"I am sure I shall," Shimona answered.

"I am leaving to you personally my wife's jewellery," The McCraig went on. "I think you will find the sapphires, which are unique, will become you, but then so will all the jewels."

"B . . . but . . . please . . . I cannot . . ." Shimona began frantically, then she saw the Duke frown and the words died away on her lips.

She knew The McCraig would think it very strange if she refused to accept the gift he offered her.

Then she thought quickly that of course the jewellery would be bequeathed in the name of Katherine McCraig, Alister's real wife.

"It is very . . . kind of you, Sir," she managed to stammer to The McCraig.

"I can think of no-one I would rather own it, than yourself."

Shimona drew in her breath.

The pretence and deception were far harder to bear than she had anticipated and she was thankful when they could move into the Dining-Room where the conversation in front of the servants was of other things.

The Attorney, who looked exactly like a caricature of his profession, Shimona thought, arrived with his black bag containing the documents and a number of large white quill pens with which they could be signed.

They sat around a table in what Shimona learnt was the Breakfast-Room, and the Attorney read aloud in a dry, crisp voice the long legal document which he had prepared on The McCraig's instructions.

Although he was very long-winded about it, the disposition of the money was quite clear and straightforward.

Alister McCraig was to receive £100,000 for his immediate use and he was, on his Great-Uncle's death, to inherit his entire fortune and any personal effects that were not already entailed onto the Chieftain.

The value of the whole amounted to a very large sum, and Shimona thought that, after he had heard the contents of the Will, Alister McCraig seemed to walk taller and to have a pride and a presence that had not been there before.

She remembered how the Duke had said that Alister's father had quarrelled with The McCraig and she thought that it was unfair that he should have suffered through a disagreement that was not of his making.

It had not only left him poor, but maybe with a sense of inferiority.

Perhaps it was for that reason that he had married Kitty Varden, she thought perceptively, as an act of defiance because he wished to assert himself.

She was sure, despite the fact that he was somewhat insignificant, that Alister McCraig was at heart a nice human being.

The Attorney's voice seemed still to rasp in their ears after he had left.

The Duke had insisted on them all drinking a glass of champagne to celebrate what he said was a special occasion, and they wished The McCraig a safe journey home.

"I am going to insist that you both come to see me in the spring," The McCraig said to Shimona and Alister. "If it had been possible I would have liked to take you back with me now.

Alister parted his lips to protest, but The McCraig went on:

"I know you will have many other commitments. But next spring I shall not take no for an answer."

"It is something we will both look forward to," Alister said.

"And so shall I," The McCraig replied with his eyes on Shimona.

She smiled at him, hoping that she would not have to lie again, feeling that every word of deception she uttered seemed to stick in her throat.

It was still early but The McCraig wished to retire to bed, and although Shimona hoped there would be some excuse for her to talk to the Duke alone they all moved in a body across the Hall and seemed to expect her to follow The McCraig up the staircase.

It may have been her imagination, but Shimona fancied that the Duke did not look at her, as he bowed in return to her curtsey.

She went to her bed-room where Nanna was waiting.

"You should not have waited up, Nanna," she exclaimed. "You must be tired and as you well know I am quite capable of putting myself to bed."

"If other servants don't know the right way to behave—I do!" Nanna answered.

"What has upset you now?"

"I told you this is a bad house, and that's what it is!" Nanna retorted. "The men-servants were drinking too much below stairs—disgusting I call it!—and the maid-servants from all I hear are no better than they ought to be!"

"What do you mean by that?"

"It's not something I should be repeating to you, Miss Shimona, but you might as well know what sort of place you are in."

Shimona was well aware that this was all a thinly disguised attack upon the Duke, and because she was quite certain that Nanna would have her say whatever she replied she asked a little wearily:

"What has happened?"

"I can hardly believe it, Miss Shimona," Nanna replied, "but on the floor above us there is at this moment a baby that had no right to be born into the world."

"A baby?" Shimona enquired. "How do you know?"

"The Head Housemaid told me about it," Nanna said. "Not that she knows her place. She wouldn't be accepted in any household I've worked in."

"What did she tell you?" Shimona asked.

"That one of the kitchen-maids, little more than a child, she is, gave birth to a baby three days ago."

"Here in the house?"

"Upstairs, as I've just said."

"Do they know who the father is?"

Shimona was almost afraid of the answer.

"Apparently one of the grooms," Nanna replied. "A married man, with a wife and three children, so he's not prepared to stand by her."

"Poor girl!" Shimona murmured.

"Poor girl indeed!" Nanna exclaimed. "And what do you expect with such an example from those who should know better?"

Shimona did not need to ask what Nanna meant, knowing she was determined to have her say.

"There's parties that take place in this house, Miss Shimona, when the Duke comes here for the hunting, that I would not soil your ears by repeating. I was told about them downstairs, and they were enough to make any decent person's hair stand up on end!"

"I do not think it is any of our business, Nanna."

"I should hope not!" Nanna retorted. "As I've already said, Miss Shimona, a bad master means bad servants, for there's always fools ready to follow those who set a bad example."

There was no use in arguing, Shimona thought.

When at last Nanna had left her, still muttering to herself, and she was alone, she could not help feeling sorry for the girl upstairs who had given birth to an illegitimate baby.

Had she perhaps been wildly in love with the man to whom she had given herself? Had she thought that nothing mattered save the feelings they had for each other?

And if she was young, had she been aware of what the probable consequences of such an action might be?

She remembered how she had said to the Duke that the circles from a stone thrown into a pond will cast ripples outwards indefinitely.

Was it really the example of the Duke that had caused his kitchen-maid to produce an illegitimate child?

How could they have known when they tried to save Alister McCraig from the consequences of an uncomfortable marriage that she would be left all the jewellery that had belonged to The McCraig's wife?

One thing led to another and it was so easy for people to be hurt or even destroyed by a wrong action.

Shimona remembered she had not said her prayers
and because she was still unhappy about the strange
barrier between her and the Duke she prayed that he
might find happiness.

"Make him happy, God," she prayed. "Let him clear
himself of all that is wrong and wicked, and please,
whatever sins he has committed, do not let there by
any ill consequences from them."

She prayed for him from the very depths of her soul,
thinking that one unavoidable consequence was that
she loved him.

For good or bad, whatever happened in the future,
she would love him and go on loving him all her life.

It was a love, she was sure with an inescapable con-
viction, which would defy time and she would never be
free of it.

She had known that, even when she thought she
would never see the Duke again, and now she had
snatched one more day with him.

He had said when he came to her home that he
would never let her go, but she had the uncomfortable
feeling he had changed his mind.

It was nothing he had put into words, she just knew
it instinctively, as she knew that her whole being
reached out towards him.

She longed for him and for the closeness they had
known when he had held her in his arms in Ravenstone House.

There they had been one and Shimona thought despairingly that perhaps never again would she know
the rapture and wonder of feeling that they were part
of the Divine which he had given her.

"I love him!" she whispered into her pillow.

Then irresistibly and unmistakably she knew what
she wanted and although she knew it was something
she should not say she prayed aloud:

"Oh God, make him love me enough to want to . . .
marry me!"

It had been a tiring day and Shimona drifted away into a dreamless slumber.

She awoke suddenly to feel she was still travelling, the wheels were still rumbling beneath her and there was the soft sway of the Phaeton, the jingle of the harness.

Then she opened her eyes and remembered where she was.

The fire had died down but the coals were still glowing and she could see the outline of the bed against them.

Everything seemed very quiet, but she felt as if something had disturbed her.

"I am being imaginative," she told herself, and yet she found herself listening.

What she expected to hear she had no idea, she just listened.

She could hear nothing but the sound of her own heart.

"I must go to sleep," she thought.

Even if The McCraig left for Scotland to-morrow, the Duke had promised at dinner that he would take her and Alister to see his horses, which meant they would not return to London until the following day.

Shimona felt her heart leap at the thought. She would be able to talk to him. There was so much she wanted to know, so much she wanted to learn from him.

She could ride well. Her mother had insisted upon that, because she herself had always been an extremely good rider.

When they could afford it they had hired the best horses from a livery-stable and either rode in the parks or even sometimes ventured outside the city into the open countryside.

Shimona thought she would like the Duke to see her

on a horse, for she was sure he would admire a woman who rode well.

But never in her wildest dreams had she imagined she would be able to ride anything so superlative as the horses which the Duke owned.

"Do you own race horses?" she had asked him at dinner.

"I have some in training," he replied, "but I really prefer steeple-chasing when I can ride my own animals. I like to do things for myself, not watch other people doing them for me."

Alister had laughed.

"Is that why I never see you at a Mill, Uncle Yvell? I believe in fact you are a rather good pugilist."

"I box sometimes at Gentleman Jackson's Rooms," the Duke answered.

"And you fence also," Alister said. "If you are not careful, they will call you a Corinthian."

"They have many other more appropriate titles for me," the Duke said cynically.

As if he thought it would be a mistake for The Mc-Craig to know too much about the Duke's reputation, Alister changed the subject.

But Shimona had heard the bitterness in the Duke's voice, and because she loved him she wanted to say something which would make him smile and forget his unpleasant thoughts, whatever they were.

"How can he be all the things they say he is?" she asked herself now. "I do not believe it. I do not believe what anyone says."

She felt she wanted to proclaim her faith in him to the world. She wanted to defend the Duke against his enemies. She wanted to hold him in her arms and protect him as if he was a child who was being bullied.

"I suppose that is love," she thought. "Love that makes me want not only the ecstasy of his loving me, but also to mother him, to look after him and save him from anything that could hurt him."

She lay in the darkness feeling that her thoughts and

prayers were winging their way towards him. Then as she lay there she was aware of something strange.

It was not what she heard, although she felt it was that for which she had been listening, but something she smelt.

She lay for some moments to make sure that she was not mistaken, then she knew that it was smoke.

She got out of bed and reached for her winter dressing-gown which Nanna had laid over a chair by the bed.

It was made of turquoise blue velvet and warmly lined with thick satin. Shimona put it on and slipped her feet into little boots of silver lame lined with fur which she always wore when it was cold.

She buttoned her dressing-gown high at the neck and down the front and as she did so she pulled the bell sharply two or three times.

It must be late she thought, but the bell would ring upstairs, and one of the house-maids would hear it.

Whether they did or not, she must arouse everyone, for now the smell of smoke was stronger than it had been before.

Even as she turned towards the door Shimona heard a bell begin to ring and the cry, far away, but coming nearer, of: "Fire! Fire! Fire!"

CHAPTER SIX

As Shimona reached the door it was flung open and the Duke stood there.

He saw Shimona and said quite calmly:

"The house is on fire. Go downstairs and out into the garden."

He did not wait for her answer but turned to run along the passage, and she knew that he was going to warn The McCraig.

She noticed that he was still wearing his evening-clothes and knew it could not be as late as she had thought, as he had obviously not yet gone to bed.

She moved out onto the landing and looking over the bannisters saw a turmoil in the Hall where men were moving pictures and furniture out of the Sitting-Rooms.

Alister also in his evening-clothes was directing them through the open front door.

Shimona was just about to descend the staircase when there was the sound of panic-stricken voices, women were screaming, and down the stairs from the top floor came a number of servants.

The women who had obviously been aroused from bed, wore shawls or blankets over their nightgowns and they were being propelled down the stairs by the men who were still in their livery.

"Come on! Get on with you! You've got to get out of here!" one of the men was saying roughly.

Shimona remembered what Nanna had said and thought he was the worse for drink.

She stood to one side to let them rush down the stairs. Then she saw that one woman was being carried by a footman and as she passed Shimona heard her cry weakly:

"My—baby! My—baby!"

No-one appeared to hear or to take any notice, but all down the staircase Shimona could hear her crying even above the noise and commotion which the others were making.

"They have left the baby behind," she told herself.

The smoke was not yet very thick although it was beginning to sting her eyes. She looked up the staircase and saw that it was clear and the fire, wherever it was, was not on the top floor of the building.

Impulsively, without thinking it might be dangerous, she ran up the stairs to see if she could find the baby who had been left behind.

Before she reached the top landing she heard it crying, and as there was an oil-lamp outside the bed-room it was not difficult to locate which one contained the child.

She found it lying on the bed and she knew the servants in their haste to get the mother to safety had overlooked the fact that the baby was lying beside her.

It was a very small baby and for its size it seemed to make quite an inordinate amount of noise.

It was wrapped in a shawl and Shimona pulled a blanket from the bed and wrapped it in that too. Then she started back down the stairs.

She could not move very quickly because she was not only hampered by the child in her arms but also by the fact that her velvet dressing-gown reached to the floor and she was unable to lift it.

When she reached the lower landing the smoke had become much thicker, and when she tried to move through it she saw the staircase down to the Hall was now in flames.

For the first time Shimona realised the danger she was in.

Now she hurried away along the passage feeling there must be another staircase which would take her down to the ground floor.

The smoke seemed to grow thicker and thicker. She groped her way through it and felt cold air on her cheeks.

A moment later the smoke cleared and she saw in front of her a long window which was open.

"I must have missed the staircase," she thought.

Looking through the window she saw that it led out onto a flat roof and realised that the window opened out from the main building onto one of the side wings which she had noticed when she first arrived.

It seemed to be the obvious thing to go out onto the roof rather than brave the thick smoke which had obscured the staircase she was trying to find.

She had to stoop to get through the window and did so with care so as not to hurt the baby.

It had ceased crying and was only whimpering as if it was hungry.

It was easy to walk on the roof and Shimona moved towards the parapet, realising that the light which made it easy for her to see her way came from the fire in the down-stairs rooms of the main part of the house.

The flames were crackling ominously even as she reached the parapet which was about a foot high.

She looked down into the garden below and saw the household congregated on the lawn.

They also saw her, because although Shimona could not hear what they said she could hear their raised voices and she saw several hands pointing in her direction.

The flames were hot and she moved further along the building until she reached the end of it.

"Now they have seen me," she told herself, "it

should be easy for someone to find a long ladder so that I can climb down into the garden."

She turned and gave a frightened gasp as she realised what a hold the flames had by now on the house.

From where she was standing she could see them belching out like crimson tongues from the lower windows and the smoke was rising in a black cloud high above the roof.

"It is a good thing I saved the baby," she told herself. "It would have had no chance of surviving."

She looked down below and saw through the smoke there were men running in the garden towards where she was standing and she thought she could discern a ladder in their hands.

Then to her consternation she was aware that the flames were not only widespread in the main part of the house, but were also now appearing at the side of the wing on which she was standing.

"This wing also must have caught fire," she thought and felt fear beginning to flicker inside her almost like the tongues of fire which were consuming the house.

Again she looked over the edge of the parapet.

The smoke made it difficult to see what was happening, but as yet there was no sign of any rescue party.

She looked back again towards the flames, then with a leap of her heart she saw a figure coming towards her from the open window and knew who it was.

The Duke came to her side and she saw that his white cravat was singed and there were dirty marks on his face.

"Why did you not do as I told you . . ." he began, then he saw the baby in her arms.

"They . . . forgot the . . . baby," Shimona answered automatically.

But her heart was singing with happiness because he had come for her and she was no longer afraid.

He looked down into her eyes, then he put his arms round her and held her as close to him as he could without hurting the baby in her arms.

"How could you do anything so absurdly brave?" he asked. "I heard a woman crying about losing her baby, but I did not realise that it was in the house."

"It is . . . quite safe," Shimona said a little incoherently.

It was difficult to speak because the Duke's arms and the closeness of him made her feel that nothing else was of any importance except the fact that they were together again and there was no longer a barrier between them.

She felt the Duke's lips on her forehead, then he went to the side of the balustrade to shout:

"Hurry up with the ladder!"

As he spoke Shimona saw the tongues of fire rising above the parapet only a few yards from them.

The Duke must have seen it too for he turned back and began to take off his evening-coat.

"It is not going to be easy," he said, "because you have to hold the baby, but I want you to do exactly as I tell you to do and not be afraid."

"You are with . . . me," she whispered, "that is all that . . . matters."

He had taken off his coat and now he made her put her arms into the sleeves and because she was so small they covered her hands. Then he pulled the rest of the coat high up over her shoulders so that it covered her head.

He covered the baby's face with the blanket and said:

"Keep your head down and on no account look up. Just trust me to guide you."

As he spoke he pulled her backwards to the edge of the parapet, then he lifted her in his arms and stepped onto the ladder.

He was holding Shimona close against him so that he covered her back; one arm encircled her waist, the other held onto the side of the ladder. Her head was bent until she could see nothing and was in complete darkness.

They went down very slowly and now Shimona

could hear the roar of the flames, the crash of falling masonry, and she knew that if the Duke had not been holding her she would have been desperately afraid.

Step by step, step by step they went lower and lower, until suddenly the Duke released her, other arms took hold of her and someone lifted the baby from her arms.

She tried to pull back the coat from over her face but she was being carried away from the noise of the fire and when finally she managed to see what was happening she was blinded by the glare of it.

The flames now out of control were leaping higher and higher and she saw the ladder on which they must have descended collapse at the same time as the roof of the building fell in.

She saw Alister's face through the smoke and realised that he had carried her away.

"The . . . Duke . . ." she murmured. "Where . . . is . . . the Duke?"

"He will be all right," Alister replied. "I am going to carry you to a place where you will be out of danger."

"The Duke . . . must have . . . been . . . burnt!" Shimona insisted.

"They are improvising a stretcher for him," Alister answered. "He will be following us."

Shimona tried to content herself with this information but, as Alister carried her across the garden and a little way down the drive, she could think of nothing but the flames leaping over the falling ladder.

She knew that as the Duke had guided her down, having given her his coat, he had protected her with his own body.

Alister carried her in through an open door and set her down on the floor in a small front room which was neatly furnished.

"This is your first guest, Mrs. Saunders," he said to a middle-aged woman who was arrayed in a red flannel dressing-gown.

"I'll look after her, Mr. McCraig," the woman replied.

"They are bringing His Grace here as well, Mrs. Saunders. I am afraid he has been burnt in the fire, and he will need the use of your best bed-room."

"It's all ready, Sir," Mrs. Saunders answered. "My husband was certain you'd wish to use the house as soon as we hears the fire had broken out."

"A lot of people will have to be accommodated," Alister said, "but if you will look after His Grace and this lady, then that is all I will ask of you."

"I'll do my best, you knows that, Sir," Mrs. Saunders answered.

Alister turned to Shimona.

"You are all right?"

"I am all right," she replied. "Please . . . find out . . . what has happened to the Duke."

Even as she spoke she heard the sound of men's feet and a moment later she saw four men carrying a narrow gate on which they had laid the Duke.

Shimona looked at him and gave a cry of sheer horror.

He was lying face downwards and his back was bare while only the tattered remnants of his fine lawn shirt remained on his wrists and round his neck. The whole of his back had been burnt raw.

"Take His Grace upstairs!" Alister commanded.

With great difficulty the men negotiated the narrow stairway up to the landing while Mrs. Saunders had gone ahead to open the door of the front room.

"We need a Doctor," Shimona said.

"I know that," Alister answered, "but he lives at least six miles away, and I am told he will not come out at night."

Shimona for the first time felt panic-stricken.

She did not need to be told how seriously injured the Duke was. Then to her relief she saw Nanna coming through the doorway.

She put out both hands towards her.

"Oh, Nanna. His Grace is terribly burnt. What can we do about it?"

It was a child crying for help and Nanna automatically responded.

"We'll look after him, Miss Shimona. Don't you worry."

Then she went up the stairs, and Shimona followed her.

As she reached the top she heard Alister say: "I will be back later."

Then he was gone and a moment later the men who had carried the Duke upstairs passed her on the small landing and also left the house.

The Duke was lying on his face in the centre of a big double bed which seemed almost to fill the room.

Mrs. Saunders was staring at his back.

In the light from the candles she had lit it was even more horrifying than it had seemed in the dim light downstairs.

"It'll kill His Grace," she said after a moment. "There's naught they can do for burns as bad as those!"

"Something has to be done!" Shimona answered fiercely. Then she gave a sudden cry. "Nanna, do you remember when you scalded your foot what Mama used to heal it?"

"Honey," Nanna replied. "But that was a small burn, nothing like this!"

"Mama always said that honey should be used on burns—and all wounds!" Shimona said. "And it will stop the pain."

"That's true," Nanna agreed, "the pain will be unbearable if His Grace recovers consciousness."

"If . . . ?" Shimona whispered beneath her breath.

Then she said to Mrs. Saunders:

"Have you any honey in the house?"

"Indeed I have, Miss. We keeps our own bees and my larder's full to bursting with the good crop we had this summer."

"Then please fetch it up here."

"And bring us some of your old sheets," Nanna added. "I'm sure anything we destroy His Grace will replace."

"I'm not worried about that," Mrs. Saunders answered. "You're very welcome to all I have."

The two women left the bed-room and Shimona stood looking down at the Duke's body.

It seemed impossible that any man could be so badly burnt and be still alive, and she knew the pain he had endured as he carried her to safety protecting her with his own body must have been intolerable.

"How could he have done that for . . . me?" she asked herself and felt the tears gather in her eyes.

She brushed them away and for the next hour she worked with Nanna to cover the whole of the Duke's body with a thick layer of honey.

They poured it over his raw skinless back, then they bandaged him with the sheets which Mrs. Saunders tore into strips.

They had also to bandage his arms and the backs of his legs where his silk stockings had been burnt away to leave nothing but skinless flesh.

Only his face and his hands were unmarked as they discovered when they turned him over, and his thick satin evening-breeches had protected him from waist to knee.

"He gave me . . . his coat," Shimona said miserably after they had been working for some time.

"I know, dearie, I saw what he did," Nanna answered. "He's a good man, whatever they may say about him."

When the Duke was bandaged so that he looked like a cocoon, Nanna sent Shimona from the room while she and Mrs. Saunders cut his breeches away and put him between the sheets.

It was only then that Shimona felt the reaction of what she had passed through sweep her like a tidal wave.

When Nanna came to find her she was sitting on the floor of the landing outside the Duke's room fast asleep.

Shimona did not even stir when she was put to bed in a small room at the back of the house.

She did not wake until Nanna came to call her in the morning looking her usual self in one of her own dresses which had somehow miraculously been saved from the fire.

The moment she was awake Shimona sat up in bed to ask:

"His Grace? How is he?"

"He has not regained consciousness," Nanna answered. "And as Mr. Alister tells us they are expecting the Doctor some time this morning I thought you would wish to get up and tell him that we can nurse him and need no interference."

If Shimona had not been so worried she would have smiled.

She knew that Nanna disliked all Doctors with the exception of Doctor Lesley and had complete faith in the potions that her mother had prepared over the years.

She realised too that if Nanna had taken the Duke under her wing she would not have to fight to stay and look after him as she intended to do.

There was however one urgent question that mattered more than anything else.

"He will . . . live, Nanna?" she asked. "We will be able to . . . save him?"

"With God's help we will," Nanna replied.

The following days seemed to pass almost in a dream.

It was difficult for Shimona to think of anything or even to remember to eat and drink in her anxiety about the Duke.

When finally he regained consciousness, Nanna gave him one of the herbal draughts she had prepared and he went to sleep again.

"The longer he's not aware of what's happened, the better!" she said when Shimona questioned her. "I'm doing what your mother would have done, and that'll prove to be right."

Shimona was sure this was true, but it was difficult not to be desperately anxious and she found it hard to think of anything but the man she loved—the man who had saved her life.

Ten days after the fire had taken place Alister asked to see her and she left the Duke's bedside to go down to the small front room where he was waiting.

He had called every day, having accepted the responsibility that the situation demanded, to find out how the Duke was, and she learnt that he had been very busy taking charge of everything in his Uncle's absence.

He was being, Shimona thought, surprisingly efficient; in fact he seemed a different person.

She had heard from Nanna after the first night that everyone had been housed in the farm cottages, and that quite a number of the valuable pictures and pieces of furniture in the house had been saved.

Even her own gowns which had been shut in a heavy wardrobe had only been slightly scorched and were in fact wearable.

But most of the rooms in the main part of the house had been damaged and the wing from which she had been rescued had been completely gutted.

The fire had started, Shimona learnt, because one of the men-servants who had drunk more than the rest had overturned an oil-lamp.

None of the others had been in a fit state to put out the fire until it was out of control.

"Mr. McCraig's sacked the agent—and not before time," Nanna told her.

"Sacked Mr. Reynolds?" Shimona questioned.

"It was his fault in letting the household staff get out of hand."

Three days after the fire Shimona had learnt that Captain Graham had come from London to supervise everything.

The Duke's valet, Harris, who was housed in a nearby cottage, was always there if they needed him and Captain Graham made no changes where their lodging was concerned except to improve the menu.

Luxuries appeared which were well beyond the cooking capabilities of Mrs. Saunders.

The out-rider whom the Duke had spoken of as being an excellent cook was now in charge of the small kitchen.

The Chef, like most of the other servants who had been at Melton Paddocks, had been dismissed.

"A clean sweep was what was wanted," Nanna said with satisfaction.

Alister was waiting for Shimona when she went into the Sitting-Room and she saw by the expression on his face that he had something grave to impart.

"What is it?" she asked apprehensively.

"I know you will be sorry, Shimona," he replied, "but my Great-Uncle died last night."

"Oh, no!" Shimona exclaimed in consternation.

"As you know he had a slight heart-attack after we got him away from the fire," Alister explained. "He seemed to get better and talked of going North in a day or so. But last night he must have had another attack and when his valet called him this morning he was dead."

"I am sorry . . . so very sorry."

"So am I," Alister said in all sincerity.

He hesitated for a moment, then he said:

"You will understand that I have to take his body north. He would not wish to be buried anywhere except among our own people."

"Of course," Shimona murmured.

141

"I will leave Captain Graham in charge," Alister went on, "but there is something I want to ask of you."

"What is it?" Shimona asked.

Alister seemed to feel for words and then he said abruptly:

"When this is all over—will you marry me, Shimona?"

Shimona stared at him in astonishment, thinking she could not have heard him correctly.

"M . . . marry you?" she replied. "But I thought . . ."

"So did I," he answered. "I knew that Kitty had been married before, but she had told me that her husband had died in prison. It was not true."

Shimona found it difficult to say anything and he went on:

"When he read what had happened in the newspapers and it was reported that I was heir to The Mc-Craig, the man came to see me and asked for £20,000 to disappear and not to make any future claims upon his wife."

"What . . . did you . . . answer him?" Shimona managed to say.

"I told him I would settle £20,000 on Kitty, who could then resume their relationship if she wished to do so."

"So you are . . . free."

"I am free," he said. "But I know that my Great-Uncle was right when he said you were exactly the right sort of wife for the Chieftain of the Clan McCraig."

He paused before he added a little self-consciously:

"I have also fallen in love with you."

"I am very honoured that your Great-Uncle should have said such kind things about me," Shimona said softly, "and that you should think the same. But I know you will understand when I say that I could not marry any man I did not . . . love."

"And if I wait, so that we get to know each other better, have I a chance?"

"I am . . . afraid . . . not!"

"You love someone else?"

There was silence and then Alister said in a low voice:

"It is—Uncle Yvell, is it not?"

"Y . . . yes."

"Oh, my dear, he will break your heart," he pleaded, "and I could not bear to think of that happening to you."

"There is . . . nothing I can . . . do about it," Shimona murmured.

Alister came to her side to take her hand in his and raise it to his lips.

"You have taught me so much," he said. "If I make something of my life in the future, if I become in any way worthy to follow in my Great-Uncle's footsteps, then it will be entirely due to you."

"Thank . . . you," Shimona said.

Then he kissed her hand and left her.

When he had gone she went upstairs to the Duke's bed-room and sat down by his bedside.

He was asleep but he was looking better.

The pallor that had been there at first had gone from his face and he looked extremely handsome. She could only think, as she had thought again and again, how much she loved him.

She told herself that he must love her a little.

What man would have suffered as he had for her sake unless he had been activated by love?

And yet she was not certain.

It was somehow ironic that Alister should have asked her to marry him, when all she prayed for in her heart, even though she told herself it was impossible, was to hear those words from the Duke.

Nanna had come into the room without Shimona being aware of it.

Now she started as she felt her come up behind her.

"Don't look so worried, dearie," Nanna said in a low voice. "I've looked at the back of one of His Grace's arms this morning when we were making the bed. There's a new skin forming. Skin as clear and as flawless as that of a new-born babe."

"Oh, Nanna, is that true?"

"Would I tell you a lie?" Nanna enquired. "The honey has worked as your mother always said it would."

"I can hardly . . . believe it!"

"Oh, 'thou of little faith!' " Nanna said almost scornfully.

But Shimona wanted to go down on her knees and send a prayer of thankfulness and gratitude up to the sky.

The Duke grew better day by day and now it seemed to Shimona that she never had a moment to herself.

She read to him, she wrote letters and memoranda at his dictation. Although she had the feeling that Captain Graham would have done it better than she did, the Duke wished to have her by him.

She even thought that when she was reading the newspapers or a book to him he was watching her face rather than attending to what she was saying.

Once or twice when she asked him a question about what she had read he certainly found it hard to give the right answer.

He did not talk very much and they had no intimate conversation—certainly nothing that could not have been said with a dozen people in the room.

But Shimona went to sleep with his name on her lips and awoke thinking of him.

When she was not with him, she felt part of herself was missing.

"I love him; I love him . . . there is nothing else in

the world but him!" she would whisper over and over again.

The Duke slept in the afternoon and then both he and Nanna insisted that Shimona went out for a walk.

Her steps nearly always took her to the stables where Saunders or one of the other grooms would be waiting with a basket of apples cut into small pieces with which she could feed the horses.

Their heads would be over the lower door of their stables and they would reach out greedily for the pieces of apple she gave them in the palm of her hand.

Saunders would talk to her about the horses.

But it was Harris who told her the things she wanted to hear about the Duke.

She soon learnt that the valet had what was almost an adoration for his master whom he had looked after, he told Shimona proudly, ever since he was a young man.

"Them as says things about His Grace don't know him as I do, Ma'am and that's the truth!" he said.

He saw Shimona was interested and he went on:

"His Grace has often warned me against speaking of his private affairs, but I don't mind telling you, Ma'am, that he's done more good in his time than a great many other gentlemen in his position, and there's as many people living secretly on his bounty as there are on his official pay-roll."

This was the sort of praise that Shimona wanted to hear, and she only hoped that Harris said such nice things about the Duke to Nanna.

In fact since the Duke had saved her from the fire Nanna had completely reversed her opinion of him.

"He saved your life, Miss Shimona," she said more than once. "If it hadn't been for His Grace, you'd have been burnt to a cinder. That roof collapsed a few seconds after you reached the ground!"

There were tears behind the words and then as if she thought she was being too sentimental Nanna would add almost angrily:

"Why you couldn't have done as you were told, Miss Shimona, and gone straight downstairs I don't know. I saw you on the landing and thought you were just behind me, but all that shoving and pushing by those hysterical women stopped me from getting to you."

"I had to save the baby, Nanna, you know that."

Captain Graham told her what had happened to it.

"The mother's more grateful than she can ever say. She wanted to come and thank you personally, but I thought you'd enough to put up with already."

"What has happened to her?" Shimona asked.

"I took her back to her parents. They're decent, respectable folk and they've taken her in. She's a pretty girl and doubtless she'll find someone who'll marry her."

"Oh, I do hope so! Perhaps . . . it would be . . . possible . . ." Shimona began a little hesitatingly wondering how much money she could afford to offer.

"There is no need for you to worry about that," Captain Graham said. "I knew what His Grace would want and I have provided her with what you might call a handsome pension."

He smiled and added:

"The other servants who have been dismissed have also been given a considerable sum of money to tide them over until they can find other employment. I have no doubt they will behave better in the future than they have here."

Shimona on her walk looked at the house with its burnt-out windows and wondered if the Duke would rebuild it.

She still did not like to bother him with fundamental questions until he was better in health.

It was now well into November and she thought that if he were leading an ordinary life the Duke might be staying at Melton Paddocks for the hunting.

She wondered if the reports of the parties he had given had been exaggerated, or if in fact they had been the orgies which Nanna had heard described.

"What happens at an orgy?" she wondered.

What did people do when they behaved in a reprehensible manner which made other people like her
father not only denounce them, but also speak of what
occurred with almost bated breath?

She felt very young and ignorant as she turned away
from the house, feeling despairingly that it was ridiculous to think that the Duke might be genuinely interested in her.

What had he in common with a girl who had seen
nothing of life, who might have been shut up in a con-
vent for all she knew of the world and the sort of entertainments that amused him?

She walked back towards the groom's house and as
the pale winter sunshine sank behind a distant wood
she forgot for a moment her sense of unhappiness because of the beauty of the leafless branches and boughs
of the trees, silhouetted against the pink and gold of
the sky.

There was a touch of frost in the air and Shimona
thought that it would freeze during the night. Then
her footsteps quickened because it was time for her to
go back and she would see the Duke again.

"If for nothing else," she told herself, "I shall always
bless the fire because I have had this time with
him . . . time when we have been together and even
when he was unconscious I was able to be near him, to
look at him."

She opened the door and the warmth of the small
house came towards her like a wave of welcome.

She pushed back her fur-trimmed cloak from her
face, unclasped it at the neck and laid it down on a
chair.

She was just about to go upstairs when she realised
that the door of the front room was open.

She could see the bright light of the fire and she
realised that someone was sitting beside it.

For a moment she could not believe it possible, then
as she went to the doorway she saw that sitting in one

of the big leather arm-chairs which had been salvaged from the fire was the Duke.

He was dressed and his high, intricately-tied cravat was very white against his face which was much thinner since he had been ill.

He looked amazingly handsome and very like his old self.

"You are . . . up!" Shimona gasped.

"It was to be a surprise," he answered. "Forgive me for not rising."

"No, no, of course, you must take things easily."

Now she ran across the room towards him, her eyes wide and shining in her small face, her lips parted with excitement.

"You are . . . not in . . . pain? You feel all . . . right?" she asked almost incoherently, the questions tumbling over each other.

"I am almost as good as new!"

Shimona laughed from sheer happiness. Then she sank down on the woolly hearth-rug at his feet.

"I am so glad, so very, very glad! I was . . . afraid when you were carried in here that you . . . would not . . . live."

"I realise it is entirely due to you that my skin has healed and without a scar on it," the Duke said. "Your Nurse told me it was you who thought of using honey."

"You saved my life," Shimona said softly.

Her eyes looked up into his, but he turned his head to stare at the fire.

"Now I am better, Shimona," he said in what she thought was a hard voice, "we have to make plans for your future."

Shimona was suddenly still.

"M . . . must we . . . talk about it . . . now?"

"We must," the Duke answered gravely. "Now that I am no longer an invalid you cannot stay with me unchaperoned."

Shimona looked at him in consternation.

She had forgotten, even if she had thought of it, that a chaperon where they were concerned was necessary.

"There are," the Duke went on after a moment, "two alternatives for you to consider."

Shimona looked at him in perplexity and he went on:

"The first is that you should go to your grandparents and this, before we came north, I promised your Nurse I would help you to do."

"I . . . thought Nanna must have said something like that to you," Shimona answered. "But I have already told her that I have no intention of getting in touch with relatives when for years they ignored my mother's very existence."

"A little while ago there was no alternative," the Duke said, "and I agree entirely with your Nurse that it was the sensible and practical thing to do."

Shimona did not speak and he did not look at her as he went on:

"Since we have been here I understand that you have had the opportunity of accepting a different position."

For a moment Shimona did not understand, then the blood rose in her cheeks as she said:

"Do . . . do you mean what . . . Alister suggested?"

"Alister wrote me a letter before he left and I read it when I was well enough to do so. He is very anxious that you should be his wife."

Shimona drew in her breath.

"I am . . . honoured that he should . . . wish it . . . but I cannot marry him."

"Why not?"

"I am . . . not in . . . love with . . . him."

"Is that really so important? You would have a great position in Scotland, and Alister speaks about you with a warmth of feeling of which I did not know he was capable."

"He was . . . very happy with the woman he

thought he had married . . . or so he said . . . until
he found that she already had a . . . husband."

"He thought he was happy," the Duke corrected,
"but The McCraig and you made him see there were
greater possibilities in himself than he had ever dreamt
of."

He paused before he went on:

"I believe when he gets older and is living amongst
his own people that Alister will develop both character
and personality."

"I think that too," Shimona agreed, "and I hope one
day he will find a woman who will love him for himself
and whom he will love with all his . . . heart."

There was an unmistakable little throb in her voice
and after a moment the Duke said:

"So you have decided to go to your grandparents."

"There is a . . . third alternative," Shimona said in
a very low voice.

He looked at her enquiringly and although she was
shy she forced herself to meet his eyes as she said:

"You . . . offered me one . . . once."

"I offered you money and you refused it."

"If I . . . accept it now . . . would I be able
to . . . see you . . . sometimes?"

She knew that he went rigid, then he said:

"That would be impossible and so I must withdraw
my offer."

"Why . . . must you?"

She raised herself onto her knees and came nearer
to his chair so that she was touching him.

Although he did not move she felt, because her body
was against his legs and her shoulders touched one of
his arms, a quiver ran through both of them.

She looked up into his face and this time their eyes
met.

They were held spellbound by a magic that was inescapable, a magic which seemed to hold them as close
and as entwined one with the other as if their lips actually met.

"Let me . . . stay with . . . you," Shimona whispered.

For a second she thought that his arms would go round her.

He did not move, but the lines of his face seemed to deepen and his eyes, which she hoped would somehow reflect the fire which she had seen in them before, only darkened.

Then in a voice that she had never heard him use, a voice that seemed to be strangled in his throat the Duke said:

"I love you, God knows, I love you, but I cannot ask you to marry me!"

CHAPTER SEVEN

There was silence for a moment. Then Shimona dropped her eyes and said:

"Of course . . . I understand that you could not . . . marry the daughter of an . . . actor . . . but . . ."

"Good God, that is not the reason!" the Duke interrupted violently. "Did you really imagine that was why . . ."

He checked himself to say in a quieter voice:

"There is no man, whoever he might be, whatever his position in life, who would not be fortunate beyond words to be your husband."

151

Shimona looked at him and he saw the bewilderment in her face.

"I will explain everything to you," he said, "but go and sit in a chair. I cannot say what I have to say when you are so close to me."

Confused but obedient, Shimona rose from her knees and moved across the hearth to sit opposite him, her eyes on his face, her fingers linked together in her lap.

The Duke looked away from her into the fire, then he began:

"I am going to tell you about myself, not to make excuses for my behaviour, or for what I am, but simply because I want you to understand what I am trying to say to you."

Shimona waited and after a long pause he said:

"I do not suppose you heard of my father, but he was known as 'The Praying Duke.' He was sanctimonious, narrow-minded and fanatical on the subject of sin."

Again there was a pause before the Duke went on:

"It is difficult for me to explain to you what it was like living with him after my mother died. I think, looking back into the past, he must have been unhinged and a little mad."

His voice was cynical as he continued:

"If anything was likely to put a child off religion it was living with my father. We had long family prayers in the morning with the whole household there and the same thing at night, and everything that was amusing, interesting or could in any way be construed as being a pleasure was forbidden."

"Why was he like that?" Shimona enquired.

"Heaven knows!" the Duke replied. "I only know that after my mother died, when I was seven, I lived in the nearest thing to a hell on earth."

Shimona made a little sound of commiseration and he went on:

"He was determined to bring me up in his own

152

image and I was therefore not allowed the company of children of my own age, nor even to be looked after by a Nurse or Governess. I was in the hands of Tutors."

"It was much too young!" Shimona murmured.

"Of course it was!" the Duke answered. "And they were always elderly, erudite men who had not the slightest idea how to look after a child, let alone to interest his mind."

"It was cruel!"

"I realised how cruel when I was not allowed to go to school."

"You stayed at home?"

"With my Tutors always in attendance giving me lessons from the time I rose in the morning until last thing at night. I was allowed to ride, but not to play games."

"It must have been intolerable . . . and very lonely."

"I think the loneliness was the worst part," the Duke agreed. "I had no-one to talk to, no companion of any sort."

"How long did this go on?"

"Until I was eighteen."

"Oh, no! It cannot be true!"

"It was true!" the Duke said grimly. "So you can imagine that when my father died it was like coming out of prison."

He gave a short laugh.

"And like a prisoner who has been incarcerated for a lifetime, I found the world a strange place and had not the least understanding of it."

"What . . . happened?"

"Can you not guess the rest?" the Duke asked mockingly. "I came to London because I was now my own master. Society welcomed a wealthy Duke with open arms."

"It must . . . have been . . . enjoyable," Shimona said in a low voice.

"It was like coming out of the darkness into the light

but I had no power of discrimination, no standards by which to judge the people I met, nothing to guide me but a wild desire to make up for the time I had lost."

"I can . . . understand . . . that."

"I wanted to do everything that I had not been allowed to do in the past. I wanted to race my own horses, shoot, fence, fight, do all the things which every young man of my age had grown up doing."

The Duke's lips twisted a little cynically as he added:

"And naturally I wanted to meet women!"

Shimona pressed her fingers together. She felt a sudden stab of jealousy that was like a dagger piercing her heart.

"My father considered women were the invention of the Devil," the Duke went on. "So for me they had an attraction that drew me to them like a magnet."

Looking at his handsome face as he spoke Shimona was well aware that women would have found him as attractive as he found them.

"Again I had no discrimination," he said, "and as I started my life in the *Beau Monde* at Carlton House, the Prince of Wales's more disreputable friends were the ones who introduced me to the amusements with which they were all too familiar."

The Duke's voice was bitter as he said:

"You can imagine what happened. I was like a small boy let loose in a sweet-shop. I gorged myself greedily and in consequence earned very aptly the title I have been given."

His lips curled:

" 'His Disgrace!' I was quite proud of it! At least no-one would be likely to accuse me of being a 'Praying Duke'!"

He drew in his breath.

"Then I met you! When you came into the room at Ravenstone House I knew you were everything I always wanted and dreamt of and had never found."

"I . . . I too felt . . . something happened when we . . . met," Shimona murmured.

"We recognised each other," the Duke said. "We belonged, and there was no need for words."

He turned his face to look at her and she saw the pain in his eyes.

"When I kissed you I knew that after all there was a God and I believed in Him."

Shimona felt herself quiver as his words seemed to vibrate through her. Then he rose to his feet.

"But because you are everything that is pure and good," he said harshly, "and because I am what I have made myself, I still have enough decency left not to drag you down to my level."

He gave a deep sigh before he said very quietly:

"I shall love you all my life, and because I love you I shall send you away to-morrow to your grandparents where you will be safe. Perhaps one day you will find happiness with a man who is worthy of you."

Shimona was very still.

She understood so many things which had not been clear before.

She too had known a life without companions, she too had known the loneliness of being kept apart from the world.

The Duke's prison had been a cruel and hard one. Hers had been comfortable and she had been encircled with love. But the enforced segregation had left its mark on both of them.

That was why she could understand exactly what he felt and also why he had behaved as he had.

She knew he was waiting for her to speak and she rose from the chair to stand beside him.

She had a feeling that he was tense.

Yet she knew by the firmness of his chin and the hard line of his lips that he meant what he said and that he was sending her away so that they would never see each other again.

She moved a little nearer to him and raised her face to his.

"I . . . I have always heard," she said softly, "that if

you . . . save someone's life . . . you are . . . responsible for them . . . forever!"

The Duke did not move, but she felt him stiffen.

"I . . . belong to you," Shimona went on. "I may be a nuisance . . . and an encumbrance . . . but I will not . . . leave you. I will follow you . . . and sit on the doorstep of Ravenstone House until you let me . . . in."

The Duke made a little sound that was half a laugh and half a sob, then he put out his arms to draw her against him.

"Do you know what you are saying?" he asked. "Do you really mean that you will stay with me? That you will marry me?"

"I love you!" Shimona answered. "I love you so . . . agonisingly that if you . . . send me away . . . I swear I shall die!"

"Oh—my darling . . ."

His voice broke as his arms tightened, and he was kissing her cheeks with hard, rough kisses as if he had lost control of his actions.

Their lips met . . . then there was the tenderness and gentleness that she had known before.

It was as if their two beings merged into each other and there was no longer any division, or any barrier between them. They became part of one another and once again there was the rapture and wonder of a Divine ecstasy.

They clung together as if they had passed through a tempestuous and dangerous sea, and had reached a harbour of safety where they need no longer be afraid.

Shimona felt as if her eyes were blinded with glory and her whole being vibrated to music which came from another sphere.

The Duke raised his head and looked down at her face. He had not known a woman could look so radiantly happy and at the same time so spiritual, and he felt as if he must kneel before her.

"I love you! My precious, my darling, my perfect little love!" he said brokenly.

Then with his face hidden against the softness of her neck he whispered:

"Help me to be—as you want me to be—because I could not bear to—disappoint you."

"I want you just as you have always been to me," Shimona replied, "kind and gentle . . . considerate and everything that is . . . fine and noble."

He raised his head.

"Do you mean that?"

"You know I mean it."

They looked into each other's eyes and the world seemed to stand still.

The Duke sat down in the arm-chair and drew Shimona into it beside him.

There was room for them both if he held her close in his arms.

"You must not . . . do too much," she said anxiously.

"You are not to worry about me."

"Can you expect me to do . . . anything else" she asked, "when I thought I might have . . . lost you?"

There was a sob in her voice, then suddenly she hid her face against his shoulder.

"You are crying," the Duke said in a voice of consternation. "My precious darling, what has made you cry?"

"It is . . . because I am so . . . happy," Shimona sobbed. "I have been so . . . afraid that I would not be able to . . . stay with you . . . that you would not . . . want me."

"Not want you?" the Duke exclaimed. "Do you know what I have been through? Thinking about you, knowing that I must send you to your grandparents, and wondering how I could live through the rest of my life when you were no longer there."

"How could you . . . think of anything so . . . cruel?"

"I was thinking of you," he said. "I still am and I know that if I did what was right I would let you go."

"I have . . . already told you that I will not . . . let you do . . . that," Shimona replied, "and besides . . . I think you worry too much about your reputation. I do not know what terrible things you are supposed to have done . . ."

"And I pray that you never will!" the Duke interposed.

Looking at the tears still wet on her cheeks, he asked:

"What were you going to say?"

"You . . . may not agree," Shimona said hesitatingly, "but I . . . thought that if we could . . . leave London for a little while and live in the country . . . in your house with the beautiful gardens, people would soon . . . stop talking about you and perhaps instead they would begin to talk about the . . . good things you are doing."

The Duke put his fingers under her chin and turned her face up to his.

"Is that what you would like?" he asked. "Tell me honestly. Would you be content with living in the country with me instead of going to Balls and Receptions and all the parties that you could enjoy in London?"

Shimona gave a little laugh.

"Since I have never been to any Balls and parties I certainly would not miss them! Besides, I would much rather be . . . alone with you than at the most splendid Ball that was ever given! I can imagine nothing more wonderful than to be in the country and be able to ride . . . and plan the gardens . . . so long as we do it . . . together."

The Duke pulled her closer against his heart.

"Together! That is the important word!" he said. "And there is in fact a lot for us to do at Ravenstone."

"What sort of things?" Shimona asked curiously.

"My father, because he disapproved of them, had

every picture, however valuable or beautiful, which depicted women, especially those who were dressed, or should I say undressed, like goddesses, removed to the attics."

He smiled as he went on:

"With them went all the furniture that was carved with hearts or cupids, and a number of beds and sofas that he considered too comfortably luxurious to be anything but an invitation to indolence."

"It must have made your house very . . . austere."

"It is! That is why I have hardly lived there since I inherited the title," the Duke replied. "But we can restore it to its previous glory, put it back as it was when my grandfather re-built the house and brought treasures from Italy and France which are now heirlooms."

"I would love to do that."

"We will do it—together," the Duke answered.

"It sounds so . . . wonderful . . . so perfect!"

"And that is what you are!"

The Duke took his soft linen handkerchief and wiped the tears from her eyes, then he kissed them one after the other, and his lips lingered on the softness of her cheeks.

Then he pulled her even closer against him and found her mouth. He kissed her passionately, fiercely, possessively and there was a fire burning in his eyes, but she was not afraid.

"I . . . love you!"

Shimona was not certain if she said the words aloud.

Her whole body vibrated with the wonder of him and the wild sensations he aroused in her.

They were no longer two people but one.

This, she thought, was what she had always wanted. This was what she had missed, a sense of belonging, of not being the "odd-person-out."

The Duke's hand was on her head, smoothing her hair.

"You are so beautiful!" he said hoarsely. "You will be the loveliest of all the Duchesses of Ravenstone."

"We will have our . . . portrait painted . . . to-gether."

He laughed.

"Why not and it will be entitled: 'Her Grace and His Dis . . . .' "

Shimona put her fingers up to cover his lips.

"You are not to say it. That is all in the past . . . it is forgotten . . . and any wrong that resulted has been forgiven."

"How can you be sure of that?" the Duke enquired.

"There is something in the Bible," she answered, "about being 'purified by fire.' That is what you have been because you were so brave, because you saved me. We have started a new life . . . you and I . . . and never after to-day will we talk about the past."

She put her arm around his neck and drew his head a little closer to hers.

"I know that the consequences of what we will do . . . together will 'ripple out' and bring . . . blessings and happiness to many, many . . . people."

"My precious," the Duke said. "I love you! I adore you! I worship you!"

Then he was kissing her until again he swept her up into a boundless sky brilliant with stars where they were alone with their happiness and very near to God.

Never Laugh
at Love

❧

Author's Note

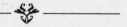

James Gillray was the first master draughtsman to make caricature a primary occupation and he became the most ferocious and brilliant caricaturist of his time.

He was so popular that there were queues outside Humphrey's print shop, over which he lived, waiting for his latest cartoon. By the end of 1811, when he was still in his middle fifties, he was already half crazy, the victim of hard drinking from the terrific pressure of work.

Thomas Rowlandson came from the comfortable Middle Class and had Art training in Paris and at the School of the Royal Academy.

He began as a painter of serious subjects. However he lost so much money gambling that he turned to satirical cartoons.

George Cruikshank's work lacked Gillray's tremendous force and Rowlandson's zest. He was sucessful in his early twenties and lived, after fifty years of aggressive teetotalism, until 1878.

CHAPTER ONE

❧

1817

"*I*t has come! It has come!"

Chloe tore into the School-Room, where her sisters were sitting at the big table in the centre of the room.

"It has come!" she repeated.

"The letter?" Thais questioned.

"What else?" Chloe answered. "I was certain when I saw the post-chaise turn in at the gate that something exciting was going to happen!"

"How do you know it is a letter from God-mama?" Anthea asked.

She spoke in a quieter tone, but there was no mistaking the excitement in her eyes.

In answer Chloe held up the letter, which the girls could all see was written on the most expensive white vellum paper, and addressed in flowery, elegant handwriting to their mother.

"She has answered quickly," Thais said. "We did not expect to hear from her until at least the end of the week."

"I am sure she has said yes," Chloe remarked. "Oh, Anthea, think how exciting it will be!"

"Shall I go and tell Mama?" Phebe enquired.

She was the youngest of the sisters and was only ten. Chloe was sixteen and Thais a year older.

Phebe had fair hair and blue eyes and was in fact a

small replica of Thais and they both looked exactly like their mother.

"No, you cannot disturb Mama," Anthea said quickly.

"Why not?" Chloe enquired.

"Because she is communicating with the Muse."

"Oh, Lord, not again!" Chloe exclaimed. "I suppose we dare not disturb her."

She looked enquiringly at Anthea as she spoke as if she hoped her oldest sister would contradict her. But Anthea said firmly:

"No, of course not. You know how it upsets Mama when she is writing to have us interrupt her train of thought."

Chloe put the letter on the mantelshelf, propped up against the clock.

She gave a little sigh and said:

"I think I shall die of curiosity if Mama does not open it soon."

"It is only eleven o'clock," Anthea said. "We shall just have to wait until it is time for luncheon."

Thais groaned.

"Why ever did she have to have a visitation to-day of all days?"

"I think she has been thinking over a poem for some time," Anthea answered. "I know what it means when she gets that far-away look in her eyes."

"If only they were good enough, we might sell them," Chloe said.

"Of course we could not do that," Anthea retorted.

"Why not?" Chloe enquired. "They say that Lord Byron has made an absolute fortune out of his poems. I am sure Mama's are nearly as good."

"I am certain she would be extremely shocked at the idea of commercialising her art," Anthea said. "So you are not to suggest it to her, Chloe—it would only worry her."

"It is far more worrying to be without money," Thais interposed in a practical tone. "Supposing your

God-mama will have you stay with her in London Anthea, what do you think you are going to wear?"

"I made myself a new gown last week," Anthea replied.

"That is not going to take you very far," Thais said. "Not if one is to believe the *Ladies Journal!* They say a débutante requires at least ten gowns for a Season in London."

"If I do go, which I very much doubt," Anthea said, "then there is only a month of the Season left. We all know that the Prince Regent goes to Brighton at the beginning of June."

"Well, even for a month you will need more than one gown," Thais retorted.

At seventeen Thais was very clothes-conscious.

Of the four sisters she resented the most having only the cheapest materials with which to make their own gowns and being unable to afford none of the ornamentation which the *Ladies Journal* said was essential if one was to be stylish.

It was true, Anthea thought, that her appearance would be lamentable if she did go to London and as her mother confidently expected, she was to move in the smart society in which her God-mother, the Countess of Sheldon, was a leading light.

Actually, Anthea had never thought for a moment that her mother's sudden idea of sending her to London for the Season would prove to be anything but a pipe-dream.

Always vague, always, as her husband had said so often, with her head in the clouds, Lady Forthingdale had failed to realise that at nineteen Anthea, her oldest daughter, might expect a more amusing existence than could be provided in the small house where they lived in an obscure Yorkshire village.

It had been, of all unexpected people, the local Vicar who had awakened her to her responsibilities.

He had been obliging enough after Sir Walcott Forthingdale's death to give the younger girls, Thais,

Chloe and Phebe, lessons in History, Scripture and Latin.

They learnt French from a Frenchwoman who, having previously taught her native language at a young ladies' Seminary in Harrogate, had retired to the village when the school had no further use for her.

Lady Forthingdale paid extremely little for the lessons, but Anthea always thought that Mademoiselle enjoyed them far more than her pupils simply because she felt lonely in her cottage and longed for someone to talk to.

The Vicar, calling on Lady Forthingdale to report on Phebe's progress in Latin, had remarked on leaving:

"I often think, My Lady, how fortunate you are to have such charming and delightful daughters. It will undoubtedly be a sad day when they marry and leave home, which of course Miss Anthea might do at any time."

"Marry?—Anthea?" Lady Forthingdale had exclaimed.

"I believe she has passed her nineteenth birthday," the Vicar replied. "A time when most young ladies, especially one as pretty as Miss Anthea, begin to think of setting up a home of their own."

"Yes, of course, Vicar," Lady Forthingdale had agreed.

But when he had gone she had sent for Anthea and said in a self-reproachful manner:

"Dearest, how could I have been so thoughtless? I had forgotten that you were nineteen! It is remiss of me to have done nothing about it."

"About what, Mama?" Anthea answered.

"About making your début," Lady Forthingdale replied.

"Me, Mama? But how could it be possible?"

"It was what your father and I always intended," Lady Forthingdale said. "But I have been so distressed, so helpless since he was killed that it never struck me how old you were."

"Very old, Mama!" Anthea laughed. "Soon my teeth will be falling out and my hair going grey!"

"I am talking seriously, Anthea," Lady Forthingdale said reprovingly. "We may be poor, but the Forthingdales have been respected in Yorkshire for hundreds of years, and my own family came to England with William the Conqueror."

"Yes, I know, Mama," Anthea said, "but being blue-blooded does not pay the bills, and it certainly will not provide for a Season in London."

Since her father's death she had taken over the running of the house and the paying of the bills.

Better than anyone else she realised how little they all had to live on, and how careful they had to be with every penny.

"I was not suggesting that we should pay for you in London," Lady Forthingdale said. "I am not quite as stupid as that, Anthea."

"Who else is likely to do so? You know how few relations we have."

"I would not ask your father's relations to help, not even if we were starving in the gutter!" Lady Forthingdale said with a sudden note of anger in her soft, musical voice. "They were always horrible to me because they expected your father to marry money. In fact they never forgave him."

"He fell in love with you, Mama," Anthea said, "and that is not surprising. You have always been the most beautiful person I have ever seen in my life."

Lady Forthingdale smiled.

"You take after your Papa, dearest, and while he was exceedingly handsome, you are very pretty."

That was certainly true, but while Anthea had her father's dark hair, she had very large green-grey eyes which sparkled mischievously and a curving, smiling mouth that was complemented by two dimples in either of her cheeks.

Ever since she had been a baby in a cradle anyone who looked at Anthea had smiled at her, and she had a laugh which made people laugh with her.

"You are flattering me, Mama!" she said now. "But do go on! I adore being paid compliments!"

"Which should not be given by your mother," Lady Forthingdale said sharply. "Oh, how could I have been so selfish and forgetful as not to have thought of this before?"

"Thought of what?" Anthea asked.

"Of writing to your God-mother, my friend Delphine, the Countess of Sheldon."

Galvanised by her remorse at being so negligent, Lady Forthingdale had sat down there and then and written to the Countess of Sheldon to ask if in memory of their old friendship she would do her a great favour and invite Anthea to stay with her in London.

She has been such a Wonderful Daughter to me since my Beloved Husband's Death, she wrote, *that in my Grief and Distress I completely overlooked the fact that this Year, now that we are out of mourning, Anthea should have appeared in Society.*

I have always remembered Your own Ball and how Beautiful You looked, Delphine, and how every man was at Your Feet. I am therefore begging You to remember Anthea, your God-daughter, and let Her, just for a few weeks, sample the Delights of London and meet a few Young Men who, you will understand, are sadly lacking in this small Village.

She went on to recall how delighted Delphine had been when at the age of fifteen and just after her confirmation Lady Forthingdale had asked her to be God-mother to her first child.

Delphine's parents had lived in Essex, a mile from Lady Forthingdale's. Their mothers were close friends and their fathers were joint-Masters of the local foxhounds.

At fifteen, Delphine had adored with an adolescent

passion, the beautiful Christobel, who three years her junior, had married the dashing Sir Walcott Forthingdale almost as soon as she left the School-Room.

Sophisticated, worldly and inclined to be somewhat of a Rake, Sir Walcott had been bowled over by Christobel the moment he saw her at her first Ball.

From that time he had never left her side, and disregarding all protests from her parents they had been married at the end of the year.

Anthea had been born when her mother was just nineteen and had gone back to her parents' house for her confinement.

Delphine had been a daily visitor, and when the baby was born she had appeared to adore Anthea as much as she had adored her mother.

It had been therefore an inexpressible thrill when Lady Forthingdale had suggested that Delphine should be one of the God-mothers at Anthea's Christening.

But after that they had seen very little of each other. Sir Walcott had settled down on his family estates in Yorkshire and he was not really to blame for the fact that the rents he raised could not pay for the upkeep.

Gradually with the passing years and the financial difficulties which arose during the war with Napoleon, their income shrunk so that when he was killed at Waterloo there was in fact very little left.

You are too old! How can you possibly leave me?" Lady Forthingdale had protested when Sir Walcott insisted on rejoining his Regiment and buying himself a Captaincy.

"I am damned if I am going to sit here rotting," he had replied, "and let all my friends fight for me."

He had however listened to her pleas until after the battle of Trafalgar when everyone had been quite certain that the war would be over very quickly.

"I have to be in at the kill!" he said. "I have shirked my fences long enough."

He had gone off to fight under Wellington but

fortunately for Lady Forthingdale's peace of mind was not posted to the Peninsula.

But when finally the Army had proceeded to Brussels for the final showdown with Napoleon, Sir Walcott was with the Cavalry.

It had been inevitable, Anthea had thought when they heard of his death, that he should be amongst those who made the wild Cavalry charge at the beginning of the battle in which there were 2,500 casualties.

"It is just the way Papa would have wished to die," she had told her broken-hearted mother, realising it was no consolation to those left behind.

But she knew that her father, who had always been a thruster in the hunting-field, would never have held back or been content not to be first in the field of battle.

They had been forced to leave the house in which they had lived all their lives, and because the Estate was in bad repair the small amount they received for it had mostly gone in paying Sir Walcott's debts.

There had been however enough to buy the small house in Smaller Shireoaks in which they now lived and to invest the surplus to bring in a minute income every year on which they all had to live.

It had never even crossed Anthea's mind that she should be doing anything else but look after her mother and sisters.

Occasionally there was a Ball in the neighbourhood to which she was invited and in fact she had attended two last winter after they were out of mourning.

But while she had plenty of partners they were mostly married men or youths whose mothers kept a strict eye on them and had no intention of allowing them to become involved with—"that penniless Forthingdale girl, however pretty she might be!"

When the letter had actually been sent to the Countess of Sheldon Anthea had allowed herself a few daydreams in which she took London by storm and found herself not only a suitable husband, but also one rich enough to help her sisters.

Now that the idea had been put into her head she realised that it was essential for Thais, who was so pretty, to "come out" the following year.

"Even then she will be older than most of the other débutantes," Anthea reasoned, "and after her there will be Chloe and lastly Phebe. I must find myself a husband who will allow me to entertain for each one of them in turn!"

At the same time she was well aware that her mother had not seen the Countess of Sheldon for more than eight years.

People altered, drifted apart from their old friends and, as Anthea was well aware, did not wish to be encumbered with other people's daughters.

She calculated without much difficulty that the Countess was now thirty-four, and although she knew little of social life she could not help feeling that it was rather young to undertake the duties of a Chaperon.

However the letter had gone to London and, while Anthea could not believe the Countess would totally ignore her mother's appeal, she was quite certain it was a 99 to 1 chance that she would say 'No'.

"I cannot wait an hour-and-a-half for Mama to open that letter," Thais said sitting down at the School-Room table. "Shall we steam it open and see what is inside?"

"Oh, yes, let us do that!" Chloe cried.

"Certainly not!" Anthea said automatically. "You know that would be most underhand and ill-bred, and certainly unbecoming to a Lady of Fashion!"

"From all I read of Ladies of Fashion," Thais said, "they do all sorts of things that would be considered unladylike. In the novel I have just finished the heroine was always listening at key-holes."

"Servants do that—not heroines," Anthea said. "I cannot think where you find such books. Certainly not in Papa's Library . . . or the Vicar's."

Thais giggled and looked exceedingly pretty as she did so.

"I borrowed it from Ellen."

"Ellen?"

Thais did not answer and Anthea said:

"Do you mean Ellen at the 'Dog and Duck'?"

"She has a gentleman-friend who brings them to her regularly," Thais admitted.

"Oh, Thais, how can you?" Anthea protested. "I am sure Mama would have a fit if she thought you were friendly with Ellen, even though she is a very kind woman."

At the same time it came home to her very forcibly that Thais ought to have more suitable friends than the barmaid at the "Dog and Duck."

She was only just seventeen the previous month, but she had already lost what her father used to call "puppy-fat" and was so pretty that even the choirboys stared at her when she was in Church.

"It is Thais who should go to London, not me," Anthea thought and wondered whether her God-mother, if she sent an invitation, would accept Thais as a substitute for herself.

"What can Mama be writing now?" Chloe asked.

"I think she is going through a religious phase," Thais answered.

"We are lucky that it did not happen before we were born. Otherwise I am certain one of us would have been christened Jezebel or Magdalene!" Chloe said.

They all laughed.

"To Chloe's heart young Cupid shyly stole," Anthea murmured beneath her breath.

But she did not say it aloud; they had teased Chloe too often with the verse.

"It could not be worse than being called Chloe," her sister went on despairingly. "Why, oh why did Mama have a William Blake period when I was born?"

"I do not think mine is much better," Thais said. "Noone can ever pronounce my name properly."

"Think how romantic it is," Phebe said.

She sprang to her feet to recite dramatically:

The lovely Thais at his side
Sat like a blooming Eastern bride
In flow'r of youth and beauty's pride.

"Oh, shut up!" Thais cried and picking up one of
the books that lay on the table threw it at her.

The girls, with the exception of Anthea, all hated
their names.

She would read Robert Herrick's ode: 'To Anthea!
Ah, my Anthea!' and wonder if it would ever come true
in her life.

Give me a kiss and to that kiss a score;
Then to that twenty add a hundred more.

Would a man ever say that to her? And what would
she feel if he did?

"I cannot think why Mama could not have chosen a
name from 'The Vicar of Wakefield'," Chloe was saying. "When she was reading it to us, I thought that if I
did anything wrong I could always quote her source by
saying:

When a lovely woman stoops to folly
And finds too late that men betray. . . .

"It might be something to remember as a precaution
rather than an excuse," Anthea remarked.

"I wonder what sort of folly the poet was thinking
about," Phebe asked.

No-one answered her and she said defiantly:

"If Papa were alive, I should ask him."

"Well, he is not!" Anthea said, "and you are not to
bother Mama."

It was a rule in the house that their mother was
never to be bothered.

They all loved the sweet, rather ineffectual person
she had become since her husband had been killed.

It was a point of honour to protect her from all the

175

difficulties that she made little effort to understand, but which gave her sleepless nights when she knew about them.

Anthea often thought that her mother wrote poetry whenever she wished to escape from anything unpleasant.

It was certainly what she had done during her husband's lifetime, and now she seemed to become more and more immersed in writing long poems which she read to her daughters and then forgot.

For the first time Anthea wondered if in fact it would be possible to sell what her mother had written.

Then she told herself that while the idea would doubtless horrify the author it was very unlikely that any publisher would be interested.

From all they had read in the magazines Lord Byron's works had been an overwhelming success.

But the scandals that surrounded him had compelled him to go abroad the previous year, and Anthea suspected that when he was no longer present to be talked about and be the centre of attraction, the sales might drop.

Who, she asked herself with practical common sense, would be concerned with poems written by a lady in the wilds of Yorkshire, who would certainly not be a talking-point for the gay, frivolous socialites who enjoyed Lord Byron's effusions?

"You know it is rather sad," she said aloud, "that none of us have any saleable talents."

"I am writing a novel," Thais said.

"Yes, I know," Anthea answered. "But you have been writing it for the last three years and as far as I can make out you have only got to Chapter 5. By the time you have finished in another twenty years it will not matter whether with the sales you can buy a pretty gown or an ugly one."

She bent her back and with shaking hands, faltered in a quavering voice:

"All my own . . . work, help a poor old

woman . . . pretty lady . . . who has given the best years of . . . her life . . ."

There was a burst of laughter.

Anthea's impersonations were always life-like and her sisters now recognised old Mrs. Ridgewell who was the village beggar.

"It is very difficult to write a novel," Thais said with dignity, "and besides it takes me so long because I cannot spell!"

"I suppose I might sell some of my water colour sketches," Anthea remarked reflectively.

Chloe laughed.

"The last time you put one in the village Bazaar it stuck and stuck. It was only when I reduced it to 3d. that it was sold and then it was only because Mrs. Briggs liked the frame!"

Anthea sighed.

"I noticed when I went to see her last week because she was ill that she had taken out my picture and the frame had a pressed rose in it which one of her grand-children had sent to her!"

"Well, it certainly does not look as if we shall make any money that way," Chloe said. "I have often thought that I might give riding-lessons for anyone who would pay me."

"And who is likely to do that?" Thais enquired. "Anyone in the village who has an animal with four legs rides it anyway and the County when they go hunting certainly do not wish to be taught by you."

Chloe sighed.

"I would give anything for a good horse! It is absolutely sickening that now Papa is dead we have only old Dobbin to take Mama out when she wants to go any-where, which is very seldom."

"We cannot afford anything better," Anthea said, "and Dobbin must be getting on for twelve years old. You are not to ride him hard, Chloe. If he falls dead, we should never be able to buy another one."

"Money! Money! Money!" Chloe declared. "No-one talks of anything else in this house."

"It all comes back to what I asked originally," Thais said. "What is Anthea going to wear if she goes to London?"

"I am going to wear the clothes I already have with the new ones which you will all have to make for me."

Her sisters stared at her wide-eyed and she went on:

"I have thought about this just in case God-mama says she will have me. I am quite certain that we are clever enough to copy the designs in the latest *Ladies Journal,* so that I shall be presentable, if not spectacular!"

"You will look like a country mouse," Chloe said frankly.

"Very well . . . a country mouse," Anthea agreed. "But if the opportunity arises I am not going to refuse to go to London, because if I get there I have a feeling it would be to the advantage of all of us."

There was a moment's silence, then Thais said:

"You mean . . . you would find a husband?"

"If I . . . can."

"I do not want you to get married," Phebe said, her voice rising to a wail. "If you get married, Anthea, you will go away and leave us. It would be horrid without you—it would really!"

She got up from the table as she spoke and rushed round to the other side to put her arms round Anthea's neck.

"We love you, Anthea! We cannot let you go away and marry some horrid man who will never be as fond of you as we are."

"Perhaps I will marry a nice man who will have you all to stay," Anthea said, "who would lend Chloe his horses to ride and give a Ball for Thais."

"Do you really think you could do that?" Thais asked.

"I can at least try," Anthea answered.

As she looked at her sisters' serious faces and wide eyes, the dimples showed in her cheeks and she said:

"If I go to London I shall wear a placard round my neck saying: *'Three sisters to support! Please help with a wedding-ring!'* "

The girls all dissolved into laughter and at that moment the door opened and Lady Forthingdale came in.

She moved slowly and there was a far-away look in her eyes that they all knew meant that she was in the midst of being inspired by the Muse.

"I need your help, girls," she said. "I cannot get any further with my poem."

It said a great deal for the respect in which her daughters held Lady Forthingdale's talent that none of them for the moment mentioned the letter on the mantelshelf.

Instead they were silent as, completely unselfconscious, their mother stood just inside the door and lifting one white hand with its long, thin fingers recited:

In dying are we born,
And if some part in this pale earth
Must fade because I hold you in my arms,
Why then I would embrace the cross itself
If through the sacrifice of self be found
The glory of a love which must be God's.

"That is lovely, Mama!" Anthea exclaimed as she finished.

"One of your best!" Thais agreed.

"But what comes next?" Lady Forthingdale asked. "That is what I cannot determine."

"You will have inspiration later on," Anthea said. "It is nearly luncheon time, Mama. I was just going to come and interrupt you anyway."

"This morning the first part of the poem seemed to flow quite smoothly," Lady Forthingdale went on, but Anthea could bear it no longer.

179

"There is a letter, Mama! It arrived over an hour ago!"

The words seemed to burst from her and Lady Forthingdale looked at her daughter in astonishment before she said in quite genuine bewilderment:

"Letter? What letter?"

"A letter from London, Mama."

"From London? Oh—from Delphine Sheldon. I had forgotten. Do you mean there is an answer to mine?"

"Yes, Mama."

Chloe jumped up to take the letter from the mantelshelf and put it in her mother's hand.

"It must have come very quickly," Lady Forthingdale said in surprise.

"It flew here on the wings of a dove!" Chloe said irrepressibly. "Open it, Mama! Open it and see what she says!"

Very slowly, as it seemed to her daughters watching her, Lady Forthingdale opened the letter.

She began to read it. Then Chloe could not bear the tension.

"Read it aloud, Mama! Please read it aloud!"

"Yes, of course," Lady Forthingdale agreed. "I was forgetting how interested you would all be, especially Anthea."

She smiled at her oldest daughter before she held up the letter to read:

> *Sheldon House,*
> *Curzon Street,*
> *London.*
> *April 28th, 1817.*

Dearest Christobel:

It was a Surprise and such a very Pleasant One to hear from You after all these Years. I have often thought about You and I was indeed most deeply Distressed to hear that Sir Walcott had been killed at Waterloo. So many of our Splendid and Brave men died there to save the world from that Monster Napoleon Bonaparte.

Of course I shall be Delighted to have my God-daughter, Anthea, to stay with Me here in London. It is a great Pity that We did not think of it Sooner as, Alas, there is not very much Left of the Season in which to present Her to the Fashionable World.

I feel however I can give Her a very Enjoyable time and suggest She leaves Immediately.

It will not be possible for Me to send His Lordship's horses as far as Yorkshire, but if you can convey Her to the White Horse at Eaton Socom this Friday I will Arrange for an Abigail to look after Her that Night, and for our Travelling Carriage to convey them both to London the following Morning.

I send You my Affectionate Greetings, Dearest Christobel, and will look forward to seeing My God-daughter whom I remember as a very attractive Child. She will bring with Her Memories of the happy times We spent together so many Years ago. Oh, Dear, how quickly Time passes!

Yours lovingly, and with unchanging Affection,

Delphine Sheldon.

Lady Forthingdale finished reading the letter and Chloe gave a hoot of joy and excitement.

"She has accepted! She has accepted! Oh, Anthea, do you hear? You are to go to London!"

Chloe glanced around the room with excitement, but Anthea, who had risen to her feet, stood looking at her mother with worried eyes.

"Friday evening," she said. "Do you realise, Mama, that that means I have only to-morrow to get ready for the visit?"

"That will give you plenty of time to pack," Lady Forthingdale replied vaguely.

"But, Mama . . ." Anthea began.

As she spoke she caught Thais's eye and realised there was no point in saying any more.

Her mother would only be distressed if she said that she had nothing to wear.

After all, she thought, even a week would not be

enough to replenish or create a wardrobe in the style which would be expected in London.

"I shall just have to explain to my God-mother," she told herself, "that she must put up with me as I am!"

"I think it is very kind of Delphine," Lady Forthingdale was saying gently. "But I was quite certain she would not fail me. As I have always said to you all, it is friendship that counts in life and really friends never alter."

In London the Countess of Sheldon was entertaining the Duke of Axminster in her elegant Salon.

He had just returned from Newmarket where he had been in attendance on the Prince Regent, and finding a note from Her Ladyship awaiting him at Axminster House had answered the summons immediately without changing his driving-clothes.

His close-fitting breeches and polished Hessian boots made him, with his grey whipcord jacket, look even more handsome and elegant than usual.

There was an expression on his face as he regarded the Countess which softened the usual rather hard arrogance of his eyes.

"I came as soon as I got back," he said. "Your note sounded urgent."

"It was," Delphine Sheldon said briefly. "We have had, Garth, the most fantastic piece of good fortune!"

"What is that?" the Duke enquired.

"I am so glad you were away the last week or you would have been as desperate as I was."

"What happened?"

"Edward suddenly decided that he would return to the country. You know how he hates London, and something had upset him at the Club! I do not know what it was, but he came back in a towering rage and said we were to leave on Tuesday and he was closing the house."

"Good God!" the Duke ejaculated. "What did you do?"

"I argued with him, I pleaded, but he was adamant! You know how he loves being at Sheldon. He was just determined to get back there."

The Countess paused, then she said:

"I loathe the country, and that ghastly mother-in-law of mine makes it a hell on earth. Besides I should die if I could not see you!"

"You know what it would mean to me also."

"Yes, of course, but I could hardly tell Edward that!"

"You said we have had a stroke of good fortune," the Duke prompted.

"I was just going to tell you about it but I can assure you, Garth, it was a very near thing that I was not swept away from you and incarcerated in that mausoleum in the backwoods of Wiltshire!"

"Well, you are still here and that is all that concerns me at the moment," the Duke said with a smile.

"And it concerns me," Delphine Sheldon said softly.

She put out her hand to him as she spoke and he kissed her fingers.

She wondered if there was any other man in London who could do it so gracefully, while looking so disturbingly masculine.

"You look very lovely!" he said. "But go on with your story."

"I was in despair," the Countess said. "When Edward makes up his mind nothing will alter it. It is like banging one's head against the Rock of Gibraltar!"

"But you succeeded in changing his decision!" the Duke again prompted.

He found it slightly irritating that the Countess always took a long time in coming to the point of a story.

"That was when a miracle happened," she said. "Out of the blue, at the very last moment, when I had given up hope and my maid was actually packing my trunks there arrived a letter from Lady Forthingdale!"

The Duke looked puzzled.

"Do I know her?"

"No, of course not. She lives in Yorkshire and we were friends when I was a girl."

The Duke waited.

"I had not heard from her for eight years, but now she has written to me," the Countess said, "asking if she could send her daughter, who is my God-child, to London for what remains of the Season."

She paused expectantly, but for a moment the Duke was unresponsive.

"Do you not understand?" she asked at length. "Oh, Garth, do not be so obtuse. When I showed the letter to Edward he quite saw that I had a duty to my God-daughter, and I could not very well refuse her mother's request."

"Do you mean that you are going to have the girl here?"

"Of course I am going to have the girl here," the Countess replied. "I would have Medusa here, or whatever that monster was called who had the snakes in her hair, if it meant I could stay in London!"

She gave a little sigh of sheer happiness.

"Do you not understand?" she asked. "It means that Edward has gone to Sheldon and I can remain here until the end of the Season!"

"He will really allow you to stay here alone?"

"Not alone," the Countess corrected, "but with my God-daughter, chaperoning her in the most respectable manner to all the most important parties, and to Almacks. In fact I shall be a Dowager, Garth, sitting on the dais and behaving with the utmost propriety."

"Not as far as I am concerned, I hope!" the Duke objected.

The Countess laughed.

"No, of course not! But that is what Edward believes and you know what a stickler he is for doing the right thing. Especially when it concerns one's duty! That is what I persuaded him I owed to . . ."

She paused.

184

"What is the girl's name? I ought to remember. I was at her Christening. An . . . Anthea! Yes, of course. Anthea!"

She laughed.

"Anthea Forthingdale! Poor girl. What a mouthful!"

"It is, as you say, a piece of good fortune. I could not have borne your being taken away from me to Sheldon. It would have been very hard for me to find an excuse to drop in there."

"There will be no need for you to have any excuses to come here," the Countess said. "And not only has Edward gone, but he has also taken that doddering old Butler with him who I am convinced was always spying on me, and of course his personal valet and the groom who has been with the Sheldons for forty years—which is far too long for any servant to stay with anyone!"

She threw out her hands in an expressive gesture.

"So I have new staff and an open door and an open heart, my dearest, irresistibly handsome Garth!"

The Duke did what was expected of him and took the Countess in his arms.

It was an hour later that the Countess, looking at herself in her mirror as she dressed for dinner, thought how satisfactory life could be when one managed to get one's own way.

She had not exaggerated when she told the Duke that she really was in despair at being taken to the country at a moment's notice, just because her husband was bored with London.

Unless Lady Forthingdale's letter had arrived to save her, she would have had to do as her husband wanted.

She had been married when she was only eighteen in the same hasty manner as her friend, Christobel, but in her case it was a very different marriage.

The Earl of Sheldon, immensely rich and of

considerable social importance, had been a widower for ten years when he saw his future wife in the crowded Ball-Room at Devonshire House.

She had been among a number of débutantes who were present at one of the lavish and exclusive Balls which were given by the Duke and Duchess of Devonshire and attended by everyone who was of any importance in the *Beau Monde*.

Delphine had not been particularly outstanding amongst the other girls of her age. It may have been her red hair which attracted the Earl, or perhaps it was her youth which to a man satiated with sophistication had a charm of its own.

Yet the explanation may simply have been that love is unpredictable and no-one can be quite certain where Cupid's arrow is likely to strike next.

Whatever the reason, the Earl who, since he had been widowed, had devoted himself to much older and more experienced beauties, had danced for the first time in many years with a débutante and lost his heart.

Delphine had been both intrigued and overwhelmed by his importance.

But even if she had wished to refuse such a matrimonial catch, it would have been impossible for her to do so.

Her father and mother were not unnaturally delighted at their daughter's success, and she was whisked up the aisle almost before she knew what was happening to her.

There was no doubt that at first she had been extremely happy.

The luxury with which her husband enveloped her and the sophisticated social world into which he introduced her had an allure which kept her an adoring and faithful wife for at least ten years.

During this time she presented the Earl with two sons and a daughter, and then began to think about herself.

The Earl was getting older and he found the country far more satisfying than London.

What was more, he had little in common with the Regent.

In fact, he resented the manner in which the Heir to the Throne, growing more and more frustrated at not being King, expected fulsome adulation, uncritical flattery and undivided attention from all who surrounded him.

The Earl was too much of an individualist and too egotistical himself to find Carlton House anything but a bore.

While too experienced socially to show his boredom, he found it so much easier to live in the country where no demands were made upon him.

Delphine, on the contrary, found in London all she desired in the way of amusement and interest.

This narrowed down eventually to any Gentleman who was prepared to succumb to her charms and cast his heart at her feet.

The years had brought her a wholehearted appreciation of her particular attractions and she had no desire to hide them under a bushel.

She was beautiful, she was *chic,* and the Earl's importance made it easy for her to become a leader of the gay, raffish and extravagant society which revolved round Carlton House.

After she took her first lover, she had felt guilty.

But by the time their numbers had multiplied considerably, she was concerned only with keeping her husband in ignorance of what was now vital to her happiness.

She was in fact rather in awe of the Earl.

Although she could beguile and entice him into doing most of the things she wished, there was a hard core of obstinate determination on which she could make no impression.

This was obvious when it came to a choice between

London and Sheldon, and on anything which concerned the honour of the family.

No amount of entreaty, pleading or defiance would move the Earl on these matters, and Delphine knew it.

It was therefore, as she had said, a miracle that she had been reprieved at the eleventh hour from having to leave London and—more important—the Duke.

She had as it happened, achieved the zenith of a long treasured ambition when she succeeded in attracting the Duke of Axminster.

He had a reputation for being not only difficult, but also extremely fastidious.

He was of course pursued by every match-making mother in the length and breadth of England.

He was also sought after, chased, and hunted relentlessly by the Ladies of Fashion who counted their successes as a Red Indian counted the scalps on his belt.

It had taken time, a great deal of manoeuvring and a lot of luck before the Duke became aware of Delphine's enticements, but finally she 'hooked' him.

It was a triumph which was all the sweeter because she was in fact genuinely enamoured of the most eligible bachelor of the "Town" and veteran of an inordinate number of amatory campaigns.

It was not only his great possessions or even his undeniable good looks.

There was a kind of arrogance about him which appealed to more women and which Delphine found very much more exciting than the humble devotion of her previous lovers.

She always had the feeling, and it was a challenge, that she was very much more in love with the Duke than he was with her.

That she used every wile, every sophistication that she had ever learnt, combined with an expertise which came from long practice, and still could not be sure of him, made the chase even more exciting!

Delphine was determined that sooner or later he

would become her abject slave like all those upon whom she had previously bestowed her favours.

"Will Your Ladyship wear the emeralds to-night?" her maid asked.

Delphine started.

She had been staring at herself for so long in the mirror that she had for the moment forgotten where she was or what she was doing.

"The emeralds, Maria!" she said. "And that reminds me—there will be a young lady coming to stay here and she will be arriving on Friday."

"On Friday, M'Lady?"

"That is what I said," the Countess answered. "She will occupy the bed-room at the back. It will be quieter for her there than the room next door to this."

"It's very small, M'Lady."

"That will not matter," the Countess said loftily. "People who come from the country, Maria, are not used to the noise of the London traffic, and as you well know the room beside mine overlooks the street."

"Yes, of course, M'Lady, I didn't think of that."

"We must do everything to make Miss Forthingdale comfortable," the Countess said.

As she spoke she thought with satisfaction of several hostesses she knew who had daughters who had just made their début.

To-morrow she would call on all of them and persuade them to include Anthea in their parties and take her to many of the entertainments to which they were escorting their own daughters.

"That will leave me free," the Countess said to herself. "Free to be with Garth."

She gave a little sigh of satisfaction. Then as the maid fixed the emerald tiara on her red hair she told herself that he was hers, completely and absolutely hers, as she was sure he had never belonged to another woman.

'And why not?' she thought with a little sigh of satisfaction. 'I am far more beautiful than any of them!'

CHAPTER TWO

*A*nthea arrived in London in a luxury which was a vivid contrast to the discomfort of the first part of the journey.

Lady Forthingdale had at first been horrified at the idea of Anthea travelling alone to Eaton Socom.

She declared it would be impossible unless Anthea went by Post Chaise and they could find someone to accompany her.

"You are forgetting, Mama," Anthea said, "that such a way of travelling would be extremely expensive. To hire a Post Chaise for me alone would cost an astronomical amount."

Lady Forthingdale knew this was true and when she did not reply Anthea said firmly:

"I shall go by Stage-Coach and I assure you I shall be very well Chaperoned by the dozen or so of my fellow-passengers."

"But I do not . . ." Lady Forthingdale began, only to be silenced when Anthea said firmly:

"Either that, Mama, or I cannot afford to go to London at all. You know you have left all money matters in my hands, and I assure you it will be very difficult to find the fare even as it is."

Only when she was alone with Thais did Anthea talk about clothes and cry despairingly:

"I know exactly what you are going to say, Thais,

but I cannot afford to buy myself even one more gown unless you are all to go hungry."

"Perhaps your God-mother will be generous enough to provide you with something to wear," Thais suggested.

Anthea smiled.

"We can pray she will do that, but of course I must not drop even the slightest hint of my fervent hopes. It would be far too pushing!"

Thais laughed.

"Take some of your old frocks which you wear in the garden and which are patched. That should bring it to her notice, if nothing else does!"

"I have a feeling, Thais, that you would fare far better in London than I shall," Anthea said. "Supposing you go in my place?"

"No, of course not!" Thais said. "And besides the Countess is not my God-mother."

"It seems extraordinary," Anthea said reflectively, "that after all these years she should be so pleased to hear from Mama and so kind as to have me to stay with her."

"Mama says: Once a friend—always a friend."

"I know," Anthea replied, "but we seem to have been sadly lacking in them since Papa was killed."

"I know this house was cheap," Thais said with a little sigh, "and that is why Mama bought it. But you have to admit, Anthea, it is a dead and alive hole. Why, you even have to travel three miles to get to the main road where the Stage-Coach passes."

This was true and Anthea could not gainsay it.

It only confirmed her determination that somehow she must save the girls from wasting their attractions and never being seen by anyone but the villagers.

It was therefore with a feeling that she was setting out on an extremely important adventure that Anthea left home the following morning, knowing she had a very long journey ahead of her.

Thais and Chloe drove her in the ancient carriage

pulled by Dobbin, which was their only conveyance, to the cross-roads where the Stage-Coaches to Harrogate passed once a day.

The Coach was not full and Anthea obtained an inside seat without any difficulty.

She passed the next fifteen miles chatting to a local farmer who had known her father and was only too pleased to have someone to whom he could air his grievances.

These concerned the disgraceful manner in which the Government, now the war was over, was treating the farming community.

"They wanted us—we were important when 'Nappy' was making threatening noises just across the Channel," the farmer said bitterly, "but now he's beat we're beat too! Nobody is interested in us any longer."

Anthea tried to be consoling, but she was in fact glad when she reached Harrogate and could change her conveyance for a more important-looking Stage-Coach. It was almost full, so that she was fortunate to get a seat.

She was however, squeezed between a fat woman with a squealing child and an elderly invalid who insisted on having both the windows up.

Before they reached the Posting-Inn where they were to rest for the night, Anthea had nursed the child, retrieved a number of ducklings which had escaped from a basket in which they were being carried to market and listened to the invalid denouncing the expense of a treatment in Harrogate.

She also found the coach insufferably hot and very uncomfortable.

She was in consequence so tired that she slept peacefully on the hard bed which was provided at the Posting-Inn.

And having passed an undisturbed night she was the only passenger who was bright and smiling at the hurried breakfast served by a tired and surly waitress at 5.30. a.m. the following morning.

All this made the comfort and attention which was waiting for her at the "White Horse" at Eaton Socom more delightful.

The Abigail whom her God-mother had sent to meet her was not, as she had feared, an elderly and perhaps disagreeable maid who would look down her nose at a young lady from the country.

Instead she was greeted by Emma, a girl of not more than twenty-two who was obviously excited at being entrusted with such an important mission.

"Miss Parsons, that's the head housemaid, Miss, always gets carriage-sick; so she works herself into such a fever when Her Ladyship said she was to come to meet you that she was a-shaking like a leaf—she was really!"

"I am sorry that I have caused such a commotion," Anthea smiled.

"'Twas a bit of luck for me, Miss," Emma said. "I feels like a real Lidy, coming all this way in a slap-up carriage. I've never been in one before."

It was quite obvious that Emma was a chatter-box and, while Anthea was too tired the night she arrived at "The White Horse" to talk to anyone, she was quite prepared to listen as they set off for London the next morning.

Emma, sitting opposite her on the small seat of the well-padded carriage, seldom drew breath.

"I have never been to London," Anthea confided.

"It's a awful big city, Miss," Emma replied. "But there's lots of gaieties and entertainments for everyone, high or low, and 'tis not surprising that Her Ladyship likes it better'n Sheldon."

She saw that Anthea was listening attentively and went on:

"We was actually packing, Miss. The trunks had been abrought down from the attics when your mother's letter arrives. I was helping Miss Maria, that's Her Ladyship's maid, and Her Ladyship rushes into the room crying: 'We're saved, Maria! We're saved!

Unpack the trunks! We are staying in London! Oh, Maria, I am so thankful!' "

Anthea was surprised.

At the same time she thought here was the explanation why her mother's letter had received so quick a reply.

"Her Ladyship does not like the country?" she ventured, not wishing to appear inquisitive.

"She hates it, Miss. We all knows that, and 'tis not surprising. I've heard her say that Sheldon Castle's like a prison, and that's what it looks like, besides being miles from anywhere."

"And you too like London?" Anthea asked.

"I've got me reasons," the maid said coyly.

"You mean you have a young man."

"How did you know, Miss?" Emma asked. "He's ever so nice, but he works in London and if I had to go with Her Lidyship to Sheldon it's ten to one he'd find someone else. You can't leave a man lying about like with no-one to look after him!"

Emma's chatter told Anthea quite a lot before they arrived.

It was obvious that the excuse of chaperoning her God-child had been very welcome to the Countess, and she also gathered that there were a profusion of Balls, parties and other festivities to enjoy on her arrival.

She could not help feeling a little worried when she knew how few clothes her trunk strapped to the back of the travelling-carriage contained.

She had brought with her her own new gown and also Thais's best and two of her mother's. They had sat up late altering the waists and shortening the hems.

All Lady Forthingdale's daughters could sew well. Their old Nurse had seen to that and thanks to Nanny's teaching they could copy a pattern quite skilfully from the latest magazines which showed the most elegant *toilettes* for every type of occasion.

The only difficulty was that judging by the sketches

the austerity of the gowns worn during the war had given way to much more elaborate fashions.

Now the skirts were scalloped with lace or frills, sometimes caught up with bunches of flowers, and bodices while still décolleté and high-waisted were decorated in the same manner.

Anthea knew the gowns she had brought with her were pretty and undoubtedly became her. At the same time they were very plain and of course made of the cheapest possible materials.

"Perhaps nobody will notice me," she told herself, then realised that was in fact the last thing she wanted.

It was important that she should be noticed, and even more important that she should be admired by at least one eligible bachelor.

She wondered what sort of gentlemen her Godmother would invite to the house to meet her, and she was to find the answer to this the very night she arrived.

It was late in the afternoon when the travelling-carriage reached Sheldon House in Curzon Street.

It was an impressive mansion despite the fact that it did not stand, as Anthea had somehow expected, in a garden of its own.

The porticoed front door opened directly onto the street, but as soon as Anthea saw the fine hall with its marble floor and curving staircase she knew that it was grander than any house she had previously visited.

She was shown into a Salon which struck her as extremely elegant and luxurious beyond her imagined idea of the house in which her God-mother would live.

She gazed around the room at the inlaid furniture, the exquisite *objets d'art* of gold and enamel, the Sèvres china, the fine portraits on the walls of previous Earls and Countesses of Sheldon.

Then the Butler announced from the doorway that Her Ladyship was resting but would Miss Forthingdale go upstairs to her *Boudoir?*

By this time Anthea was feeling over-awed and

nervous—a feeling that was not assuaged when she entered the *Boudoir* and saw her God-mother.

She had known that the Countess of Sheldon was younger than her mother but not by very many years. So she had expected her to be getting on into middle-age, in fact someone well past the lissomness of youth.

Her first glance at the Countess told her how mistaken she had been.

Lying on a *chaise longue* and wearing a diaphanous and very revealing négligée of emerald-green gauze, she appeared to Anthea to be little older than she was herself.

Never had she imagined that any woman could be so alluring!

Then as she drew nearer to her God-mother she felt embarrassed at the transparency of her négligée revealing a slim exquisitely curved body which it seemed impossible could belong to anyone over the age of twenty.

"Anthea, my dear child!" Delphine Sheldon said holding out both her hands. "It is delightful to see you! I hope you have not had too exhausting a journey?"

Anthea curtsied, then advanced to take the soft white hands in hers.

"It is so kind of you to have me, God-mama," she said.

"I am pleased—I really am," the Countess said. "But it is very remiss of your mother not to have written to me before and I am afraid I had forgotten that you would not be grown up. So you must forgive me!"

Two green eyes looked up in the most charming manner into Anthea's face. At the same time she felt they were taking in every detail of her appearance.

"You are pretty, Anthea," the Countess said after a moment, "but not as lovely as your mother was at your age."

"I take after my Papa," Anthea said, "but Thais and Phebe look exactly like Mama, and they have her fair hair and blue eyes."

"I thought, when I was fifteen, that your mother was the most beautiful person I had ever seen," the Countess said.

There was no doubt, Anthea thought to herself, that her God-mother was the most beautiful person she could have imagined.

Never had she thought any woman could have such vivid red hair, such attractive green eyes slanting at the corners, and such a provocative red mouth.

"You must tell me all about your family," the Countess said, "but later after you have rested and changed for dinner. I have arranged a party to-night in your honour, and afterwards I will take you to Almack's."

"To-night?" Anthea asked breathlessly.

"Why not?" the Countess enquired. "The sooner you are launched into the Social World the better! I have managed to obtain a voucher for you from my dear friend the Princess Esterhazy. I assure you, Anthea, it is very exceptional for a girl to receive one of these much-coveted vouchers the moment she arrives in London."

"I am very grateful, God-mama."

She thought that the Countess stiffened before saying:

"I have been thinking, Anthea, what you should call me. God-mama sounds quite old, almost like Grand-mama, and Aunt is nearly as bad!"

Anthea waited and the Countess continued:

"I think therefore it would be best if you called me Cousin Delphine. Cousins can be any age, can they not?"

"Yes, of course," Anthea agreed.

"Your Mama and I might easily have been related. We were so close to each other and our parents' houses were adjacent. So that is the solution."

"Yes, of course," Anthea said.

"Then Cousin Delphine it is and do not forget."

"I will remember," Anthea promised.

The Countess rang a little gold bell which stood beside her *chaise longue.*

The door was opened almost immediately by her lady's-maid.

"This is Miss Forthingdale, Maria," the Countess said. "Take her to her room. I expect the maids will have unpacked for her by now."

"Yes, M'Lady," Maria answered.

"Then good-bye, Anthea. We will meet before dinner in the Salon. Wear your prettiest gown, and remember, first impressions are always important."

Anthea was to remember her God-mother's words later in the evening when she was at Almack's and realised that she was without question the worst dressed girl in the room.

At dinner her appearance had not seemed to matter as nobody paid any attention to her. But she was well aware that on the dance floor her plain white muslin with one frill was conspicuously inadequate as a Ball-gown.

The gauzes, satins, silks, lamés, lawns, batistes and tulles were all embroidered with gold and silver tinsel and bestrewn with lace, motifs, flowers and ruches.

Each gown was a work of art, and the tiny puff-sleeves were as elaborate as the skirts.

It was little wonder that Anthea felt like a charity-child from an Institution.

"I am a country mouse," she told herself, "and no-one could mistake me for anything else."

The Dinner party had consisted of twenty exquisitely bejewelled and expensively garbed ladies and gentlemen, all of whom obviously knew one another well and, Anthea gathered, were close friends of her God-mother.

She was introduced to them all, but the Countess omitted to mention their names, while she was presented as a cousin who had come to London for what was left of the Season.

The gentlemen bowed, the ladies gave her a

condescending nod before resuming the conversation they were having before being interrupted.

At dinner Anthea had a good-looking youngish man on one side of her who from the moment they sat down was deep in conversation with the lady on his left.

As she frequently called him "darling" in a soft, purring tone, Anthea gathered they were closely acquainted.

On her other side was a red faced, jovial Peer who talked throughout the meal with a man two places away from him about racing.

Apparently both had horses in training and were rivals for the Gold Cup at Ascot, although Anthea gathered there were several other competitors to challenge them.

As neither of her partners spoke more than two or three words to her, she was able to observe the rest of the company with interest.

She was in fact memorising everything that she heard and saw so that she could relate it to her sisters.

"Do not forget a single thing that happens!" Chloe had admonished before she left. "You know we want to hear every detail, who the people were, what they looked like, how they dressed, and of course what they said."

"If I write it all down it will be as long as a book," Anthea said.

"Write as much as you can," Thais begged, "and store the rest in your mind."

"I will do that," Anthea promised.

She had already rehearsed to herself as she travelled in the Stage-Coach how she would make her sisters laugh when she impersonated the passengers—the querulous invalid, the woman with the baby and the farmer's wife who had inadvertently let loose the ducklings.

Looking round the dining-table she began to see

that it would be easy for her to portray some of her God-mother's guests.

She thought that she would also make little sketches of some of them on the letters which she was determined to write home at every opportunity.

Never had she seen such silver ornaments, so many flunkeys, so much glitter and expensive jewellery, or such low-cut gowns.

At the Balls she had attended in the country the gowns worn by the lady guests had been neither transparent nor had their décolletages been anything but discreet.

It seemed to Anthea that her God-mother was wearing a gown that was just as revealing as the négligée in which she had rested in her boudoir, and when some of the other ladies bent forward she felt herself blushing to see how much their ample charms were disclosed.

But it was really the gentlemen who intrigued her most.

They were so much smarter, so very much more impressive than any men she had ever met before. There was no doubt that black knee-length breeches and high, meticulously-tied cravats were exceedingly becoming.

She was well aware that her God-mother was "doing her proud," as her father would have said.

Almack's was the most severely exclusive and most despotically controlled Club in the whole of London. As she had read:

Many diplomatic arts, much finesse and a host of intrigues are set in motion to get an invitation to Almack's. Persons engaged in Commerce have no hope of ever setting foot inside the strongly-guarded door.

"I will see everyone of importance," Anthea told herself when after dinner the party set off from Curzon Street.

A procession of carriages conveyed the Countess's guests drawn by thoroughbred horses which made Anthea long to have a closer look at them.

She found herself seated beside her God-mother in a carriage which struck her as being smarter and more luxurious than any of the others.

She was also quite certain after only a quick glimpse that the two horses which drew it could not be excelled by any other animals in the street.

It was only as they drove along that she learnt that the carriage did not belong to her God-mother, but to the gentleman who accompanied them.

"It is a long time since I have been to Almack's," he remarked. "I had hoped that I should never have to be bored again by the autocratic pretensions of its host-esses."

"Now, Garth, do not be difficult!" the Countess begged. "You know that I have to take Anthea there so that she can meet The Town, and if we do not attend tonight's Ball, we shall have to wait a week for the next."

She turned to Anthea.

"Everything depends, my dear, on your making a good impression on Lady Castlereagh, Lady Jersey, Lady Cowper, the Princess de Lieven and, of course, my dear friend, the Princess Esterhazy."

"I hope I shall do that," Anthea said a little nervously.

"As the Duke has said, they are very autocratic."

Anthea started.

She had not realised that the gentleman sitting opposite her was a Duke, and she thought how thrilled the girls would be to know she had met one.

She looked at him in the lights that shone through the carriage windows as they drove up Berkeley Street.

He was, she decided, the best-looking man she had ever seen, and yet there was something about him that she felt was rather repressive.

She had not noticed him before dinner among the

number of other gentlemen to whom her God-mother
had introduced her.

Now she realised that he had a great distinction and
an air of consequence which was unmistakable.

'He certainly looks like a Duke,' she thought to herself.

"Perhaps you will meet the Duke of Wellington,"
Chloe had said before she left home. "If you do, ask
him if he remembers Papa."

"I shall never meet anyone half so important or so
grand," Anthea replied, "and if I do, I shall be far too
nervous to ask questions."

This is not the Duke of Wellington, but probably,
Anthea thought, his was an older title and that was the
explanation for his aloofness and a pride which was
very obvious even when he was not speaking.

"How long shall we have to stay?" the Duke enquired.

"No longer than I can help," the Countess replied,
"and I hope, Garth, you will ask me to dance. I am
wearing a new gown especially so that I can show it off
in a Ball-Room that is not as crowded as the one we
were in last night."

The Duke did not answer, and after a moment the
Countess said:

"You must not fail me to-night, and remember we
owe so much to Anthea."

Anthea turned her head to look wide-eyed at her
God-mother.

She could not understand, and when she was about
to ask a question she saw the Countess hold out one
hand towards the Duke.

He raised it to his lips.

"Have I ever failed you?" he asked in a low voice.

"Never!" she replied.

It was quite obvious to Anthea that for the moment
they had forgotten her very existence and she kept
silent. But she was listening with intense curiosity.

Almack's was all she had expected.

The large Ball-Room lit by huge crystal chandeliers, the long windows draped with elegant pelmets, the gilt-framed mirrors, the Band high above the dancers on a special balcony, were all just as she had imagined them.

There were also the Dowagers and their charges seated on gilt chairs around the room, and the hostesses introducing prospective partners to the girls who, immediately the dance was over, were returned to their Chaperons.

Princess Esterhazy greeted Anthea charmingly and having found her two dance partners obviously felt she had done her duty.

After dancing with a dull and unresponsive young man who was obviously not interested in her, Anthea found herself seated beside her God-mother who was conversing with the Duke.

She watched the dancers and realised that while some of them were proficient and graceful, others were clumsy and almost grotesque in their movements.

She was so busy observing all she saw that it was with a start of surprise that she heard a voice say beside her:

"Who are you? Why have I not seen you before?"

She turned her head to see an elderly gentleman with white hair and a deeply lined face. But his dark eyes were shrewd and there was the suspicion of a twist to his thin lips.

"Because I have not been here before," Anthea replied.

"This is your first time?"

"I arrived in London this afternoon."

The old gentleman had an ivory-handled stick on which he rested a blue-veined hand.

One leg was stuck out in front of him and Anthea thought he must be lame.

He was however most elegantly dressed, although perhaps he was slightly old-fashioned in that he was wearing a fob and there was a large diamond ring on one of his fingers.

203

Anthea had read somewhere that Beau Brummell, when he was an arbiter of fashion, had declared that for a man jewellery was in bad taste, and that therefore none of the Bucks and Dandies surrounding the Regent wore any jewellery.

"So you are congratulating yourself," the old gentleman said, "that you have entered the holy of holies."

"I am thinking how lucky I am," Anthea answered.

"I do not know that there is much luck about it," her companion growled, "unless you are referring to the fortunes of birth. The colour of your blood gets you in here—talents are not considered an asset."

Anthea laughed.

"I am glad about that."

"Are you telling me you have no talents?"

"Not many," Anthea confessed, remembering her conversation with her sisters.

"A good thing too!" the old gentleman said positively. "Far too many women to-day are trying to push themselves forward. All I ask is that a woman should be a woman. I have always liked them that way."

He glanced at Anthea in what she thought was a mischievous manner.

Because she liked him she said impulsively:

"Would it be very rude, Sir, if I asked you to tell me who some of the people are? You see I want to know about them, so that I can tell my sisters when I get home."

The old gentleman chuckled.

"If you keep your ears open while you are in London you will have plenty to repeat," he said. "What is your name, young lady?"

"Anthea Forthingdale, Sir."

"I am the Marquess of Chale."

Anthea gave a little gasp.

"I think I have heard of you, Sir."

"And nothing to my advantage, I'll be bound!" the Marquess said. "If you want to know who these creatures are—there is one that will amuse you!"

He pointed out a rather heavily built man who was dancing energetically with a very pretty woman wearing an egret in her hair.

"That is Alvanley," he said. "He has plenty of wit and enjoys two things."

"What are they?" Anthea asked.

"Gambling and cold apricot tart!"

Anthea looked at him to see if he was joking.

"It is true!" the Marquess said. "He once found an apricot tart so delectable that he ordered his Chef to have one on the side-board every day throughout the year."

"How extraordinary!" Anthea exclaimed.

"A popular fellow, but a nuisance to his hosts and hostesses when he stays with them."

"Why is that?"

"They always have to order one of their servants to sit up all night outside his bed-room."

"Whatever for?"

"After reading late, he extinguishes his candle either by throwing it on the floor, aiming a pillow at it, or pushing it, still alight, under the bolster!"

Anthea laughed.

"Is that really true?"

"It is indeed!" the Marquess said. "If you intend to observe Society you might as well learn of their eccentricities."

"Tell me more," Anthea begged.

"See that chap?"

The Marquess pointed with his stick at a handsome man with bold dark eyes, dancing with a pretty girl who was however on the fat side.

"Colonel Dan McKinnon—a great jokester," the Marquess said. "Notorious for practical jokes!"

"What sort of jokes?"

"Once in Spain he impersonated the Duke of York and kept it up, with the connivance of his Regimental friends, for several hours."

"What happened?"

"When a huge bowl of punch was served by the Mayor at a banquet given in his honour he suddenly dived into it throwing his heels into the air!"

Anthea laughed again.

"You make everyone sound very funny!"

"They are, if you watch people, as I do. I'll tell you another story about Colonel McKinnon. He is a favourite with your sex. Women go mad about him, but they soon bore him and when he leaves them they weep their eyes out."

"I can understand that," Anthea said.

She thought that Colonel McKinnon with his dark eyes and athletic figure was unusually attractive.

"One lady," the Marquess went on, "wrote McKinnon a letter full of reproaches. She threatened suicide and demanded the return of a lock of her hair she had given him."

"Did he return it to her?"

"He sent his Orderly with a large packet containing several locks of hair ranging from blonde to red, from black to grey. With it was a message—'Pick out your own!'"

"That was cruel!" Anthea cried.

The Marquess was obviously pleased to have an audience and he continued to chatter on, telling Anthea stories which she knew would enthrall the girls.

The Duchess of York, she learned, had an obsession for dogs that was making her look ridiculous.

At one time she had a hundred, many of them rather dirty, sharing her apartment.

A man called Akers—Anthea never learnt if he had a title or not—who enjoyed driving a four-in-hand, had had his front teeth filed, and paid fifty guineas to 'Hell-Fire Dick' the driver of the Cambridge Telegraph Coach, to teach him to spit in the familiar coachman style!

Anthea was so enthralled with what the Marquess was saying that she did not realise that the Countess, at whose side she was sitting, had risen to dance with the Duke.

As they passed by the Marquess looked at them and said:

"That is the Countess of Sheldon—devilish pretty woman, but hot to the touch. I imagine Sheldon has a hard time keeping her within bounds."

Anthea was not certain what this meant, so she was silent as the Marquess continued:

"Well, she will have met her match with Axminster! He is another who leaves a trail of broken hearts behind him."

"He looks very proud," Anthea ventured.

"Got something to be proud about!" the Marquess retorted. "Ancient family, great wealth! They have all tried to catch him, but the betting in White's is that they will fail."

"You mean—girls want to marry him?" Anthea asked.

"That is right but he likes them already married and sophisticated. Who shall blame him? And it is safer, unless the husband turns nasty."

Anthea watched her God-mother and the Duke with renewed interest.

From what the Marquis was suggesting it sounded as if the Duke was in love with the Countess.

Then she told herself that the married women her mother knew all behaved with the utmost circumspection. If people were saying unkind things, it was undoubtedly a piece of malicious gossip because her God-mother was so beautiful.

She was wondering whether she ought to reveal to the Marquess that she was in fact staying with the lady he had just described as "devilishly attractive" when the Countess stopped dancing and came across the room to Anthea.

"Dearest child," she said, "I have been most remiss in not finding you a partner. The Duke would be delighted if you would finish this dance with him."

"Oh, no!" Anthea tried to protest.

But the Countess moved away and the Duke put his arm round Anthea and without speaking started to waltz.

She was fortunately not afraid of disgracing herself on the dance floor, having practised the waltz with her sisters and always been in demand at local Balls.

At the same time she had never danced with anyone as important as a Duke, and she looked up at him from under her eye-lashes hoping he would not find her too countrified or not proficient enough to follow his lead.

She realised with some consternation that he was in fact looking extremely bored.

There was no misunderstanding the expression on his face and she was sure as he swung her round the room that he had been forced by her God-mother into dancing with her against his will.

Because her mother had always said that silence was boring and people should try to make polite conversation whoever they were with, Anthea said after a moment:

"The Marquess of Chale was telling me the most interesting things about some of the people here."

"I should not believe more than half he tells you," the Duke replied coldly. "His Lordship is known as the most inveterate gossip in the whole of White's!"

Anthea knew that this was the most important Gentlemen's Club in London, and she remembered hearing that the Dandies lounged in a bow-window eyeing the women passing in the street and making rude remarks about them.

She would have liked to ask the Duke about White's, but there had been something crushing in the manner in which he had spoken of the Marquess.

She thought to herself that it was obviously an effort for him not only to dance with her, but also to converse with anyone so unimportant.

It was therefore with a sense of relief that she heard

the Band stop playing and realised that the dance was over.

The Duke took her back to her God-mother, moving so swiftly that it was in itself an insult. Very different, Anthea thought, to the languid way in which he had moved while dancing.

"I hope you enjoyed your dance," the Countess said as they joined her. "After all, it is not every débutante who has the privilege of dancing with a Duke the very first night she makes an appearance at Almack's."

She glanced up at the Duke with a mischievous twinkle in her eyes as she added:

"I am sure you would like to stand up with Anthea in the Quadrille."

"I think it is time for me to return home," the Duke said. "I do not like keeping my horses out late."

He spoke sharply and Anthea fancied there was an almost defiant look in his eyes as he met the Countess's.

Just for a moment it seemed as if it was a battle of wills, then she capitulated.

"It *is* getting late, Garth," she agreed, "and Anthea has had a long day. I am sure she has seen all she wants of Almack's."

They said good-night to the Princess Esterhazy, Anthea thanking her Highness prettily for having been her sponsor.

"It has been a pleasure, Miss Forthingdale," she said, "and you must persuade your Cousin to bring you here again next week."

"I shall try to do so, Ma'am," Anthea answered.

There was a great deal of curtseying and a large number of gentlemen who seemed to wish to kiss the Countess's hand before finally they were outside and stepping into the Duke's carriage.

As they drove back to Curzon Street, neither the Duke nor the Countess seemed to have much to say.

As they stepped out onto the pavement the Countess held out her hand to the Duke and said:

"I thank Your Grace for your kindness to me and to my guest. We are both very grateful."

Anthea curtsied. They went into the house, and the Butler who had let them in stood at the open door until the Duke's carriage drove away.

"We will go straight up to bed, Dawson," the Countess said as he closed the front door. "As His Lordship is not here, there is no need to leave a footman on duty in the hall to-night."

"Thank you, Your Ladyship," the Butler said. "James will be very grateful for your consideration."

The Countess smiled at him and started up the stairs.

"Come along, Anthea," she said. "You need your beauty sleep and I have a great many delightful things planned for you to-morrow."

"You are very kind," Anthea answered. "I cannot tell you how grateful I am and how thrilling it was to visit Almack's this evening."

"I can see I am going to enjoy having you here," the Countess said.

They reached the top of the stairs and she moved her head forward, obviously inviting Anthea to kiss her cheek.

"Sleep well, dear child," she said. "There will be no reason for you to hurry in the morning. I never breakfast before ten o'clock."

She moved away as she spoke towards her bed-room and Anthea saw that her maid, Maria, was waiting for her.

Emma too must have heard their arrival for she came hurrying into the bed-room almost as soon as Anthea reached it.

"Did you have a nice time, Miss?" she asked.

"I had a lovely time, Emma!" Anthea replied. "And Almack's was all I expected it to be."

"The ladies at dinner had very fine gowns," Emma enthused. "We was all peeping over the banisters when the company left and we thought the jewellery alone must be worth a fortune!"

"I thought that too," Anthea replied.

It only took a short time to put on her nightgown and brush her hair. As soon as Emma left her she got into bed.

She thought she would fall asleep the moment her head touched the pillow, but instead she found herself remembering everything that had happened, all the people she had met, and what the Marquess had told her.

"I must not forget anything," she said to herself.

An hour later she was still awake.

She got up and lighting the candle by her bed looked around for a piece of paper.

"I will write down the names," she said and wondered how one spelt "Alvanley."

Her room was too small to contain a writing-desk, and unfortunately when she had come away she had left in such a hurry that she had not brought a writing-pad or even her sketching book with her.

She had however packed her paint-box and several pencils, but they were of no use without paper to write on.

She remembered that she had noticed in the Salon when she was waiting to be shown upstairs to her Godmother's *Boudoir* a very elegant Louis XIV *secretaire* standing in one of the windows.

It had been open and she had seen on it a blotter embellished with the Sheldon coat of arms, and a silver rack containing the thick white vellum paper on which the Countess had written to her mother.

"I will go downstairs and get some," Anthea decided.

She put on a wrap over her nightgown, and thinking she would be quieter if she moved bare-foot, she did not bother to put on the slippers which Emma had arranged beside a chair in her room.

She opened her door quietly.

The house was very quiet. There were only two or three candles alight in the silver sconces in the hall and on the stairs, but they gave enough light for Anthea to find her way without difficulty.

She reached the Salon and found that by leaving the door open she was able to find her way to the *secretaire*.

As she had suspected, there was plenty of paper in the silver rack and she took several sheets.

As she would doubtless awaken long before her hostess she thought she would write a long letter to the girls telling them all that had happened to date.

She came from the Salon and as she did she heard a sound at the front door.

She stood still, thinking she must have been mistaken. Then it came again and it seemed as if someone was interfering with the lock.

Thoughts of burglars and robbers swept through Anthea's mind and she wondered whether she should scream or run for help.

She had an idea that the servants slept in the basement, but she was not sure.

She had seen only the first two floors since her arrival and had no idea where the men-servants' quarters might be.

Then the front door opened and a man came into the house.

He turned round to shut the door behind him and as Anthea stood watching, feeling as if she was paralysed and could neither move or make a sound, he turned towards the stairs.

To her complete and utter astonishment she saw that it was the Duke!

At the same time as she recognised him he saw her standing in her white wrapper staring at him.

"What are you doing here?" he asked sharply.

"I . . . I thought you were a . . . burglar!" she faltered. "I was . . . just going to . . . scream!"

There was a moment's silence. Then the Duke said:

NEVER LAUGH AT LOVE

"I remembered something—important that I had to tell—Her Ladyship."

Anthea walked towards him.

"C . . . cousin Delphine has retired. If it is . . . important, I could . . . take her a message."

The Duke was standing with one foot on the stairs.

In the dim light of the flickering candles he looked very large and overpowering.

"I will convey the message," he said after a moment.

"But . . . Cousin Delphine is in . . . bed," Anthea insisted.

Again there was a pause before the Duke with a note of amusement in his voice said:

"My good girl, go to bed yourself and do not interfere in other people's affairs."

He did not wait for a reply.

He walked up the stairs as he spoke and on reaching the landing turned in the direction of the Countess's room and disappeared from sight.

Anthea stood staring after him.

Then as the full implication of what he had said and what he was doing swept over her, the colour rose in a crimson tide up her pale face.

CHAPTER THREE

*A*nthea was both shocked and embarrassed.

Although she had read the passionate love-poems which interested her mother, she had never mentally translated them into actual physical activity.

The fact that the Duke was, as she now realised, the lover of her God-mother seemed to her to be shocking and an outrage against decency.

She had never imagined that older people, or rather women of her mother's age, would have the type of liaison that she connected with the Kings of France or Charles II.

They had just seemed to be mythical figures which had no real semblance of humanity about them.

To be confronted with the fact that her God-mother was having a clandestine affair with the Duke of Axminster was a revelation which exploded in her mind like a bombshell.

She also felt very ignorant, and the blush which had suffused her face when the Duke told her not to interfere in other people's affairs seemed to burn its way into her consciousness all through the night.

If she could have had a choice, Anthea when morning came, would have sped back to Yorkshire to hide herself amongst the familiar objects she knew and understood.

She wondered frantically whether the Duke had told her God-mother what had occurred.

She was in fact sure he had done so when at 9.30 a.m., half an hour earlier than her God-mother usually was called, she was summoned to the Countess's bed-room.

As Anthea walked along the passage she tried to think of what she could say, what explanation she could make, but could only feel that being gauche and countrified was hardly an excuse for making such a *bêtise*.

The Countess, looking more alluring than ever, was propped up against a profusion of lace-edged pillows, her red hair falling over her shoulders, her eyes very green in the morning light.

Anthea stood just inside the doorway, wondering ap-prehensively what her God-mother would say, and was surprised when the Countess said with a smile on her red lips:

"Good-morning, Anthea. I thought you might like to drive with me in the Park this morning, and after that I feel we should visit Bond Street and see if there is some little object which takes your fancy and which I might give you as a present."

Even as she spoke Anthea realised she was being bribed.

It affronted her pride and her self-respect that her God-mother should think for one moment that she could not be trusted to be discreet without an induce-ment to keep her lips closed.

She was just about to reply that there was nothing she needed when the Countess gave a cry so shrill and sharp that Anthea was startled.

"Is that the best gown you have?" she asked. "And I noticed the one you wore last night! Oh, Anthea, how remiss of me! How inexcusable that I should not have thought of it!"

"Thought of . . . what, Cousin Delphine?" Anthea asked bewildered.

215

"That you would need new gowns coming to London from Yorkshire, and I forgot too that your father was not wealthy. How could I have been so negligent?"

Without giving time for Anthea to answer the Countess picked up the bell beside her bed and rang it violently.

When Maria ran in she exclaimed:

"Why could you not have told me, Maria, that Miss Forthingdale required new gowns! We knew she was coming from the country. I am mortified that we have been so obtuse as not to have had some ready for her."

"I do not . . . wish to be a . . . nuisance . . ." Anthea began, only to have anything she might have said swept to one side!

Her God-mother imperiously commanded Maria to bring from the wardrobes everything that she did not need and which could be altered immediately.

"I will buy you some new gowns," the Countess said, "but they will of course take time. What we must do in the meanwhile is to contrive that you look fashionable and well-dressed in my clothes, and there are in fact plenty for which I have no further use."

This was an understatement, Anthea found an hour later, when she was being presented with dozens of gowns all so smart, so exquisitely made, that she could not understand how her God-mother could bear to part with them. But the Countess had a valid excuse for everything she gave away.

Maria would hold up a dream of sparkling gauze.

"I wore that at the Duchess of Bedford's Ball," the Countess explained. "It was the envy of every woman present, but I cannot appear in it again."

When Maria showed a dress and coat of cream satin with appliqué work of green velvet leaves, she said:

"I have worn that ensemble twice at Carlton House and the Prince Regent admired it enormously, so he will not wish to mention it another time!"

There were Ball-gowns and complete *toilettes* for the afternoon, for the morning and for travelling.

There were high-crowned bonnets to go with them festooned with feathers, flowers and ribbons.

There were reticules to match the gowns and slippers dyed to the same colour which fortunately fitted Anthea, being only just a trifle larger than her own.

She lost count of how many different garments Maria brought from the wardrobes and from another room, and yet there still seemed to be a multitude left.

All the clothes she was given, Anthea realised, were in the hues which suited the Countess best: greens to match her eyes, jonquil yellow and gold to bring out the lights of her hair, deep blue to accentuate the white of her skin.

There were also a number of white gowns which, as her God-mother pointed out, were extremely suitable for a débutante.

Anthea was too overwhelmed to realise that very many of the gowns she was given were really too sophisticated and too elaborate for a young girl.

But even when she thought later that some of them were a trifle overwhelming, they were certainly preferable to the plain muslins she had made herself.

Muslin, she learnt from Maria, was a material which had gone out of fashion since the war ended.

Some of the coats were trimmed with bands of expensive furs like ermine and sable. But when Anthea suggested humbly that she should cut them off, the Countess held up her hands in horror.

"You must not alter the style, child!" she cried. "Besides, what would I do with the strips of ermine or the lengths of sable except throw them in the waste-paper basket!"

Anthea shuddered at such extravagance!

Yet while occasionally she protested that her God-mother was giving her too much, she could not help realising that she now had enough clothes not only to dress herself but also Thais and Chloe.

"How can I ever thank you?" she asked.

But she understood perfectly what her God-mother meant when she replied:

"You can thank me, Anthea, by being my loyal friend, as your mother was when we were young together."

"I should be honoured," Anthea managed to say politely.

At the same time she could not help wishing that the Countess had not supposed that her silence must be bought.

In the days that followed Anthea found that her God-mother had arranged in an extremely efficient manner that she was seldom in Sheldon House.

There were several ladies, two of whom were related to the Earl, who were introducing their own daughters to Society.

They had apparently been coerced into including Anthea in the parties, the expeditions and the Balls to which they took their own progeny.

It was after a week of being passed from hand to hand and of associating with girls of her own age that Anthea decided that she much preferred the fascinating social figures who made up her God-mother's particular circle.

She went with the Countess to a dinner-party which was very like the one which had taken place on the night of her arrival.

Now that she had found her feet and was not so bewildered, Anthea found the conversation exciting, witty and informative.

It was very unlike the inanities and incessant giggling that she had to endure from the other débutantes.

What was more, she found it a delight to look at the gentlemen in her God-mother's parties.

The beardless youths who partnered the young were, she found, so half-witted, that she had to force herself to be polite to them.

Fortunately, even though she dined with her young

acquaintances, they afterwards attended the Balls given by the great political or social hostesses.

There Anthea invariably found the Marquess of Chale.

"I have something amusing to tell you, Miss Forthingdale," he would say as soon as she appeared.

At the first opportunity she would sit beside him, listening to his anecdotes and to his often spiteful but invariably amusing tales about the people in the Ball-Room.

"I cannot think why you waste your time with that old gossip," one of the Dowagers who was chaperoning Anthea said to her.

She would not have understood if Anthea had replied that it was the Marquess's conversation which made her letters to Yorkshire sparkle as brightly as the diamonds round her God-mother's neck.

As the Countess rose late and Anthea, however late she went to bed, could not get out of her country habit of waking early, a day seldom passed without a fat envelope being placed on the Hall-table for the Butler to frank.

Determined that her sisters should feel they were a part of her own experiences, Anthea not only described all she saw, she also drew sketches of the people she met.

She of course made no mention of the Duke's special place in her God-mother's life, but she related that she had met him and drew a picture of him looking extremely disdainful and very autocratic.

She could not help feeling shy and tense when they met, even though he behaved towards her with the same polite indifference he had shown the night of her arrival.

She told herself that he had probably never given another thought to her stupidity in not understanding why he had called at Sheldon House in the middle of the night.

But even to think of how obtuse and foolish she had

been was to bring the colour to her cheeks and to increase her dislike of the Duke for having inadvertently placed her in such an humiliating position.

She learnt that he was much younger than her God-mother and in fact had only just passed his twenty-eighth birthday.

But this, she felt, did not excuse the fact that he was behaving extremely reprehensibly in pursuing another man's wife and actually making love to her in her husband's house.

There was however no doubt that, as the Marquess had said, the Countess was a 'devilishly pretty woman'.

Anthea used to watch the enticing manner in which she would look at the Duke from under her long, mascaraed eye-lashes, the way she had of touching him with her soft white hands, and of pouting her red lips provocatively.

She was not surprised that he could not resist such blandishments and found from what she had learnt in other houses that her God-mother had in fact succeeded in capturing a citadel which had resisted many other attacks upon it.

"I always thought that Axminster would marry the Duke of Brockenhurst's daughter," one Dowager remarked to another in Anthea's hearing.

"So did the Duchess!" the other replied. "But he was far too wily. They have all tried to catch him, but he confines himself to women who are already married."

"He never leaves Delphine Sheldon's side," the first Dowager said tartly.

"Are you surprised?" was the reply. "She is certainly in good looks, and she might as well make the most of what is left of her youth."

"You are too charitable, my love! Personally it would give me a great deal of pleasure to see His Grace marched down the aisle by some determined young female. He has been a distrubing influence in the Social World for far too long!"

"All handsome, wealthy Dukes are that!" her friend

laughed. "It will have to be a very early bird who finally catches Axminster!"

Because the Duke was constantly in her mind Anthea knew without even seeing him that he was always in Sheldon House.

She longed to discuss him with the Marquess, but she realised that would be disloyal to her God-mother and with difficulty she contained her curiosity.

The two new gowns which the Countess ordered for her in Bond Street were pink and therefore very becoming to Anthea's dark hair.

She wore them for all really important parties and the more elaborate of them to Carlton House when she was presented to the Prince Regent.

When she rose from a deep curtsey he informed her with the charm for which he was renowned that she was "pretty, very pretty indeed," but he doubted if she would ever eclipse her cousin, Delphine.

"I would not presume to attempt such a thing, Sire," Anthea replied.

She found to her surprise that she was not at all nervous and that in fact the Regent was not half so awe-inspiring in person as he appeared in his pictures and caricatures.

"All women want attention," he answered, "and they all wish to compete with their own sex."

"Only in an effort to capture the attention of gentlemen who are exceedingly fastidious and critical, like yourself, Sire," Anthea answered.

The Prince chuckled in delight at what she had been half-afraid he would think an impertinence.

But he had taken it as a compliment and later in the evening he singled Anthea out to show her a new picture he had recently acquired.

"You were a success with His Royal Highness," the Countess said when they were driving home. "It is a pity that that is the last party he will give. He is leaving London for Brighton next Friday."

"Does that mean it is the end of the Season?" Anthea asked.

"I am afraid so," the Countess replied with a note of regret in her voice.

"Then I . . . shall have to . . . go home."

"There is no hurry, my dear."

But three days later a letter from the Earl made it clear to his wife that he was aware of the Prince Regent's plans and that it was time for her to return to the country.

"Nothing can save us now," the Countess said miserably to the Duke.

Anthea descended from the Stage-Coach at the cross-roads to find Thais and Chloe waiting for her with Dobbin.

As she walked towards them and the guard on the Stage-Coach began to unload half-a-dozen large leather trunks, they stared at her too astonished for the moment to say anything.

"I am home!" Anthea cried, "and oh, how thrilled I am to see you!"

Her voice was the same, there was still the same sparkle in her eyes, the same dimples in her cheeks, but otherwise it was hard to recognise the Anthea who had gone away from them.

This was someone they had never seen before, in an emerald green travelling gown and coat to match with a high-brimmed bonnet trimmed with emerald green ostrich feathers.

"Anthea! Can it really be you?" Chloe exclaimed.

"I have never seen anything so smart, so absolutely breath-taking!" Thais cried.

The guard from the Stage-Coach set the trunks down on the road-side, then accepting the tip Anthea handed him, touched his high hat respectfully and climbed back onto the box.

The coach rumbled off and Chloe climbed from the carriage to ask excitedly:

"What is in those trunks? What have you brought, Anthea?"

"Clothes!" Anthea answered. "Gowns, all like the one I am wearing! There are dozens of them . . . dozens and dozens!"

"I cannot believe it!" Thais cried. "How can you have got them? Where did they come from?"

"God-mama gave them to me," Anthea explained. "But I have something far more important to tell you than that!"

"What is it?" Thais asked.

"We are rich!"

"Rich?"

The girls gasped and Anthea said:

"I cannot wait to tell you everything! But first let us find someone to help us with these trunks. I dare not try to lift them myself or I shall split the sleeves of my gown."

"No, no! Do not touch them!" Thais said quickly.

Several small boys were summoned and for two pennies lifted the trunks onto the carriage.

Thais turned Dobbin's head homeward and they set off moving slowly because it was quite a load for the old horse.

"What do you mean—you are rich?" Chloe asked.

"I have discovered how to make money," Anthea replied. "Oh, girls, it is so exciting! I have so much to tell you that I felt as if I should never get here. Even her Ladyship's carriage in which she sent me to Eaton Socom seemed to crawl though it was drawn by four horses. Think of that!"

"Tell us about the money," Chloe pleaded. "Have you won a lottery or been gambling? I cannot think . . ."

She stopped suddenly and said with a different note in her voice:

"You do not mean you are engaged to be married, Anthea?"

"No, no, of course not!" Anthea said. "It is something much more exciting!"

"How could it be?" Thais asked.

"It is," Anthea answered, "because I can make money myself; and what is more, I can make as much as I want, as much as we need!"

"But how? How?" Thais enquired.

"By selling my sketches!" Anthea replied.

It took Anthea some time to explain what had happened only a week before she was due to return home.

It was after her visit to Carlton House that she realised that while she had greatly enjoyed her time in London and it had been an experience which she felt had in some ways changed her outlook on life, she had not achieved what she had set out to do.

She had not found herself a husband!

Many of her partners had paid her compliments and several had flirted with her in a manner which made her think their intentions might be serious.

But she had not in fact received a single offer of marriage.

There was no doubt that after she was dressed in the latest fashion and, on her God-mother's insistence, Maria added a touch of cosmetics to the clearness of her skin, she received quite a lot of attention.

She was never without partners at any of the Balls, and two gentlemen went so far as to try to kiss her in the garden between dances.

But while they declared that their hearts were irretrievably lost, she learnt from her friend, the Marquess of Chale, that both would be obliged to marry wealthy wives if their Estates were to remain intact.

"The men who are wealthy enough to choose a wife without any other assets than a pretty face, are few and far between," the Marquess informed her.

Anthea was well aware that he was warning her not to be too cast down at not receiving an offer.

"Besides most of them, like Axminster," he went on, "have a very inflated idea of their own importance."

Anthea could not help feeling dispirited when she realised that when the Season was over her hour of glory would be over too.

She must return to Yorkshire, go back to scrimping and saving for the family, making one penny do the work of two, looking forward to nothing more thrilling than the local Hunt Ball in December.

Then fate took an interest in her predicament.

She was waiting for her God-mother the next morning and as usual the Countess was late.

She had a habit, Anthea discovered, of getting completely dressed in one expensive and fascinating ensemble, then deciding she would wear something quite different and changing everything from her bonnet down to her slippers.

The carriage was outside the door and Anthea had waited for over twenty minutes in the Hall, when feeling restless she entered a room she had not seen since she had arrived at Sheldon House.

It was, she knew, the Earl's special Sanctum, and it made her think of her father because she was certain it was the sort of room he would have liked to have if he could have afforded it.

There was a deep, comfortable leather sofa and armchairs to match, a huge writing-desk, and against one wall there stood a large Chippendale bookcase with dozens of beautifully bound books behind the glass.

Anthea moved towards them, feeling she had been somewhat remiss in not discovering them before.

Then on the other walls of the room were framed a number of caricatures and cartoons which she saw had been done by the famous satirical artists, James Gillray and Thomas Rowlandson.

She had heard these often referred to in conversation, and she had learnt that everyone found most amusing those which had been published recently by a third cartoonist called George Cruikshank.

She stood staring at the drawings, seeing that they were extremely clever and that she could easily recognise the better known figures in them.

There was no mistaking the Prince Regent and the ample proportions of Lady Hertford.

There were a large number of wartime cartoons depicting Napoleon in various guises. In one by James Gillray, he was shown as Belshazzar, seeing the writing on the wall.

They fascinated Anthea and she went from picture to picture.

She was just feeling disappointed because there were no more to see, when she found a portfolio lying on a table and realised it contained dozens of unframed sketches.

The one on the top was a sarcastic reference to the payment of £35,000 for the Elgin marbles when John Bull and his numerous family required bread.

"That is brilliant! Really brilliant!" Anthea said to herself and turning over the cartoons found herself laughing first at one, then at another.

Quite suddenly she realised that some of them were not unlike the sketches she herself had drawn for the girls!

"I am sure," she thought, "I can learn a great deal from studying Gillray, Rowlandson and Cruikshank."

Rowlandson, she could see, used a reed pen and added washes of brilliant colour. His crowds, his absurd men, his plump women showing their legs, were slightly coarse.

At the same time Anthea thought there was a rollicking zest about his cartoons which made them very funny.

She heard her God-mother calling her and hurried into the Hall to find the Countess descending the staircase looking quite dazzling in a daffodil-coloured gown, her long white neck encircled with topazes and with feathers to match in her enormous bonnet.

"What are you doing in His Lordship's room?" she asked.

"I hope it was not wrong of me, Cousin Delphine, but I was looking at the cartoons," Anthea replied.

"Oh, the Earl collects them all! Personally I find them very tiresome and so exaggerated that it is difficult to recognise anybody."

Anthea knew this was untrue. When they drove down St. James's Street the following day she saw crowds outside Humphrey's Print Shop and guessed that a new cartoon by either Rowlandson or Cruikshank had been issued.

She questioned the Marquess the same evening about the Cartoonists.

"Those fellows make a fortune!" he said. "But they make people laugh and that does nobody any harm."

"Is James Gillray still alive?" Anthea asked.

"No, he died of drink in 1811," the Marquess replied. "I have always understood that it was the terrific demand for his work that drove him to the bottle."

"I was looking at some of his drawings to-day."

"In the Earl's collection? Seldom misses a new one, but there are now not as many published as there used to be. Rowlandson is past his prime and is getting lazy. There is only Cruikshank who is very young, in fact in his early twenties!"

"As young as that?" Anthea asked. "And yet people buy his cartoons?"

"People will buy anything for a good laugh," the Marquess replied.

Anthea was rather pensive for the rest of the evening.

When Emma had left her in her night gown ready to get to bed, she took from the drawer a sketch-book she had bought since coming to London, in which she had done a number of drawings to show her sisters.

They all portrayed the Social figures she had seen at Almack's and at the other parties.

She realised as she looked at them that she had

caricatured everyone in a manner which was in fact not unlike Gillray's work.

The coloured wash she had added made her finished pictures resemble Rowlandson's and Cruikshank's.

She examined some of her sketches critically, then with a determined expression on her face she got into bed.

The next morning she rose early before her Godmother was called and taking Emma with her she hired a Hackney carriage and drove to 27 St. James's Street.

She left Emma outside and went in and asked for the Proprietor.

She was surprised to find he was a she, and to meet Mrs. Humphrey, an elderly be-spectacled lady, square-faced with a small, tight mouth, wearing a white bonnet.

"What can I do for you, Madam?" she enquired.

Anthea felt rather shy as she produced her sketch-book.

"I am . . . wondering," she said, "whether it would be . . . possible for me . . . to sell one of these?"

She knew, as Mrs. Humphrey took the book from her, that she was calculating how she could refuse, politely and without giving offence, to buy anything.

Then as she turned over the pages, her expression altered.

"Have you done these yourself?" she enquired, an incredulous note in her voice.

"Yes."

"Have you offered them to anyone else?"

"No," Anthea replied. "I drew them to amuse my sisters who live in the country. Yesterday I was looking at some of Mr. Gillray's cartoons and I saw the name of your shop on the back."

"Mr. Gillray is a very great loss indeed."

"I am sure he must be," Anthea answered, "but I see you publish the work of Mr. George Cruikshank."

"A clever young man," Mrs. Humphrey said, "but not the artist that James Gillray was or indeed his successor, Thomas Rowlandson."

She turned some more pages of Anthea's sketch-book, then she said:

"You say you wish to sell these?"

"Are they worth anything?" Anthea asked.

"If you will excuse me a moment," Mrs. Humphrey said, "I would just like to speak to my associates."

She disappeared into the back of the shop and Anthea stood looking around her.

There were not only caricatures on the long tables but also some rather delightful water-colours, which made Anthea realise that she certainly could not compete in that field.

Mrs. Humphrey returned.

"You have not told me your name, Madam," she said.

Anthea thought quickly.

She was quite certain it would be a mistake, if she did publish any of her caricatures, to allow anyone to know the name of the artist.

"My name is Dale," she said. "Miss Ann Dale."

"Very well, Miss Dale," Mrs. Humphrey said. "I would like to tell you that my associates and I think very highly of the sketches you have just brought me."

"You do!" Anthea exclaimed.

"We would be willing to publish them all."

"All?" Anthea questioned faintly.

She thought she could not be hearing correctly.

"You can accept payment by subscription or receive a sum of money outright for copyright."

"I am afraid I do not understand," Anthea said.

"There are two ways for an artist to sell cartoons and caricatures," Mrs. Humphrey explained. "Sometimes the artist will sell his work outright to the printer.

"The other way is for him to receive a small sum down and to take fifty per cent of every copy which is bought. These as you will see if you look around the shop, are usually sold at 1/6d. to 2/-d. each. Yet a Thomas Rowlandson occasionally fetches as much as £3."

Anthea thought for a moment, then she said:

"If you bought my drawings outright what would you give me for them?"

Mrs. Humphrey looked down at the sketch-book and seemed to be calculating.

Then she said:

"Seeing that we are short of cartoonists at the moment and these sketches illustrate a social angle that has not been portrayed before, I am prepared, Miss Dale, to offer you £10. each for them!"

For a moment Anthea thought she must be joking. Then in a voice which hardly seemed to be her own she answered:

"I would like to accept that, Mrs. Humphrey."

From that moment it seemed to her as if she was in a dream from which she was afraid she would awaken!

Even now as she told her sisters what had happened she could hardly believe it had really been true.

"£10!" Chloe said in an awe-struck voice.

"How many did you sell?" Thais asked.

"There were ten in the book," Anthea replied.

"A hundred pounds!"

"It cannot be true!"

"And they will take as many more as I like to send them," Anthea said.

The burble of noise which came from Thais and Chloe's lips made it difficult to say any more until they had travelled for at least a mile.

Then as they neared home, Anthea said:

"I was thinking as I drove north that it would be a mistake for us to tell Mama. You know she would be shocked at me trading my drawings, and she would also be afraid that someone might discover my identity."

"Yes, you are quite right," Thais said in a serious tone. "It would only worry her."

"I will just pay more of the money into the bank," Anthea said. "I persuaded Mrs. Humphrey to give me cash."

She remembered that she had to wait for quite a while while Mrs. Humphrey procured the £100, and she had been afraid that when she got back to the house her God-mother would ask where she had been.

She swore Emma to secrecy by saying that she had been to buy a special present for the Earl to thank him for having her to stay at Sheldon House.

This story was easily substantiated by the fact that Mrs. Humphrey had given her George Cruikshank's latest cartoon as a gift and Anthea had shown it to Emma.

"I can't make head nor tail o' them drawings," Emma said. "My young man enjoys them, but I thinks, if you asks me, Miss, a man likes a laugh more'n a woman."

"What makes you think that, Emma?" Anthea asked.

"Well, I'm always wanting to talk about love and how much we matters to each other," Emma said. "But Jim—he just wants to 'ave a good laugh. 'Come on, Em.,' he says, 'Yer knows I love yer. We don't have to look all gloomy abaht it.' "

Anthea before she left London, had bought her God-mother a pretty paper-knife that she had admired in a shop in Bond Street, and asked her to convey the Cruikshank cartoon to the Earl.

"That is a very sweet thought, Anthea," the Countess had said. "I am so glad you have enjoyed your visit and you know how delighted I have been to have you as my guest."

The Countess had paused, then added:

"Perhaps it would be possible for me to invite you another time."

"Or perhaps you would have Thais," Anthea suggested tentatively.

"I might. Indeed, I might do that next year," the Countess replied.

Anthea knew that the invitations would be given if once again her God-mother needed an excuse to stay in London.

Anthea was sure that Thais, if she had the opportunity, would be far more successful than she had been in finding herself a husband.

But what did husbands matter when she had found a way to augment their income?

She would in the future be able to provide plenty of the luxuries they had been unable to afford.

"I have been so lucky!" she said aloud. "I have brought back clothes and discovered I have a talent that is really saleable."

"You are clever, Anthea!" Chloe said in undisguised admiration.

Thais was more practical.

"How can you go on doing caricatures of people if you are not in London?" she asked.

"It will not be so easy," Anthea admitted, "except for the fact that I have made friends with the Marquess of Chale."

"A Marquess?" Chloe interposed. "Oh, Anthea, is he in love with you?"

"Not in the slightest!" Anthea laughed. "The Marquess is a very old man, over seventy, but he knows everybody and is the greatest gossip in the *Beau Monde*. I have asked him to write to me."

"Will he do so?" Thais asked.

It was a question that Anthea had already asked herself.

But she discovered that the Marquess was an inveterate letter-writer and corresponded with his relatives and friends in the same prolific manner in which he talked.

"I am sure he will write to me," Anthea said confidently. "And if we search through magazines and newspapers, now that I know what the people look like, I am sure I can do sketches of them and make whatever they are doing appear funny."

"It is the most exciting thing that has ever happened!" Chloe exclaimed. "I wish we could tell Mama and Phebe but I suppose we will have to keep it to ourselves."

"We must indeed," Anthea answered, "and no-one must guess the real identity of Miss Ann Dale or . . . and listen to this girls . . ."

They turned their faces obediently towards hers as she said:

". . . or of the tiny little mouse that will appear in the corner of every one of my drawings."

"The country mouse!" Chloe exclaimed. "Did you really put it in?"

"It will be my trade mark," Anthea answered. "I drew it to amuse you. Now I have decided that that will be my signature and, who knows, I may go down to posterity—just like James Gillray!"

"It is a thrilling idea," Chloe said, "but rather disappointing that nobody will ever know it is you. I cannot help thinking, Anthea, that by being anonymous you will miss half the fun."

"I shall also miss the recriminations," Anthea laughed, "and the brick-bats from those who think they have been insulted!"

"Will they really be angry?" Thais enquired.

Anthea shrugged her shoulders.

"I do not expect so," she replied. "The people in Society live in a world of their own. They think themselves too grand and too important for it to matter what the common people think!"

As she spoke she thought of the Duke.

She was quite sure he would not value anybody's opinion but his own.

He was, Anthea told herself, quite insufferably conceited and puffed up with his own importance!

At the same time she could not help remembering that he was in fact the most handsome man she had seen during her visit to London.

CHAPTER FOUR

*T*he Duke left his Phaeton with the groom and walked across the grass towards the Achilles statue.

At six o'clock in the morning the mists in Hyde Park were still insubstantial round the trunks of the trees and the grass was wet with dew.

There was a puzzled expression on the Duke's face as, moving behind the statue, he saw a veiled figure rise from a seat and utter a little cry.

"What in the name of God is all this about, Delphine?" he enquired as the Countess threw back her veil and raised an anguished face to his.

"I had to see you," she replied, "and it was the only way I could do so without Edward being aware of it."

"I thought I must be dreaming when I received your note an hour ago," the Duke said.

"Edward returned last night," the Countess said with a little quiver in her voice.

The Duke looked at her enquiringly and she went on:

"He had a very good reason for doing so. I have brought it with me."

She held out to the Duke what looked like a small scroll. He took it automatically before he said:

"Suppose we sit down? I see no point in being needlessly uncomfortable."

"Uncomfortable!" the Countess exclaimed. "Wait

234

until you hear the reason why the Earl has come posting to London!"

She spoke in such an agitated manner that the Duke, after a quick glance at her face, seated himself on one of the park chairs which stood behind the statue and unrolled the scroll she had given into his hand.

He saw immediately it was a cartoon and remembered that the Earl of Sheldon had a collection of them.

As he looked at it in the pale morning light he saw it depicted a very superior and autocratic-looking lion wearing a coronet seated on a cushion which was emblazoned with his own coat of arms.

In front of him clawing at him beseechingly, pleadingly, enticingly, were a number of small cats, all with the faces of very young girls.

But one of the lion's paws was placed protectively round a ginger cat with slanting but adoring green eyes, whose face undeniably resembled that of the Countess.

Beneath the cartoon was written simply:

The Love of the Pussycats.

"Dammit!" the Duke ejaculated. "This is too much! Who the hell has done this?"

"I have no idea," the Countess said, "but you can imagine what Edward feels about it."

"It is not signed by either Rowlandson or Cruikshank."

"Does it matter who drew it?" the Countess asked with a querulous note in her voice. "Edward is furious, as you can well imagine! For the first time he suspects that I have taken a lover, and I have had the greatest difficulty in convincing him otherwise."

"You have convinced him?" the Duke asked in a note of relief.

The Countess gave a deep sigh.

"Edward arrived at ten o'clock last night in a

towering rage, swearing that he was considering divorcing me and citing you as co-respondent!"

The Duke stiffened.

"I thought at first he would strike me, he was so incensed," the Countess went on. "Then he said that whether he divorced me or not he intended to close Sheldon House for good!

" 'You will stay in the country where I can keep an eye on you,' he said. 'I have put up with your predilection for London and the raffish Society you prefer for too long. In future you will remain at the Castle, and to make sure we will re-open the Nurseries and add to the numbers of our family.' "

The Countess gave a little sob.

"I could hardly believe it was Edward speaking to me in such a manner, but he meant it, Garth. I swear to you, he meant it!"

The Duke said nothing and after a moment the Countess continued:

"You know how I loathe the country and I am too old to have any more children. Besides without being in London, without being able to go to parties and meet amusing people, I swear if I did not die from sheer *ennui* it would be because I had killed myself first!"

"But His Lordship changed his mind?" the Duke asked hopefully.

He realised that as usual the Countess was taking a very long time to come to the point.

"It took me two hours to persuade him that he was mistaken," the Countess answered. "Two hours when I felt as if I were a martyr being tortured on the rack."

"How did you persuade him?"

The Countess drew a deep breath.

"I told him that the cartoon was a sheer malicious lie and that the reason we had been seen together so much these past weeks was that you were engaged to be married to my God-child, Anthea Forthingdale!"

"You told him what?"

The Duke's voice was as sharp as the report of a pistol.

"I told Edward you were going to marry Anthea, and Garth, you will have to do so because otherwise Edward swears he will not be convinced by my explanation."

"You must be crazy!" the Duke exclaimed. "I have no intention of marrying a girl to whom I have spoken hardly more than half a dozen words."

"You danced with her. You have seen her at the parties I have given and those we have attended together."

"I saw her because she was staying in your house," the Duke said. "That does not say I have any wish to marry her."

"Of course you have no wish to marry her," the Countess agreed. "You love me, and I love you. But if you love me, Garth, you have to save us both from this terrible, ghastly situation."

The Duke said nothing. His lips were tight and his chin was very square.

He stared down at the cartoon.

"If you do not substantiate my story," the Countess said, "I am certain that Edward will go back to his original plan of divorcing me, and you can imagine what a scandal there will be."

"I do not believe he would do such a thing," the Duke said slowly.

"He would! You do not know Edward as I do," the Countess said. "His pride is hurt. There is no-one more proud than Edward and no-one more determined when he makes up his mind about something."

The Duke knew this was more or less true, but he said aloud:

"Perhaps I had better speak to the Earl."

"What could you say?" the Countess asked. "Except that the cartoon is a filthy libel. Do you suppose Edward will believe you?"

"Why not?" the Duke enquired.

"Because for one thing I am quite certain it is not only the cartoon which has upset him," the Countess replied, "but that someone has been talking."

The Duke did not speak and she continued:

"You know my mother-in-law, old though she is, has cronies who report to her everything I do. She always lets me know that she is *au fait* with my latest conquest."

She paused to say:

"And one can never trust servants."

"I thought you said you had new staff."

"Not all of them," the Countess answered. "And besides, I do not suppose they are above gossiping to the servants from the Castle, without perhaps even realising what harm they are doing."

That was, the Duke knew, something that could not be avoided, and too late he realised how indiscreet he had been to visit the Countess so frequently at Sheldon House in her husband's absence.

"There is only one thing to be done to save ourselves," the Countess said, "and that is for you to marry Anthea as quickly as possible."

"How can I do that?" the Duke asked impatiently, "and why the haste?"

"Because Edward has said that until you are married he absolutely forbids me to speak to you again, and I am to stay shut up in the Castle until Anthea is actually a Duchess.

" 'A broken engagement would be only too easy for Axminster,' he said. 'He can get out of his obligations, if in fact they have ever been made. You have made a fool of me for too long, Delphine, and this time I intend the laugh to be on your paramour—not on me!' "

"There must be a better way of coping with this," the Duke said slowly.

There was silence for a moment then he said:

"I must of course ask you if you would prefer to come away with me."

The Countess looked at him in surprise.

"Do you mean that?"

"The only honourable thing I can do is to offer you my protection," he replied, "until such time as your husband can get a divorce passed through Parliament."

The Countess gave a little cry.

"Oh, Garth, it is adorable of you! But do you really imagine either of us could bear to live abroad as the Herons had to do for years and years?"

She put her hand on the Duke's arm in a gesture of affection as she said:

"I shall never forget that you asked me, but the answer is—no. Definitely no, dearest Garth, because we would both hate every moment of our exile and would be clawing at each other's eyes within a month of reaching Paris."

The Duke took her hand in his and raised it to his lips.

"Whatever the penalties," he said, "I believe it would be preferable to what you are asking me to do."

"Nonsense!" the Countess said briskly. "Anthea is a very sweet girl. You have to marry sometime, and though the Forthingdales may be poor, their blood is as blue as your own. She will make you a commendable Duchess, and you know as well as I do that you must have an heir."

There was no gainsaying this, but the Duke had never contemplated surrendering his freedom until it was absolutely necessary.

He had thought there was no need for him to think of marriage for at least another five years, or perhaps longer.

As if she read his thoughts, the Countess said softly:

"I am sorry, Garth, but there really is no alternative."

The Duke looked down at the cartoon as if he thought there might be some other way of repudiating its insinuation.

There was no denying that the expression on the

lion's face, while a caricature, was unmistakably his own, or that the slanting green eyes of the ginger cat were all too obviously the Countess's.

It was a clever drawing and far more skilfully executed he thought, than George Cruikshank's crude, vulgar style.

But its very delicacy made the cartoon all the more dangerous, and to be honest he well understood the Earl's anger at his wife being publicly pilloried.

"You will do it, Garth?" the Countess asked anxiously.

The Duke had been silent for some time.

"It is the only way you can save us both," she murmured.

"Then I suppose the answer is—yes," the Duke said grudgingly.

Anthea was in the kitchen rolling out the pastry for a chicken-pie she was making for dinner.

A large white apron covered her gown and because she had washed her hair the previous day, she had covered it with a protective white handkerchief.

All the girls could cook well, their old Nurse had taught them when they were quite small.

When she retired to look after her sister who was ill, they had taken it in turns to prepare meals and often vied with each other in seeing who could produce the most delicious dishes.

As she worked Anthea was thinking that now she could make money, they would be able to afford Mrs. Harris from the village to come in two or three days a week to do the scrubbing.

That was the side of the housework they all disliked, and Thais always managed if it was possible, to get out of her share.

Anthea was sure that her mother would be too vague

to ask any awkward questions as to why Mrs. Harris was employed or how they could afford to pay her.

Anthea thought with satisfaction that waiting on the School-Room table were three more cartoons neatly packed up and waiting to be despatched to Mrs. Humphrey in London.

The main difficulty, she found, was to keep her drawings out of sight of her mother.

Rising early in the morning and working late after Lady Forthingdale had gone to bed was, she discovered, a better way than trying to hide what she was doing when her mother came unexpectedly into the School-Room.

"Tell us about the pictures you have sold," Thais had asked.

"To tell you the truth," Anthea replied, "I have almost forgotten which they were. I drew them in my sketch-book whenever I had a moment, and I never anticipated when I showed them to Mrs. Humphrey that she would take the lot!"

She smiled.

"I just thought how lucky I would be if she bought one and gave me perhaps £1. for it so that I could buy you all a present."

"£10. for each!" Chloe exclaimed. "It seems an unbelievable amount for those scrawls you have been doing ever since I can remember."

"You used to make us laugh with your drawings when we were children," Thais said. "It seems funny you should make the smart people in London laugh at them now."

"It seems funny to me too," Anthea agreed. "But I had better draw everything I can while it is all fresh in my mind. It would be mortifying if Mrs. Humphrey should return anything I sent her."

"I asked you to tell us about the ones you have sold," Thais said.

"There is no need for me to do that," Anthea said.

241

"You will see them. Mrs. Humphrey has promised to send me one of each issue as soon as it is printed."

"You gave her this address?" Chloe asked.

"How could I help it?" Anthea asked. "But I can assure you that no-one in London is interested in Yorkshire except that some of the gentlemen occasionally attend the races at Doncaster, and elderly ladies take the waters at Harrogate."

"And of course no-one will have heard of Miss Ann Dale," Thais laughed.

"Or the Country Mouse," Chloe added.

"No, that is my safe-guard," Anthea had agreed.

She put the pastry over the pie-dish and cut the edge into an elegant pattern.

The girls all liked chicken pie, and Anthea had found time to make one this afternoon, as everyone was out.

Chloe and Phebe were having lessons and Thais had gone with Lady Forthingdale to Doncaster.

Once or twice a year an elderly Squire who lived two miles away would drive into Doncaster for a meeting with the race-course officials.

When he did so he invariably invited Lady Forthingdale to accompany him.

As she seldom went out her daughters always persuaded her that the drive would do her good.

"As a matter of fact," Lady Forthingdale had said yesterday when the Squire's invitation arrived, "I want to go to the Library in Doncaster. There is a book of poems by Lord Byron that I particularly wish to purchase."

"Lord Byron, Mama?" Anthea questioned. "Are you going romantic again?"

"I feel that His Lordship's work might be of assistance in the poem I have been considering this last week," Lady Forthingdale replied.

"I thought you would get back to love eventually!" Chloe said irrepressibly.

" 'Love is a malady without a cure'," Anthea quoted with a smile.

"It is also 'a sickness full of woes'," Thais interposed who was as knowledgeable on her poets as Anthea was.

"I think you are making fun of me," Lady Forthingdale said with dignity. "But I do not wish any of you to laugh at love. It is something very beautiful which I hope one day will come into the lives of all of you."

"Nanny said once that it was unlucky to laugh at love," Phebe remarked.

"And so it is!" Lady Forthingdale said. "That reminds me, Anthea, I never asked if you had lost your heart to anyone while you were in London."

"No, Mama," Anthea replied. "I did not fall in love simply because I met no-one as charming, handsome or attractive as Papa."

She knew that her words would please her mother and Lady Forthingdale's eyes were suspiciously misty as she thought of the husband she had loved so dearly.

Irrepressibly the thought came to Anthea that, however handsome her father had been, the Duke undoubtedly would take the prize in a contest between them.

The pie was now ready to put in the oven and she wondered as she opened the door of the ancient stove whether any of her God-mother's elegant friends were capable of cooking anything, even an egg.

The idea of their doing so in their elaborate gowns and glittering jewels made Anthea smile.

She was just wondering if that might give her an idea for a cartoon, when there came a loud knock on the front door.

She felt it might be the letter she was hoping for from the Marquess.

She had written to him on her return home to make quite certain that he would keep his promise and write to her.

Without bothering to remove her white apron she

ran from the kitchen through the Hall and pulled open the front door.

As she did so she gave a gasp of sheer astonishment.

Outside there was an extremely elegant Phaeton pulled by four horses. Behind it were two out-riders in blue and gold livery and behind them, just coming down the drive, was a Travelling Chariot also pulled by four horses, escorted by two more out-riders.

As Anthea stared as if she could not believe her eyes the servant who had knocked on the door said sharply:

"His Grace the Duke of Axminster calling on Lady Forthingdale. Is Her Ladyship at home?"

He spoke in the superior tone of a Senior servant addressing an underling.

While Anthea was finding it impossible to reply, the Duke stepped down from the Phaeton and came to the front door.

"Forgive my unexpected appearance, Miss Forthingdale," he said, "which I gather is a surprise."

"A . . . surprise?" Anthea repeated stupidly.

"It is obvious that you were not expecting me," the Duke said. "I wrote to your mother three days ago, but the posts are lamentably slow, and I imagine she could not have received my letter."

His eyes flickered over her apron as he spoke and Anthea realised how strange she must look.

"No . . . no," she faltered. "Mama has not . . . heard from you . . . and she is out this . . . afternoon."

"I still hope that I may have the pleasure of seeing her," the Duke said.

With an effort Anthea remembered her manners.

"Will you come in, Your Grace?"

"Thank you," the Duke said gravely.

He walked into the Hall. Anthea pulled the handkerchief from her head but was so bemused that she made no effort to take off her apron.

Instead she led the way into the Drawing-Room and was relieved to see that it was quite tidy.

Three long windows opened onto the garden and there was a sweet fragrance from the freshly picked flowers in the big bowls which Anthea had arranged the previous day on various tables round the room.

"You are on your way to the Doncaster Races, Your Grace?" she managed to say when they reached the hearth.

She indicated a comfortable chair on which the Duke could sit.

It was the only thing she could think of to explain why the Duke had called.

"I, in fact, intend to stay the night with Lord Doncaster, who is a distant cousin," he replied, "but the races will not take place until next month."

"I had . . . forgotten."

There was a little silence. Then the Duke said:

"As your mother is not here it would perhaps be best if I explained myself to you."

"Explained what?"

"The reason for my visit."

She looked at the Duke enquiringly, thinking that he must have a message from her God-mother.

After a moment's obvious hesitation the Duke said:

"In my letter, which should have arrived by now, I asked your mother if she would permit me to pay my addresses to you!"

Anthea's eyes opened so wide that they seemed to fill her small face. Then after a moment she faltered:

"I do not . . . think I . . . understand."

"I am asking you to marry me, Miss Forthingdale!"

Again there was a silence that seemed to fill the whole room, before Anthea asked in a strange voice:

"Is this a . . . joke?"

"I assure you I am completely serious."

"B . . . but you . . . cannot . . . I mean, you . . . cannot . . ."

Anthea stopped stammering and said sharply:

"Why do you want to . . . marry me?"

"It is time I took a wife," the Duke answered baldly,

"and I thought when we met in London that we seemed to be well suited."

Anthea rose to her feet.

"I cannot imagine, Your Grace, that you intended to be . . . insulting . . . but I cannot . . . credit for one moment that you expect me to . . . accept such an extraordinary and unexpected . . . suggestion."

"Why not?" the Duke asked. "I am usually considered extremely eligible."

"I am well . . . aware of that," Anthea answered, "but Your Grace is also aware that there are . . . reasons why I could not . . . contemplate such . . . a . . . an . . . i . . . idea."

She stammered over the last two words feeling it impossible to express what she was thinking in words, knowing quite well that he would understand what was in her mind.

The Duke did not answer and after a moment Anthea said without looking at him:

"I think we have . . . nothing further to say to each . . . other . . . Your Grace, and as my mother will not be home for some hours . . . there is no point in your . . . waiting to see her."

As she spoke she had an urgent desire for the Duke to leave as quickly as possible.

She could not possibly imagine his motive for coming to ask her to marry him.

But she was certain that if he had spoken to her mother, it would be very difficult without involving her God-mother, to explain why she could not accept him.

She had every intention of remaining loyal to the Countess, and she could only be thankful that she was alone in the house when he called.

Now the sooner he departed the less likelihood there would be of having to make difficult explanations of his presence.

"Please go," she said.

"I think I had best be frank with you, Miss Forthingdale," the Duke said.

"About what?" Anthea asked suspiciously.

"I had not intended to tell you the real reason why I am asking you to marry me," the Duke replied, "but perhaps it is the only way I can make you understand the urgency of it."

"I cannot imagine what you are talking about," Anthea said. "Let me make it quite clear that nothing Your Grace can say would make me agree to be your wife, and unless we mean to be involved in difficult explanations to my family, you should leave at once!"

Anthea glanced towards the clock on the mantelshelf as she spoke and saw with relief that it was only two o'clock.

That meant that unless anything unforeseen happened, it would be at least an hour before Chloe and Phebe returned from the village.

She could imagine only too well how curious they would be to say the least of it, in fact astounded, by the Duke's entourage which was waiting in the drive.

"I thought you seemed fond of your God-mother, Miss Forthingdale," the Duke said surprisingly.

"I am," Anthea answered.

"Then if you could save her from something very unpleasant, from a scandal which would completely ruin her life, would you not be prepared to do so?"

"Y . . . yes, of course," Anthea agreed, "but I . . ."

"The Earl of Sheldon is threatening either to divorce your God-mother, citing me as co-respondent," the Duke said, "or to incarcerate her in the country and never permit her to visit London again!"

He spoke coldly and quite unemotionally.

"Oh, poor Cousin Delphine!" Anthea exclaimed. "Why should the Earl do that? What has happened?"

"I dare say you have seen those scurrilous caricatures of which the Earl has a notable collection," the Duke said.

Anthea was very still.

"The one that has caused all the trouble," he went

on, "portrays your God-mother and me in a manner to which the Earl has taken great exception."

Anthea found it almost impossible to breathe as he continued:

"The only way your God-mother could prevent His Lordship from putting his threats into action was to tell him that the reason I had been at Sheldon House so frequently during his absence was that you and I were engaged!"

"He . . . believed . . . that?"

Anthea's voice was so faint it was hardly audible.

"He agreed to accept such an explanation," the Duke replied, "on condition we were speedily married."

Anthea walked across the room to stand staring into the garden with unseeing eyes.

She could hardly believe that what she had heard was the truth.

She could hear the Marquess saying that a good laugh hurt nobody, and yet it was her cartoon which had precipitated this drama and caused the Duke to ask for her hand in marriage!

Her cartoon!

She had drawn it two days after the Duke had looked so bored when he danced with her at Almack's and after she had seen him enter the house later and thought he was a burglar!

She had disliked him and wanted to portray him at his most arrogant and autocratic!

She would not have cared if it hurt him, but she had never wished to hurt her God-mother or cause her a moment's unhappiness.

The Countess had been most kind and generous to her and she owed her a debt of gratitude.

Now the only way she could repay that debt was to marry the Duke!

"How can I . . . marry him? How . . . can I?" she asked herself.

Then she was sure that not only had the Duke

spoken the truth but also that the Earl's threats were seriously intended.

She had not stayed for over a month at Sheldon House without realising that her God-mother was in fact considerably frightened of the Earl. The servants too spoke of him with an awe that invested him with an ominous presence, even when he was not there.

Although Anthea had heard a great many remarks about her God-mother, some of them disparaging, no-one had ever spoken of the Earl except with respect, sometimes grudgingly, but nevertheless respectfully.

"If you will do this for your God-mother," the Duke said from behind her, "I assure you that not only will she be extremely grateful, but so will I."

"But how . . . could we be . . . married in such . . . circumstances?" Anthea asked.

"I see no difficulty about it," the Duke answered.

There was a challenging note in his voice.

Anthea realised without his putting it into words that anyone to whom he proposed marriage would be expected to accept eagerly and gratefully so distinguished a suitor.

It was only, she thought, because she had inadvertently learnt of the more intimate details of the Duke's love-life that she must look on him in a different way than any other girl would do.

It flashed through her mind that if in fact she had found in London the husband she was seeking, there would almost certainly be a skeleton in his cupboard of which she had no knowledge.

And yet she could remember all too vividly what she had felt when she had seen the Duke going up to her God-mother's bed-room.

She could still hear the amused contempt in his voice when he had told her not to interfere in other people's affairs!

At the same time she had no-one to thank for the predicament she was now in except herself.

"How could I have been so foolish," she asked

herself frantically, "as to include that particular cartoon with the others?"

She had in fact forgotten all about it.

"It was madness to have sold a cartoon which included Cousin Delphine," she told herself now. "Madness and at the same time unkind!"

Anthea had never been anything but kind; that was
characteristic of her nature. She was always deeply
touched by suffering or unhappiness.

She could be moved to tears by a tale of cruelty or
privation.

She would listen with sympathy and patience to the
grumbles and complaints of the villagers and would go
to endless trouble to help them.

Yet without intending to, merely because she was
bemused by the large sum of money which had been
offered her, she had hurt the Countess.

'It was a malicious drawing in the first place,' she
thought miserably. 'But it is too late now for recriminations.'

"I cannot believe that you are so heartless as to refuse to help your God-mother," the Duke remarked
almost beguilingly.

Anthea found it impossible to reply and after a moment he said:

"Perhaps you are waiting for me to go down on one
knee in the conventional fashion?"

Now there was a note of mockery in his voice and
Anthea turned round to say sharply:

"There is no need for play-acting, Your Grace. You
have been . . . frank with me, and I will be equally
frank with . . . you. I have . . . no wish to . . .
marry you, but in the . . . circumstances you make
it . . . impossible for me to . . . refuse."

"I thought you would see sense," the Duke said,
"and I assure you, Miss Forthingdale, I will do my best
to make you happy."

"Thank . . . you."

Anthea thought as she spoke and her eyes met the

Duke's that they seemed to be challenging each other to a duel in which both were determined to be the victor.

"You will wish to be alone when you break the news to your mother," the Duke said after a moment. "So I hope she will be gracious enough to receive me to-morrow afternoon when we can talk over the details of the wedding."

"That would be . . . best," Anthea conceded.

"Then I will continue on my journey," the Duke said, "but I would like to thank you in all sincerity for agreeing to my proposition."

Anthea inclined her head a little and he went on:

"I can assure you that your God-mother will be as grateful as I am. You have saved us both from something which would inevitably bring a lot of unhappiness and unpleasantness to a number of people."

Anthea knew he was speaking of his family.

She realised that he must have a great number of relations, all of whom she was certain would be absolutely astounded when they learnt who he was about to marry.

There seemed to be nothing more to say and for the first time Anthea was conscious of the white apron that covered her gown and that in their small house the Duke looked very large and overpowering.

As they were walking towards the Hall, the Duke noticed the portrait of Sir Walcott which stood over the mantelpiece.

"Is that your father?"

"Yes," Anthea replied.

"I see he was in the Scots Greys."

"Yes."

"I understand from your God-mother that he is dead. Was he perhaps killed at Waterloo?"

"Yes."

"I saw the charge," the Duke said. "It was magnificent! There has never been anything like it in the annals of British history."

"You were at Waterloo?"

"I was," the Duke replied. "We must talk about it sometime. I would like to learn more about your father."

Anthea knew he was trying to be pleasant but she felt as if she was frozen inside.

She pulled open the front door before he could reach it and drew a deep breath of fresh air.

The Duke's cavalcade and the livery of his servants made a vivid patch of colour and the whole entourage seemed even more incongruous than it had on its arrival.

It had nothing in common, Anthea thought, with the overgrown, unkept drive and the shabby exterior of the house, any more than she had anything in common with the tall, handsome, elegant man who stood beside her.

"I shall see you to-morrow," the Duke said.

She held out her hand and he raised it to his lips.

"Let me say once again how very grateful I am," he said in a low voice.

She did not answer.

He walked towards his Phaeton, swung himself up onto the high seat, took the reins from his groom and turned his horses with an expertise which Anthea knew ranked him a Corinthian.

Then as he raised his high hat and his servants imitated him by raising theirs, the procession of carriages and horses swept back down the drive under the low branches of the oak trees and disappeared into the distance.

Anthea stood looking after them. Then she closed the door and put her hands up to her face.

It could not be true!

She must have dreamt the whole thing! How could she have known, how could she have guessed, that one cartoon, just one, should cause so much trouble and involve her in such a fantastic tangle?

Then as if galvanized by the horror of it, she ran to

the School-Room to pick up the envelope lying on the table and tear it into a dozen small pieces.

"How could I have been so crazy, so naïve, so unimaginative?" she asked herself, "as to think that I could caricature the people I met and not expect repercussions?"

She could see now how mischievous her drawing had been, though she had done it merely to amuse her sisters.

As they had never seen her God-mother, she had known they would have no idea who the ginger cat might be.

It had merely amused her and balanced the picture to put the Countess in it.

When she had been sketching she had never for one moment expected the cartoons to be seen by anyone except Thais, Chloe and Phebe. So she had exaggerated the characteristics of everyone she had drawn.

Now she was sure they must inevitably give offence.

There was one of Lord Alvanley, she remembered, with his cold apricot tarts and bed-side candles being extinguished under the bolster which was very amusing. But he might not think so!

There was an even more provocative one of Colonel Dan McKinnon counting his locks of female hair and saying to his batman:

"I really must look around for an Albino, otherwise my collection is not complete!"

She had depicted him in the guise of a Sultan, with the concubines he had discarded and on whom he had turned his back weeping bitterly.

'I should not have done it,' Anthea thought. 'I should never have sold anything so intimate, so unkind.'

She wondered wildly whether she should rush to London to try to persuade Mrs. Humphrey to sell her back the cartoons which had not yet been published.

Then she told herself that while Mrs. Humphrey

had seemed very pleasant she was undoubtedly a business woman.

Having sold her drawings outright Anthea was quite certain that she would not now relinquish them, and she could only pray that none of the nine remaining cartoons would cause as much trouble as the first.

"No-one must ever know that I drew them," she thought.

She felt herself trembling at the thought of how angry the Duke would be if he ever discovered that instead of being grateful to her he should in fact be cursing her for having involved them all in this frightening situation.

"The only thing I can do," Anthea thought miserably, "is to try to put things right by saving God-mama and the Duke from the Earl."

At the same time, she thought, she would rather marry anyone . . . any man in the world . . . than the Duke.

She believed that he would, as he had promised, try to make her happy.

But how could she be happy, knowing that he not only loved her God-mother, but also that she had been instrumental in revealing their affection to the one person who should not have known of it—the Earl.

Anthea felt as if her head was whirling and it was impossible to think clearly.

She only knew the future seemed terrifying and full of quicksands.

"Supposing he ever discovers the truth?" she asked herself.

She was sure that if her God-mother was afraid of the Earl, she was likely to be far more frightened of the Duke.

"He is a very frightening person," she thought.

She remembered his arrogance and unconcealed boredom when he had been forced to dance with her at Almack's.

"How can I bear a lifetime of that?" she asked.

As she did she heard voices in the Hall, and knew that Chloe and Phebe had returned.

CHAPTER FIVE

*A*nthea stared at herself in the mirror and realised that she had never before looked so attractive—in fact almost beautiful.

She could indeed hardly believe it was her own reflection that she was seeing.

The exquisite and extremely elaborate wedding-gown which her God-mother had sent her from London was undoubtedly every woman's ideal gown for the most important moment in her life.

On her head Anthea wore a lace veil that had been in the Duke's family for generations, and surmounting it a diamond tiara fashioned in the shape of a wreath of flowers which glittered and quivered with every movement she made.

"I did not believe anything could be so lovely!" Thais had said in an awed voice before she left for the Church with her mother and the other girls.

In fact the whole family, it seemed to Anthea, had been breathless with excitement ever since she had told them in an embarrassed manner that she was to marry the Duke.

After she had announced it on her mother's return

from Doncaster, for a moment they had stared at her speechless.

Then there had been a babble of excitement which made it difficult for Anthea to make herself heard.

"The Duke of Axminster!" "But you hardly mentioned him in your letters!" "Why did you not tell us about him?" "How could you have been so secretive?"

The Duke's letter to Lady Forthingdale had in fact arrived the next day, but by that time the Duke had met Anthea's family.

She had expected them to hate him as she told herself she did, but to her astonishment he charmed them all.

"He is so handsome and exactly what a Duke should be!" Chloe cried.

Thais was beguiled into thinking him more romantic than any hero she had ever read about in a novel.

"He said such kind and complimentary things about Papa," Lady Forthingdale said later with a little throb in her voice, "and I know, Anthea, that he is just the husband Papa would have chosen for you had he been alive."

It was hard at times for Anthea not to cry out that she was acting a lie, that the Duke did not care for her; and that if she had a choice she would not marry him.

But because she felt so guilty and because she was so afraid he might discover her treachery, she forced herself to act the part which was expected of her.

The Duke had not only made himself extremely pleasant to her mother and to the girls, but he had also proved unexpectedly considerate.

Because he realised they had no servants, when he came to a meal he brought with him delicacies that required no cooking, and insisted that his servants should wait at table.

For the first time Thais, Chloe and Phebe ate pâté de foie gras, boar's head, succulent hams and game cooked in a manner which bore no resemblance to the plain boiling and roasting which had been the limit of Nanny's repertoire.

Exotic fruits from Lord Doncaster's greenhouses were also produced, and there were chocolates and bon-bons which were so expensive to buy that none of the girls had ever been given them before.

Besides all this the Duke, having discovered that his future mother-in-law was interested in poetry, brought her leather-bound volumes from the most expensive bookshop in Doncaster, which was a sure way to win her heart.

"He is bribing the family!" Anthea told herself scornfully, "just as my God-mother bribed me when she realised I knew her guilty secret!"

Although it made her try to disparage everything the Duke brought with him to the house, she could not help realising that there was really no need for him to put himself out as she had already agreed to do what he wished.

As it was, she found it hard to remain coldly aloof from the adulation which the Duke evoked in her sisters.

"He is wonderful! So kind, so understanding!" Thais would say.

"He remembers that I like sugared almonds," Phebe said. "I hope I find a husband as nice as him when I grow up."

It was Chloe however who was thrown into a state of stupefaction when the Duke said he would give her a horse to ride to hounds and would also provide and pay for a groom to look after it.

Overcome at achieving her greatest ambition Chloe had thrown her arms round the Duke's neck and kissed him.

"Thank you! Thank you!" she cried. "It is the most wonderful thing that has ever happened to me!"

Anthea thought that the Duke for a moment stiffened with surprise at Chloe's demonstrativeness. Then he asked:

"If you are so grateful when you are given one hunter, what will you do when you receive a diamond necklace?"

"Who wants a necklace?" Chloe said scornfully. "I would much rather have a string of horses!"

The Duke laughed.

"I expect you will change your mind when you get older. All women like diamonds."

Because of what he had said to Chloe, Anthea had expected him to give her a diamond engagement ring, doubtless one which already was part of the Axminster collection.

But instead he gave her a ring which showed that he had at least considered her as an individual.

After he and Anthea had announced their engagement and a notice of it had been sent to the *London Gazette* the Duke returned to London.

Although she was glad to see him go, Anthea found the curiosity of the neighbourhood hard to bear alone.

It was extraordinary, she thought cynically, how many people claimed her acquaintance now that she was to marry a Duke.

People she had no idea even existed called on Lady Forthingdale, and invitations to Balls and parties from every part of Yorkshire arrived every day.

"How kind people are!" Lady Forthingdale exclaimed.

"Kind?" Anthea replied. "They are not kind, Mama, they are only sucking up to us now because I am to marry a Duke! They paid no attention to us in the past."

"I expect they thought we were still in mourning for your dear father," Lady Forthingdale replied.

"You would make excuses for the devil himself, Mama!" Anthea said. "Personally I would like to throw all their invitations in the fire and not bother to answer them!"

"I think that would be very rude, dearest, and even if you and His Grace do not wish to accept such hospitality it would be nice for Thais, and later Chloe, to be included on their visiting lists."

"They will be included in the future," Anthea prophesied in a hard voice.

At the same time it was difficult to be cynical when everyone was so anxious to be friendly and the wedding presents began to arrive.

"Who are the Leightons, Mama?" Anthea asked as she opened a parcel containing a most magnificent pair of candelabra.

"I cannot recall their name for the moment," Lady Forthingdale replied. "Perhaps they are friends of the Duke's."

"The parcel is addressed to me and they live in Yorkshire."

"Then they must certainly be asked to the wedding," Lady Forthingdale said.

"It will be impossible to get any more into the Church," Anthea replied.

But even as she spoke she knew her mother would invite the Leightons and there was nothing she could do to prevent it.

She had hoped that the Duke would not be in a hurry to be married.

But she thought, although he did not say so, that he was being urged by the Countess to get the ceremony over as soon as possible so that the Earl's suspicions could be finally laid to rest.

The wedding-day was arranged for the second week in July and the Countess wrote to Lady Forthingdale saying that she wished not only to give Anthea her wedding-gown and a most comprehensive trousseau, but also to provide bride's-maids' dresses for Thais, Chloe and Phebe.

The girls were ecstatic with excitement and could talk of little else.

It was the Duke who brought the news of this act of generosity when he returned to Yorkshire for his second visit.

He arrived at the house late in the afternoon when the family were all together in the Drawing-Room and Lady Forthingdale was reciting to them a poem she had written in celebration of Anthea's marriage.

She had only just started the first line when there was a knock on the front door which, because it was so imperious, made Anthea know at once who had arrived.

"Who can that be?" Lady Forthingdale asked, arrested in the midst of her recitation.

"I will go and see," Chloe answered before anyone else could reply. "Wait until I come back, Mama, I do not want to miss a word."

She ran across the Hall and as Anthea had expected gave a cry of delight when she saw who was outside.

A moment later they heard her call out:

"It is the Duke! It is the Duke! He is back! Oh, is it not exciting?"

They had expected him shortly but had not been quite certain which day he would arrive.

Now as he walked into the Salon he seemed to Anthea to be far too big and overpowering in the low-ceilinged room, and so elegantly and faultlessly dressed that he made even the furniture look shabby.

He raised Lady Forthingdale's hand to his lips, then turned towards Anthea.

She curtsied but kept her eyes downcast feeling they might reveal that she was the only person present who was not pleased to see him.

Her coldness, if he realised it, did not perturb him.

Completely at his ease he gave Lady Forthingdale the letter from the Countess in which she described the gifts she intended to make to all the family.

"How kind! How very kind!" Lady Forthingdale said as she read what her friend had written.

"I also have brought gifts," the Duke said and obviously noted with a faint smile the light that appeared in Thais, Chloe and Phebe's eyes.

"Sugared almonds!" the Duke replied, "and other things as well!"

"Where are they?" Chloe asked.

"You will find them being unloaded in the Hall," he answered. "There is a very special present for your mother."

"Come and look! Oh, Mama, come and look!" Chloe cried.

Half-protesting and yet intrigued Lady Forthingdale allowed herself to be swept out of the Sitting-Room into the Hall.

The Duke and Anthea were left behind and although she had no wish to be alone with him she would not lower herself to run after her family.

"I have a present for you also, Anthea," he said.

"There is no need to give me one."

"I think everyone would consider it strange if I did not do so."

She realised then that he spoke of an engagement ring, and because she thought she had been rude the colour rose in her cheeks.

He drew a jewel-box from his pocket and when he opened it she saw not the diamonds she had expected but instead a very beautiful ruby.

It was exquisitely set with diamonds and in its depths glowed a mysterious fire.

"I thought rubies would become you," the Duke said. "This is your own and not part of the family collection."

He took her left hand as he spoke and put the ring on her third finger.

"Thank . . . you," Anthea managed to say and wondered why her fingers, because he touched them, trembled a little.

"I hope it will make you happy," he said unexpectedly.

She longed to say that neither jewels nor gifts of any sort could do that, since happiness must come from the heart. But she was sure that he would not understand.

Anyway how could she make him happy when she knew that he was yearning for the Countess and that they were being married only to save her good name?

Fortunately there was no question of saying anything more because the girls having collected the gifts the Duke had brought for them from London, poured back into the Drawing-Room.

They were wildly excited over a collection of new books, a habit and a riding-whip for Chloe, a silk shawl for Thais and a whole number of small things for Phebe which would keep her amused for months.

'I wonder who chose them for him?' Anthea thought.

Then she told herself that doubtless he had well-trained secretaries and servants who would be well aware what sort of expensive presents he would be expected to give his fiancée and her family.

Then she remembered he had brought the Countess's letter with him!

So they had been seeing each other!

Perhaps now that their engagement was announced to the newspapers the Earl was satisfied that his suspicions were unfounded.

Or were they meeting clandestinely, prepared to risk discovery because they could not deny their love?

Anthea wondered what the Countess really felt about the Duke being married.

"If I were in love with a man," she thought, "I would hate him to marry someone else! I would be desperately jealous!"

Then she told herself she was being conceited in making herself of such importance. How could her beautiful, alluring, seductive God-mother be even remotely jealous of her?

The idea was ludicrous!

She was nothing but a country mouse!

But now, waiting to leave for the Church, Anthea had to admit to herself that the Duke had acted his part well, and that not even the most discerning on-looker would have suspected that their marriage was anything but a love-match.

Certainly not her mother or her sisters.

They were convinced that the Duke had fallen in love with her at first sight and she with him.

"Why did you not tell us about him?" Thais enquired over and over again.

Lady Forthingdale had the answer.

"When one is falling in love, dearest," she said, "it is so magical, so ethereal that one is almost afraid to breathe lest the wonder of it should disappear."

She smiled at Anthea.

"That is, I know, darling, something of what you felt, though it cannot be put adequately into words."

She gave a deep sigh.

"It is what I felt for your father and have always prayed that one day you would all feel the same."

"And that is how I would like to feel," Anthea said to her reflection in the mirror.

In two minutes time she had to leave for the Church.

Downstairs the Colonel of her father's Regiment had come to Yorkshire especially to give her away.

The little grey stone Church which was only a short distance from the house would be, she knew, packed with not only their neighbours, but also relations and friends of the Duke's who were staying in all the big houses in the vicinity.

Lord Doncaster had a house-party of thirty. Some could find accommodation no nearer than York.

At first Anthea had felt shy and a little frightened of the ordeal that awaited her. Then she told herself there was no point in feeling anything but coolly practical.

This was a wedding where, instead of the bride being on the threshold of a new and wonderful experience, she was merely a means to an end.

It was as if she had no identity of her own, but was just serving as a life-line for the Duke and the woman he loved.

"Yet how can I feel resentful," Anthea asked herself, "when it is entirely my own fault and I have no-one to blame but myself?"

Mrs. Humphrey, as she had promised, had sent her a copy of 'The Love of the Pussycats' and another cartoon which had been issued at the same time.

When they arrived Anthea had taken them to the kitchen and burnt them in the stove.

She was always terrified that the girls would forget her instructions and make some reference to her talent for drawing to the Duke.

But she had made them swear on everything they considered holy that they would never speak of the cartoons or the money she had made by selling them.

"He would never forgive me," she said, "if he had the slightest idea that I had drawn anything so reprehensible."

"They might amuse him as they have amused us," Thais suggested.

"He would be very shocked," Anthea replied, "and unless you want him to go away and never speak to any of us again, be very careful to keep my secret."

She knew this threat would be effective.

But to make quite certain there was no evidence that could be used against her, she extracted the letters she had written from London from her Mother's *secrétaire* and burnt those too.

Even the funny little sketches with which she had illustrated some of her letters could, if he saw them, give the Duke the idea that she might somehow be connected with the cartoon which had caused so much trouble!

The clock on the mantelpiece struck the hour and Anthea realised it was noon.

She must leave at once for the Church.

Because her home was far too small to accommodate so many guests, the Reception was to take place in Lord Doncaster's house.

It was nearly an hour's drive from the Church and

the Duke had suggested that it would be best as they had a long way to go south if he and Anthea should leave after the ceremony.

"I cannot believe," he said, "that we will be greatly missed and I have no desire to make a speech or listen to one."

"No, of course not," Anthea agreed.

He had therefore arranged that they would return alone to the house for a light luncheon and for Anthea to change into her travelling-clothes.

Everyone else who was present at the Church would go on to Doncaster Hall where there would be a 6 ft. high wedding-cake and an enormous wedding-breakfast which would last late into the afternoon.

"How can you bear to miss all the fun?" Chloe had asked Anthea.

"I do not think I should enjoy it very much," she answered.

"Do not be so stupid," Thais said. "She wants to be alone with her husband, just as I would want to be."

She spoke with a quiver in her voice and a romantic look in her eyes and had no idea that her oldest sister gave a little shiver as she thought how frightened she was of being alone with the Duke.

"What shall I say to him?" she wondered frantically.

Then she told herself it was absolutely essential that she should try to behave normally and not be in the least hysterical.

She remembered her father saying how much men disliked scenes.

"Women enjoy them!" Sir Walcott had said with a smile, "but I assure you, that any normal man will run a mile rather than be involved in dramatics, hurt feelings, or tears."

"This would obviously come under the heading of 'dramatics' " Anthea told herself and she was determined to behave as her father would have wished.

She picked up her bouquet of roses and lilies-of-the-valley and turned to leave the bed-room.

As she did so the diamonds on her head glittered and the sunshine coming through the window seemed to envelope her like a blessing.

"I am acting a part in a play," Anthea said to herself, "and the only thing that matters is that I should prove a competent actress."

The Duke and Duchess of Axminster arrived at the Earl of Arksey's mansion shortly after five o'clock.

Situated in a large park it was a notable example of Elizabethan architecture and looked extremely impressive as the four horses the Duke had been driving since they left home crossed the bridge over the lake.

"It is very large!" Anthea remarked.

"It has been added to over the years," the Duke replied. "But Arksey has redecorated a lot of the rooms recently and I think you will find it quite comfortable."

"I should imagine," she smiled, "it will certainly be more comfortable than a Posting-Inn which would probably have been our alternative accommodation."

"I loathe Posting-Inns," the Duke remarked.

"I cannot imagine you have stayed in many of them," she replied. "When I travelled to London by Stage-Coach I was horrified at what the average traveller encounters in such places."

"You travelled by Stage-Coach?" the Duke asked in surprise.

"Unfortunately," Anthea replied, "we did not think that Dobbin would be able to complete the journey!"

The Duke, who had seen Dobbin, laughed.

"You keep forgetting that I am Cinderella," Anthea said, "or would you prefer to be King Cophetua while I am the Beggar Maid?"

"I think you resemble neither at the moment," the Duke said with a slightly dry note in his voice.

Anthea had to admit he was right.

The travelling coat of rose-pink satin which the

Countess had sent her, with a high-brimmed bonnet trimmed with pink ostrich feathers to match, made her look like a Princess in a fairy-story.

However she found herself thinking again as she entered Arksey Hall that the whole thing was in fact more like a theatrical programme and everything she did and felt pretence.

The great house formed the impressive backcloth, and when she found there were three maids to wait on her in the huge State Bed-Room in which, she was told, Queen Elizabeth had once slept, it was only another Act of the play.

After a bath scented with rose-oil Anthea put on a lovely gown of white gauze embroidered with silver which had silver ribbons and silver shoes to match.

As she walked down the broad staircase to the Salon, she almost expected to find an audience waiting to applaud her.

The Duke was waiting in the large room which overlooked the rose garden and had long windows opening onto a terrace.

He was standing with his back to her and as Anthea entered she thought how tall and commanding he was —a very fitting hero for the play in which she was envisaging herself.

She did not speak but he must have sensed her presence because he turned with a smile on his lips.

"You are very punctual," he said, "and may I say I appreciate that?"

"I have cooked too many meals myself not to be sympathetic with the Chef who finds his soufflés falling flat and his meat over-cooked," Anthea replied.

She walked towards the Duke as she spoke and joined him to stand looking out into the garden.

"I love roses," she said. "And I am sure there is nothing more beautiful than an English garden like this one."

"Are you telling me," the Duke asked, "that you

would rather have stayed in England for our honey-moon?"

"No, of course not!" Anthea replied. "You know how thrilled I am at the thought of visiting the battlefield of Waterloo, and it means so much to Mama."

"I am glad it pleases her," the Duke said lightly. "At the same time I want to show you not only where your father died but also where I fought."

"I understand you received the Waterloo medal."

"I will show it to you when we are in London."

Anthea moved away from the window towards the mantelshelf.

The Salon was very elegant. At the same time it was a trifle stiff and she thought they too, were being stiff and over formal.

"I think I should tell you," the Duke said, "how very becoming that gown is. What is more it shows off your rubies to perfection!"

Anthea put her hand up to her neck.

She had almost forgotten that a jewel box had been delivered early in the morning, containing a magnifi-cent ruby necklace to match her ring.

"I am afraid I have not thanked you," she said. "It was shamefully remiss of me, but there has been so much to think about."

"Of course," he replied. "One does not get married very often!"

"Thank goodness for that!" Anthea exclaimed. "Imagine if one had to have a commotion like this every year, or even every five years."

"I think we will be quite content to wait for twenty-five," the Duke said, "until our Silver Wedding."

"That is too long to contemplate," Anthea thought in her heart, but aloud she said:

"I cannot imagine, after all the presents we have received, that we shall need any more silver. What will you do, as it is, with over fifty entrée dishes?"

"We might give a party."

"Or perhaps," Anthea said, "keep so many dogs that they can each eat out of a silver dish!"

The Duke laughed at the idea, but it flashed through Anthea's mind that she had sold a cartoon of the Duchess of York's one hundred dogs, with one complaining that he could not find his bowl!

Because she was embarrassed by her own thoughts it was with relief she heard the Butler announce that dinner was ready.

They went into the Dining-Room where the Earl's Chef had surpassed himself by providing them with a meal that excelled any that Anthea had eaten in London.

There was champagne to drink and when the servants withdrew the Duke raised his glass.

"Your health, Anthea!" he said. "You have come through to-day with flying colours. I cannot think of anyone who would have carried off this somewhat difficult situation so magnificently!"

She was surprised at his praise and the note of sincerity in his voice. She felt the colour rising in her cheeks.

"Now you are embarrassing me!" she said. "I thought you behaved extremely commendably yourself, considering you were a reluctant bridegroom."

The Duke frowned as if he thought her remark tactless, but after a second's pause he said:

"I feel that we are starting out on a voyage of discovery. We really know very little about each other and we have seldom been alone together until now."

He smiled as he added:

"Your sisters, quite unintentionally, I am sure, are extremely effective chaperons!"

"We have always done everything together," Anthea said. "In fact I feel to-night they will be depressed because they cannot be with me!"

"I think it would cause a great deal of comment," the Duke said in an amused voice, "if I set off for

France not only with my bride but also with her three sisters!"

"They would have loved to see the battlefield," Anthea said a little wistfully.

"Perhaps we will take them another time," the Duke suggested.

Her eyes lit up.

"Do you mean that?"

Then she told herself that he was only speaking conventionally.

Once the formalities of their marriage were over he would be able to return to the Countess, and she would doubtless be left to amuse herself in the country or any where provided that she did not intrude on his private life.

Because the idea was somewhat depressing she said quickly:

"Do you wish me to leave you while you drink your port?"

"I hope you will do nothing of the sort," the Duke answered. "I do not want any port, but I will tell the Butler to bring a decanter of brandy to the Salon."

Anthea rose to walk ahead of him down the long passage which led to the Hall.

As she did so she could see them both reflected in the gilt-framed mirrors on either side of the corridor.

The feeling of their enacting a play was intensified, and the Salon with its crystal chandeliers lit and the dusk falling outside the windows was very theatrical.

Because she had no idea what they should talk about Anthea went round the room looking at the *objets d'art,* exclaiming in delight over snuff-boxes set with precious stones, at miniatures depicting the Earls of Arksey down the ages and at exquisite pieces of Dresden china.

"I have a great many treasures at my houses in London and in the country," the Duke said, "which also I think will please you."

"Mama used to tell me how great noblemen

possessed such beautiful things," Anthea said, "but it is always difficult to visualise them without actually seeing them."

"That is true," the Duke said, "and not only of seeing but of feeling."

"Yes, indeed," Anthea agreed. "One reads about people's emotions, of sorrow, of happiness, elation, ecstasy, and of course, love, and one wonders what it would feel like to experience any of those one's self."

"Usually to be disappointed," the Duke said.

"Disappointed?" Anthea questioned.

"Particularly when it comes to love."

Anthea looked at him uncertainly.

"But, surely," she said, "it is very wonderful and very exciting being in love?"

"It never quite reaches one's expectations," the Duke replied.

"Oh, but you must not say that!" Anthea exclaimed. "That means you are not really in love! Mama says that loving my father was far more marvellous, far more wonderful than she ever dreamt it could be."

"Perhaps she was very lucky," the Duke remarked.

Anthea glanced at him a little uncertainly and wondered if he had quarrelled with the Countess or perhaps in some way she had failed him.

Because she had slept very little the night before and because she was so tired, Anthea suggested after they had talked a little while longer that she should go to bed.

"But of course," the Duke said. "And we have before us tomorrow another long stage of our journey south, so I am afraid you will have to rise early."

"Then I will certainly go to bed at once," Anthea smiled.

He escorted her into the Hall where there was a footman waiting to give her a candle in a silver candlestick.

Because the servant was present Anthea felt it

embarrassing to say good-night, so she merely smiled a little shyly at the Duke and walked up the staircase.

She thought as she did so how once again it seemed part of a play that maids should be waiting for her in her bed-room with candles alight on each side of the great, silk-canopied bed.

She put on one of the exquisite lace-embroidered night-gowns that her God-mother had sent her from London.

She slipped into bed as the maids extinguished all the candles except the two at the bed-side and as the door closed behind them Anthea lay back on the lace edged pillows looking around her.

Now she felt like a Princess in the fairy-story who was so blue-blooded and sensitive that she felt a pea under a dozen mattresses.

"It is all very exciting!" she thought. "Exciting seeing this magnificent house, and very exciting to think of going abroad!"

She gave a little sigh which was almost one of happiness.

"There is nothing to be frightened of," she admonished herself. "The wedding has gone off smoothly, the Duke is good-tempered, in fact everybody is happy!"

She lay thinking of how pretty the girls had been in their pink gowns which made them look like rosebuds, and how her mother had shed tears of joy when she and the Duke had signed their names in the Vestry.

"In the future I will be able to look after the girls and Mama," she thought.

The idea suddenly came to her that perhaps, after all, it was a good thing she had drawn the cartoon.

"If I had not done so I should be at home again skimping and saving," she realised. "Instead Chloe has a horse to ride, I can give a Ball for Thais at Christmas—she need not wait until the Season—and Phebe can go to a really good School."

She smiled as she turned over to blow out the candles by her bed and as she did so the door opened.

The Duke came into the room and Anthea looked at him in surprise.

He was wearing a long brocade robe in a plum-coloured red which was becoming to his dark hair, and there was a touch of white at his neck which showed up the squareness of his jaw.

He walked towards her and only as he reached the bed did Anthea say:

"What is . . . it? Why are you . . . here?"

"You were not expecting me?" the Duke asked.

"Expecting you?" she asked in a puzzled voice, then added quickly: "You mean . . . you cannot mean . . ."

The Duke sat down on the side of the bed.

"I can see you are surprised, Anthea," he said, "but frankly I meant to talk to you before now about our marriage."

"What . . . about it?" Anthea asked nervously.

Her long dark hair was falling over her shoulders nearly to her waist, but the soft muslin of her nightgown was very transparent and did not disguise the whiteness of her neck or the soft curves of her breasts.

Her eyes were very large in her small face and there was an apprehensive look in them that had not been there before.

"We have been married in rather exceptional circumstances," the Duke said after a moment's pause, "but I think, Anthea, you will be sensible and wise enough to realise that it would be a very great mistake for our marriage to be anything but a normal one."

"What do you . . . mean by . . . normal?" Anthea asked a little above a whisper.

"I mean," the Duke said, "that we are man and wife, and that we should behave as an ordinary married couple would do."

"You . . . mean," Anthea said hesitatingly, "that you would . . . sleep here with me and make . . . m . . . make . . . love to me?"

"That is what would be expected, Anthea," the Duke

said, "and that would be the right way to ensure that
our marriage is successful."

"But . . . you could not . . . do that," Anthea
said. "I could not . . . let you!"

"Why not?"

"Because . . ."

She found it difficult to go on and after a moment he
said:

"You are thinking that my interests lie elsewhere.
But, Anthea, you are old enough to realise that a wife
has a very different position in a man's life to any other
woman."

"B . . . but you are . . . in love with . . . someone else."

The Duke was silent for a moment, then he said:

"It may seem a difficult thing to ask, but surely you
can forget what happened when you were in London?"

Anthea made a little gesture and he went on:

"You must have moved in the social world long
enough to realise that most men have liaisons of one
sort or another before they marry. Usually their wives,
especially if they are as young as you, do not hear of
them, But—and perhaps it is a good thing—there is no
need for any pretence between us."

"I . . . I married you," Anthea said, "because I
knew it would . . . help my God-mother, but I never
thought . . . I never dreamt that I should be expected to be your . . . real wife."

"I hoped you would not feel like that," the Duke
said, "simply because it would make our relationship in
the future extremely difficult, if not impossible for
both of us."

"If you . . . made love to me," Anthea said, "you
would be . . . thinking of Cousin Delphine."

She thought the Duke stiffened before he said:

"I should be thinking of you and that you are my
wife."

"I do not think that is possible," Anthea said. "How

could you . . . kiss me and even by . . . shutting
your eyes not be . . . thinking—'It should be
Delphine! It should be Delphine?' "

She saw the Duke's lips tighten and thought he was
angry, but for the moment she did not care.

"It would be just the same," she went on, "as when
my Nanny used to give me nasty medicine as a child
and say 'If you hold your nose you will not taste it.' But
it did not work!"

As if he could not help himself the Duke laughed.

"Really, Anthea, it is hardly a very apt simile!"

"I think it is very apt!" Anthea contradicted. "And I
think it . . . wrong of you to . . . suggest what you
. . . have!"

"I assumed you would be reasonable over this."

"It is not a question of being reasonable," Anthea
answered. "You belong to Cousin Delphine. I have always thought it was wicked for someone to try to take
away another woman's husband, and just as I would
never do that, I would never try to take you away from
the woman you love. You are hers . . . not mine."

The Duke rose to his feet to walk across the room to
the fireplace, then he walked back again.

"I never envisaged for a moment that you would feel
like this," he said.

"I do not know how you . . . expected me to feel!"
Anthea said. "I think you are very handsome . . . You
are much nicer than I thought you would be. You have
been very generous to the girls and to Mama . . . a
. . . and . . . to me. But I do not . . . love you!
How . . . could I?"

"Love is not entirely essential to marriage," the
Duke said. "You are my wife, you bear my name. All I
am suggesting is that we lead a normal married life."

"How can it be . . . normal," Anthea asked, "when
if you make . . . love to me you would be . . . wishing you were . . . making love to Cousin Delphine?"

"Oh, my God!" the Duke ejaculated. "Is it not possible to make you understand what I am trying to say?"

275

Anthea did not answer and after a moment he came back to the bed to sit down on it and say:

"I do not want to sound exasperated or cross—I am not! It is just that I realise I am looking at it from a man's point of view, and you from a woman's."

"And because I am a . . . woman," Anthea said in a very small voice, "I could not . . . let you . . . touch me, when you . . . love someone else."

She sounded suddenly very weak and rather helpless and she added almost tearfully:

"I am . . . sorry. I am very . . . very sorry, when you have been so . . . kind to us all, but I cannot do it . . . I cannot really!"

She looked at the Duke and put out her hand.

"Please try to understand. I will do everything else you want of me. I will look after you . . . I will obey you . . . and because I know you would hate it I will not make . . . scenes . . . never again after this one . . . but please do not . . . do not . . . touch me!"

The Duke looked at her for a long moment and because she could not help herself Anthea could not look away from him.

Although she was appealing to him she felt somehow it was a battle of wills. She felt he was drawing her, compelling her, forcing her!

Then when she was conscious that her heart was beating and her mouth was dry he capitulated.

"Very well, Anthea," he said. "It shall be as you wish. I will sleep in my own room."

"Thank . . . you," Anthea said. "Thank you very much . . . indeed . . . and please . . . try to . . . understand."

"I am trying," the Duke said.

Anthea gave a little sigh.

"As I have already said . . . you are much kinder and nicer than I ever expected."

He rose to his feet and as he would have moved away she said:

"You are not very . . . angry with . . . me?"

She put out her hand as she spoke. He took it and raised it to his lips.

"Perhaps I am more disappointed than angry," he answered.

Then he went from the room closing the door behind him.

CHAPTER SIX

Riding out from Brussels towards the battle-fields of Waterloo Anthea thought that she had never been so happy.

It seemed to her that every day she was with the Duke it was easier to talk to him and everything became more exciting.

She had felt constrained and embarrassed the morning after their wedding-night. But she told herself that the worst thing she could do would be to erect a barrier between them which would make it impossible for her to talk to him naturally.

Everything was easy because she fancied, although she was not sure, that the Duke had speeded up their progress to the Continent.

Certainly they had stayed only one night at each of the important houses where they had been offered hospitality.

As they usually arrived late in the evening and left early in the morning and were therefore somewhat tired, there was not time to be bored by each other's conversation.

The weather was hot and sunny so the Duke drove his Phaeton.

The Travelling Chariot either went ahead with the luggage so that everything was in readiness when they arrived, or was not far behind should they wish to ride in it.

Their cavalcade with four out-riders was very impressive and Anthea enjoyed the commotion they caused when they passed through small villages to be stared at open-mouthed by the yokels.

They passed one night at Axminster House in London and Anthea saw that it was in fact filled with the treasures of which the Duke had spoken, but she had little time to examine them.

By the time they had dined she was ready for bed, and they left early in the morning for the drive to Dover where they were to embark on the Duke's yacht.

Having never been at sea before, Anthea was apprehensive in case she should be sea-sick.

"Even though the Duke is not in love with me," she told herself, "I cannot imagine anything more undignified or unromantic."

But fortunately the sea was flat and there was only a breeze blowing in the right direction to carry them across the Channel.

Everything to Anthea was so new and exciting that her enthusiasm was irrepressible and the Duke found himself responding to her high spirits.

What was more she made him laugh.

He could never remember spending a long time in the company of any woman unless he was enamoured of her and she was doing everything in her power to entice him and being very intense in the process.

Anthea, having made up her mind to be natural with the Duke, behaved as if he were one of her family or perhaps the brother she had never had.

She was wise enough to remember two things; first

that a man is always willing to give advice and to instruct and secondly that, just as she had been amused and entertained by the tales of the Marquess, so in the same way she could amuse the Duke.

Not of course with the tales of the *Beau Monde,* a world he knew better than she did, but of the life familiar to her by which she had always managed to make her sisters laugh.

Because it came naturally to her she usually impersonated the people of whom she was talking: old Mrs. Ridgeway—the village beggar, the Vicar who frequently found Phebe's inquisitive questions embarrassing, the farmers who were always at odds with the rent-collectors, and a dozen other country characters.

She even included the loony boy who wandered round the village singing tuneless songs but was not so simple that he did not steal when he got the opportunity.

The Duke found himself amused by what Anthea was telling him, and he also found himself watching the sparkle in her eyes and the dimples in her cheeks.

Their honeymoon, although Anthea did not realise it, was a new experience for him as well as for her.

When they reached Brussels the Duke found that he had an attentive pupil who would listen with wide eyes to everything he told her and who never ceased asking pertinent and intelligent questions.

He had not brought his own horses with him, but he had sent a Courier ahead who had not only rented for them an impressive mansion, but had also procured some fine blood-stock so that they would either drive or ride.

"It would be best for us to ride to the battle-field," the Duke had said this morning.

"I would prefer that," Anthea replied, "although I have not ridden a spirited horse for some time, so I hope I shall not disgrace myself."

"I will see you are on a mount that is not too frisky," the Duke promised.

When the horses were brought round Anthea was delighted with the chestnut mare which had been provided for her.

The Duke on the other hand was riding a headstrong, obstreperous stallion which was obviously in need of exercise.

He frisked about the road shying at passers-by but soon found that his rider intended to master him and there was no chance of his getting his own way.

Anthea knew the Duke was enjoying the tussle, and there was in fact a look of satisfaction on his handsome face that was unmistakable.

The Countess had included in her trousseau an extremely attractive habit of deep red silk, almost the colour of her rubies, which was frogged with white braid matching the long gauze veil which encircled her high-crowned hat.

She looked exceedingly elegant, and although her face was a little serious as she concentrated on her riding as they moved through the town the Duke knew she was enjoying herself.

He showed her the house in the Rue de la Blanchisserie which the Duke and Duchess of Richmond had rented before the battle and where they had given the Ball which had been immortalised by Lord Byron's poem.

"Why did the Duchess of Richmond want to give a Ball?" Anthea asked.

"The Duke of Wellington always believed that psychologically it was wise to appear in public unconcerned and for ordinary life to carry on as usual."

The Duke smiled.

"I was there when one day the Duchess of Richmond said to the Duke of Wellington:

" 'I do not wish to pry into your secrets, Duke, but I wish to give a Ball, and all I ask is, may I give my Ball?'

" 'Duchess,' the Duke replied, 'you may give your Ball with the greatest safety, without fear of interruption!' "

"But he was wrong!" Anthea cried.

"Operations were not expected to begin before the 1st of July."

"Tell me about the Ball. Was it very gay?"

Anthea smiled as she added:

"I know that 'The lamps shone o'er the fair women and brave men'."

"The Ball-Room," the Duke replied, "had been transformed with rich tent-like draperies and hangings in the royal colours of crimson, gold and black. The pillars were wreathed in ribbons, leaves and flowers."

"Oh, I wish I had seen it!" Anthea exclaimed.

"Byron's 'lamps'," he went on, "were in fact the most magnificent crystal chandeliers, and the 'brave men' were headed by His Royal Highness, the Prince of Orange, and of course the Duke of Wellington himself."

"And you were with him?" Anthea questioned.

She already knew that the Duke had been on the Duke of Wellington's staff.

"I was," the Duke replied. "And I was at his side when the Duke learnt that some of the advance Prussian forces had been repulsed by the French less than eight miles from Quatre Bras.

"The Prussians, under Marshal Blücher, were to join up with the British at Quatre Bras. Napoleon had however begun his advance far sooner than was anticipated."

"How frightening!" Anthea said. "And what happened after that?"

"The news rapidly circulated round the Ball-Room that we were off the next morning," the Duke answered. "Most officers hastily said good-bye and departed. I waited for my Commander-in-Chief."

Anthea drew in her breath.

"Were you afraid?" she asked.

"Not in the slightest!" the Duke replied. "We were all extremely anxious to get to grips with the French."

They left the city behind and as they drew nearer to the battle-field Anthea was not surprised to see men and even women searching like beach-combers for souvenirs.

She had already learnt that there were stalls in the market-place offering for sale bullets and buttons, badges and pieces of uniform.

And the Duke had told her that hundreds upon hundreds of English visitors had come to Belgium every month since the battle to wander about, sight-seeing and scavenging.

But Anthea was not interested in anything but the battle itself.

The Duke related how the three days had been wet and miserable with at times torrential rain.

"I remember," he went on, "how chilly the cross-roads to Quatre Bras were at 6 a.m. on June 17th, as we waited in a draughty hut made of branches, for news of the battle."

The Duke's voice deepened as he said:

"It did not feel any warmer when we learnt Blücher's troops had been badly mauled just before night fall, and had begun that morning to withdraw towards Warre, eighteen miles back."

Anthea could see he was re-living the disappointment and apprehension they had all felt at the time.

"What happened?" she asked.

"We withdrew northwards about half-way towards Brussels. We had had practically no sleep since fighting all the previous day, to hold Quatre Bras!"

The Duke paused before he continued:

"We were all soaked to the skin. Many of the soldiers were so covered in mud that it was hard to recognise their uniforms."

Anthea and the Duke reached the ridge of Mont-Saint-Jean where Wellington had made his headquarters in the village of Waterloo.

From there the Duke looked over the battle-field as if he was seeing it all happen again.

He could point out to her the Fort of Siogres on

their left, La Haye Sainte and Hougoumont ahead, both scenes of desperate fighting.

"The rain had poured incessantly," he said, "and the ground became squelching mud. But if our Army was wet and miserable, so were the French!"

"We learnt afterwards," he went on, "that Napoleon had said confidently 'The Prussians and English cannot possibly link up for another two days!' He therefore decided to launch an assault on Wellington.

" 'The battle that is coming,' he told them, 'will save France and be celebrated in the annals of the world!' "

"When did the battle actually start?" Anthea asked.

"First there was desperate fighting for Hougoumont at about mid-day," the Duke replied, "and Wellington always said it was the gallantry of the Coldstreams there which saved the battle of Waterloo.

"Then the situation on the crest above La Haye Sainte became critical," he continued. "But many of us who had served in the Peninsula with Wellington were there. The 92nd were ordered to advance."

He gave a sigh.

"The Brigade had been reduced to 1,400 men by the fighting at Quatre Bras, but the Gordons, the Black Watch and the 44th flung themselves with bayonets on the 8,000 Frenchmen—then . . ."

He paused dramatically.

"As the Gordons staggered under the weight of the massed French, they were aware of huge grey horses thundering down behind them with their riders uttering wild, exultant cries."

"It was the Scots Greys!" Anthea said hardly above a whisper.

"They swept through in a mad whirlwind of a charge such as had never before been launched by the British Cavalry."

Anthea felt her eyes fill with tears at the thought that her father had been amongst them.

"Behind them came the heavy Cavalry," the Duke went on. "As the bugle sounded the 'charge' I heard someone shout: 'To Paris!' They went through like a torrent, shaking the very earth!"

Anthea shut her eyes.

She could visualise the Life Guards and the King's Dragoons wearing the classical helmets with horse-hair crests and plumes designed by the Prince Regent.

She could hear them thundering deep into the enemy lines until the French turned and fled!

Buglers sounded the rally, but no-one listened!

Two eagles were captured and fifteen guns in Napoleon's great battery disabled, while the French gunners sat on their limbers and wept.

"But they had charged too far," Anthea murmured, who had read the story of the Battle of Waterloo a thousand times.

"The whole valley behind them was flooded with French Troops. They were cut off."

"And yet it was a victory."

"Despite the heavy casualties," the Duke said. "No Cavalry had ever before routed so great a body of Infantry in formation."

"It was the way Papa would have wished to die."

Then because Anthea did not want the Duke to see the tears which had suddenly begun to run down her cheeks she spurred her horse forward.

She was riding, she thought, over the same ground that her father had ridden in that wild charge when 2,500 Cavalry had lost their lives.

The Duke rode after her and only came to her side when she had wiped away her tears.

"It was just here," he said quietly, "where we are now standing, that in the afternoon Wellington turned to one of his *Aides-de-Camp* and asked the time.

" 'Twenty minutes past four, Sir,'

" 'The battle is mine,' Wellington said, 'and if the Prussians arrive soon there will be an end to the war.' "

The Duke paused.

"As he spoke we heard the first Prussian guns."

"And that was the end?"

"Not for some hours yet," the Duke replied. "In fact not until 8 p.m. and our Army was down to some 35,000 men. The French were shaken, but not yet routed."

"Were you worried?" Anthea asked.

"Things had gone wrong. The Prussians had not yet been able to break through, and yet I think that everyone was supremely confident that the Duke could not fail."

"What happened?"

"At about 7.30. p.m. the Duke was standing up in his stirrups at his Command Post by that tree. A ray of the setting sun threw into relief an unforgettable and indescribable expression on his face."

"What was happening?"

"We could see that the French extreme right was under cross-fire. Then someone cried: 'The Prussians have arrived!' "

"They had got through!" Anthea cried.

"This was the decisive moment," the Duke answered, "and every soldier knew it. I heard one of the Commanders advise limited action, but Wellington knew better.

" 'Oh, dammit!' he exclaimed. 'In for a penny—in for a pound!'

"He took off his hat and waved it three times towards the French. In a flash his signal was understood."

The Duke paused.

"Three deafening cheers of relief and exaltation rang out as the Light Cavalry swooped onto the plain."

"And that was the end?" Anthea asked.

"Nothing could stop Wellington's men," the Duke replied. "Napoleon formed a reserve of his Old Guard into squares to stem the torrent, but it was impossible. Eventually he just had time to swing into his *berline* and escape before he could be overtaken by the Prussians."

Anthea drew a deep breath.

The Duke had made it seem all so real.

"It was 9 p.m. on Sunday the 18th June and nearly dark when Marshal Blücher and Wellington rode forward to greet one another."

"Napoleon was finally defeated!"

"But at a terrible price!"

"Papa," Anthea whispered to herself.

"And 15,000 other British," the Duke said. "But the French had lost 25,000!"

"I hate war!" Anthea exclaimed.

"So did the Duke of Wellington. He said: 'I hope to God I have fought my last battle. It is a bad thing to be always fighting!' "

Anthea turned her horse towards the plain.

She felt as if the ghosts of those who had died there rode beside her.

Then something, perhaps it was the emotions surging within her, spurred her quiet horse from a trot to a gallop.

She felt the turf pounding beneath her hoofs and she thought that she could understand the wild elation the Scots Greys had felt as they swept towards the French.

She remembered being told that in a charge the horses felt the same excitement as their riders.

"Those terrible grey horses—how they fight!" Napoleon had said watching from his mound.

Then she recalled how the Scots Greys had been cut off and that the Colonel was last seen with both his arms shot off and holding his bridle in his teeth. A friend of her father's Captain Edward Kelly had three horses shot under him. But he lived to survive the battle!

"My dearest, dear love," he wrote to his wife next day, who showed the letter to Lady Forthingdale. "All my fine Troopers knocked to pieces . . ."

A little shame-faced Anthea pulled on her reins and checked her horse.

She looked back over her shoulder and realised in

consternation that something had happened to the Duke.

She had thought he was following her, but now she saw that his horse was down on the ground and he himself was sprawled beside it.

Hastily she rode back.

As she reached him the stallion staggered to his feet and she saw that the animal must have caught his foot in a shell-hole and pitched the Duke over his head.

He was lying very still and she dismounted quickly.

Feeling that her horse was too quiet to wander far away she left him free and crouched down at the Duke's side.

She turned him over onto his back and realised that he was unconscious. His eyes were closed and there was mud on his forehead. The skin was broken and she guessed that in the fall he must have struck his head on a stone which had knocked him out.

She felt suddenly desperately afraid and wondered frantically what she should do!

The Duke came slowly back to consciousness to real-ise he was lying on something soft and above his head he heard a voice say:

"Will you or will you not fetch help? I have prom-ised you three louis, but I will make it five if you hurry."

Anthea was speaking in French and the man who answered her spoke in a rough *patois* difficult to under-stand.

"I'll go, but I'll take one of the horses. It'll be quicker."

"You will do nothing of the sort!" Anthea said firmly. "How do I know that you will come back?"

"You'll have to trust me."

"I do not intend to trust you with a horse."

"What is to prevent me from taking one?"

287

"I will prevent you," Anthea said quietly.

The Duke felt her hand go into his pocket and draw forth the pistol that she knew he always carried when they were travelling.

She pointed it at the man and he spat at her:

"All right, *Madame*, but you're an Amazon—not a woman!"

"I would rather be an Amazon than a ghoulish sneak-thief from the corpses of dead men. Get on with you and be quick about it if you want your money."

The man must have gone, for the Duke heard Anthea give a little sigh of relief and realised he was lying in her lap.

"We will be—gone before he—returns," he managed to say with difficulty.

Anthea gave a cry.

"You are all right? I was so afraid when I found you that you might have broken your collar-bone."

"I am—all right," the Duke said. "Give me a moment—or two—then we will—ride back."

"Do you think you can do that?" Anthea asked. "I imagine the man I was just talking to will wish to earn five louis."

"I shall be—surprised if he is any—help to us," the Duke muttered. "Assist me to my—feet."

It was not as easy as it sounded, because although he disliked having to admit it he felt very dizzy. It took time and a great deal of effort before he could hoist himself onto the saddle of his horse.

Finally with Anthea's help he managed it and they moved at a very different pace back towards Brussels.

Afterwards Anthea often wondered how the Duke had managed to stay in the saddle.

She knew he was in pain and she learnt after the doctor had seen him that he had, as she suspected, a concussion.

"He will be all right, Madame, after two or three days in bed," the doctor said cheerfully, "but these big men fall heavily and he is lucky there are no bones broken."

They had been forced to ride home very slowly not only because the Duke was injured but also because the stallion was lame.

"It was my fault," Anthea told herself.

She realised it had been crazy to gallop over the battle-scarred field where there were deep holes made by the guns of the opposing Armies.

'I was fortunate,' she thought. 'But how could I have been so foolish as to involve the Duke for the second time in trouble?'

She felt chastened and rather depressed the first night when she had to dine alone.

Although she peeped into the Duke's bed-room to say good-night, he was asleep and could not speak to her.

Two days later he was better if rather disagreeable, and to make amends for having been so stupid Anthea determined to be cheerful and not, as her father would have deprecated, to bore him with dramatics.

Instead she amused him with some toys she had bought at the stalls in the Market-Place.

A toy monkey which had string to make him climb a pole, a puzzle fashioned from horse-nails on which the Duke spent a considerable time before he mastered the trick of it, and some funny little pictures of the battle showing Wellington with an enormous beak-nose to distinguish him from a moon-faced Napoleon.

"I have also brought you a special delicacy," Anthea said.

She sat down on the side of the Duke's bed and produced a cardboard box in which reposed the rich, succulent and creamy *patisserie* for which the Belgians were famous.

"Do you feel like eating one?" she asked.

"I do not!" the Duke replied.

"Then as I could not bear to waste them," Anthea

said, "I shall eat them myself! If they make me disgust-
ingly fat I can always blame you!"

The Duke watched fascinated as she bit into a cake
from which coffee cream oozed out between thin layers
of sponge.

"How Phebe would enjoy this," Anthea said.

"I hope you are not suggesting that we take some
back for her?" the Duke remarked.

Anthea considered the question for a moment.

"I suppose such delicate confections would not
travel."

"I can assure you they would not!"

"It is a pity," Anthea said. "I think they are without
exception the most delicious cakes I have ever tasted!"

The Duke shut his eyes as if the sight of them made
him feel somewhat sick.

"I am not boring you, am I?" Anthea asked anxiously.

"Not in the least," he replied. "I intend to get up to-
morrow. I am tired of staying in bed."

"No, no! You must not do that!" Anthea said hur-
riedly. "It is very important when one has had concussion to rest, otherwise, as Nanny used to say, one becomes 'addle-pated'! Think what a disaster that would
be for His Grace the Duke of Axminster!"

"I wonder if it would matter very much?" the Duke
remarked.

"But of course it would matter!" Anthea said. "What
will happen if you father a long line of half-witted
Dukes?"

There was silence, and as Anthea realised what she
had implied, the colour rose in her cheeks.

"It is of course a question," the Duke said, "of
whether I shall produce a long line of any sort, intelligent or, as you say, addle-pated!"

Anthea jumped down from the bed and went to the
window.

"Oh, look!" she exclaimed. "There is a man with a
barrel-organ with a monkey on top of it. The sweetest

little monkey, in a red coat. I wish the girls could see him!"

"It is a pity you cannot draw pictures of all you wish your sisters could see," the Duke remarked.

Anthea held her breath.

Just for a moment the idea came to her that she might tell him the truth.

Supposing she told him? What would he say?

Then she knew it would be impossible. He would be furiously angry. And he would never forgive her!

They had in a strange sort of way, she thought, become friends on this journey; but that was not to say that he was not counting the days until he could return to the Countess.

They would have to be careful how they saw each other in the future, but the Earl presumably had believed her story now that the Duke was married.

"Once we get back to England," Anthea told herself, "the Duke will return to his own friends and his own interests. We will of course appear together on formal occasions, and perhaps he will want me to entertain for him occasionally, but otherwise . . ."

Her thoughts came to a full-stop and she felt her spirits drop depressingly.

She was quite certain that the ease with which they now talked to each other, the way in which she could make him laugh, was only because they were alone on a conventional honeymoon from which it was impossible for him to escape.

"What are you thinking about, Anthea?"

She heard the Duke's voice from the bed and realised she had been silent for a long time.

"I . . . I was watching the monkey," she said quickly.

"And wishing your sisters were with you!" the Duke said.

Anthea did not reply and after a moment he said with a faint laugh:

"I must admit it is the first time in my life that I have

been alone with a lady who was pining for the company of someone else!"

"Did I sound rude?" Anthea asked in consternation. "You know I have liked being with you. It has been very exciting and I have loved all that you have told me."

She looked at him anxiously as she went on:

"Although you are perhaps annoyed about what happened on the battle-field, to me it was a very moving experience to be there with . . . you."

She spoke very earnestly and for once she was not laughing or even smiling.

"I too have liked being with you, Anthea," the Duke said in his deep voice.

"Have you really?" Anthea asked. "You see, I have been very much afraid of boring you. You are so experienced. You have lived such a full life, while I have done nothing!"

"But you have thought and felt," the Duke said. "I realised when we were on the battle-field and you were thinking of your father that you were capable of deep feelings."

"I loved Papa," Anthea answered, "but I was not only thinking of him. I was thinking of those other men who died and how their wives, their mothers and their sweethearts must have wept at their loss."

"As I have just said, you can feel, Anthea. That is very important. Most women do not feel very deeply about anything."

"Perhaps that is true of the women you know," Anthea replied. "But when Papa was killed, part of Mama died too. They loved each other so much. One had only to see them together to know what love is like."

"And that is what you hoped to find!" the Duke said.

Anthea looked away from him.

"I suppose . . . everyone has secret . . . dreams."

"And yours have been spoilt by me," the Duke said. "I am sorry, Anthea."

NEVER LAUGH AT LOVE

Anthea gave herself a little shake and suddenly her dimples re-appeared.

"Can you imagine how your friends in the *Beau Monde* would laugh if they heard you?" she asked. "Apologising for marrying a Little Miss Nobody from Nowhere—a girl with no assets, who should be down on her knees thanking the Gods of fortune for having sent her a real, live Duke!"

"If you talk to me like that, I swear I will spank you, Anthea!"

"You will have to catch me first," Anthea teased, "and that you will be unable to do until you have recovered from the wounds inflicted on you at the battlefield of Waterloo!"

She made a little grimace at him as she spoke.

Then before he could answer her she whisked out of the room, leaving him laughing rather weakly and trying to think of an answer to cap her *repartee*.

He was well aware that Anthea with an ingenuity all her own, was entertaining him.

He knew that ordinarily, had he stayed in bed with nothing to do and a persistent head-ache, he would have loathed every moment of his enforced captivity.

But Anthea had contrived to keep him amused, and he found himself waiting impatiently for her to return to him and watching the door for her to appear.

His bruised head and the fact that at times it ached intolerably kept them in Brussels longer than the Duke had intended.

It was only because Anthea flatly refused to leave until the doctor permitted it, that he was forced to bow to the medical dictum which made them stay an extra week.

Finally they left for England, their luggage considerably increased by the amount of presents that Anthea had bought for her family.

"Are you really very rich?" she had asked the Duke soon after he was laid up.

"I am not going to answer that question," he said, "until I know what it is you wish to buy."

The first purchase was an amusing peasant-costume which she knew would fit Phebe and which she would find fascinating.

The next day it was a gown for Thais, a riding hat for Chloe and an exquisitely painted picture for her mother.

"What about yourself?" the Duke enquired after he had assured her he would not be bankrupt if she purchased all she wanted for her family.

"Me?" Anthea enquired wide-eyed. "I want nothing. I have all these beautiful gowns. In fact so many of them that I think they will be out of fashion before you have seen them all!"

"They certainly become you," the Duke said. "You look very different from how you appeared that first night at Almack's."

"Do you remember that?" Anthea asked. "I shall never forget it. I hated you!"

"Hated me?" the Duke exclaimed in surprise.

"You did not want to dance with me, and when you did you looked so bored I thought you were insufferable!"

There was a note in her voice which told the Duke that he had hurt her and he put out his hand to say:

"I was obviously very remiss and exceedingly ill-mannered."

"It certainly made me hate you," Anthea said, "which was why . . ."

She bit back the words on her lips knowing that quite inadvertently she had been about to say this was why she had caricatured him.

He was watching her face.

"What were you going to say?"

"Which was why . . . I was glad you never asked me for another . . . dance."

But he knew that was not the true answer.

Although the Duke swore he was completely well

Anthea had a feeling that when he was tired his head-aches returned.

"You are not going to molly-coddle me any longer," he said. "You and my valets are nothing more than a lot of old women! You forget I was a soldier and used to hardships."

"You are getting older," Anthea said mischievously as she rose to leave him. "What you could put up with when you were a young man is not so easy when you are nearly middle-aged!"

They were talking alone in the Duke's bed-room. He had, with the doctor's permission, dressed and was sitting in the window getting the fresh air.

He reached out and caught her wrist.

"I assure you I am well enough to give you the spanking you deserve! I have had quite enough of your sniping at me."

He pulled her towards him as he spoke and Anthea pretended to be frightened, striving to free herself as she cried:

"No, no! You must not over-tax your strength! Remember how weak you are!"

"I will not be called weak!" the Duke said grimly.

He caught hold of her other arm and held her in front of him so that it was impossible for her to escape.

"You are my prisoner! I have to decide now whether I shall beat you or kiss you!"

Laughing, her eyes met his and suddenly they were both very still.

Something passed between them, something magnetic and strange Anthea had never known before, and yet it was unaccountably exciting.

It was difficult to breathe and her eyes seemed to fill her small face.

Then the Duke released her.

"I think it is . . . time for your . . . tea," Anthea murmured incoherently and fled from the room.

They left Brussels two days later and reached London without mishap, having stayed the night at

Canterbury rather than do the journey from Dover in one day as they had done on the outward journey.

They therefore arrived at Axminster House at four o'clock the following afternoon.

"Welcome home, Your Grace," the Butler said to Anthea as she stepped into the huge marble Hall.

"Is everything all right, Dorkins?" the Duke enquired.

"Everything, Your Grace. There's tea in the Library, and wine, if Your Grace prefers."

"I think you should have a little wine," Anthea said before the Duke could speak. "I am sure you are feeling tired."

"I am feeling nothing of the sort!" the Duke said firmly, conscious of a head-ache which he had determined not to acknowledge.

Anthea glanced at him in a way which told him that she was not deceived, then walked ahead of him.

The Library which looked onto the garden was at the back of the house. She had learnt the Duke habitually sat there.

Although it was called the Library, it was in fact a very large and very beautiful Sitting-Room and in Anthea's mind far more comfortable and less formal than the big Salons on the first floor.

There was a tea-table glittering with silver drawn up beside an arm-chair, and on it every type of delicacy to tempt their appetites—sandwiches, scones and a number of different sorts of cake.

"Can you really be hungry?" the Duke asked in an amused voice as Dorkins poured him out a glass of champagne.

"It is tea-time," Anthea replied a little reproachfully. "At home we always have Nursery tea with hot buttered toast and crumpets in the winter, and cucumber sandwiches in the summer."

"I have a feeling you ate a large number while you were preparing them!" the Duke said.

"That is why I am hungry now," Anthea smiled.

"If there is anything else you require, Your Grace, if you will just touch the bell," Dorkins murmured.

"I am sure we have everything!" Anthea answered.

"A great number of letters have arrived for Your Graces," the Butler said. "I have placed them on the table with the presents which came after you left. Some of them have been sent on from Yorkshire."

Anthea jumped to her feet.

"Yorkshire!" she exclaimed. "Then of course there should be a letter from home!"

She hurried across the room without waiting for Dorkins to bring the letters to her and found, as she had expected, one in her mother's hand-writing and one in Thais's.

"How exciting!" she cried. "We shall know now whether they received the letters I sent to them!"

She took the letters in her hand and returned to sit at the tea-table.

The Duke who had followed her across the room, stood looking at the pile of presents.

They had been opened by his secretary but were arranged neatly with the card of the sender tied onto each one.

"More entrée dishes!" he groaned.

"Just listen to what Thais says," Anthea cried. "She is very funny about the Reception and she says that without us it was like 'Hamlet' without the Prince! Phebe ate six pieces of wedding-cake and felt sick all the way home.

"Oh, and listen to this . . ." she continued.

Everyone said You were the most beautiful Couple they had ever seen. The Duke was so handsome that Chloe swears She saw several Women almost fainting when He walked down the Aisle, and You looked lovely, Dearest, you did really!

We were all so proud of You. Come back soon! We long to see You and We want to hear all about Your Honeymoon.

Mama says that that is when two People visit 'the blessed Isles of Bliss.'

> *All our love, Your affectionate sister,*
> *Thais.*

P.S. . . .

Anthea was just about to read the postscript out aloud when she stopped. She saw that Thais had written:

> *A lot more of Your Cartoons arrived, and as I thought You would like to see Them I have put them in the same Box as a quite nauseatingly ugly Garnet Necklace which has been sent to You by a Cousin that no-one has ever heard of! They are very funny, Anthea, and made Chloe and me laugh a lot!*

Hastily Anthea folded the letter and put it into the pocket of her travelling-gown.

For the first time she realised that the wedding presents had been unpacked and feeling suddenly afraid she walked quickly across the Library to where the Duke was standing.

As she reached him he held out a letter he had been reading and said in a voice she hardly recognised:

"Perhaps you would like to explain this?"

Anthea saw the heading on the writing-paper and felt as if she was turned to stone.

Automatically, hardly knowing what she did, she took it from him and the words seemed to flash in front of her eyes like a streak of lightning.

> *Dear Miss Dale:*
> *I enclose Copies of the other eight of your Cartoons which we have published all together as there has been such a demand for the first Two.*
> *I know You will be interested to hear that 'The Love of the*

*Pussycats' has now sold over Three Hundred Copies! Please
let Us have some more of your Work as soon as possible.*

> *I remain,*
> *Yours respectfully,*
> *Hannah Humphrey.*

Anthea looked up at the Duke, saw the expression
on his face and gave a little cry.

Clutching the letter tightly in her hand, she turned
and ran from the room in a panic, frightened as she
had never been frightened before.

CHAPTER SEVEN

*A*nthea came out of the back door of the cottage and
threw a basin of water over the marigolds.

When she had done so, two cats followed her back
into the house to sit watching her with unblinking
green eyes as she stirred a saucepan on the ancient
stove.

"Dinner is not ready yet," she said to them, "so you
will have to wait."

She found it comforting to talk to the cats.

Having always lived in a family, she found the silence and the loneliness of Elderberry Cottage at times
so oppressive that she felt she could bear it no longer.

And yet, she asked herself, what else could she do?

She had run away from Axminster House because
she could not face the Duke.

Afterwards she wondered how it could have been so easy? She had not had to think or plan but had acted merely on impulse.

She had rushed from the Library upstairs to her bed-room and found there were three housemaids unpacking her trunks.

She saw that her travelling cape and bonnet were laid on a chair. Beside them she noticed a valise which during their travels had contained most of what she required for one night.

Without considering, hardly realising what she was doing, Anthea put on her bonnet and cape and said to one of the maids:

"Carry this valise downstairs for me."

She had gone ahead down the Grand Staircase to find there was only one footman on duty in the Hall.

"I require a Hackney Carriage."

The flunkey looked surprised but hurried out obediently into the street to find one.

Two minutes later Anthea was driving away from Axminster House and the Duke.

She had told the coachman to drive to "The Lamb" at Islington, meaning to take a Stage-Coach home. But as she drove there she had thought that Yorkshire was the first place the Duke would look for her.

She was afraid not only of his anger but also of her mother's distress.

Anthea realised only too well how horrified Lady Forthingdale would be that she had lampooned her God-mother and precipitated such a disastrous sequence of events.

It would be impossible to keep from her the knowledge that the Duke had proposed not out of affection but merely to save himself and the woman he loved from being implicated in a divorce.

"Mama would be shocked and miserable!" Anthea told herself.

By the time the Hackney Carriage had arrived at Islington she had made up her mind.

She would not go back to Yorkshire. Instead she would go and stay with her old Nurse.

No-one would suspect that she was there and in weeks, or perhaps months, everything would have calmed down and she herself would be able to face the music.

It was not going to be easy, Anthea was aware of that.

The thought of the Duke's anger made her tremble, but it was not only his anger she feared.

As she journeyed towards Cumberton in Worcestershire where her Nurse lived, she began to face the truth.

She was indeed afraid of what the Duke might say to her, but most of all she regretted losing his friendship.

"I liked being with him. I enjoyed listening to him talking to me. It was wonderful when I made him laugh," she thought.

Then even as she half put into words what she felt, she knew it was not just friendship she had for him but something far deeper and far more disturbing.

"I love . . . him! I love . . . him!" she finally admitted to herself when she stayed the night at a Posting-Inn and was allotted a small, hard bed in the attic.

It was very different from the luxury she had enjoyed on her honeymoon.

That had all been so comfortable and extravagant and unlike anything she had known before, but she knew now it was not the material comforts which had mattered.

Everything had seemed gay and exciting simply because the Duke was there.

"How blind of me not to realise it before," she told herself!

She wondered how she could have failed to understand her feelings when her heart had leapt whenever she saw him, how it had been an enchantment to drive beside him and to hear his deep voice explaining so many things which she wanted to know.

"He understood what I felt about Papa on the battle-field."

She had tried to hide her tears, but he had seen them.

"You can feel, Anthea," he had said, "that is very important. Most women do not feel very deeply about anything."

"What did he mean," Anthea asked now, "by saying it was important? Important to whom?"

She knew the answer to that.

He was in love with Cousin Delphine and although he might have found his honeymoon less tedious than he had anticipated, she was nothing in his life except the wife he did not want.

"I . . . love him! Oh, God, I love . . . him!" Anthea cried despairingly into the darkness.

The misery she was feeling was worse than anything she had experienced in her life before.

It was an agony and a despair which made her wish that she had never gone to London and never met the Duke.

How could she have guessed that love would be like this?

It was not the blissful emotion of which her mother had talked, but something agonizing which tortured her because she knew her love could never be requited and that because of it she would never laugh again.

She wished now that she had let the Duke make her truly his wife as he had wanted to do.

If he had kissed her, if he had held her in his arms, whoever he might have been thinking of, it would have been better than to know that she would have no memories of love in the empty years that lay ahead.

"If only he had . . . kissed me . . . just once," her heart cried.

It took Anthea the whole of the next day to reach Pershore in Worcestershire, and from there she found a Carrier's cart to take her to Cumberton.

It was a small village, just as her Nurse had often described it to her, with a dozen black and white thatched cottages standing around a village green.

There was an ancient Inn called 'The Pelican' and a duck-pond in which witches had endured trial by water in mediaeval times.

The Carrier, who was conveying some barrels of ale to "The Pelican," set her down and seeing a small boy eyeing her with curiosity Anthea asked him the way to Elderberry Cottage.

"T'be at th'end o'th'village," he answered.

"Will you carry my valise for me?" Anthea asked. "I will give you 2d. if you will do so."

The boy, whose name she learnt was Billy, was only too willing to oblige and they set off side by side.

Anthea was aware that several faces had appeared at the cottage windows obviously surprised not only at her smart appearance, but also at the arrival of a stranger.

"I expect you know Miss Tuckett," Anthea said to Billy.

"Aye, Oi knows 'er all right, but 'er be dead!"

"Surely not?" Anthea exclaimed. "You must mean her sister, Mrs. Cosnet who I knew was ill."

"They both be dead," Billy insisted. "Missie Tuckett, 'er be buried two weeks ago cum Thursday."

"I cannot believe it!" Anthea exclaimed in consternation.

She had known that Nanny's widowed sister was very ill when she had left Yorkshire to nurse her, but she had written several times to say she was better in health.

Nanny had written to congratulate her on her approaching marriage and she had written back to thank her and say how much she wished she could be at the ceremony.

But dead!

When she fled from London she had thought child-like that Nanny would always be there to look after her.

It was an unhappiness she could hardly bear to know that Nanny was dead and she would never see her again.

"What am I to do?" she asked helplessly of the small boy beside her.

"Mrs. Weldon, 'er who lives next door, 'as th'key," he volunteered.

"Then I will go to the cottage," Anthea decided.

She was to learn in the next few days that the whole village had in fact been expecting her to arrive.

"Your Nurse and a wonderful woman she was, wrote a letter to you," the Vicar said, "saying that she was ill and telling you that if anything should happen to her the cottage and its contents were to be yours and your sisters."

He paused to add:

"She was a little rambling, but I think I am right in saying that you are Miss Anthea and your sisters are Thais, Chloe and Phebe?"

"You are quite right," Anthea answered.

She realised as the Vicar went on talking that Nanny had not mentioned the fact that she was to be married and he had no idea that she was not still Miss Forthingdale.

She was relieved that she did not have to tell him her real name and surreptitiously, when he was not look-ing, she removed her wedding-ring.

"I am quite certain you would not wish to settle in Cumberton, Miss Forthingdale," the Vicar was saying, "but it is a nice little cottage and, if you should wish to sell it, I am quite certain I can find a purchaser."

"Thank you, Vicar," Anthea said, "but for the mo-ment I will stay and tidy up Nanny's things."

"That is right, Miss Forthingdale, do nothing in a

hurry," the Vicar smiled. "It is always wise to sleep on a decision, whatever it may be."

Anthea found however that there was little to tidy.

Nanny had always been meticulously particular when she lived with them and her house was as 'clean as a new pin' as she would have said herself.

Mrs. Weldon had looked after Nanny's two cats, which as soon as they found that Anthea was staying at Elderberry Cottage returned to their home demanding food at least twice a day.

This meant that Anthea had to cook, however depressed she might feel.

She often thought that if she had been alone she would just have sat and moped and made no effort to feed herself.

But Antony and Cleopatra, as she had named the cats, were very sure what they required and had no compunction about complaining noisily if their meals were overdue.

She stirred the pot now in which a large rabbit was cooking and thought they were more importunate than any husband might be.

Even to think of the Duke was to feel a sharp stab of unhappiness within her, and she wondered if she would ever be free of the heavy weight of misery that was like a stone within her breast.

She wondered if he missed her, or if in fact he had been glad to be rid of her.

He would suppose she had gone back to Yorkshire, and this would have relieved him of feeling any embarrassment about being with the Countess again.

Cleopatra's green eyes reminded her of Cousin Delphine's and she thought again and again, as she looked at the cat, of the mischief-making cartoon that had caused all the trouble.

"How could I have done it?" she asked herself for the thousandth time.

She heard again the sharp note in the Duke's voice

as he had handed her Mrs. Humphrey's letter and asked:

"Perhaps you would like to explain this?"

How could she explain it? How could she explain anything except that he would never forgive her.

A tear dropped onto the stove and made a little sizzling sound.

Fiercely Anthea wiped her eyes with the back of her hand. What was the point of crying? It only gave her a head-ache.

There was a knock at the door and she thought it must be Billy bringing her some purchases from the small shop at the other end of the village.

She turned from the stove, walked towards the door and opened it to stand transfixed.

It was not Billy who stood there, but the Duke!

She looked at him with a stricken expression.

"Good-evening, Anthea!"

It was impossible for Anthea to find her voice.

She could only stare at him, thinking he looked even more handsome, larger and more overpowering than when she had last seen him.

"I would like to come in!" the Duke said after a long silence, "but I am not quite certain what to do about Hercules."

Anthea looked with bemused eyes to see a black stallion tethered by his bridle to a wooden paling next to the gate.

She opened her lips to speak but no sound came, and at that moment Billy appeared.

"That be a fine 'orse, Missie!" he said appreciatively.

"Will you . . . lead him to . . . Mr. Clements and ask him to put . . . the horse . . . in his stables, rub him down and . . . feed him?" Anthea asked in a voice that sounded strange even to herself.

"That Oi will, Missie," Billy said with relish. " 'Ere's th'things ye wanted."

He thrusted a package into Anthea's hand and

lifting the bridle from the fence started to lead the horse down the road.

"Clements was a . . . groom before he . . . retired," Anthea explained to the Duke. "Your horse will be quite . . . safe with . . . him."

She walked back into the cottage to put the package which Billy had brought her down on the table.

"I can see you are very cosy here," the Duke said. "I am sure your Nurse is looking after you well."

"Nanny is . . . dead!"

There was a throb in her voice. It was difficult to speak of it.

"I am sorry about that. Then you are here alone?"

"Y . . . yes."

She glanced towards him and looked away again. She had not realised before how very small the cottage was.

He seemed too big for the tiny room and his head almost touched the oak beams crossing the ceiling.

"I have ridden a long way," the Duke said. "I wonder if I could have a drink?"

"Of course," Anthea replied. "I have some cider, or when Billy returns he can fetch you something from the Inn."

"Cider will do well."

The Duke sat down on a hard chair beside the table as Anthea brought a bottle from a cupboard and put a tumbler down in front of him.

She then went back to the stove to stir the rabbit in the pot, her back to the Duke.

He watched her as he drank the cider. Then he said:

"I have also had nothing to eat since noon and then it was not a very substantial meal."

"I have nothing to offer you but rabbit," Anthea said, "and that is really for the cats."

"I have a feeling they are already over-fed," the Duke said, "while you are looking very thin, Anthea."

"I . . . have not been . . . hungry."

The Duke glanced at Antony and Cleopatra, who eyed him balefully.

"I am very fond of rabbit!" he said firmly.

Anthea brought a clean linen cloth from a drawer and laid it over the table.

Then she set a knife and fork in front of the Duke and put a plate near the stove to warm.

"I have a dislike of eating alone," the Duke said, "and although I have a feeling your cats will accept an invitation with alacrity, I would rather you joined me, Anthea."

She put another plate to warm and laid another knife and fork without looking at him. She also put a cottage loaf of fresh bread and a pat of butter on the table.

"That looks extremely good!" the Duke said.

"There are a few strawberries and a small cream cheese, otherwise the larder is empty."

"I am too hungry to be particular," the Duke answered. "I am looking forward to the rabbit."

There were no vegetables, so Anthea went into the garden and cut a lettuce. She also found several tomatoes which had ripened in the sun.

She thought as she went back into the cottage that the Duke looked very much at his ease. But his riding-boots were dusty and she knew that he must have ridden hard.

"How did you . . . find me?" she managed to ask as he cut himself a large crust from the cottage loaf.

"Thais told me."

Anthea started.

"Thais? You have . . . been to . . . Yorkshire?"

"I thought you would have gone home," he replied, "but when I realised you were not there I was very tactful."

"You did . . . not tell . . . Mama?"

"No, of course not," he answered, "and when I realised that none of them had heard from you I took Thais on one side and told her the truth."

Anthea was unable to meet his eyes.

The thought of the Duke and Thais discussing the cartoons she had drawn made her feel more humiliated than she had before.

"It was Thais," the Duke went on, "who guessed that you would come here, so you can realise that I have done a lot of travelling in the last week."

Anthea started.

"Your head!" she exclaimed. "You have not had your head-aches again?"

"Occasionally," the Duke admitted, "but it was only because I was doing more than perhaps was expedient."

"I . . . I am . . . sorry."

She told herself this was one more thing she had done wrong, one more way in which she had damaged the Duke.

She was quite certain he should never have undertaken such an arduous journey as going all the way to Yorkshire and then down to Worcestershire so soon after he had returned from the Continent.

The rabbit was ready and having tipped it from the saucepan into a china dish, she brought it to the table.

She remembered there was vinegar in the cupboard for the salad and also a pot of home-made redcurrant jelly.

Nanny would never let a season go by without making the fruit into jams, and Anthea had not forgotten that ever since she was a child she had always found them delicious.

"I suppose it is because I am very hungry," the Duke said, "but I do not think I have ever tasted a more delectable rabbit!"

Because she thought it would please him Anthea put a little on her own plate.

Now she surreptitiously gave morsels of it to Antony and Cleopatra who were moving restlessly around the table, rubbing themselves against their legs and making it quite clear that it was their dinner-time.

The Duke took a second helping of rabbit.

There was a knock on the door.

"It will be Billy," Anthea said. "He has come to tell you about your horse."

The Duke put his hand in his pocket and drew out a handful of change.

"Can you afford 6d?" Anthea asked. "He has been very helpful to me."

"In which case why not a shilling?"

"We must not spoil the market!" she answered.

For a moment he saw a suspicion of her irresistible dimples.

She gave Billy the 6d, then remembered that the Duke had only had cider with his dinner.

"Is there anything you would like Billy to fetch you?" she asked. "I imagine 'The Pelican' has some port."

"I would rather not risk it!" the Duke replied.

"That will be all, then, Billy."

"Good-night, Missie," he answered. "Oi'll be around early in th'morning with th'eggs for ye breakfast."

Anthea closed the door behind him.

The Duke had eaten practically all the rabbit and she put the few pieces which were left on a plate on the floor for Antony and Cleopatra.

He finished the strawberries in a few mouthfuls and helped himself to the cream cheese which Anthea had made from the milk the cats had not required.

Anthea took the empty plates into the Scullery. When she returned the Duke was cutting himself another piece of the loaf.

"I am afraid I can not give you an adequate meal," she apologised in a worried voice, "but doubtless you can get something to eat at Pershore or wherever you are going to stay to-night."

The Duke finished the cheese before he replied:

"I think it would be sheer cruelty to take Hercules any further, and quite frankly, I am tired."

"Why could you not have come here more slowly?"

Anthea asked. "You know the doctor said you were to be careful not to do too much too quickly."

"I have a feeling," the Duke said with a note of amusement in his voice, "that is exactly the way your Nurse would have spoken to me were she here!"

"She would at least have made you behave sensibly!"

"If I am to be sensible," the Duke replied, "then I refuse categorically to go any further to-night!"

He looked round the tiny room before he added:

"I do not mind sleeping on the floor. I have slept in far worse places when we were fighting in Portugal."

"That is a ridiculous suggestion and you know it!" Anthea said sharply. "I can manage very well in the armchair, and I will show you where you can sleep."

She walked towards the very narrow, twisting staircase which was just beside the front door.

The Duke followed her.

"Be very careful of your head!" Anthea admonished. "Even I have difficulty coming up these stairs."

Doing as she told him the Duke followed her and she opened the door of the room above.

The walls sloped under the thatch but there were two low diamond-paned windows to let in the light and the Duke could see the whole room was filled with a bed which made him stare in astonishment.

Anthea saw his face and for the first time since he had arrived she gave a little laugh.

"It is surprising, is it not?"

"It is indeed!" the Duke agreed.

"Nanny's brother-in-law weighed over twenty stone," Anthea explained, "and he always said he was so uncomfortable in an ordinary bed that he invented this one. He made the frame of oak and collected goose-feathers for his mattress."

Anthea's dimples were showing as she went on:

"When we were children Nanny used to tell us stories about this bed and how her sister, to make the sheets for it, had to sew two large ones together, and the same applied to the blankets.

"We used to talk about it as 'the Giant's Bed', and when I saw it I knew it had been aptly named!"

"It certainly solves our problem," the Duke remarked.

"Yours, at any rate," Anthea answered. "I do not believe there is a bed at Axminster House as large as this one."

"There is not," the Duke agreed, "and that is why, as I have already said, it solves *our* problem."

Anthea looked at him enquiringly and he said:

"There is no reason for either you or me to sleep downstairs. If you take one side, and I the other, we might as well be in two different countries, France and England, for instance, with the Channel between us."

Anthea was silent and he said after a moment:

"It is a sensible solution and to-morrow, if you want me to, I will move on to Pershore, or any other place you suggest. But to-night I am going no further!"

He looked at Anthea challengingly as if he expected her to argue. Then she said after a moment:

"Very . . . well. As you say, we have the Channel . . . between us . . . but I must point out that in the village they know me as 'Miss Forthingdale'."

"Then we will certainly give them something to talk about!" the Duke said. "Unless of course you would like to put on your wedding-ring again."

Anthea was surprised he had noticed.

"The Vicar did not realise I was married and I thought it might be . . . uncomfortable to explain who I . . . was."

"I feel certain the Vicar will require an explanation after to-night!" the Duke said mockingly.

He turned towards the door.

"I am going to find Hercules because I have razors and various other necessities in my saddle-bag."

Anthea did not speak and he went on:

"When I come back I will want to wash and as I imagine the only place I can do so is downstairs, I suggest, Anthea, that you get into bed. If you are asleep when I come upstairs I will not wake you."

"Thank . . . you," Anthea said faintly.

She felt as if the Duke had taken command and there was nothing she could do but obey him.

He turned and left her, bending his head to get through the low door, and she heard him going rather cautiously down the twisting stairs.

She put her hands up to her cheeks as if to prevent them from burning.

She heard the door close and hurried down the stairs to take a kettle of hot water from the stove and stand it in the basin in the tiny scullery.

Then she returned to the bed-room and hastily began to undress.

It was growing late. Outside dusk was falling, but there was still the last glow in the sky to throw a golden light through the open windows.

There was a fragrance of roses and stocks and Anthea could hear the rooks going to roost.

She did not light the candles knowing that would bring in the moths. Instead she left the curtains undrawn and having put on one of the thin, lace-trimmed nightgowns which had been in her trousseau she slipped into bed.

"I will pretend to be asleep," she told herself. "Then to-morrow I will make all the explanations that have to be made."

It seemed incredible that the Duke had eaten, they had talked, and yet they had not mentioned the reason why she had run away.

"He is tired," Anthea told herself, "and he probably feels he could not face a scene at the moment."

She was determined there should not be one.

He might have endangered his health in travelling all that way to Yorkshire and she thought that once again it was her own thoughtlessness which was responsible.

"I should not have run away," she told herself accusingly.

She lay tense and trembling a little because there was so much for which she felt responsible.

And yet, even though she was nervous, it was impossible not to feel that the hard lump of unhappiness which had lain in her breast ever since she left London had vanished.

She was with the Duke again! He was there! She could listen to his voice and he was even more wonderful than she had remembered!

She did not dare ask herself why he had troubled to follow her.

Could it be that he was so angry that he wanted them to separate from each other for ever?

She knew this was a thought that had lain at the back of her mind all the time and which frightened her more than anything else.

"Oh, please God, let me see him . . . sometimes," she prayed. "Please God . . . please . . ."

She heard his footsteps coming up the garden path. He shut the door, locked it and she heard him crossing the room downstairs.

He was undressing, then she knew from the sound that he was washing in the small scullery at the back of the cottage.

She hoped he would find the soap and a towel.

She should have put everything ready for him but she had been so bemused that she could think only of obeying his instructions and getting into bed as he had ordered her to do.

Now she could hear him coming up the stairs, and because she was shy, she shut her eyes as he opened the door of the bed-room and came in.

His side of the bed was only a few feet inside the door.

With her eyes shut Anthea felt him get in and sink down in the feather mattress.

She held her breath, wondering if he would turn

over and go to sleep. But after a moment, as if he knew she was awake, he said conversationally:

"This is the most comfortable bed I have ever slept in."

"As you are so . . . tired I am sure you . . . would sleep . . . anywhere."

"I am not as tired as I was," he said, "and I am no longer worried about you, Anthea."

"You were . . . worried?"

"Of course I was! How could you do anything so damnable as to run away without telling me where you were going? It was only after Dorkins announced dinner that I learnt you had gone!"

"I . . . I am . . . sorry," Anthea said in a very small voice.

"Why did you go?"

Anthea was so surprised at the question that she turned her head to look at him.

It was difficult in the little light that remained in the room to see clearly, but although his head was on the pillow, he was looking towards her.

"Y . . . you . . . know why I . . . went," she managed to say after a moment.

"You thought I would be angry," the Duke said, "and I can understand that. But I wish you had trusted me."

"I . . . I wanted to tell you . . . when we were in . . . Brussels, but I was . . . afraid."

"Thais told me that you were trying to make some money because you were all so poor. I should have realised how very poor you were, Anthea."

There was a kindness in his voice which made Anthea feel suddenly very weak.

She had expected him to be angry, she had expected him to demand an explanation, but kindness was something she had not expected.

She stared at the window in front of her feeling the tears come into her eyes.

"Thais told me that the £100 you obtained for the

cartoons enabled you all to have extra food which you had never enjoyed before. As always, Anthea, you were thinking of your family."

The tears ran down Anthea's cheeks but she did not wipe them away.

"If I do not move," she thought to herself, "he will not notice."

There was silence before the Duke asked:

"Are you crying, Anthea?"

"N . . . no."

It was not a very convincing reply and after a moment he said:

"Are you sure you are not crying?"

It was impossible for Anthea to answer him.

"To make certain," the Duke said, "I am going to cross the Channel to see for myself. I do not want you to be unhappy."

Anthea gave a little sob and then her hands went up to her face.

"I . . . I am . . . sorry . . ." she began to say, then burst into tears.

She had not felt him move but he was beside her and his arms went round her as she cried:

"I am . . . s . . . sorry . . . I did not . . . mean it . . . I swear I did not m . . . mean it . . . I did not want to be . . . u . . . unkind to God-mama or really to . . . y . . . you . . . it just . . . h . . . happened and I am so . . . ashamed . . . so terribly a . . . ashamed at . . . what I have . . . done."

It was impossible to say any more.

She could only cry despairingly against him, all the misery of the last fortnight accumulating in a tempest which shook her whole body.

"It is all right," the Duke said gently. "It is all right."

She went on crying, realising she should stop herself, but quite unable to do so.

There was something very comforting about feeling his arms holding her close. Then as her tears abated a little he said softly:

"It is all over. We can forget about it."

"We . . . cannot! We cannot do . . . that!" Anthea
sobbed. "It was unlucky to . . . laugh at . . . love
. . . and because . . . I did so . . . you . . . had
to . . . marry me."

"I have realised that," the Duke said quietly, "and
that is why I have something to tell you."

Anthea stiffened.

She knew, she thought, what he was about to say.

"When I thought it over," he said, "I realised that it
was very lucky for me that you did draw that particular
cartoon."

Anthea thought she could not have heard him
aright.

She raised her face wet with her tears to look up at
him.

"It is quite simple, my darling. If you had not drawn
it we would not have been married and we would not
be here now."

As the Duke spoke he bent his head and his lips
found hers.

For a moment Anthea was too astonished to breathe.
Then as his mouth took possession of her she felt a
strange streak like quicksilver flash through her.

It was so vivid, so poignant, that for a moment it was
sheer pain, until it turned into an unbelievable rapture.

He drew her closer and his lips became more posses-
sive, more insistent, and she felt her whole body in-
vaded with a warmth and a wonder she had never
known before.

It was an ecstasy which was beyond words, almost
beyond thought, and it made her quiver with the glory
of it.

"This is love!" she thought. "This is what Mama said
it was like and it is even more marvellous!"

Instinctively she drew closer to him, her body
against his, her heart beating wildly, her lips very soft
as she surrendered herself to the wonder of his.

The Duke raised his head.

"My darling one! My sweet!" he said unsteadily.

"I love . . . you!" Anthea whispered. "I love . . . you!"

Then the Duke was kissing her again, kissing her passionately, demandingly, masterfully, until she could no longer think.

She only knew that her love reached out to him so that she gave him not only her lips, but her heart, her soul and her . . . body.

They were one and there was nothing else but love.

The moon shone through the small window throwing a silver light onto the bed.

"Are you . . . asleep?" Anthea whispered.

"I am too happy to sleep," the Duke answered.

"But you must try. You have ridden such a long way to-day."

"Are you still molly-coddling me?" he asked with a note of amusement in his voice, and pulled her nearer to him. "Oh my precious little love, I cannot tell you how much I missed you when you were not there to bully me, to make me take care of myself!"

"I thought . . . you would be . . . glad to be . . . rid of me."

"I think what I missed most," the Duke said, "was your laughter. I have never known that days could be so long, so dull and lifeless!"

"I laughed . . . at love . . ."

"Which you will never do again, my adorable wife! We will laugh together, but like the gods only from sheer happiness."

"To-gether."

Anthea's cheek was against his shoulder.

"I suppose I fell in love with your dimples," he ruminated. "They fascinate me. And your voice has some lilting quality in it that I have never heard in any other woman's."

Anthea gave a deep sigh.

"I was . . . always thinking how much I must . . . bore you after the brilliant and beautiful women you have known and . . . loved."

Her voice trembled on the last word.

"I know now," the Duke answered, "that I have never really been in love before. I have been attracted, enamoured, passionately aroused by many women, but I have never laughed with them."

"But you wanted to . . . make love . . . to them," Anthea murmured.

"I wanted to make love to you, too, but you would not let me."

"I have often . . . thought during these . . . last weeks how . . . foolish it was of me."

"No, you were right!" the Duke said. "I was not offering you real love, Anthea, not at that moment! But when we were in Brussels I found it increasingly hard not to touch you, and not to come to your room after we had gone to bed."

"Why did you . . . not do . . . so?"

"I suppose the truth was that I was too proud to risk being rebuffed for the second time," he answered, "but every day I wanted you more. Every night was a frustration I hope never to repeat, knowing you were so near, and yet the doors between us were closed."

"Is that . . . why you suggested we . . . sleep here . . . tonight?" Anthea asked.

"I will admit that fate played into my hands by producing a bed like this," the Duke answered, "but I had no intention, Anthea, of letting you escape me a second time!"

She gave a little cry.

"I am glad . . . so very glad!"

"Thais was sure you loved me, even if you were not aware of it."

"Thais?" Anthea questioned. "But how could she have known?"

"Perhaps you are so close as a family that the girls know more about you than you know yourself. That is something I missed by being an only child."

"Thais was right!" Anthea said. "I love you more than I can ever tell you! I love you with . . . every breath I draw . . . with every thought . . . I think. There is only . . . you!"

The Duke kissed her forehead, her eyes, her mouth and then her neck where a little pulse was beating madly.

"I had no idea any woman could be so sweet, so soft, so adorable!" he said.

There was a note of passion in his voice that made Anthea quiver.

"I will . . . try to be exactly as you . . . want me to be, and I promise I will . . . never draw a picture again!"

"I have every intention that you shall draw."

"You . . . want me to?" Anthea asked incredulously.

"Not cartoons, my precious, except to amuse me," he said. "But you obviously have an extraordinary talent which I do not think should be wasted!"

Anthea waited, wide-eyed.

"What I suggest and I have been planning this all the time I have been trying to find you, is that you should have lessons from an artist who is really qualified to teach."

"Perhaps I can only . . . caricature people?"

"We will find out for certain," the Duke replied, "and I suggest we start by going to Italy."

"To Italy?" Anthea exclaimed.

"I have, my sweet darling, been defrauded of a proper honeymoon!"

He kissed her small nose before he said:

"I have always understood that a honeymoon is a time for love-making."

He paused before he asked:

"That is if you agree, my sweetheart?"

Anthea felt a little flame within her vibrate to the note in his voice.

"I . . . agree," she murmured against him.

He kissed her hair.

"I want to teach you about love, my darling, and I promise you that you will never escape me again."

"I . . . will . . . not want . . . to do so . . ."

He kissed both her dimples before he continued:

"I do not think either of us wishes to go back to London at the moment. So I suggest we cross the real Channel again and travel to Italy, the Paradise of artists."

"I would love that!" Anthea cried. "I would love anywhere with you . . . but especially Italy!"

"You shall study the works of Michelangelo in Florence," the Duke said, "and perhaps we will find someone to give you some lessons there before we visit Venice, and then come home via Paris. There are some drawings in the Louvre I particularly want you to see."

"It sounds too . . . thrilling . . . too perfect!"

"And when we get back," the Duke went on, "I think there are many things at Axminster House in Hampshire that will please you. But I know now it has always lacked something which you and I must provide."

"What is that?" Anthea enquired.

He held her very close to him and his lips moved over the softness of her skin before he answered:

"A family, my adorable wife. It is what I missed when I had no Thais, Chloe or Phebe with whom to laugh."

His lips were touching hers as he asked:

"Will you give me beautiful daughters like you, my lovely one?"

He felt the quiver which ran through her before she whispered:

"Only if . . . you will . . . give me lots of . . . sons exactly like you . . ."

She was unable to finish the sentence because he was

kissing her with a passion that revealed the fire within him.

It evoked an answering flame in Anthea and she clung to him knowing that once again he had aroused the incredible rapture and the blinding glory that she had always known was a part of real love.

It was everything which was beautiful and sacred, everything that she had heard in music, seen in painting and found in poetry.

It was divine and she must surrender herself to it completely and wholeheartedly.

The Duke's lips became more insistent.

She could feel his hand touching her body, she could feel his heart beating against hers.

Then there was only love and the laughter of the gods.

A Touch
Of Love

CHAPTER ONE

1820

"*I* am afraid, Miss Selincourt, that I have bad news for you!"

"Oh, no! I was hoping you would not say that!"

"I assure you I have done everything in my power and spent many sleepless nights worrying as to how I could have something different to report, but it is hopeless."

Mr. Lawson, the senior partner of Lawson, Cresey and Houghton, had a note of sincerity in his voice which was unmistakable.

The girl to whom he was speaking gave a deep sigh and sat down in the chair opposite him, her eyes large and worried in her oval face as she asked:

"Are things really . . . bad?"

Mr. Lawson gave her a look of sympathy before he replied:

"You shall judge for yourself."

A grey-haired man of about fifty, he had to put on his spectacles before he could find the paper he wanted amongst a number of others on his desk.

Then he held it in front of him, obviously reading it over to himself as if he hoped by doing so he might find some salient point he had missed.

Finally he laid it down and said:

"You know, Miss Selincourt, that I had a great

admiration for your brother-in-law, Lord Ronald, and I was very proud that he extended to me his friendship."

Tamara Selincourt nodded and he went on:

"I begged him on numerous occasions to make some provision in the event of his death, but he merely laughed at me."

"But why should he have expected to die?" Tamara asked. "After all, he was only thirty-three and my sister was just six months younger."

"Thirty-three!" Mr. Lawson repeated to himself. "You are right, Miss Selincourt, at thirty-three one does not think about death."

"And their new boat was considered to be especially sea-worthy," Tamara cried. "After all, it cost a great deal of money."

"I am well aware of that," Mr. Lawson answered, "and it is one of the things which now have to be paid for."

"Ronald thought that he might make a little money out of her, perhaps taking a cargo from one harbour to another."

Tamara spoke almost as if she was speaking to herself and unexpectedly she laughed.

"That was really nonsense, as we both know! Ronald and my sister just loved the sea. They were only happy when they were sailing over the waves, setting out on what seemed to them an exciting adventure and . . . leaving us . . . behind."

Tamara's voice dropped on the last words. Then she added hardly above a whisper:

"What will . . . become of the . . . children?"

"That is what has concerned me," Mr. Lawson replied. "After all Sándor is nearly twelve and should soon be going to school."

"He is a very bright boy," Tamara said. "In fact they are all unusually intelligent, which is not surprising when you remember how clever my father was."

"I have always regretted that I never had the pleasure of meeting him," Mr. Lawson answered.

"He was brilliant!" Tamara exclaimed, "and although his books did not make very much money they will always be re-printed for the use of scholars."

"I am sure of that," Mr. Lawson agreed, "and because I am also sure Sándor has inherited his grandfather's brains he must be well educated. There is only one way that can be accomplished."

"How?" Tamara asked.

She raised her eyes to Mr. Lawson's as she spoke, and he thought, as he had thought many times before, how lovely she was.

She certainly had a beauty not usually found in a small Cornish village.

"She is like an exotic orchid," he told himself and wondered how many young men, if they had the opportunity, would think the same.

Tamara certainly did not look English.

Her red hair, such a dark, rich auburn that it could only have come from South-East Europe, framed the perfect oval of her face and gave her skin a translucent whiteness which again was very un-English.

Her eyes were so dark as to be almost purple, and yet Mr. Lawson could not help thinking that despite her exotic appearance there was something very young and very innocent about her.

"How old are you, Miss Selincourt?" he asked unexpectedly.

She smiled at him.

"I thought that was a question you should never ask a lady," she replied. "To be truthful I am nineteen, thirteen years younger than my sister, Maïka, but then there was a brother in between us who died when he was only a child."

"Nineteen!" Mr. Lawson repeated to himself. "You are too young, if I may say so, to have so much responsibility thrust upon you."

"But I have to look after the children. Who else is

there?" Tamara asked. "And anyway, I love them and they love me."

She looked at the worried expression on Mr. Lawson's face and said:

"I am prepared to work for them, to do anything that is necessary; but I was hoping you would tell me there is enough money left so that in the meantime we should not starve."

"I know that is what you hoped, Miss Selincourt," Mr. Lawson replied, "but, unfortunately . . ."

"I made £40 out of the first book I wrote," Tamara interrupted. "It seemed a lot at the time, but I am very hopeful that my second one, which is now in the Publishers' hands, will make me a great deal more."

"When is it to be published?" Mr. Lawson asked.

"Any day now. They did not give me an exact date, but they told me it would be some time in June."

Mr. Lawson looked down at the piece of paper that was in front of him, before he said:

"Supposing you make another £40, or even double that amount, you still could not keep yourself and three children on such a small sum."

There was silence. Then Tamara said:

"Are you telling me there is no other money?"

"That is the truth."

She stared at him incredulously.

"But how . . . I do not understand?"

"The allowance your brother-in-law, Lord Ronald Grant, received every quarter ends with his death, and I am afraid that the last amount which arrived a week ago has already been anticipated."

"To pay for the boat!"

"Exactly!"

"But the house . . . ?"

"The house, as I expect you know, is mortgaged and you are extremely fortunate in that there is a purchaser ready to buy it."

Tamara looked at the solicitor in a startled manner.

"But . . . I thought we could . . . stay here."

"You must see that is impossible," Mr. Lawson said. "The house was always too big and too expensive for Lord Ronald's means, but he and your sister fell in love with it and believed they could make ends meet."

Tamara was silent.

She knew only too well how both her sister and her brother-in-law were prepared always to leave everything to chance, good luck, or just hope.

She had had a suspicion for some years that they were running more and more hopelessly into debt.

But Lord Ronald had insisted on building a new boat because their old one was unseaworthy, and he blithely ignored the question of how he was to pay for it.

Now a storm had brought catastrophe and tragedy to them all.

Lord Ronald Grant and his wife had been drowned when a sudden and unexpected tempest had burst out of what seemed a cloudless sky.

The 'Sea Lark' had been swept away to be wrecked, they learnt later, on the rocks.

The shock had been all the more terrible because it was two days before Tamara could learn what had happened.

She only felt within herself that the worst had occurred when her sister and her husband did not return.

Some fishermen had gone out as soon as the storm had abated, but all they had discovered were fragments of the 'Sea Lark' floating on the waves and, pathetically, a little woollen cap which had belonged to Lady Ronald.

It had all happened so unexpectedly, so suddenly that it was hard for Tamara to realise that her good-tempered, charming brother-in-law was dead and that she would never see again her sister, whom she adored.

Now, as if her thoughts went to what Mr. Lawson had been saying a little earlier on, she said aloud:

329

"They gave me a home after Papa died. I was so happy with them, and you know, Mr. Lawson, if it is the last thing I do I have to repay that debt."

There was a note in Tamara's voice which showed she was not very far from tears, and after a moment Mr. Lawson said:

"I understand only too well what you are feeling, Miss Selincourt, and that is why you will appreciate that the only sensible course for you to take is the one I am about to suggest to you."

"What is that?" Tamara asked curiously.

"It is," he said slowly, "that you should take the children to their uncle, the Duke of Granchester!"

If he had exploded a bomb in front of her Tamara could not have looked more astonished.

"Take them to the Duke?" she repeated, her voice incredulous. "How could you suggest such a thing?"

"Who else is there?" Mr. Lawson asked. "As far as I know your brother-in-law has not kept in touch with any member of his family, and the children are undoubtedly, now they are orphans, His Grace's responsibility."

"It is impossible!" Tamara protested. "Surely you are aware of the manner in which the Duke has treated his brother . . . and my sister?"

There was an unmistakable note of hostility in her voice and Mr. Lawson said quietly:

"I know the story only too well, but we cannot entirely blame the present Duke for his father's attitude when Lord Ronald wished to marry your sister."

"It was inhuman! Barbaric!" Tamara stormed, and now her dark eyes were flashing. "Do you know what happened, Mr. Lawson, when Ronald wrote to his father to say he wanted to marry Maïka?"

Mr. Lawson did not reply and she went on angrily:

"He stormed down to Oxford where Ronald was in residence and told him that if he married Maïka he would never speak to him again!"

"You must understand," Mr. Lawson said mildly,

"that the Duke, who was a very pious man, had a horror of anything connected with the play-house!"

"He said because Maïka appeared on the stage that she was an actress. But in fact she was nothing of the sort!"

Tamara's voice seemed to ring out as she continued:

"Maïka was a singer and because at the time my mother was desperately ill and my father could not afford the high fees asked by the best doctors, she sang in an Opera Company."

Mr. Lawson was about to speak but Tamara went on:

"In two years she made enough money to pay for all the treatments my mother required."

"Surely this was explained to His Grace at the time?" Mr. Lawson murmured.

"Do you suppose he would listen?" Tamara asked furiously. "He would not even allow Ronald to speak in my sister's defence."

She drew in her breath before she said:

"Ronald told me that he spoke as if Maïka was a prostitute, a woman beyond the pale, whom he had picked up in some gutter! He would neither meet her nor hear about her. He just repeated his ultimatum!"

She paused before she added:

"When Ronald told him that, whatever he said, he intended to marry my sister, the Duke walked out and never spoke to him again!"

She threw out her hands as she asked:

"What sort of father was that? What sort of man is it who would repudiate his own son without allowing him even to speak a word in his own defence?"

"The Duke has been dead for some time," Mr. Lawson remarked quietly.

"The present Duke is no better," Tamara snapped. "He is only a year older than Ronald and you would think he might have understood and perhaps sympathised! But he slavishly accepted his father's decision that the family should sever all connections with the 'black sheep'."

Her voice broke on the last word.

She rose and walked to the window to stare out fighting her tears before she said:

"You know how sweet, gentle and wonderful in every way my sister was. Actually she hated the stage and everything to do with it."

"She once told me so," Mr. Lawson replied.

"As soon as she made enough money to save my mother," Tamara went on as if he had not spoken, "she left the Theatre just to be Ronald's wife, as she had always wanted to be, and they were blissfully happy."

"I do not think I have ever known a couple who were so happy," Mr. Lawson agreed almost enviously.

"And they died together," Tamara murmured. "I do not think either of them could have gone on living alone."

Mr. Lawson adjusted his spectacles.

"Now to get back to where we started, Miss Selincourt," he said briskly, "and that is the financial position of you and the children. The only possible thing to do is to take them where they belong."

"Do you really think I would do that?" Tamara asked. "That I would humiliate myself and them, to ask favours of a man who has behaved so abominably to his own brother?"

"What is the alternative?" Mr. Lawson asked.

"There must be something . . . something we could . . . do," Tamara said desperately.

She walked back towards the desk and sat down in the chair in which she had been sitting before, almost as if her legs would no longer support her.

"If there is, I have no idea of it," Mr. Lawson said. "Quite frankly, Miss Selincourt, I think it only right and just that the Duke should be made responsible for his brother's children."

Tamara did not speak and after a moment he went on:

"Mr. Trevena says he will take over the house and pay enough money to rid you of the mortgage and all

Lord Ronald's other debts, provided he has possession immediately."

"I suppose he wants it for his son who is getting married," Tamara said dully.

"That is right," Mr. Lawson replied. "He is a difficult man, and if we put him off he may buy a house elsewhere."

Tamara was silent, realising that to sell a house of the size of the Manor in that isolated part of Cornwall was not easy.

They might go for months, if not years, without finding another buyer, and it would be impossible to feed the children, let alone provide them with clothes, and education.

"Is the Duke aware that his brother is dead?" she asked after a moment.

Mr. Lawson looked slightly uncomfortable before he said:

"I have not yet informed His Grace."

Tamara looked at him. Then suddenly there was a little light in her eyes.

"I know why . . . because you were waiting for Ronald's allowance to come in. That was kind of you . . . very kind."

"And strictly unethical!" Mr. Lawson said with a smile.

There was silence for a moment, before Tamara asked:

"Must we tell him . . . now?"

"I am afraid so," Mr. Lawson replied. "You would not wish me to behave in such an illegal manner that I should no longer be allowed to practise as a Solicitor."

"No, of course not," Tamara answered, "and you have been so kind already. I am sure my brother-in-law never paid your firm for the many times he had to consult you over the many documents appertaining to the Estate and of course the boat."

"It is not of any great consequence," Mr. Lawson replied. "As I have said, I valued your brother-in-law's

333

friendship and I do not think anyone could have known your sister without loving her."

"It is a pity the Grant family could not hear you say that," Tamara observed.

"Would you think me very impertinent, Miss Selincourt, if I suggested that when you meet the Duke of Granchester you do not fight old battles," Mr. Lawson asked. "Content yourself with trying to make him interested in the three orphans and accept them as his sole responsibility?"

"Supposing he refuses to do anything for them?" Tamara asked. "It is quite likely, considering they are my sister's children."

"I cannot believe that the Duke would allow anyone with the name of Grant to starve," Mr. Lawson replied. "Furious though the old Duke was with Lord Ronald, he continued his allowance all these years."

"The same allowance he made him when he was an undergraduate at Oxford," Tamara said scornfully.

"It was nevertheless a substantial one," Mr. Lawson insisted, "and the Duke could in fact have cut his son off with only the proverbial penny."

"If you think I am going to be grateful to the family . . . I am not!" Tamara said in a hard voice. "As for the present Duke, from all I have heard about him . . ."

She gave a sudden cry and put her fingers up to her lips.

"What is it?" Mr. Lawson asked in astonishment.

"I have just remembered . . . I did not think of it until now, but I cannot . . . I cannot take the children to the Duke of Granchester. If they go, they must go . . . without me!"

"But why?" Mr. Lawson asked.

"Because I have . . . based my . . . novel on him!"

"On the Duke?"

Tamara put her hand up to her forehead as if she was trying to think clearly.

"You remember my first book, which although it was a fairy-story was also slightly satirical?"

"Indeed I thought it very amusing and original," Mr. Lawson said.

"Well, this book, the one which is being published at the moment, is a novel about a spiteful, unkind, wicked Duke, who is in fact the present Duke of Granchester!"

"But you have never seen him, and you know nothing about him."

"I know all that Ronald has told me, and because I was interested I always looked for anything written about him in the newspapers and magazines."

She looked at Mr. Lawson in consternation as she went on:

"When Ronald's friends whom he had met at Oxford came to stay with us, they always told us stories about the Duke and I stored them up in my memory."

"And you think the Duke would recognise himself?" Mr. Lawson asked. "In which case your book might be libellous."

"I do not think he would care to acknowledge the portrait as a true one," Tamara answered. "I have no reason to think he would even read it, but . . ."

She was silent and after a moment Mr. Lawson said:

"Exactly what have you said that could identify His Grace as being the character portrayed in your novel?"

"Well, for one thing the book is called 'The Ducal Wasp' and the Duke is the villain who goes about making everybody miserable and unhappy. He drives Phaetons and Curricles which are always black and yellow, and his servants wear a black and yellow livery."

"Which are the Grant family colours," Mr. Lawson said.

"Exactly!" Tamara answered, "and, oh, there are lots of other things about him which Ronald told me and about the Castle. There are also incidents I have invented like a race meeting where the villain pulls the favourite so that he can make a lot of money by betting on another horse from his stables, which of course wins."

Mr. Lawson put his hand up to his forehead.

"Why did you not let me read it before you sent it to the Publishers? You will undoubtedly be prosecuted for libel and ordered to pay enormous damages."

Tamara laughed.

"That is easy, at any rate. If I have no money, I cannot pay."

"Then you may go to prison."

"Then I will plead that every word I wrote was true and therefore justified."

Mr. Lawson groaned.

"That is something which cannot happen! You will sit down, Miss Selincourt, here and now, and write to the Publishers withdrawing your book!"

"Withdraw my book?" Tamara cried. "I shall do nothing of the sort!"

"You must! You must see it is the only possible course for you to take," Mr. Lawson insisted.

He saw the light of defiance in Tamara's eyes and said quietly:

"You have to think of the children. Knowing what you believe the Duke to be like, could you bear to send them alone to Granchester Castle? I know they would be unhappy without you."

There was a long silence. Then Tamara capitulated.

"No, you are right. I will send the letter."

"I will draft it for you," Mr. Lawson said. "In the meantime, I will despatch a letter to-morrow morning to the Duke, informing him of his brother's death and telling him that the children will arrive at the beginning of next week."

"As soon as . . . that?"

"We have to remember Mr. Trevena."

"Y-yes . . . of course."

Once again Tamara rose to walk to the window.

"I am thinking," she said, "that if I must . . . go with them, and I realise that Vava is too young to go

without me, then it might be best not to go as . . .
Maïka's sister."

Mr. Lawson considered for a moment what she had
said. Then he said:

"No, of course not, I should have thought of that. It
would be best to say that you have looked after them
as . . ."

". . . as a Governess," Tamara interposed. "At least
then he will have to give me my wages, so that I shall
not be entirely dependent upon him."

Mr. Lawson looking at her and seeing the sunshine
touch the dark red of her hair to a flaming gold,
thought she would look very unlike the usual run of
Governesses to be found in charge of small children.

He did not however express his thoughts, he only
asked aloud:

"What name shall I call you?"

"Does it matter?" Tamara asked. "No, wait, it had
better be something that the children can remember."

"Why not Miss Wynne?"

"Excellent. I will tell them that is what we are going
to do."

"But I hope you will not try and win a battle against
the Duke," Mr. Lawson said. "It is important, Miss
Selincourt, that he should like the children. He is a
very rich and powerful man, and there is nothing he
could not do for them if he takes a fancy to them."

"I think he is far more likely to fling us all into a
dungeon and keep us there on bread and water until
we die," Tamara said dramatically.

Mr. Lawson laughed.

"I think if that was discovered it would cause a scandal which would reverberate throughout the whole
country! I assure you that from what I have heard of
the Duke he does not like scandals."

"No, of course not," Tamara agreed. "That is what
his father thought Ronald was causing by marrying an
actress."

There was no mistaking the bitterness in her tone and Mr. Lawson said quickly:

"I do beg of you to try to forget the past. As close relatives of His Grace, the children cannot only have everything they have ever desired, but also a unique opportunity for happiness in the future."

Tamara did not speak and after a momemt he said:

"It seems strange that we should be talking about it now when Kadine is only ten, but in seven years time she will be a débutante and a very beautiful one. The whole social world will be open to her and her sister as the nieces of His Grace the Duke of Granchester."

Tamara looked at him in surprise, then with a quick change of mood which Mr. Lawson knew was characteristic of her, she said:

"You are right! Of course you are right, and I must think of the girls. They will both be very beautiful, as you say, and perhaps they will be able to pick and choose the right sort of husbands . . . men who are rich but whom they also love."

There was a sudden softness in her dark eyes which made Mr. Lawson think to himself that long before Kadine and her little sister Validé were grown up, their aunt would be married, or at least she would have had the opportunity of it not once but a hundred times.

He rose from his desk.

"If you will wait a few minutes, Miss Selincourt, I will draft a letter for you to write to your Publishers, and also a letter from myself to His Grace telling him to expect you."

"I will wait," Tamara said.

Mr. Lawson smiled at her and went to the outer office where there were several clerks sitting at their high desks, their white quill pens moving busily over the books and documents which proved Lawson, Cresey and Houghton one of the busiest Solicitors in the town.

Tamara rose from the chair in which she had been sitting and once again walked to the window.

She felt as if everything that had happened this morning was going round and round in her head in a manner which made it hard for her to think straight.

For one thing it was more of a blow than she was willing to express to Mr. Lawson to know that she must withdraw her novel.

She had had such high hopes of making quite a considerable sum of money from it, considering how much she had made with her first book.

That had been a very slim volume, but the Publishers had sent her several reviews which had been complimentary.

She thought that a novel might capture the imagination of the smart social world that had made a hero out of Sir Walter Scott and a great financial success of Lord Byron.

Hers combined adventure, villainy and a certain amount of romance in what she had thought was an agreeable mixture which should please almost everybody's taste.

Living so quietly in Cornwall, she had had little opportunity of meeting social celebrities.

But her imagination had been excited by the tales of the cruel, unpleasant Duke of Granchester who had ostracised his brother as his father had done before him.

Tamara had adored her brother-in-law, and every time she dipped her pen in the ink to write something scathing and vitrolic about the villain in her novel, she felt she was somehow paying back the Duke for his unkindness.

She had deliberately not shown Lord Ronald her manuscript before it went to the Publishers.

He was such a good-humoured, gentle person that she felt he might have protested against the picture she had drawn of his brother, even though there was no reason for him to defend any member of his family.

They had certainly treated him as if he were a pariah, an out-cast, and yet, though he often laughed about their various eccentricities, he had never been unkind.

"I cannot understand," Tamara's sister Maïka had once said to her, "how they could bear to lose Ronald. He is so charming, so kind and so sympathetic you would think he must have left a great void in his family which no-one else could fill."

"They are stiff-necked, autocratic and altogether contemptible!" Tamara had answered, but Maïka had merely laughed at her.

"I do not mind being outside the Castle gates," she answered. "It is just that sometimes I hate to think that Ronald cannot afford the horses he ought to ride, or the clothes he ought to wear, or be able to attend the races at Newmarket and Ascot."

"I have never seen anybody so happy as Ronald," Tamara answered. "It does not matter what clothes he wears down here, and I believe he is just as amused by racing the children on the sands as he would be watching a jockey come in first carrying his colours at Newmarket."

Her sister had kissed her.

"You are such a comfort to me, Tamara," she said. "Sometimes I feel it is wrong that I should have deprived Ronald of so much, but as far as I am concerned in him I had the whole world and Heaven in my arms."

Tamara had only to see her brother-in-law and sister together to know that Mr. Lawson was right when he said it would be impossible for two people to be happier than they were.

There seemed to be a light in their eyes when they looked at each other that held a radiance which was not of this world.

If Ronald had been away from her for a few hours Maïka would be waiting for him when he returned, to throw herself into his arms and pull his head down to hers.

They would kiss each other closely and passionately

as if they had only just fallen in love and the wonder of it was irresistible.

But now they were both gone and Tamara knew, as if it were a sacred trust, the children were in her care and there was no-one else to love them or to look after them except herself.

'Mr. Lawson is right,' she thought. 'The Duke must think of me as the children's Governess and as he will surely not wish to be bothered with finding anyone else, he will be content to keep me on in such a position.'

Mr. Lawson came back into the room.

"Here is the letter to your Publishers," he said. "It is quite brief and to the point, and I have asked if they will send the manuscript to this office. It will be safer here. If you left it lying about at Granchester Castle it might be uncomfortable for you."

Tamara turned and slowly walked to the desk and as he saw the expression on her face Mr. Lawson said:

"I am sorry. I know this represents for you a lot of wasted work, but it is really the only thing you can do."

As Tamara picked up a pen, he went on:

"You must write another book, and perhaps you will find something pleasant to write about at Granchester Castle—even its owner!"

"If wishes were horses, beggars might ride!" Tamara answered and laughed.

She signed the letter and put the big quill pen back in the pen-holder.

"I shall try to forget it," she said, "but I suppose every author feels when publishing a book that they have produced a baby. I cannot help mourning my poor little still-born child."

Mr. Lawson laughed but he said.

"That, Miss Selincourt, is the sort of remark you should certainly not make at Granchester Castle. It would undoubtedly shock the elderly Grant relations."

"I shall guard both my tongue and my pen," Tamara promised, "and my next manuscript will come here to you. You shall cut out every libellous word in it before it goes to the Publishers."

"I shall keep you to that promise." Mr. Lawson smiled. "I have no wish, Miss Selincourt, to have to defend you in court."

"And I have no wish to see the inside of a Debtors' Prison," Tamara replied.

"I will send this letter and the one to the Duke to-day," Mr. Lawson said, "and I will come over to the Manor the day after tomorrow to see if I can help you with your packing. By then I shall have made arrangements for your journey."

"You are very kind."

She put out both her hands towards him.

"I know that Ronald and my sister would want me to thank you for the friendship you have shown me and the children."

Mr. Lawson held both Tamara's hands very tightly. Then he said:

"You are being very brave, my dear. I only wish I could have had better news for you, but perhaps, who knows, it will all turn out for the best."

"If it is the best for the children, then I shall be content," Tamara said. "As far as I am concerned, if I am honest, I am apprehensive of what awaits us at Granchester Castle."

Riding back on the old horse which had served the family well for many seasons, Tamara felt the wind from the sea blowing on her face and thought she would always be homesick for the beauty of Cornwall.

She had come to live with her sister after their father died and found the wild beauty of the furthermost point of England so lovely and so unlike anything she had ever seen before that she had not missed the crowded, busy life she had left in Oxford.

She was just fifteen when her father, Conrad Selincourt died of a heart-attack.

She had looked after him during the last years when he had been alone without her mother and she was therefore older in her ways and in her outlook than most girls of her age.

She was also a great deal better educated.

Living at Oxford, the daughter of a Don, she had been acquainted with and listened to a great number of men as intelligent and cultured as her father.

Besides which she had studied and had access to fine Libraries ever since she was old enough to learn.

If Conrad Selincourt had given his daughters his brains, their mother had undoubtedly contributed their beauty.

It was not only Maïka's voice which had gained her a place in an Opera Company but also her beauty.

It had in fact been her teacher at Oxford who had secured her position and seen to it that she was given a salary which far exceeded what she might have expected as an amateur with no experience.

The Opera Company was not the usual impecunious company which toured from city to city, but was financed privately by a Committee of benevolent Music Lovers who thought it important that people outside London should have the opportunity to hear good music.

It was when they were performing at Oxford that one of the leading ladies was taken ill and Maïka had the chance to take her place.

She not only sang outstandingly well but she also looked so lovely that it was obvious to the Producer and the Manager that she was just the person to fill the gap in their company.

For the Duke of Granchester to speak of her as being "a common actress and little better than a prostitute" was a gross insult and completely inaccurate.

All the ladies in the Company were in fact models of virtue, and the Committee who watched very closely over the affairs of their performers would not have tolerated licence of any sort.

Maïka, who sang at places like Bath, Tunbridge Wells and some of the lesser cities, was as untouched and unaffected by what was spoken of as a loose theatrical life as if she were a closely chaperoned débutante.

Whenever she was not actually performing she returned home, and it was in her father's house at Oxford that Lord Ronald met her and fell immediately head-over-heels in love.

That he was not yet twenty-one was sufficient excuse for his father to deprecate such an early marriage.

But the Duke, in trying to break off the attachment, was so tactless and so unnecessarily unpleasant that it achieved the very effect he wished to avoid of precipitating Lord Ronald into marriage.

Faced with the ultimatum of "never speaking to that woman again," no young man with any spirit could have accepted it without besmirching his own honour and self-respect.

The Duke had stormed back to London and Lord Ronald had married Maïka the following month.

She finished her contract with the Opera Company, then as Lord Ronald had taken his final examinations they had left together to seek a place where they could live.

Because they found they both had a passion for the sea, it was obvious that their home must be at the seaside, and someone had told them that Cornwall was cheap.

They had gone there to find it, as Lord Ronald had said, the Eden they both desired and no Adam and Eve could have been happier.

The Manor was certainly very attractive, Tamara thought as she arrived home, and she felt a pang of distress to think that they must leave it as well as all the memories she had shared there with her sister and brother-in-law.

As the sounds of her horse's hoofs clattered outside the front door the children came running out.

Sándor was first, running to the horse's head and saying as he did so:

"I will take Firefly round to the stables, Aunt Tamara."

"You are very late, Aunt Tamara," Kadine said, while Validé who was five and who was always called Vava, standing at the top of the steps merely cried:

"I want my tea! You are late! I want my tea!"

"You shall have it in a moment, pet," Tamara said, picking her up in her arms. Then followed by Kadine she went into the kitchen.

There was an old woman there who helped in the house with the children and with everything else that was required.

"Ye're back, Miss Tamara," she said as Tamara entered carrying Vava in her arms.

"Yes, I am back, Lucy," Tamara answered. "Can we have tea? As Vava said I am late."

"They wouldn't eat without ye, Miss," Lucy answered, "even when I tells them there were hot scones and cream for ye all."

"It would have been greedy not to wait for you, Aunt Tamara," Kadine said.

At ten she already showed promise of a beauty which would undoubtedly make dozens of young men's hearts miss a beat once she was grown up.

Strangely enough, Tamara thought, none of the children had the dark red hair of their mother which had been a crowning glory handed down from their Hungarian grandmother.

They were all fair like their father, but Kadine and Vava had eyes with long dark lashes that made people look at them, then look again in astonishment.

Sándor's hair was more brown than gold, but he had his father's clear-cut features and was undoubtedly an extremely handsome little boy.

Looking at him when he came in from having taken the horse to the stables, Tamara thought how closely he resembled his father and wondered if there was also a resemblance to his uncle.

In which case, if the Duke of Granchester was

outstandingly handsome, the portrait of him in her novel had been incorrect.

It was impossible for her to allow the villain to be too good-looking. He had to have a sardonic, cynical expression which proclaimed his wickedness at first sight.

'Anyway, I shall soon be able to judge for myself what he really looks like,' Tamara thought.

She felt her heart sink at the news she had to tell the children as soon as tea was finished.

CHAPTER TWO

*T*amara had not realised there were so many people to whom she would have to say good-bye.

As soon as it was learnt locally that she and the children were leaving the Manor, the friends they had made over the years called hourly to bid them "Godspeed."

There were a few local dignitaries from the County, but the majority were fisher-folk, farmers and villagers, who all expressed with deep sincerity how sad it was to see them go.

Over and over again as the visitors said something touching about her sister and Lord Ronald, Tamara felt the tears gather in her eyes and, when finally they were driven away from the Manor by Mr. Lawson in the gig pulled by their old horse, she could barely get a last glimpse of it through her tears.

Mr. Lawson had arranged that he would drive them

into Truro in their own conveyance, and from there they would take a stagecoach to carry them on the first stage of their journey to Granchester Castle in Gloucestershire.

As they set off the children were excited at the thought of travelling and Vava did not understand that they were leaving the place that had been their home all their lives.

They had, Tamara thought, an enormous amount of luggage, not only because she had added her sister's clothes to her own, but also because she could not bear to leave behind many little objects she had known ever since she had lived in her brother-in-law's house.

There were snuff-boxes, not of any particular value, but which he had treasured; there was a work-basket belonging to her sister, and there were pieces of embroidery that they had done together.

There were even things like a very special shell the children had picked up on the sea-shore and a flag that had floated behind Lord Ronald's first boat, all mementoes of happiness.

Because she realised that in the future she was going to be very poor, and any money she had must be kept for the children in case the Duke was not as generous as Mr. Lawson hoped, she was determined to spend as little as possible on herself.

She therefore did not buy mourning and, while Sándor wore a black armband, she and the girls only added black sashes to their ordinary gowns and black ribbons to their bonnets.

Actually, with her red hair and the children's fair curls, black was exceedingly becoming and threw into prominence the clearness of their skins.

But Tamara was at the moment not concerned about her appearance although she was quite well aware that before she reached the Castle she must, as a Governess, make every effort to look subdued and perhaps dowdy.

As they drove along in the gig, Mr. Lawson tried to cheer them all up with stories that he had heard of the magnificence of Granchester Castle, and also of Granchester House in London.

"Of course the Duke is often in waiting on the King," he said, "although I cannot believe that he approves of the raffish life His Majesty enjoyed when he was the Prince of Wales."

Tamara did not answer.

For the moment she only felt the idea of meeting the Duke hanging over her like a menacing cloud.

She had hated him for the manner in which he had treated her brother-in-law and she now hated him on her own account because in a way he had been instrumental in preventing her novel from being published.

'I must write another book,' she thought.

But for the moment her mind was blank. All she could think of was the misery of leaving behind everything that was familiar and the happiness which had made her and her sister so close to each other.

The day before they left, despite the thousands of things there were to be done, Tamara had gone to the Church-yard to say a last farewell to her brother-in-law and Maïka.

Their bodies had never been found, but she had arranged with the Vicar for a plaque to their memory to be set in a special place in the Chancel.

She had asked Lucy and other women in the village who had loved them to see there were always flowers in front of it, both summer and winter.

They had promised her they would do this, and Tamara knelt in the pew where they had sat every Sunday and prayed that she would not fail her sister's trust in looking after her children.

"You must help me, Maïka," she said. "It is not going to be easy for them to remember all the things that you taught them about kindness, sympathy and understanding."

She had the feeling as she prayed that those virtues were very unlikely to be found at Granchester Castle.

When she went back to the Manor it was to find

Sándor almost in tears because he had only just realised that his pony would not be able to go with them.

"He will be well looked after, Sándor," she told him,
"and there will be plenty of horses for you to ride at
the Castle."

"I want my own Rufus," Sándor answered. "You
know, Aunt Tamara, I have had him ever since he was
a foal."

"I know, dearest," Tamara answered, "but I promise
you he will be well looked after in the home Mr. Lawson has found for him."

As Sándor still looked so depressed she said:

"Perhaps later we could ask your uncle if we could
buy him back for you."

"Do you think he would agree to that?" Sándor
asked, a new light in his eyes.

"We can but try," Tamara answered.

But as she spoke she could not help thinking that if
the stories of the Duke's stables were true he would
hardly want a not very outstanding or well-bred pony
among his pedigree stock.

There were many other crises, such as when Vava
brought in a whole collection of stones from some secret place in the garden which she insisted must be
included in the luggage.

And Kadine wished to take a new litter of kittens, all
six of them, because she said there would be no-one to
look after them properly once they had gone.

Finally they had set off, and now as they neared
Truro Tamara knew they must say good-bye to their
last friend in the person of Mr. Lawson.

They drew up outside the Coaching Inn, and while
they were standing rather forlornly waiting for Mr.
Lawson to arrange for the luggage to be put on the
roof of the coach Tamara gave a sudden cry.

"Look children," she exclaimed. "There is Erth Veryon!"

They looked in the direction in which she pointed
then ran across the street to where a tall man with

349

white hair was walking hand-in-hand with a boy of about sixteen.

As they reached him Tamara said:

"Erth, it is good to see you, and I am so glad we are not leaving Cornwall without saying good-bye to you."

The man, who was about fifty years of age, put out his hand and Tamara lay her fingers into it.

He was blind, but he had a smooth unwrinkled face with a remarkable expression of an inner spirituality.

"You are leaving Cornwall, Miss Tamara?" he asked.

"You recognised my voice," Tamara smiled.

"I never forget a voice," Erth Veryon replied.

"And do you remember mine?" Kadine asked.

"It is Miss Kadine!"

"And me? You remember me?" Vava questioned.

"Little Miss Vava!"

"I am here too," Sándor said. "How are you, Erth?"

"Very well, thank you, Master Sándor, and if you are setting off on your travels, I am also setting off on mine."

"Where are you going?" Tamara asked.

"I shall go where the Lord directs me."

"If He directs you to Gloucester, please come and call on us," Tamara begged. "We shall be at Granchester Castle. To see you, Erth, would be like meeting a little bit of Cornwall in a foreign land."

There was a note in her voice which made the blind man reach out again to take her hand.

"You are unhappy and worried," he said.

"Yes," she answered. "I have to take the children to live with their uncle the Duke of Granchester, and as you can guess, if it were possible, we would much rather stay here."

"I heard of Lord Ronald's death," Erth said, "and that of your sister. It was sad, very sad for you; but, you know, they are together with God."

"I hope so," Tamara said with a little quiver in her voice.

"You can believe it because it is true," Erth said in his

deep Cornish voice. "But you are not only grieving for them. Something else is disturbing you."

Tamara did not think it strange or uncanny that he was so perceptive.

She had known him ever since she had lived in Cornwall and she had seen him heal her brother-in-law's broken ankle so that the doctor had been amazed that Lord Ronald was so quickly on his feet.

Erth Veryon had also healed a child in their village who had been so ill that everyone was sure he would die, and an old woman whose relatives had given her up for dead.

Holding his hand now she felt as if some vibration passed from him into her own body, and after a moment he said:

"You have hate in your heart. It will poison you. Replace it, child, with love; for only through love can you find happiness."

Tamara drew in her breath.

She might have expected that Erth would know what she was feeling. At the same time he was asking the impossible.

"You must try," he said as if she had answered him aloud. "Try to give love, then you will receive it. That is what God has promised us, and we can believe Him."

When Tamara would have answered, she heard Mr. Lawson call her from the other side of the road.

"I must go," she said. "Come and see us if ever you can, Erth."

She took her hand from his, fumbled in her handbag, found a half-sovereign and pressed it into the hand of Erth's grandson who was his constant companion.

As she did so she put a finger to her lips so that the boy would not thank her. Erth would never take money for his services and in consequence would often go hungry.

His grandson smiled at her and the Healer was not

aware of what was happening because the children were clamouring for his attention.

"Good-bye, Erth! Good-bye!" they cried.

"Trust in God," he said to them, "and He will deliver you safely to your destination."

"We will," Kadine replied.

Then they were running across the road to Mr. Lawson.

Tamara joined them and the Solicitor hurried them into the Stage-Coach.

He had procured the best seats facing the horses for Tamara and the two girls and a place on the box with the other men for Sándor, where he much preferred to travel.

"Write to me . . . please write to me," Tamara said as she said good-bye.

"You know I will do that and I shall be waiting to hear from you."

"If it is too frightful," Tamara said in a low voice, "we shall all come back and camp in your garden or shelter in a cave on the beach."

Mr. Lawson laughed but Tamara knew he was really unhappy to see them all go.

Fortunately there was little time for long farewells as the Guard of the Stage-Coach was hurrying everyone into their places, and almost before the door was shut the horses began to move off.

The girls hung out of the window waving and shouting good-bye, but Tamara sat back in the corner of the seat and shut her eyes to prevent the tears over-flowing and running down her cheeks.

'This is really good-bye,' she thought, 'good-bye to the old life and Heaven knows what lies ahead in the new one.'

It was a very long and tiring journey to Gloucester. They stayed every night at a wayside Inn and changed frequently from one Stage-Coach to another, each time with the worry of transporting their baggage and making quite sure nothing was left behind.

Tamara grew used to the surliness of porters who disliked Stage-Coaches because the passengers seldom gave large tips, and the indifference of Inn-keepers who set aside the worst rooms and the most inedible meals for those who travelled cheaply.

To the children it was an adventure.

Only on the last day, when after being held up because of an accident on the road their coach was over three hours late, did Vava become fretful and Kadine too sleepy to take an interest in anything.

It was with a sense of apprehension that Tamara realised they would not reach the small town of Tetbury until nearly seven o'clock.

This meant, she thought, that by the time they arrived at the Castle the Duke would doubtless be at dinner, and if they interrupted his meal it would immediately start them off on the wrong foot.

She had hoped that at Tetbury there might be a carriage from the Castle to carry them the last five miles.

She had learnt from Mr. Lawson that he had not exactly asked that they should be met at Tetbury but he had informed the Duke that they would arrive there during the afternoon.

But when the Stage-Coach stopped at the rather inadequate Inn there was no sign of a private carriage, and when Tamara enquired she was told there was no-one there from the Castle.

She then had some difficulty in obtaining the hire of a chaise.

Only because the Duke's name obviously galvanised the Inn-keeper into some sort of action did he finally produce a very old vehicle drawn by an equally ancient horse.

The luggage was piled on the roof and Tamara and the children sat inside.

There was the smell of hay, old decaying leather and horse-flesh. When they set off and when the horse moved so slowly Tamara could not help thinking that he and the driver were half-asleep.

Finally after what seemed hours on the dusty road their conveyance turned in through a pair of enormous wrought-iron gates with stone lodges on each side of them.

The last part of the journey was down a most impressive drive, flanked on either side with ancient oak-trees.

"Now we shall see the Castle!" Tamara cried with what she hoped was a gay note in her voice even though her heart felt heavy.

But only Sándor seemed interested, for the two little girls were too tired to care.

Quickly Tamara tidied their hair and straightened their bonnets, and tried to smooth the creases out of their white frocks.

She herself had spent more time than usual, on rising, in re-arranging her hair in a different style from what she had ever worn before.

She had in fact pulled it back straight from her forehead and pinned it into a bun at the back of her head.

"I must look plain and insignificant," she told herself.

However when she looked into the mirror she thought with dissatisfaction that her eyes were far too large and her lips too curved for her to look in any way an ordinary Governess.

She had chosen the very plainest of her gowns. It was a green crêpe for, as she was not supposed to be a relation, she would not be expected to wear mourning.

Tamara and Maïka had always made their own clothes and they were extremely skilful needle-women.

But Maïka had also some very lovely gowns which Lord Ronald had bought for her as presents, because he loved to see his wife looking beautiful even though she had so small an audience to admire her.

Tamara thought it was unlikely she would ever have occasion to wear the exquisite evening-gowns that her sister had possessed or the special ones that she used to wear on Sundays when she went to Church and when occasionally they entertained friends in the neighbourhood.

'When I have time,' Tamara thought looking at her own wardrobe, 'I shall make myself some severe garments in drab colours that will make me as anonymous as I wish to be.'

She was well aware that her own dresses made of light muslin or those she had copied from 'The Ladies Journal' with embroidery and small frills of lace were most unsuitable for her present position.

There had not been time after Mr. Lawson had told her they were to leave the Manor to alter anything, and the green gown which made Tamara's skin look almost dazzlingly white was in fact the plainest frock she possessed.

Even so, it could not conceal the perfection of her figure, the tininess of her waist or the soft curves of her breasts.

She changed the ribbons on her bonnet from black to green, then half-regretted that she had not left them as they were.

Then she told herself that whatever she wore it was unlikely that the Duke would condescend to notice anything so lowly as a Governess, and all she had to do was to keep in the background and be as unobtrusive as possible.

They were drawing nearer to the Castle and now Tamara could see how enormous it was.

Lord Ronald had told her that it had originally been Norman, but had been altered and built on to all through the centuries until it was a pot-pourri of many different architectural styles.

"My grandfather spent a fortune in adding new and very impressive State-Rooms," Lord Ronald said, "but he also built up the old Norman tower, repaired the

Elizabethan wings and improved on the interior decorations which were made at the time of Queen Anne."

From the way her brother-in-law spoke Tamara had known that Lord Ronald loved the Castle, even though she sensed that his childhood there had not been a particularly happy one.

He never disparaged his parents, but both Maïka and Tamara were aware that they had been an austere couple who found children a nuisance and left them, where possible, in the care of servants.

"I often think that Ronald gives his own children the love he missed when he was a child," Maïka said once.

And there was no doubt that from the time Sándor was born Lord Ronald had been content to spend hours every day with the small replica of himself.

But later, Tamara thought, he loved his daughters best, while Maïka made no pretence of not putting her son first in her affection.

"He is so like you, darling," she heard her sister say once to Lord Ronald, "and how could I help loving to distraction your son simply because he is yours?"

'I must try and make up to the children for what they have lost,' Tamara thought now.

At the same time the Castle was so huge and overwhelming that she almost felt as if it came between her and her nephew and nieces and they were being separated by the very magnificence of it.

"It is very big and very old!" Sándor said as they drew up at the front door. "It ought to be filled with Knights, and there should be jousting."

Tamara was pleased that it excited his imagination, while as far as she was concerned, she could only think that it was oppressively large. She would have given everything she possessed in the whole world to turn round and go back to the cosy comfort of the Manor.

The carriage door was opened by a footman with powdered hair and she noticed that he was wearing the black and yellow livery that she had described in her novel.

Holding Vava by the hand she walked up the steps to find an elderly white-haired Butler looking at them in surprise.

"You have an appointment with His Grace, Madam?" he asked.

"His Grace is expecting us," Tamara answered. "Will you inform him that his nephew and nieces have arrived?"

"His nephew and nieces?"

There was no mistaking the astonishment in the Butler's voice.

"That is what I said," Tamara replied.

She moved into the centre of the huge marble-floored Hall which had a curved staircase rising on one side of it and on the other a great mediaeval fireplace.

"I think, Madam," the Butler said in a respectful voice, "there may be some mistake. You are aware that this is the home of the Duke of Granchester?"

"I am aware of that," Tamara answered, "and as I have already told you, this is the Duke's nephew, Master Sándor Grant and his nieces, Miss Kadine and Miss Validé."

The Butler was obviously thrown into confusion by the information, but he said after a perceptible pause:

"His Grace is at dinner, Madam, but I will inform him of your arrival. Will you wait here?"

He opened a door at the far end of the Hall, showed them into a Sitting-Room, then still with a look of surprise on his face he left, closing the door behind him.

"I am tired! I want a drink!" Vava said.

"I know you do, dearest," Tamara answered, "but you will have to wait until you have seen your Uncle Howard."

"Is that what we call him?" Sándor asked, turning from his inspection of a collection of miniatures which covered a table.

"Yes . . . Uncle Howard," Tamara answered.

She lowered her voice.

357

"And do not forget, children, to call me Miss Wynne."

They had been practising all the days of their journey, but Tamara knew that when Vava was tired it would be difficult for her not to say 'Aunt Tamara.'

"I will remember," Kadine said.

"Do you think Uncle Howard will be glad to see us?" Sándor asked.

Judging from the reception so far, Tamara thought, it was rather unlikely, but aloud she said:

"Of course he will, and you must remember that he is Dadda's brother and Dadda would want you to be very nice and polite to him."

"I want Mumma," Vava said. "I do not want to stay here, I want to go home to Mumma!"

Tamara put her arms round the child and drew her close.

Vava was very tired. The journey had been tiring for all of them, but most especially for a child of only five, who wanted to run and jump and not sit cooped up all day in the heat and restriction of a Stage-Coach.

Sometimes they had been fortunate in having it half-empty, but at other times it had been packed and most of the passengers disliked having the windows down, with the result that they felt almost as if they were being suffocated.

"As soon as we have met your uncle," Tamara said to Vava, "I will pop you into bed and bring you a lovely drink. While you are drinking it I will tell you a story."

This promise usually worked like magic, but Vava was too tired to listen.

To make her more comfortable Tamara took off her bonnet, tidied her hair, then held her close in her arms. The child was almost half-asleep when the door opened.

Tamara had expected the Duke to look impressive, but what she had not anticipated was that he should be not only the most magnificent man she had ever seen but also the most handsome.

Lord Ronald had been exceedingly good-looking and the Grant features had been passed to Sándor.

But combined with being over six-foot-three inches tall, broad-shouldered and carrying himself as if he commanded the whole world, the Duke had classical features.

But he had also a cynical and bored look which gave his face an almost sardonic expression.

'He *is* like the villain in my book!' Tamara thought.

Then at the hard look in his eyes as they met hers she felt her heart beat apprehensively as she rose to her feet.

She had thought Lord Ronald looked elegant and smart when he wore evening-clothes, but the Duke dressed for the evening was overwhelming.

Never had she imagined that a man could wear such a dazzlingly white cravat so intricately tied, that his satin evening-coat could fit him as if he were moulded into it, or his knee-breeches and silk stockings give him such a distinguished air.

With an effort she dropped him a low curtsey.

"Who are you and what are you doing here?" the Duke asked.

"You have not received a letter from Mr. Lawson, the Solicitor?"

"A letter?" the Duke queried. "I have heard from no-one, except from the servants who tell me these children are my relatives."

Tamara drew in her breath.

Because the Duke spoke in such a cold, authoritative voice, she felt anger beginning to replace her fear.

"Then Your Grace cannot be aware that your brother Lord Ronald is dead," she replied.

"Dead? Why was I not informed?"

"You should have received a letter telling you of the tragedy two or three days ago."

The Duke was frowning as he came further into the room to walk to the fireplace and stand with his back to it.

"Kindly tell me what happened," he ordered.

"Lord Ronald and his wife were recently drowned at sea, and as there is nowhere else they can go I have brought their children, your nephew and two nieces to you."

Tamara spoke slowly and clearly, her eyes on the Duke's face.

"And who are you?"

"My name is Wynne, Your Grace. I am Governess to the children."

He gave her what she thought was a hostile glance, then he said:

"Surely my brother made some provision for his family?"

"I am afraid not, Your Grace, and as there was nowhere else they could go and they have no money, Mr. Lawson, Lord Ronald's Solicitor, asked me to bring them here to you."

"The devil he did!" the Duke ejaculated. "And what am I supposed to do about them?"

Tamara felt her temper rising.

"I imagine, Your Grace, you will hardly allow them to starve or to be dependent upon charity."

There was a glint in the Duke's eyes as if he resented her tone. Then he turned to look at Sándor who was watching him with curiosity.

"What is your name, boy?"

"Sándor, Uncle Howard."

"How old are you?"

"Nearly twelve."

The Duke looked at Kadine and Tamara thought he must realise how pretty she was with her fair hair and her blacklashed eyes.

Before he could speak Kadine, who was never shy with grown-ups, said:

"You are like my Dadda, only taller. He told me when you were little boys you used to climb to the top of the Castle tower. Can we do that?"

"What is your name?" the Duke enquired.

"Kadine."

"And this is Validé," Tamara said quickly, "only she is always known as Vava which is what she called herself as a baby."

"All extremely theatrical names," the Duke remarked, and Tamara knew he was sneering at her dead sister.

She felt herself quiver with rage but managed to say in a cold, restrained voice:

"As we have travelled for three days, Your Grace, the children are very tired. I think it would be best if I put them to bed and other matters can be discussed later."

"So you intend to stay here," the Duke said.

"Are you suggesting we should go anywhere else?" Tamara enquired.

She thought as she spoke that her hostility was too obvious, but she was hating him as she had expected to do.

She hated his superiority, the way he sneered at the children's names which she felt was a direct insult to her sister, and the manner in which he seemed to be deliberately making them feel uncomfortable and unwanted.

"I suppose there is nothing else to be done to-night, at any rate," he conceded.

"I am tired," Vava wailed suddenly. "I want a drink."

"I am sure that is something, dearest, you will be able to have in a few moments," Tamara answered.

As she spoke she looked at the Duke almost as if she challenged him.

He stared back at her and she thought the lines of cynicism on his face were even more pronounced than when he had first come into the room.

The door opened.

"You rang, Your Grace?"

"Take these children and their Governess to Mrs. Henderson. Inform her that they will be staying in the Castle."

361

"Yes, Your Grace."

Without saying any more the Duke turned and walked from the room.

Tamara stared after him, wishing there was some way in which she could hurt him, some way in which she could express the violence of her hatred.

Instead she could do nothing but follow the footman who led them upstairs to the second floor.

Here they waited for some minutes while the Housekeeper was fetched from a different part of the Castle by a maid-servant.

When she arrived, obviously annoyed at being disturbed so late in the evening, Tamara saw she was an elderly woman dressed in the rustling black of her calling with a silver chatelaine hanging from her waist.

"Am I right in understanding that you are the Governess to His Grace's nephew and nieces?" she asked Tamara.

"I am," Tamara answered. "My name is Wynne, and I am very glad to meet you, Mrs. Henderson."

The Housekeeper barely touched her fingers.

"It is an extremely inconvenient time of night to arrive and as you were not expected naturally no rooms have been prepared for you."

"The posts must be blamed on that account," Tamara explained. "A letter was sent to His Grace over a week ago."

"From where, may I ask?"

"From Cornwall."

"Oh, Cornwall!"

Mrs. Henderson's intonation of the word could not have been more disparaging had Tamara said it was from hell itself.

"Well, you are here," she said after a moment's pause, "and I suppose I shall have to do something about it. And it must obviously be the Nurseries."

Tamara did not answer but followed the Housekeeper up another long flight of stairs to the third floor of the Castle.

Here were the Nurseries which she realised as they opened the first door, had obviously not been used for many years.

Closed windows had left them smelling stale and airless, and the fact that the floor had not been brushed or the furniture dusted for some time was very obvious when the candles were lit.

Tamara longed to suggest that there must be other rooms in the Castle that were more habitable, but she thought it really was too late in the evening to enter into any arguments.

The only thing that really mattered was to get Vava to bed for by this time she was almost asleep on her feet.

"I would like some supper for the children, if you please, Mrs. Henderson," Tamara said. "Miss Kadine and Miss Vava usually drink milk, but Master Sándor prefers lemonade."

"I doubt if the Chef has any lemonade ready," Mrs. Henderson replied, "and I cannot imagine what there will be for you to eat."

"Something light, eggs, or soup will do," Tamara said. "I think they are too tired to feel hungry."

"I'll see what can be done," Mrs. Henderson said, "and the house-maids will make up the beds."

She went from the Nursery and Tamara hurried to open the window, then looked around her in dismay.

It must have been years since there had been any painting or decorating on the walls and the furniture was shabby.

She had the feeling that, if once it had been a pleasant, cosy nursery for children, the atmosphere had certainly changed in the years it had lain empty.

The Night-Nurseries were very sparsely furnished, and even when two rather sullen house-maids had made up the beds the rooms seemed to have almost a charity-like austerity.

"I will not be depressed about it," Tamara said to

herself. "I am sure by to-morrow things will seem better."

The supper that was finally, after a long wait, brought upstairs did nothing to relieve her depression.

It was obvious that nothing could be cooked so late at night. There were some pieces of very dry-looking cold chicken on a plate, half a loaf of bread, a pat of butter, a jug of milk and one of water.

The servant who brought it plonked it on its tray down on a table and disappeared before Tamara could ask for a tablecloth.

Vava was far too tired even to want the milk. Tamara put her straight into bed and she was asleep as her head touched the pillow.

"This is a jolly rotten supper," Sándor remarked.

Tamara agreed with him, but thought it best not to say so.

"They were not expecting us and we are causing a lot of work late at night, so we cannot be particular."

"There is no salt," Sándor said.

"Never mind," Tamara answered. "This is just a picnic and people always forget things on a picnic."

Kadine was too tired to fancy cold chicken, but Tamara managed to persuade her to eat a very thin slice of bread and butter and drink some milk. Then she too went to bed.

"My room is much smaller than the one I had at home," Sándor said. "I expected to have a big room in such a huge Castle."

"We will see if we can find you a better one to-morrow," Tamara answered.

"Shall I ask Uncle Howard if I can ride his horses?" Sándor enquired.

"We will ask him at the first opportunity," Tamara promised.

But she could not help thinking that if this was a sample of the hospitality they were to receive at the Castle any concession might be hard to obtain.

But there was no point in arguing about things

to-night, and when their luggage was brought up by the footmen she took out only the night clothes they needed, deciding to leave all the rest of the unpacking until the following day.

She too was tired, but when she got into bed she found it difficult to sleep.

Instead she lay awake hating the Duke, and yet at the same time acknowledging that he was without exception the most impressive man she had ever seen in her life.

'He is just as a Duke should look,' she thought, and the description of him in her novel was rather apt.

The fictitious Duke had been called Ullester, and although his villainy had projected itself in the expression on his face he used his physical attractions like his rank, to further his nefarious ends.

'I wish Mr. Lawson had not made me withdraw the book from publication,' Tamara thought. 'I am quite certain that this Duke would not read novels and if he did, he would be far too conceited to recognize himself.'

Yet from what she had seen already of the Castle, her descriptions had been surprisingly accurate and combined with the servants' liveries and other details in the tale, there was an uncomfortable resemblance to the truth.

The hero, the Duke's brother, Lord Tristan, was everything a hero should be—kind, generous, bighearted, a champion of the down-trodden and a protector of the poor.

When he wished to marry the entrancingly lovely heroine with a face like an angel, the wicked Duke had forbidden the marriage and threatened all sorts of dreadful vengeance and penalties if his brother should disobey his command.

What was more, he persecuted the heroine's family, turning her father out of his house with the result that her mother died of privation and her sisters and brothers came to the verge of starvation.

Needless to say, the Duke's accidental death and his brother's inheritance of the title brought the novel to a happy conclusion.

"I will change the description of the Castle and the liveries," Tamara decided. "I can make the Duke the hero's cousin rather than his brother, then I can publish the book, with a differnt title."

It was a pity because she thought "The Ducal Wasp" was an amusing and provocative name.

At the same time, if the children had to live under his roof it would be a mistake for the Duke to be made more incensed than he was already.

It was long after midnight before finally she ceased thinking of the changes she could make to her novel.

She fell asleep, only to dream that the Duke of Granchester was tearing the pages from her book and throwing them out from the tower up which they were all climbing to reach him.

"I hate you . . . I hate you . . ." Tamara was calling out in her dream.

CHAPTER THREE

*T*amara awoke with a start and jumped out of bed.

She pulled back the curtains and as the sunlight flooded in she told herself that to-day would be better. Things would be brighter both for herself and the children.

The Nurseries looked out at the back of the Castle

and she could see flower-gardens which were a kalei-doscope of colour, walls of Tudor red brick and woods which rose dark green and mysterious to the skyline.

It was very beautiful and Tamara felt her spirits rise.

'There will be lots of places to explore and the children will love that,' she thought to herself. 'I will ask the Duke if they can ride, and perhaps I can go with them.'

Her eyes shone at the thought of riding really fine horses.

There had been friends of her father's at Oxford who had often allowed her to exercise their horses in the summer when they were unable to hunt.

She knew that she rode well and that if she had a choice she would rather ride than take any other form of exercise.

But she had the uncomfortable feeling that the Duke would perhaps expect his grooms to accompany the children and she would be left behind.

"I will explain," she told herself, "that I have been giving Vava lessons; then surely he will not refuse me?"

With a little grimace she told herself that the Duke could do anything he wished to do, and it was doubtful if anyone could persuade him to agree to anything that did not concur with his own selfish interests.

Determined not to let anything depress her, Tamara dressed then woke the children.

Sándor was up already and when she appeared he asked:

"May I go downstairs and explore before breakfast, Aunt Tama . . . I mean Miss Wynne? I can see some deer under the trees in the Park and I want to get a closer look at them."

"Yes, of course, you may," Tamara agreed, "but do not be late for breakfast. I expect they will bring it up at about half-past-eight."

But that, unfortunately, was wishful thinking.

At ten-minutes-to-nine Tamara rang the bell and

when a housemaid appeared she asked if they could have their breakfast.

"Breakfast, Miss?" the housemaid repeated as if it was a meal she had never heard of. "I don't think Mrs. Henderson gave orders for any to be brought up-stairs."

"Well, we can go downstairs, if that is more conve-nient," Tamara answered, "but we would like it as soon as possible. We are all rather hungry after such a small supper last night."

The maid disappeared and it was nearly half-an-hour later before she came back with a tray.

She set it down on the table with a thump and looked surprised when Tamara asked her to fetch a table-cloth.

On a dish which was uncovered there were four poached eggs which were already cold, reposing on some plain untoasted pieces of bread. There was also a loaf of bread on the tray, butter and a pot of plum jam, which all the children disliked.

There was a large pot of very strong tea and a small jug of milk.

The plates for the eggs had, Tamara felt sure, never been heated and once again there was no salt or pep-per and only three cups and saucers.

She asked the maid to fetch some more milk, an-other cup and salt.

It was so long in coming that when it did arrive the children had eaten what they could of the very unap-petising breakfast and were longing to go out into the sunshine.

"I do not like my egg cold," Vava said fretfully.

"Nor do any of us," Tamara agreed. "I will speak to Mrs. Henderson and see if something better cannot be arranged for to-morrow morning."

She felt, however it was important for her first to see the Duke.

She felt there would be many questions he would

wish to ask regarding his brother and even more about the children, but she was not sent for.

When she finally enquired of a footman whether the Duke wished to see her she was informed that he had gone out early in the morning and would not be back until just before dinner.

This at least left them free to explore the gardens and the stables where Sándor went into ecstasies over the horses and Vava begged to be lifted up onto one.

The Head Groom, who seemed to be the only pleasant servant they had met so far, answered Vava's pleadings by leading her around the stable-yard on a horse that was just going out for exercise.

When Tamara explained that they were Lord Ronald's children he became very interested in them.

"Oi remembers Lord Ronald—a fine rider His Lordship were," he said. "Fearless, and would ride anythin' however wild. Oi can see the young gentleman has the very look of him."

"I would like to have the chance to show that I can ride as well as my father," Sándor said.

"Ye must talk to 'is Grace, young Sir," the groom replied, "and p'raps he'll be buying a pony for th' young ladies."

He looked at Tamara enquiringly as he spoke and she smiled.

"We are hoping that," she answered, "and I think you will find that Miss Vava is also as fearless as Lord Ronald."

Vava in fact disgraced herself by screaming and yelling when she was taken down from the horse's back.

"I want to go riding!" she kept crying.

Only the suggestion that they would go and look for fish in the lake prevented her from running after the grooms when they set out to exercise the horses.

"I wish I could go with them," Sándor said wistfully.

"We must ask your uncle first," Tamara replied.

There was so much to see however that the children

enjoyed every moment of the morning until they went back to the Castle for luncheon.

Tamara had asked to see Mrs. Henderson before they went out, but was told she was busy. When she asked for her now the Housekeeper came up to the Nursery with what Tamara knew was an unco-operative expression on her face.

"I am afraid there was not enough breakfast for the children," Tamara said, "and as the eggs were left uncovered they were quite cold by the time they reached here."

"That's not my business, Miss Wynne," Mrs. Henderson replied coldly. "I told the Chef you required breakfast, as I've told him you'll require luncheon. The menus are left to him as His Grace entrusts him with the food that's required for the Dining-Room."

"I do appreciate that it is a long way for everything to be brought," Tamara said, "but surely there are other rooms in the Castle which are more accessible?"

"There are many rooms in the Castle, Miss Wynne," Mrs. Henderson replied, "but they are certainly not suitable for children!"

"I think you will find that these children are not destructive in any way," Tamara said.

She gave the Housekeeper what she hoped was an ingratiating smile as she went on:

"They have been so much with their parents and in fact always used the best rooms at home, so they appreciate fine things and can be trusted with them."

It was true, she thought, that Lord Ronald and his wife had loved their children so much that only the best was good enough for them.

At the Manor the children had occupied the bedrooms which other people would have kept for guests, and when they were not with their parents they had what was called 'The Nursery'.

This was on the ground floor and one of the most charming and well-furnished Sitting-rooms in the whole house.

Mrs. Henderson, as though she had nothing more to say was moving away when Tamara said:

"Will the housemaids be coming up to clean these rooms to-day? I am sure you will appreciate that having been shut up for so long they are somewhat dusty."

"I am afraid my girls are too busy," Mrs. Henderson replied. "Perhaps later in the week they may have an hour or two to spare, but for the moment I cannot promise you any assistance, Miss Wynne, in keeping these rooms clean."

She stalked away and Tamara knew that she was resenting the children simply because it meant extra work and the disruption of what she was quite sure was a lazy way of life.

"It is what might be expected of the servants of a man like the Duke," she told herself angrily.

She went back to the Nursery to make their beds while waiting for luncheon which was again over half-an-hour late.

This time it was quite inedible. There was a piece of mutton that was so badly cooked that the children could not get their teeth into it and it was again cold when it reached them.

There were no vegetables, only a dish of over-cooked potatoes, and half a heavy and unappetising suet pudding with no custard or treacle to go with it.

The food at the Manor had always been plain but extremely well cooked either by Maïka or Tamara, or by Lucy, whom they had taught to be nearly as good a cook as they were themselves.

Because Maïka could not bear her husband to suffer in any way because he had married her she would devise for him the most delicious continental dishes which she had been taught by her mother.

In the evening the three of them used to eat meals that Lord Ronald said were unequalled by anything he had ever tasted before.

While it was not good for the children to have the

rich sauces which their father enjoyed, everything they ate was not only beneficial but also delicious.

Lord Ronald would grow special vegetables and fruit in the garden which they had learnt to appreciate and Tamara knew that not only would they miss these but their absence must affect their health.

"I cannot eat this," Sándor said after he had struggled manfully to cut up the mutton and failed.

"Nor can I," Tamara said helplessly.

"I am hungry!" Vava wailed. "I am hungry!"

"I will see your uncle and maybe everything will be better to-morrow," Tamara promised.

She thought as she spoke it was not going to be easy and she had the feeling that the Duke's attitude towards them of indifference and lack of attention was only being echoed by his servants.

"Let's go into the garden and pick some peaches," Sándor suggested as he pushed aside the suet pudding. "I saw dozens of them when I was exploring this morning."

Although Tamara thought perhaps that would be a mistake, the mere fact that his suggestion cheered up Kadine and Vava made her agree somewhat weakly to follow him into the kitchen-garden.

She expected they would find a gardener there whom she could ask if they could have some fruit, but there seemed to be no-one about and Sándor disappeared into the peach-house.

He came back with four huge peaches, all ripe and so juicy and delicious that Tamara forgot her scruples and enjoyed them as much as the children.

In another house they found grapes, huge purple muscats, and they cut off a bunch and ate them.

Then wandering round the garden they discovered greengages and nectarines, and rows of raspberries in a cage made of netting so that the birds could not get at them.

"We shall all have tummy-aches if we eat any more

fruit," Tamara warned. "Suppose we pick the raspberries and take them back for supper?"

"Let us ask for some cream to go with them," Kadine cried. "You know how Dadda always said raspberries and cream were his favourite fruit."

"Mumma liked peaches best," Sándor said.

"I want another peach," Vava said greedily, but Tamara said firmly that she had had enough.

She noted however as they walked back through the garden that there were plenty of peas ready to pick and every other sort of vegetable, including crisp lettuces.

"Cut one of those," she told Sándor, "and if nothing nice is sent up for tea I will make you some lettuce sandwiches."

The children liked these and Sándor cut two lettuces with his pen-knife. They also pulled some radishes which they found in another neat row to take back to the house.

It was certainly not a very substantial meal, but at least it was better than feeling the pangs of hunger, and when teatime came and, as Tamara had expected, the only thing that was brought upstairs was the inevitable loaf of bread, and plum jam, she made the children lettuce sandwiches.

They ate the radishes with them and although they missed the dainty cakes, the scones and all the other delicacies they would have enjoyed at home, they did not complain.

The raspberries, which had made a considerable mess of Sándor's cap, Tamara was keeping for supper.

By this time she was feeling very hungry herself and when the meal came up it was again pieces of cold chicken, although this time there were four thickly cut slices of ham.

There was however a big jug of milk and she made Vava bread and milk and persuaded her with some difficulty to eat a little of the chicken which she cut up very small.

373

Although she had asked for cream they received none and had to make do with raspberries and milk, which was however, better than nothing.

"I will speak to the Duke to-night and tell him this cannot go on," Tamara told herself.

When Vava and Kadine were in bed she went down to the Hall to ask if the Duke would see her. She was however informed that His Grace had gone out to dinner, leaving early as he had some distance to drive.

The fact that he had come back to the house and made no effort to see her or the children was infuriating, but there was nothing Tamara could do about it.

She asked if the Duke would see her without fail tomorrow morning, as it was of importance.

"I'll give His Grace your message, Miss," the Butler said in a voice which showed her all too clearly that he thought her insistence was an impertinence.

She went back upstairs and after the children had gone to bed tried to read one of her favourite books which she had brought with her in the luggage.

But she found it impossible to do anything but think of the uncomfortable position they were in, the way they were being treated at the Castle, and the fact that the Duke obviously intended to ignore them.

"If this goes on, what am I to do?" she wondered.

She asked herself the same question the following morning when, after waiting to hear from the Duke, she went downstairs at ten o'clock to be informed that His Grace had once again left the Castle early and the servants had no idea when he would return.

"Is there no-one else with any authority to whom I can speak?" she asked the Butler, with a peremptory note in her voice which made him look at her in surprise.

"His Grace's comptroller is in London at the moment," the Butler replied. "We are expecting Major Melville to return at the beginning of next week. I am sure then, Miss, he will deal with any enquiries you may wish to make."

"The beginning of next week!" Tamara exclaimed.

That was four days ahead and she had the feeling that by that time they would all be hungry and the children's health might well suffer for lack of proper food.

They went out during the morning, but Tamara was very quiet. She was thinking what she could do.

When once again a quite inedible meal was sent up at luncheon-time she looked at it, then told all three children to follow her.

"Where are we going?" Sándor asked.

"You will see," Tamara answered grimly.

She knew where the back stairs were by this time, and they went down to find themselves as she expected on reaching the ground floor, in the kitchen quarters.

She walked resolutely along the flagged passage until she came to the big high-ceilinged kitchen where there was a Chef and a number of scullions grouped around a huge stove.

They were cooking, she thought, a meal for the staff and it certainly smelt better than the food that had been sent upstairs.

"Good-morning!" she said to the Chef.

He turned to look at her and stared with surprise at the three children who followed her.

"*Bonjour!*" he said after a moment.

"*Bonjour, Monsieur!*" Tamara replied in French, then continued: "We have come, *Monsieur,* to see you, because I cannot imagine the food that is being brought upstairs for His Grace's nephew and nieces can have been sent by you."

The Chef looked surprised, then he replied truculently:

"What is wrong with it?"

"You can hardly expect me to explain to a Frenchman what is wrong with food which is inedible," Tamara replied.

Her answer stung him into a retaliation and he burst into a flood of volubility, saying that it was not his job to cook for Nurseries and he had not enough help in the kitchen except to provide meals for His Grace and his friends, and for the present staff.

Tamara waited while he talked himself to a standstill, then said:

"If you have not enough help then I will cook a meal for these children; for I do not intend them to become ill from eating food which could only be intended for pigs."

Her words were ruder in French than in English and, as she had intended, the Frenchman was infuriated by her insult.

He worked himself to a frenzy, gesticulating in almost incoherent rage, and ending:

"As I said, I have not enough help and you either eat what I send you or go without!"

"I have no intention of doing either of those things," Tamara replied. "As we are very hungry, I intend now to cook a meal for my charges for they can no longer go without proper food."

She walked resolutely to the kitchen-table as she spoke and the Frenchman throwing up his arms shouted furiously:

"Do as you like! I will leave! I will not be insulted in my own kitchen!"

He walked away towards the door as he spoke and Tamara looking at the open-mouthed scullions said in English:

"Bring me a clean pan, eggs, butter, salt, pepper and a basin."

They looked at her in astonishment, then because her voice was firm and she had an air of authority about her they obeyed.

"Please put a cloth on that table and lay it for four," and to the children she said: "Sit down, darlings, and you will have some decent food as soon as I have cooked it for you."

She put a large lump of butter into the pan and set it on the stove to melt. As she did so she saw there were several chickens on a spit and she told one of the scullions to start turning it.

As he did so she first threw some salt and pepper on the nearest chicken, then broke a dozen eggs into a basin, stirring them with a fork while the butter was melting in the pan.

There were some tomatoes on a sideboard. She told a scullion to put six into hot water, then peel them and remove the seeds.

Just before she poured the eggs into the pan she told the boy who had been preparing the tomatoes to put them in another pan with a little butter.

She folded these into the omelette at the last moment and then she turned it over onto a hot dish which a scullion had taken from the oven with four plates. It was moist at the centre and perfectly rounded and golden brown on the top.

She carried it to the table and set it down in front of the children.

"Help yourselves, darlings," she said. "I will see to the chicken."

She threw more salt and pepper on it and now it was beginning to smell delicious as it turned and turned in front of the hot fire.

She set some small mushrooms to simmer on the stove and asked the scullions for a wooden bowl, but that was not procurable.

When they brought her a glass one, lettuces and a knife, she told them knives should never be used on a green salad.

"You must pull off the leaves gently with your fingers," she instructed, "then toss them in the dressing."

She made the dressing, which was the one the children liked with oil, vinegar, mustard and a little sugar.

By this time the chicken was ready and she carved it deftly, jointing it in a foreign fashion, garnished it with watercress and small mushrooms which she had set in another pan to cook.

There was only a small piece of the omelette left for

her when she sat down for a moment at the table. The children told her how much they had enjoyed it and were now waiting eagerly for the chicken.

She gave the white meat to Kadine and Vava while she and Sándor enjoyed the darker portions.

It was delicious with the fresh salad and the little button mushrooms which had been cooked exactly right.

Tamara ate quickly, then she rose from the table to ask if there was any fruit.

The scullions said there were raspberries and red currants and she told them to bring her the latter together with the white of egg and icing sugar.

They looked at her in surprise and watched with interest as she held a string of red currants between her thumb and first finger, dipped it in the white of egg, let it drip, then rolled it in the icing sugar.

It was a dish the children loved and a whole plateful of white-sugared currants quickly disappeared. Vava said grace and they rose from the table.

"Thank you for all your help," Tamara said to the scullions. "It would be a great kindness if you would bake us a cake and some scones for tea."

They smiled at her encouragingly and she looked towards the Chef who was still standing just inside the kitchen watching her as he had done all the while she was cooking.

"I must thank you, *Monsieur*," she said in French, "for your hospitality. It is the first decent meal we have eaten since we came to stay with His Grace, and I am hoping it will not be the last!"

In response the Frenchman made a sound which was one of mingled fury and derision, then he said:

"I resign! I will not stay here and be insulted, then we shall see what matters most to His Grace—a lot of tiresome brats, or his food!"

With that he stormed out of the kitchen and Tamara looked at the children.

"We have caused a storm," she said, "and I have a feeling there is even rougher weather ahead."

The two little girls did not understand, but Sándor laughed.

"You are very brave," he said, "but I think Mumma would have done the same thing."

"I am quite certain she would!" Tamara answered. "And that is why, Sándor, we are, none of us, going to be afraid!"

Kadine and Vava lay down after luncheon and Tamara helped Sándor to study one of his Latin books.

In Cornwall he had been taught by the Vicar, although in fact Tamara was extremely proficient in Latin.

"What is going to happen about my lessons?" Sándor asked.

"The inevitable answer is that we have to wait until I have seen the Duke," Tamara smiled, "but I am sure there is a big Library somewhere in this building. I can remember your father telling me about it."

"Let us go down and see the Librarian, if there is one," Sándor suggested.

They found an old man in what Tamara thought was one of the most magnificent Libraries she had ever seen.

He told them that his name was Aitken and he was the Curator of the whole Castle.

Sándor immediately bombarded him with questions about the Norman Keep, the dungeons and a dozen other things that particularly interested him.

Mr. Aitken remembered Lord Ronald well and told them that as far as he was concerned they were welcome to take any book they required from the Library.

Tamara felt excited to know how much reading she could do and how many volumes there were that would be of particular interest not only to her but also to Sándor.

They could not stay long because she did not like to leave the little girls and when Kadine and Vava rose after their rest they all went on Sándor's insistence back to the stables.

Because luncheon had been so delayed it was getting late in the afternoon but Abbey, the old groom, was pleased to see them and once again allowed Vava to sit on the saddle of one of the horses.

"Do you train a lot of race horses here?" Sándor asked eagerly.

"A great many, young Master," the groom replied, "and His Grace is running two o' them at Cheltenham Races this week. Wer're a-hoping one will win th' Steeple-Chase Cup."

'The Cheltenham Races,' Tamara thought to herself.

So that was where the Duke had been these past days, and there was perhaps some excuse for his leaving the problem of the children until after the race-meeting.

At the same time he might, she thought, have sent them a message to inform them why he was so busy.

"How do you train the horses?" Sándor was asking.

The old groom chuckled.

"Oi'll show ye, young Sir."

He took them the whole length of the stables to where at the far end they saw in an open field a miniature race-course.

Tamara remembered that Lord Ronald had once said there was such a thing in the Castle grounds and she had incorporated it in her novel.

It was therefore somewhat uncanny to see the huge jumps just as she had described them.

"They look quite easy," Sándor said after inspecting the course for some time.

The old groom laughed.

"Ye'd not be saying that if ye were a-riding, Master Sándor. There'll be many a horse falling at Cheltenham this week over exactly th' same jumps as ye see here."

Sándor said nothing but he went on looking at the artificial hedges and wide water-jump. Then he noticed that not on the race-course but at the side of it there was a five-bar gate.

"Do you train the horses over that, too?" he enquired.

"That's His Grace's new jump which he keeps exclusively for himself," the groom replied. "It's not for th' racing horses but for th' hunters."

"It is a good idea," Sándor said enthusiastically.

"His Grace has had it set up in th' new manner," the groom explained. "If the horse he's training doesn't clear the top bar th' gate falls."

"That saves a lot of broken knees," Sándor laughed.

He ran up to the gate and inspected it and saw that, as the groom had said, it was only lightly attached to two posts on either side.

A horse striking the top bar with his hoofs would simply knock the gate down and would therefore not be in danger of falling himself.

Tamara heard Vava calling to her and went to the child's side.

"I want to go faster, much faster!" Vava was saying to the young groom who was leading her.

"You are going fast enough," Tamara smiled. "This is a much bigger pony than you rode at home."

"I want to gallop," Vava said obstinately.

"Her's got a sporting instinct in her, like her brother," the old groom said beside her.

Tamara looked round to see that somehow Sándor had persuaded the old man in her absence to let him mount one of the horses which had just come into the yard after being exercised.

It was a large black stallion and as the young groom swung himself down from the saddle he had said:

"Samson's fair pulled me arms out o' me sockets. But Oi've ridden him hard an' some o' th' devil's gone out o' him."

"That's good," the Head Groom approved.

Sándor was riding down the yard obviously delighted at being mounted on such a fine horse.

"He is magnificent, is he not, Miss Wynne?" he called.

"And very much larger than Rufus," she replied.

Sándor turned the stallion's head and rode a little faster to the end of the cobbled yard, then as if he suddenly made up his mind he took the stallion onto the race-course.

The old groom started forward with a cry.

"Come back, young Sir, ye're not to go a-jumping that horse. He be too big for ye."

But either Sándor did not hear him or had no intention of doing so, for he started to ride round the course, taking the first jump in fine style and going on to the next.

"It's not right, if the young gentleman has a fall His Grace'll be a-blaming me," old Abbey muttered.

"You need not worry," Tamara said calmly. "Master Sándor is a very good rider and although he has never been on anything so magnificent as that animal he has in fact ridden a number of different horses over the years."

Sándor cleared another fence and now he was going to the water-jump.

Watching him, Tamara realised the boy was using all his intelligence. He was approaching each fence under control and at exactly the right moment lifted the stallion in a manner which made the horse sail over the obstacles in a way which might have been expected of any professional rider.

Because she was so pleased with what he had achieved she gave a little cry and clapped her hands together.

"Good! That is very good!" she exclaimed. "I knew he could do it!"

Then a voice behind her asked harshly:

"May I enquire what is going on here?"

With a leap of her heart Tamara realised that while they were watching Sándor, the Duke had approached them from the yard and they had not heard him.

She and the groom turned round hastily.

The Duke was looking even more magnificent and authoritative than before in champagne-coloured pantaloons and brilliantly polished Hessians.

He had a high hat on the side of his dark head and with him was another gentleman, older than he was, but also arrayed in the height of fashion.

The latter was looking at Tamara through a quizzing glass which made her suddenly conscious of her appearance.

She had not expected the Duke until later and as it was very hot she had put on one of her thin muslin gowns and wore her hair in a less formal style than the way she had arranged it when they first arrived.

Because she was only with the children she had taken off her bonnet which was dangling from her arm by its ribbons.

Without seeing the criticism in the Duke's eyes, she knew she was not behaving with the propriety that he might have expected of a Governess.

She curtsied and looked apprehensively at him to see that he was watching Sándor.

"Who allowed that boy to ride my horse?" he asked.

"Oi lets him just mount Samson in the yard, Your Grace," the Head Groom said apologetically, "but the young gentleman takes him onto the race-course afore Oi could stop him."

Sándor cleared another fence and the old man added:

"Th' spit and image of his father, he be! He'll be as good a rider as Your Grace in a few years."

The Duke's lips tightened in what Tamara thought was an ominous manner then the gentleman beside him said with a laugh:

"I was not aware, Howard, that you had children at the Castle, but will you not introduce me to the very charming young lady who apparently is in charge of them?"

"This is their Governess," the Duke said in an uncompromising tone.

"I should still like to meet her," his friend insisted.

To avoid further embarrassment Tamara turned away to go to Vava who was still being led around the yard.

"It is time to go back for tea," she said.

"I want to go on riding," Vava replied almost fiercely, "I want to go faster."

"I want my tea," Kadine said.

She had been feeding the horses in the stalls with pieces of carrot which one of the stable-boys handed to her.

"We will go in as soon as Sándor has finished riding," Tamara said.

Kadine looked in the direction of the race-course and saw the Duke.

"There is Uncle Howard," she exclaimed. "I am going to ask him if he will give me a pony."

She ran up the yard before Tamara could stop her and, quite unabashed by the Duke, slipped her hand into his.

He looked down at her with astonishment as she said:

"Please Uncle Howard, may I have a pony? I had one at home and I want to ride like Sándor, but I would like a pony of my own."

Her face was turned pleadingly up to his and the Duke's friend laughed.

"If you can refuse a request put so prettily, Howard, I shall be astonished."

He dropped his quizzing glass and picked Kadine up in his arms.

"What is your name, little lady?"

"Kadine," she answered, "what is yours?"

"My name is Cropthorne."

"That is a funny name!"

"Do you think so? Your name is very pretty. As pretty as you are."

"I am not as pretty as my Mumma."

"Then she must be very pretty indeed."

Kadine suddenly struggled in his arms.

"I want to go and have my tea," she said. "It was horrid yesterday, but I think we will have a cake to-day."

She was put down on the ground. The gentleman took hold of her hand and walked back to Tamara.

"I hear you are having cake for tea," he said. "Am I invited to join you?"

There was something in the way he spoke and the look in his eyes which made Tamara feel he was dangerous.

"I hardly think you will enjoy nursery tea, Sir," she replied.

"It is certainly a long time since I partook of one," he answered, "but I would enjoy anything, if it was in your company."

There was no mistaking the flirtatious note in his voice or the way he was looking at her, and the colour rose in Tamara's face as she helped a protesting Vava down from the saddle.

As she did so, she realised that Sándor had finished the course and was bringing the stallion back to the stables.

His cheeks were flushed with excitement, his eyes shining and when he saw the Duke he cried out:

"This is a wonderful horse, Uncle Howard! Please, may I ride him again?"

"You did not have my permission this time," the Duke said severely.

"Miss Wynne was going to ask you this morning," Sándor answered, "but you had gone out, and I did want to try out your jumps."

"Ye' shouldn't have gone over them without asking Oi first," the Head Groom said. "Ye might have had a fall, young Sir, and ye'd have got me into trouble."

"I have had lots of falls," Sándor boasted. "My father

385

always made me get on again immediately, so I am not afraid."

He sprang down from the stallion's back and walked to the Duke's side.

"You will let me ride your horses, Uncle Howard, will you not?" he begged.

"It depends on a great number of things," the Duke replied coldly. "I will discuss the matter with your Governess when I have the time."

He walked away as he spoke leaving Sándor staring after him.

He passed Tamara who was holding Vava by the hand and walked with immense dignity and presence back towards the Castle.

His friend followed him but paused to say to Tamara in a low voice:

"Even if I am not invited to tea we shall meet again, fair Enchantress, I will make sure of that!"

Tamara did not reply, but he smiled at her in what she felt was a far too familiar manner before he followed the Duke down the yard.

"Do you think Uncle Howard means to let me ride?" Sándor asked.

"I hope so," Tamara answered, "but he is certainly very unpredictable. It is unfortunate that he returned from the races far earlier than we expected."

Because she did not wish the children to be oppressed by her feelings she said brightly:

"Thank Abbey for letting you ride, Sándor, and now we will all run back as quickly as we can to have our tea."

They went upstairs to the Nursery to find the scullions had not failed Tamara's request: there was a cake and scones for their tea besides a comb of honey and a pot of home-made strawberry jam.

"Things are getting better," Tamara said brightly.

But she could not help wondering whether they were getting worse where the Duke was concerned.

He certainly did not seem proud of his nephew's

riding ability, but rather the opposite, and she had a feeling that his friend's compliments would make her position in the Duke's eyes even more difficult than it was already.

She had a sudden longing to escape.

If only they could go back to Cornwall, if only they had not been obliged to leave the quiet happiness of the Manor.

Once again she felt she was being over-powered by the Castle, the hostile servants and most of all by the Duke!

"I hate him," she said again to herself as if it was a talisman to give her courage!

CHAPTER FOUR

*T*amara anticipated that the Duke would send for her later in the day, so she changed into her green gown and rearranged her hair, pinning it into a bun at the back of her head as it had been on her arrival.

She could not help feeling that the severity of the style seemed to make the size and darkness of her eyes even more prominent.

But she hoped that the Duke would notice her as little as possible and, more important than anything else, think she looked older than she was.

The summons came at six o'clock, just as she was putting Vava into bed. A footman came to the Nursery door.

"His Grace wishes to see you, Miss."

"If you will wait two minutes," Tamara answered, "you can take me to His Grace."

"He's in the Blue Salon, Miss."

"As I have no idea where that is I should be grateful if you would wait for me."

The footman acquiesced, but leant somewhat familiarly against the jamb of the door thinking, Tamara knew, that as she was only a servant like himself, there was no need to be particularly respectful.

She carried Vava to the Night-Nursery and put her to bed, then made Kadine promise that when she had finished her milk she would go to her own room.

"Look after them, Sándor," she begged.

He was sitting reading by the window and he answered:

"All right, but do not forget to ask if I can ride all the horses in the stables."

"You will be lucky if you get permission to ride one," Tamara answered, "but I will do my best."

She took a last glance at herself in the mirror, smoothing her hair down at the side of her forehead where a few tendrils had escaped when Vava had flung her arms around her neck.

She told herself it was absurd to be frightened.

Yet she knew as she followed the footman down the stairs and through the great Hall that she was nervous as she had never felt nervous of any other person in her whole life.

"It is not because I am afraid of him personally," she thought, "but because he may try to prevent me from looking after the children."

The footman opened a door.

"Miss Wynne, Your Grace!" he said and Tamara walked into the room.

The Duke was alone, standing at the far end of the Salon with his back to the fireplace.

Because it was summer there was no fire and she thought that he made the hearth-rug seem almost a dais from which he reigned supreme and she was nothing but a suppliant coming before him almost on her knees.

He was looking extremely handsome, she admitted, but the lines of cynicism were very pronounced and his expression looked like one of contempt.

Even before he spoke she resented his attitude, her chin went up and there was a defiant look in her eyes, that she could not suppress as she came nearer to him.

She curtsied and stood waiting; she felt he was looking her over in a searching fashion which made her temper begin to rise.

"You seem to have taken a great many liberties since you arrived in my house," the Duke said at length.

Tamara did not speak and he went on:

"I have been informed that the children, who are obviously out of hand, have been stealing fruit from the greenhouses and that you and they have caused a commotion in the kitchen, to such an extent that my Chef has threatened to leave."

Tamara could not help feeling slightly amused.

She had been quite certain that the Chef would not actually hand in his notice as he had said he would. He would merely make trouble.

"Well, what have you to say for yourself?" the Duke asked.

"A great deal, Your Grace," Tamara answered coolly. "First I am not prepared to stand by and watch the children starve or be made ill by eating unsuitable food, and I should not have thought that the picking of fruit in their uncle's garden would come in the category of stealing."

"What is wrong with the food?" the Duke asked.

"It is both insufficient and inedible!"

"In your opinion?"

"In anyone's opinion. The children were able to eat practically nothing yesterday and were therefore so hungry that I was forced to cook them a decent meal myself, the first they have had since they entered the Castle."

"I can hardly credit that my Chef, whose cooking has been acclaimed by a great many connoisseurs, is not good enough for three children and yourself, Miss Wynne."

"It is hardly a question of cooking," Tamara answered. "The eggs that were sent up for breakfast were cold before they reached the top floor. The left-over pieces of cold chicken and mutton that were too tough to be eaten in the Servants' Hall were considered to be good enough for children in whom Your Grace obviously has no interest."

She thought he was about to speak and went on quickly:

"Servants ape their masters, and the fact that you have not welcomed your brother's children is of course reflected in the way they are treated not only by the kitchen staff but also by everyone else in the household."

She raised her chin a little higher as she added:

"In case Your Grace is not aware of it, it is not the place of a Governess who is employed to teach and to take general charge to have to make beds and clean floors because there are no housemaids available to perform these tasks."

"You surprise me, Miss Wynne," the Duke said slowly.

"I have something to suggest to Your Grace."

"What is it?" he enquired.

"If you will give me the same allowance for the children that you gave your brother, I will take them away from here back to Cornwall. The house in which they lived there would be too big and anyway it is sold, but I should be able to find another house we could afford."

"I have never heard such a preposterous suggestion in the whole of my life!" the Duke said sharply. "It is not your place, Miss Wynne, to be the Guardian of these children, nor are you old enough to act in such a capacity."

Tamara did not speak but she made a little gesture with her hands. The Duke said:

"I received yesterday the letter from my brother's Solicitors in Cornwall telling me what had occurred and informing me that you and the children were arriving here. The letter had been delayed en route owing, I understand, to an accident to the Mail Coach which was carrying it."

"It was unfortunate that we arrived first," Tamara said.

"Very," the Duke agreed. "But now you are here, I presume I must make arrangements that you, Miss Wynne, will consider suitable."

He was being sarcastic, and there was a note in his voice that made her feel as if he flicked her with a whip.

"And the first thing I would ask Your Grace," she said, "is that Sándor, who is nearly twelve, should go to school."

"He has been well taught?"

"I think you will find he is well in advance of most boys of his age."

"And you have been his teacher?"

There was a mocking twist to the Duke's lips which she did not miss.

"I have taught Sándor languages," she replied. "He speaks fluent French and good Italian, and he has learnt Latin with our Vicar, who is a classical scholar."

"Is that all?"

"I have taught him Arithmetic, Geography and English Literature, Your Grace."

"And yet you do not look English."

"My father was English."

"And your mother?"

"Hungarian."

"Which of course accounts for the colour of your hair."

Tamara did not answer. She merely raised her eyebrows.

"Well, let us hope," he said after a moment's pause, "that my nephew will not be unmercifully ragged at school for having such a fanciful, or as I said before, theatrical name."

"Your Grace's knowledge is lamentably at fault," Tamara replied. "Sándor is not a theatrical name. It is the name of one of the oldest and most respected families in Hungary. Count Andressy Sandor was in fact a National hero, and most students of history have heard of him."

She had meant to score off the Duke and she succeeded, for she saw the surprise on his face and added before he could speak:

"Actually Count Andressy Sandor was Lady Ronald's grandfather!"

"She was Hungarian!" the Duke exclaimed. "I had no idea."

Then almost to himself, as if he could not let the opportunity pass he added:

"But she was an actress."

"She was nothing of the sort!" Tamara said sharply. "Lady Ronald was a singer. She had an exceptionally fine voice and she sang for two years with a private Opera Company because her mother had had a long illness and the bills could not have been paid otherwise."

She saw the Duke raise his eyebrows in surprise and continued:

"The Opera Company has recently come under the patronage of the Countess of Rockingham who could tell you more about it if Your Grace is interested."

The Duke was obviously startled.

"The Countess of Rockingham? But she is a relative of mine," he said. "I have heard of this Opera Company she sponsors, in fact I believe I have subscribed to it."

"Then you will understand that Lady Ronald was

not an actress in the usually accepted meaning of the word."

"You certainly know more about her than I do, Miss Wynne."

There was an unmistakable note of sincerity in his voice and Tamara said in a different tone:

"I not only acted as Governess to Lady Ronald's children, I had also the privilege of being her . . . friend."

"Because you were both Hungarian."

"I have already said, Your Grace, that my father was English."

"And do you really believe that being somewhat of a foreigner you are capable of teaching English Literature to my nieces, and apparently also to my nephew?"

There was no mistaking now the little note of triumph in Tamara's voice as she replied:

"My father, Your Grace, was an Oxford Don. He was a Classical scholar with a great reputation. He published eight books on the Classics which are very highly spoken of by experts!"

As Tamara spoke she thought that she had meant to confound him and succeeded.

At the same time she could not help a little tremor of fear in case she had gone too far and he would dismiss her instantly because she had defied him.

Instead after a moment he said:

"You have certainly given me a great deal of information that I had not expected, Miss Wynne. Now shall we return to the present problem? I am sure you have many suggestions as to how the children's position in the household could be improved."

"I would like to suggest first, Your Grace, that we are moved to a different part of the Castle," Tamara said quickly. "The children have been used to living with their parents and they always occupied the best rooms in their house in Cornwall.

"They will do no damage, that I promise you, but there must be rooms which are more congenial than the dilapidated Nurseries where we are housed at the moment."

"I take your point, Miss Wynne," the Duke said coldly.

"And I think it would be a good idea if we were allowed a small Dining-Room nearer to the kitchens so that the food will not be cold when we receive it," Tamara said. "And if I might be allowed to suggest menus which are suitable for children and good for their health, it would save a great deal of future argument."

"Anything else?" the Duke enquired.

Tamara drew in her breath.

"You know how much the children want to ride, and as an outstanding horseman yourself you will understand how frustrating it is to see other people well-mounted while being only in the position of an on-looker."

"I have a feeling, Miss Wynne, that you are pleading not only on behalf of the children, but also on behalf of yourself."

"I am . . . teaching Vava to ride," Tamara answered.

"There are plenty of horses in the stables," the Duke said, "and I imagine that you and Sándor could exercise them quite as well as any of my grooms. I will see if something can be done about acquiring ponies for the two little girls."

Tamara's eyes lit up.

"Do you mean that? Do you really mean it? It would mean more to them than anything else and help them to forget that they have lost their father and mother."

There was a soft note in her voice that had not been there before and the Duke said:

"I hope, Miss Wynne, that when all these innovations are put into practice you will be satisfied."

Once again she knew he was mocking her and she answered:

"There is one more thing, Your Grace."

"What is it now?"

"You will not forget that Sándor should go to school? He needs companions of his own age as well as lessons."

"I have already said that I will give it my consideration."

"Then I can only thank you for being so generous."

Tamara curtsied, conscious as she did so that the Duke's eyes were on her face. Then as she turned to walk away he said:

"Your father's books were of course written under his name? I shall make enquiries to see if I have any of them in my Library. If not, it is an omission which should be remedied."

For a moment Tamara held her breath, then because she could think of nothing to say she curtsied again.

"I thank Your Grace," she murmured.

As she walked away she thought wildly that she had made an irrevocable slip and unerringly the Duke had put his finger on it.

As she ran upstairs to the children she was thrilled at what she had to tell them, but at the same time she could not help thinking how foolish of her it had been to say it was her father who was the Don at Oxford.

Why had she not said her uncle, or some other relative?

However the Duke knew so little about her sister that it was extremely doubtful if he knew that her name had been Selincourt.

'I won the battle on so many points,' she thought, 'but I have left myself very vulnerable, and he may shoot me down at any moment!'

It was a disquieting thought but for the moment she set it aside because she was so excited at being able to tell the children about the horses.

With a slightly better grace, although it was obvious she was somewhat affronted by the instructions she had received, Mrs. Henderson moved Tamara and the children downstairs into the West Wing.

The rooms were large and attractively furnished.

There was a delightful Sitting-Room overlooking the front of the Castle, the lake and the Park and a separate bed-room for each one of them.

"This is better!" Sándor exclaimed. "I can watch the deer from here."

"I can watch them too," Vava cried, "but I would rather see the horses."

"So would I," Sándor said with a grin.

When Tamara told him that the Duke had promised they could ride his horses, he had flung his arms around her.

"It was wonderful of you, Aunt Tamara, to make him agree," he cried.

Because she too was so excited, she forgot to rebuke him for not calling her Miss Wynne.

"The Adam Dining-Room is to be at your disposal, Miss," Mrs. Henderson said in a repressed voice, "and I understand that one of my housemaids is to be allotted to these rooms. There will also be a footman to wait upon you at mealtimes."

"The Duke is doing us royally," Tamara said to Sándor when Mrs. Henderson left them.

"So he ought," Sándor answered. "After all, if he died I should be the Duke!"

Tamara looked at him in a startled fashion.

"I never thought of that!"

"Of course I would," Sándor answered. "Papa was his heir until he died. He once showed me the family-tree we had at home, and now that Papa is dead I would be the next Duke."

"I should not think about it too much," Tamara advised. "After all, the Duke is still young. He may marry and have ten of his own children!"

Sándor grinned.

"There is plenty of room for them in the Castle!"
Tamara laughed.

"To-morrow I am going to climb to the top of the
tower," Sándor told her.

"You must be very careful," Tamara answered.

"I will," Sándor promised. "I do not want to have a
broken leg and not be able to ride."

The children could talk of nothing else but their
riding and Vava asked over and over again how soon
she would have her pony.

"We will go to the stables and talk to Abbey about it
to-morrow morning," Tamara promised.

But it was hard to get either Kadine or Vava to sleep
because they were so thrilled at what lay ahead.

The two little girls had milk and biscuits for supper
after their big tea, but Sándor and Tamara went downstairs to the Adam Dining-Room.

Because she always changed for dinner Tamara put
on one of her pretty gowns and arranged her hair in
her usual style, certain that she was unlikely to meet
the Duke again during the evening.

The dinner was very different from the meals they
had previously endured. Tamara had the idea that it
was identical to what the Duke was enjoying in the Dining-Room.

When they had finished Sándor said:

"It is warm to-night. Do you think we could go outside and walk in the garden before we go upstairs?"

Tamara smiled at him.

"It is a good idea. It is not yet dark, so we will not fall
over the flower-beds or end up in the lake."

They let themselves out of a side door and walked
across the lawns that were like velvet beneath their
feet.

There was the scent of stock and lavender on the air
and the pigeons were going to roost in the high trees in
the wood.

There was a golden glow in the sky where the sun
was setting on the horizon.

The Castle seemed very high and mysterious with just one or two lights showing in the downstairs windows.

Sándor ran ahead and Tamara paused in the rose garden beside a sunken pool filled with gold-fish. She watched their glimmering golden bodies as they moved amongst the flat green water-lily leaves.

It was all so beautiful she felt as if her heart went out to so much loveliness and she became a part of it.

Then suddenly a voice beside her said:

"You look like a goddess of the night, only far more desirable!"

She turned and saw the gentleman who had been with the Duke in the stable-yard.

He came far too close to her and she moved a step away from him.

"Sándor and I were just returning to the Castle," she said quickly.

As she spoke she looked for Sándor, but there was no sign of him.

"There is no hurry," the gentleman said.

"I have things to see to indoors, Sir."

"Not so fast," he answered, "we have not yet been formerly introduced. My name is Cropthorne, Lord Cropthorne—and yours?"

"Miss Wynne . . . and I am the children's Governess as Your Lordship is well aware."

He laughed.

"You are trying to put me in my place. But your lips are far too attractive to speak in such a severe tone. They were meant for kisses, not for rebukes."

"I would thank Your Lordship not to speak to me in such a manner," Tamara answered coldly.

She would have walked away, but he reached out and took hold of her wrist.

"I shall talk to you as I like," he said. "How could I have expected to find anything so lovely and so very alluring in Granchester's gloomy Castle?"

"Let me go!" Tamara said sharply.

"On one condition," he answered.

She did not reply and he said:

"I will tell you what it is—that you let me kiss you as I have desired to do ever since I saw you this afternoon."

"I have no intention of allowing you to do any such thing," Tamara said angrily. "You will please let loose my wrist at once. I cannot believe that the Duke would think it commendable of you to behave in such a manner."

"Has the Duke a prior claim?" Lord Cropthorne asked.

In answer Tamara struggled to free herself, but he held on to her and laughed softly.

"I have no intention of letting you go, you glorious creature," he said. "I have a penchant for women with large, dark eyes and red hair. They are more quickly aroused than their paler sisters."

As he spoke he drew Tamara relentlessly towards him.

She knew that in a battle of strength she would be helpless.

At the same time she found herself suddenly panic-stricken at the thought of what he intended to do.

He was the type of raffish Rake that she had written about in her novel, but had never actually encountered in real life.

Now she knew this was just the sort of situation in which her villainous Duke had been involved, and which had disgusted her even as she wrote about it.

She struggled but Lord Cropthorne's arms were round her, and although she twisted her head away from him she felt it was only a question of time before he overpowered her.

Then she had an idea!

For one moment she let herself go limp in his arms, so limp that he thought he had triumphed and his lips were on her cheek.

Then with all her strength she pushed him away

from her. His feet slipped on the paving-stones around the water-lily pool and he fell backwards into it with a loud splash.

Tamara did not wait even to see what had happened but turned and ran, hearing a string of oaths as she went.

Reaching the lawn she sped across it towards the Castle only to run full tilt into someone whom she had not seen in the shadow of the building.

Only as she was halted violently by the contact and put out her hands to save herself did she realise it was the Duke.

His hands steadied her. Then as she gasped for breath he said in his most sarcastic tone:

"You appear to be in somewhat of a hurry, Miss Wynne. What can have caused such impetuosity?"

Tamara forgot everything but her anger at what had happened.

She pulled herself out of the Duke's arms and said in a voice which strove to be disdainful, but which in reality was very young and breathless:

"You will find your . . . friend . . . Your Grace, in the water-lily pool . . . and I hope he . . . drowns!"

With that she walked into the Castle without looking back.

Only as she reached the Sitting-Room in the West Wing did she wonder what the Duke had thought and told herself furiously that it was of no consequence.

He could hardly dismiss her for resenting the advances of his guest, even if her behaviour was unconventional.

At the same time she was afraid he might be persuaded that it was her fault for having encouraged Lord Cropthorne in some way or other.

She was standing at the window trying to collect her scattered thoughts and breathe more naturally when Sándor came into the room.

"Where did you get to?" he asked. "I went back to find you at the water-lily pool, but the gentleman who is staying with the Duke was standing in the middle of it, and he was swearing, as Papa would have said, like a trooper! I have never heard such a string of oaths!"

"Was the Duke with him?" Tamara asked.

"He was standing beside the pool," Sándor said, "and what do you think? He was laughing! I never thought he could laugh—he seemed stiff and starchy."

"He was . . . laughing!" Tamara repeated.

It was of course absurd of her but she was relieved that the Duke was not angry but amused.

The following morning Tamara went to the stables wearing her riding-habit and she and Sándor were mounted by Abbey on two of the fine horses which filled the Duke's stables.

A young groom rode beside Kadine with her horse on a leading rein and old Abbey himself took charge of Vava.

"Don't worrit about th' young ladies, Miss," he said to Tamara. "You have a good gallop with Master Sándor, and Oi'll look after 'em 'till ye returns."

"You are to do exactly what Abbey tells you," Tamara admonished the two little girls. She was as excited as Sándor as they set off across the Park.

They rode for about two miles, then turned their horses for home.

"I am beginning to feel glad that we came to the Castle," Sándor said. "I thought at first that I was going to hate it."

"So did I," Tamara replied, "but being able to ride horses like these makes up for a lot of other things."

"Even for the odious advances of Lord Cropthorne," she told herself.

She had felt a little guilty when she went to bed and thought over what had occurred.

Then she decided he had thoroughly deserved what she had done to him.

He was, she was sure, the type of roué who thought that unprotected governesses and young housemaids were fair game. But Tamara hoped she had taught him a lesson.

However much she disliked the Duke, she could not believe he would behave in such a despicable manner.

'He would be too proud to condescend to a creature so much below him in social standing as a Governess!' she thought.

That might be reassuring; at the same time it was depressing to think that in the whole Castle there was no-one she could turn to as an equal and a friend.

In fact she had an idea that she was going to find it very lonely with no-one to talk to.

They did not see the Duke that day.

In the afternoon Tamara collected some books from the Library and took them up to their Sitting-Room.

There had been a wide variety of choice which had delighted her. At the same time she knew she was going to miss discussing what she read with Lord Ronald as she had done in Cornwall.

Maïka was as well educated as herself and they had often read together books in French, in Italian and Hungarian.

"It would be a shame for us to forget Mama's native tongue," Maïka had said often enough, "or to become too English."

She smiled as she spoke and added:

"Ronald said he fell in love with me because I looked different from any other girl he had ever seen, and he likes me when I am wildly Hungarian and unpredictable."

"I, on the other hand," Tamara told herself, "have now to be very English."

She could not forget the disparaging note in the Duke's voice when he had spoken of her being foreign.

'He is ridiculously insular,' she thought.

Somehow she could not help thinking about him even though she hated him.

But she was beginning to realise that she was not the only person in the Castle or outside who disliked the Duke.

It was obvious that the servants were not fond of him, as the servants in Cornwall had loved her sister and brother-in-law. She had learnt too from old Abbey that there was trouble on the Estate.

It was just something he had said rather vaguely, but she asked:

"Are you having riots and protests in this part of the country as I believe there has been in other places?"

"We 'as our difficulties," Abbey said in a rather repressed manner which made her think he could say more if he wished to do so.

"You mean there is unrest amongst the labourers?"

"They 'as their grievances an' there's not enough policemen t' stop 'em here as there be in London."

"Have they taken their complaints to His Grace?" Tamara asked.

"Aye, an' he'll not listen to them! But Oi thinks afore Oi gets much older than th' landlords 'll have t' listen, as those as be in Parliament 'll have t' listen sooner or later!"

Tamara was surprised that in Gloucester of all places there should be unrest.

She knew from what she had read in the newspapers and from what Lord Ronald had told her that the working conditions both in towns and in the country the previous year had caused riots which seemed to verge on revolution.

In August a meeting of malcontents had taken place at St. Peter's Fields in Manchester resulting in what had been called "The Battle of Peterloo".

Hundreds of unarmed men, women and children had been cut down by the sabres of mounted yeomanry and left wounded or dead.

The event had shocked the whole country and evoked a class-hatred which Lord Ronald was certain would recoil on the Landed Proprietors and the Mill owners for years, if not for generations.

It had all begun with the growing concern about the terrible crimes against children that were taking place in the great cities like London.

Tamara had heard of the 'Flash Houses', of the iniquitous treatment of sweeping-boys, the growing numbers of child prostitutes which were a disgrace to any civilised or Christian country.

But she had not thought this would particularly concern people who lived in out-lying districts until she learnt that injustice and low wages had caused revolts and riots amongst the country labourers also.

Ricks had been set on fire and the leaders when they were caught had been savagely punished and either hanged or transported.

She wondered what the Duke's attitude was to all these things.

She could not help thinking that by his very arrogance and the manner in which he seemed to look with disdain on those who were weaker than himself, he would incur their enmity.

She found that after the Duke had read the newspapers the day they arrived, she could obtain them next day from the Curator in the Library.

She read the Parliamentary debates and the reports of what was happening in other parts of the country and wondered if the Duke, being such a large land-owner, was perturbed about what might happen on his own Estate.

She talked to the old Curator, but he was concerned only with the Castle and its contents and she had the idea that he had long since ceased to realise that a world existed outside it.

She did not see Lord Cropthorne again and learnt that he had left the Castle.

While she half-expected the Duke to rebuke her for her behaviour towards his friend, she learnt from the servants that he had gone away that day with friends.

It made her feel that she and the children now had a freedom to move about in a way they had not been able to do before. They explored the great State Rooms, the Chapel, the Orangery, the Ball Room, and of course the Norman tower which for Sándor had a fascination all of its own.

"If we had other children we could play 'hide-and-seek'," Kadine said rather wistfully.

"It is certainly an idea," Tamara replied. "We shall have to find out if there are any local children we can ask to tea."

She thought that Kadine and Vava were rather bored with the tour of the Castle, so the next day she suggested that they should go down to the hay-field and take a picnic tea with them.

Their footman, who by this time was only too willing to do anything Tamara suggested, brought them a picnic basket and they set off, the little girls wearing their sun-bonnets and Tamara carrying her sunshade.

Hay-making had always been a time for festivity in Cornwall.

The children loved to help, or more often hinder, the women who turned the corn and stacked it in what they described as small wigwams so that it could dry out in the sun.

A large field which they found beyond the gardens had been cut, but the hay had been left to dry in the sun and there was no-one there but themselves.

Sándor started to tease Kadine by throwing hay at her, Tamara joined in and they all pelted each other until finally as Tamara sat down exhausted the children began to bury her in the hay, shouting with delight as they did so.

She was almost completely buried and she had shut her eyes against the stalks which tickled her face when she heard Sándor exclaim:

"Hello, Uncle Howard! We thought you had gone away."

"I have returned," the Duke replied.

Tamara sat up.

Beside them was the Duke riding one of his fine horses and she was immediately conscious of how undignified she must look up to her chin in hay!

There were pieces of it in her hair which, while she was playing, had lost its pins and was falling over her shoulders like a red tide.

She rose, shaking her skirt as she did so and trying to pull pieces of hay out of her hair.

"You appear to be enjoying yourself, Miss Wynne," the Duke remarked.

She did not reply and after a moment he said:

"Have you no complaints? I can hardly believe that my hay, if nothing else, is to your satisfaction."

Tamara pulled back her hair and tried to twist it in a bun at the back of her neck as she replied:

"I have not only no complaints, Your Grace, but a great deal for which to thank you. We have all ridden these last two mornings and enjoyed it exceedingly."

"I find that most reassuring, Miss Wynne."

He was being sarcastic but Tamara was too conscious of her appearance to feel defiant.

"I can ride," Vava said suddenly. "I can ride, Uncle Howard, a horse as big as yours!"

Before the Duke could reply Sándor said:

"I, too, would like to thank you, Uncle Howard. It is thrilling to ride your horses, and I know Papa would be pleased that you are so kind to us."

"That is not the reputation I usually have," the Duke answered.

Without another word he rode away.

"He really is the most exasperating and unpredictable man," Tamara said to herself angrily. "He turns up when he is least expected and behaves in a manner in which no other man would."

She had a feeling that he was watching her.

Perhaps he wanted to find an excuse for dismissing her from her post or maybe he resented the criticisms she had made and was determined to fault her.

Whatever the reason he made her feel uneasy.

Somehow the excitement had gone from the afternoon, and even when they had their tea in the shade of a tree the sunshine seemed a little dimmed and their laughter not so frequent.

'The Duke spoils everything!' Tamara thought petulantly.

She told herself there was no doubt that there was a very close resemblance between him and the fictitious Duke of Ullester in her novel.

CHAPTER FIVE

*T*amara rode into the stable-yard with Kadine at her side.

They had been in the Park together and Kadine was now allowed to ride without a leading rein, as she had a pony of her own.

It was a nice, quiet animal and a little bigger than the one that Abbey had found for Vava.

Kadine enjoyed riding, but she was not adventurous like Sándor or obsessed with it like Vava.

"You rode very well, darling," Tamara said.

Kadine smiled at her, looking so pretty as she did so that Tamara thought again how irresistible she would be when she grew up.

Old Abbey and Vava were outside the pony's stall. Vava as usual was refusing to dismount, insisting that she wanted to go on riding.

"Hurry up, Vava!" Tamara said as a groom helped her from her own horse. "It is time for tea."

"I do not want any tea," Vava said obstinately, "I want to go back and look at the little piebald pony."

Tamara looked at Abbey enquiringly and he explained:

"There's some gypsies at th' far end o' the Park, Miss, and Miss Vava was taken with a small piebald foal they've got there."

"It was so pretty!" Vava cried, "I want it! I want it all for my own!"

"That is greedy," Tamara replied, lifting Vava down from the saddle. "You have Butterfly, and no-one could have a nicer or prettier pony."

"I want two ponies!" Vava insisted.

"You are asking too much!" Tamara said firmly, "and I know you love Butterfly."

Vava kissed her pony's nose and gave it a piece of carrot which one of the stable-boys had ready.

Tamara was just about to take her away when she saw Major Melville coming down the yard towards them.

He was a middle-aged man who had been Comptroller to the previous Duke and had therefore lived at the Castle for many years.

Since he had returned Tamara found that everyhing seemed to be running more smoothly, the servants were more obliging, and she was quite certain that the Duke found him irreplaceable.

"Good afternoon, Miss Wynne," Major Melville said raising his hat.

"Good afternoon, Major, we have all had a most enjoyable ride, and it is a lovely day."

"I want a horse, please, Abbey," Major Melville said to the groom.

"At once, Sir," Abbey replied. "Will ye be a-going far?"

"No, only to the end of the Park. His Grace wants me to turn away the gypsies."

"Turn away the gypsies?" Tamara exclaimed. "But why?"

"You must not send them away!" Vava cried leaving Butterfly and running to Major Melville's side. "They have a dear little piebald pony and I want him all for my own."

"His Grace does not wish the gypsies to camp in the Park," Major Melville said to Tamara.

"They've come here for many a year, Sir," Old Abbey remarked, "an' they don't make no trouble. They're on th' way t' Evesham for the fruit picking."

"I am aware of that, Abbey," Major Melville replied, "but I have my orders."

As he spoke a horse which had been saddled was brought from its stall and he mounted it.

"You are not to send away the piebald pony!" Vava cried.

Major Melville merely smiled at her, then lifting his hat to Tamara he rode away.

"Why does the Duke not like gypsies?" Kadine asked as Tamara and the two little girls walked back to the Castle.

"I do not know," Tamara answered. "We used to see them in Cornwall, if you remember."

"Mumma always bought clothes-pegs from them," Kadine said, "and they had pretty painted caravans. I thought I would like to live in one."

"You would find it very cramped after your big bedroom here," Tamara smiled.

"It would be fun in the summer," Kadine said, "but perhaps rather cold in the winter, except that gypsies always have big fires."

Vava was silent. Tamara thought it was because she was thinking of the little piebald pony and changed the subject.

She knew, if Vava became interested in some particular object, how she would talk about it incessantly, which at times could be very wearying.

Tea was waiting for them upstairs in their Sitting-

Room and Tamara noticed with satisfaction that it was a very different meal from what they had been given when they first arrived.

The Chef had gradually mellowed towards the children, and now there was not only a variety of cakes and scones for tea and little coloured jellies but also fruit from the garden and thick cream.

Tamara looked at the clock and realised they had been riding rather later than usual and that Sándor should be home soon.

When Major Melville had returned to the Castle the Duke had obviously spoken to him about Sándor's education. She was informed he would attend a local school and he had started at the beginning of the week.

He had not said very much when he returned the first two evenings, but yesterday Tamara had thought that he seemed unusually silent and had lost his high spirits.

She supposed it was because he was finding it strange to be amongst other boys and thought he would naturally take a little time to settle down.

She had hoped that the Duke would suggest sending him to a Boarding School like Eton or Harrow.

But she thought perhaps the day-school was only a preliminary experiment and it would be a mistake for her to say too much until she saw how Sándor got on.

Kadine and Vava finished their tea but there was still no sign of their brother.

They played for a while with their toys. Then as Vava seemed to be tired Tamara called Rose, the maid who looked after them and suggested the little girl should be put to bed.

"Shall I read you a story, Kadine?" Tamara asked.

Kadine eagerly fetched a book which they had begun several days ago and which was an adventure story which she particularly enjoyed.

They were sitting on the sofa and Tamara had only read half a page when the door opened.

She looked up with a smile, knowing it must be
Sándor, then gave an exclamation of horror.

He came into the room obviously walking with difficulty, and dragging one leg behind the other. His coat
was torn, his shirt was open at the neck, one eye was
swollen and almost closed.

There was blood running from a cut lip and his nose
had been bleeding too.

"Sándor! What has happened?" Tamara exclaimed
hurrying towards him.

She put her arms out as she spoke and the boy almost collapsed into them.

She helped him to the sofa and laid him down, fetch-
ing a cup of milk from the tea-table, and holding it to
his lips.

He found it hard to drink and after a few sips he
waved it away and shut his eyes.

She took off his shoes, noting they were dusty and
scratched, then fetched some warm water to bathe his
eye and his lip.

It was some time later when he seemed a little relaxed that she said to him quietly:

"Tell me, darling, what happened?"

Tamara ran down the front stairs and across the
Hall.

She did not wait to ask a footman where the Duke
was likely to be, because she was quite certain that at
this time in the evening he would be in the Blue Salon.

It was where he habitually sat reading the newspapers which did not arrive at the Castle until the afternoon.

Her eyes were stormy and her lips were in a tight
line, and anyone who knew her would have been
aware that Tamara's Hungarian temper was flaring as
fiery as the hair on her head.

She walked into the Blue Salon but the Duke was not there.

Then as she paused, wondering where she should look for him, she heard the sound of voices and realised a door which communicated with the Study next door was ajar.

She walked towards it and was just about to pull the door further open when she heard Major Melville say:

"If you sued the author of this iniquitous book I am quite certain, Your Grace, you would get very substantial damages—certainly not less than £5,000, I should imagine."

"You are right, Melville," the Duke replied. "I have never in my life read anything so scurrilous or so poisonously offensive!"

The Duke paused, then added:

"I wonder who the author is? The mere initials 'T.S.' might hide the identity of a man or a woman."

"I hardly think, Your Grace, that a woman would be so vitriolic."

"One never knows," the Duke answered. "There are some women who, when it suits them, can be just as spiteful as any man."

"I will take Your Grace's word for it," Major Melville replied, "but what steps shall I take on your behalf?"

There was silence and Tamara held her breath.

She was only too well aware what they were discussing.

Yesterday she had received a letter forwarded to her by Mr. Lawson from her Publishers.

They informed her that her instructions to withdraw the book had arrived after the novel had actually been distributed to the book-sellers and there was therefore nothing they could do about it.

They had gone on to say:

We deeply regret, Madam, that you wish to take this step seeing that in our opinion the novel will sell well and in fact we are quite certain that in a month's time we shall be obliged to re-print it.

In the meantime we enclose a cheque for £20 for advance sales which we hope will be to your satisfaction.

Tamara had read the letter and was upset and somewhat perturbed by the information it contained.

"There is nothing I can do about it," she told herself. "At the same time I hope the book will not sell and no-one will give the Duke a copy."

It had been one thing to write about him in a vitriolic manner when she had never seen him, and she had thought when she first came to the Castle that every word her book contained was fully justified.

But as time passed she had found it increasingly hard to go on disliking him so violently, when he had allowed her to ride, given the children ponies, and acquiesced in her demands regarding their accommodation and food.

She still thought he was overwhelmingly autocratic, that he looked on her in a disdainful manner and was waiting to find fault.

But she had to admit if she was honest that he had, once they had settled in, not been half as much of an ogre as she had expected him to be.

She had looked again at the Solicitor's letter and walked to the window to look out at the beauty of the lake outside and wonder if truthfully she could say she was sorry she had come to the Castle.

"He will never read the book," she told herself reassuringly.

It was a statement that seemed to repeat and re-repeat itself in her brain.

Now she was proved to be wrong.

The Duke had read her novel and it was quite obvious what he thought about it.

"I have been sent copies of this scurrilous novel by three people already," she heard him say slowly. "Two of them are relations who are furious that what they

413

call 'the family honour' should be dragged in the mud
and the other is a friend who has offered to horse-whip
both the author and the Publisher."

"I think you should take some action, Your Grace."

"On the other hand, as you well know, Melville, to
bring a case like this into Court is to give the author,
who is obviously an extremely unpleasant individual,
just the sort of publicity he would wish to have."

"You can hardly let the whole thing pass without
making a protest," Major Melville answered.

"No, I realise that," the Duke replied, "and I have
decided what I shall do."

"What is that, Your Grace?"

"You will send to London immediately and buy up
every available copy of the book. Take over the Publisher's stock, search the book-sellers for every unsold
volume and have them brought back here."

"What will you do with them all, Your Grace?"

"Burn them!" the Duke answered. "It is the only
way to dispose of filth!"

"It will cost a considerable sum of money."

"That is completely immaterial," the Duke replied,
"but make it quite clear to the Publishers that if they
bring out another edition I will sue them for every
penny they possess."

There was a forceful determination in the Duke's
voice which Tamara had heard before.

Then so suddenly that she started nervously he
walked in to the Blue Salon through the half-open
door to find her just on the other side of it.

"You wanted to see me, Miss Wynne?"

"Yes, Your Grace."

He shut the door behind him and made a gesture
towards one of the sofas.

"Will you sit down?"

"No!"

He raised his eye-brows and stood facing her, an
enigmatic expression on his face.

"What is it?" he asked.

"Sándor—he has just returned from school. I wish Your Grace to see the state he is in."

The Duke smiled cynically.

"He has been fighting, I suppose. Do not distress yourself. All boys fight and I expect it will take him a little time to find his own level."

Tamara drew in her breath.

"He has come back in a state of collapse. I think several of his ribs may be broken and he cannot see out of one eye."

"Sándor is growing up and he has to fight his own battles," the Duke said indifferently.

"I agree he has to fight his *own* battles," Tamara said sharply, "but not yours."

"What do you mean by that?"

"Sándor has been deliberately beaten up because of you and your behaviour."

She spoke rudely but she did not care.

The Duke's indifference was the last straw and her feeling of fury at what had happened to Sándor grew.

He had not wanted to tell her about it but she had coaxed it out of him because she had to know.

She could not bear to have him treated in such a way and not understand the cause of it.

"Are you telling me that Sándor has been fighting to save my good name?" the Duke asked mockingly.

It was the last straw which broke through Tamara's effort at self-control.

Her eyes flashed and her words when she replied came tumbling through her lips as if she could no longer suppress them.

"Sándor was deliberately set upon by three boys older and bigger than himself who had been told by their fathers to take it out on him because they hate you!"

"Hate me?" the Duke asked.

"Does that surprise you?" Tamara asked. "You must realise that there are a great number of people who

415

hate you, but there is no reason why Sándor should be practically murdered in consequence."

"I can hardly credit what you are telling me," the Duke said.

"Then perhaps you will remember turning a tenant-farmer off your land because you said he did not farm well enough? His son was one of the boys who attacked Sándor."

She saw the Duke knew who the man was she had mentioned.

"Another was the son of the local saddler," she went on, "whose bill you refused to pay for what you called inferior workmanship. The third, was the son of your butcher, whom you accused of overcharging."

Tamara paused for breath, then she continued:

"Sándor's wounds will heal, but I am wondering why, unless you were striking at your brother through his son, you sent him to such a school."

She saw the anger in the Duke's face, but she stormed on:

"I asked you to send Sándor to school so that he could have proper companionship. Do you really consider such boys the right companions for your nephew and heir? If so, are you prepared to entertain them here at the Castle and invite their fathers to come with them?"

Tamara's voice seemed to ring out.

When she finished speaking there was silence, a silence when she and the Duke stood looking at each other, both with their eyes dark with anger.

Tamara's hands were clenched and her whole body tense. Then as she waited for his reply to her challenge he turned away and walked across the room.

"I will see Sándor for myself," he said and crossing the Hall walked slowly up the staircase.

Tamara was trembling and was so shaken with fury that for the moment she could not follow him.

"I am glad I wrote my novel!" she told herself. "I am glad it shocked and affronted him! Perhaps now he will

realise that he is just as horrible as the Duke of Ullester—in fact he is worse!"

It was a few minutes before she could force herself to
leave the Blue Salon and walk up the stairs. Then as
she moved slowly towards the West Wing she encountered Mrs. Henderson.

"Oh, Miss Wynne! I've never heard such a thing, I
haven't really!" the Housekeeper cried. "Poor young
gentleman, it's a crying shame, that's what it is! But
there, I always knew that school was full of a lot of
rough, common boys. I can't understand His Grace
sending Master Sándor there, that I can't."

"I shall not let him go there again, Mrs. Henderson," Tamara assured her.

She was not surprised at the Housekeeper's agita-
tion over Sándor because now she had got used to the
children there was no doubt that he was her favourite
and could do no wrong in her eyes.

"I'm just going downstairs, Miss Wynne," Mrs. Henderson continued, "to tell the Chef to make some
nourishing soup for the poor little fellow. He'll not be
able to eat anything solid."

"No, I am afraid not," Tamara agreed. "I had intended to ask the Chef myself for a bowl of soup but it
would be very kind if you could do it for me."

"It's a pleasure, Miss Wynne," the Housekeeper
said. "And I've some salve in my room which I'm sure
would help Master Sándor's bruises. I've used it many
a time and very efficacious it's proved."

"Thank you very much, Mrs. Henderson."

The Housekeeper hurried away, her chatelaine
clanking, her black dress rustling.

She had certainly changed from the woman who had
refused to have the Nurseries cleaned and had thought
the better rooms were too good for the children.

Tamara reached the part they occupied in the West
Wing, but she did not go into the Sitting-Room.

She could hear the Duke's deep voice speaking to

417

Sándor, and she went first to say good-night to Vava only to find her asleep, then into Kadine's room.

"You have been a long time coming to me," Kadine said. "As you could not go on reading the book, will you tell me a story?"

"A very short one," Tamara replied.

It was a story that Kadine particularly liked about a little girl who had the most fantastic adventures. She encountered giants and dragons, was assisted by a number of good fairies, and escaped in dark woods from goblins and witches.

It was difficult for Tamara to tell the story with her mind on Sándor and while she was seething with anger against the Duke.

But she forced herself to concentrate and as the story wound to a dramatic climax she realised that Kadine's eyes were dropping, and as she finished the last word the child was asleep.

It was only then she realised they were not alone in the bed-room for standing by the open doorway was the Duke.

She looked at him and knew that he intended to speak to her.

She put her fingers up to her lips, tucked the sheet under Kadine's chin, then rose to lower the blind over the open window.

Very softly she went out of the room and the Duke followed her.

"I want to speak to you, Miss Wynne."

She stood waiting and he said:

"Shall we go into the Sitting-Room? I have carried Sándor to his own bed."

"You carried him?"

"He was not too heavy for me," the Duke replied sarcastically.

Tamara did not answer. She was surprised that the Duke should concern himself so closely with one of the children, especially Sándor.

She walked into the Sitting-Room and as the Duke followed her he said:

"I sent for Watkins, my own valet, who actually is an extremely good nurse and told him to undress Sándor. He will, I assure you, do it as gently as any woman could."

"I suppose I should thank Your Grace."

"That is quite unnecessary," the Duke answered, "but I am, although you may not believe it, extremely perturbed at the state the boy is in."

"I am very glad to hear it."

As she spoke she suddenly realised she should not speak to the Duke in such a way.

After all, she was supposed to be a humble and sub-servient Governess, a servant he could dismiss at a moment's notice without a reference if she offended him.

Because she knew she could not bear to leave the children she forced herself to say in a somewhat milder tone:

"I hope Your Grace will now realise that your choice of a school was at fault?"

"I am aware of that, Miss Wynne, and I have told Sándor so," the Duke answered. "He will go to Eton at the beginning of next term, and I wish to consult you as to which tutors you consider are necessary to teach him until September."

"You will send him to Eton?" Tamara asked.

"I have promised him that I will do so."

"It is where Lord Ronald went and where I always wanted him to go."

"As it happens, it is also where I was educated," the Duke answered.

"Then why . . . ?" Tamara began.

She saw the expression on his face and the words died away from her lips.

"All right," the Duke said in an irritated tone. "I made a mistake, and I am not too proud to admit it. If you want to know the truth, I resented the fact that you assumed that I should automatically take over the upbringing of these children."

"It was because there . . . seemed to be . . . no-one else," Tamara answered weakly.

She suddenly saw that she had been very demanding and peremptory. Because Mr. Lawson had convinced her there was nowhere else they could go she had been concerned only in forcing the Duke, whom she hated, into doing what she wanted.

"There are actually quite a number of relations who would have been only too pleased to more or less adopt my brother's children," the Duke said, "but you did not think to discuss it with me, Miss Wynne."

"What you are implying, Your Grace, is that what has happened to Sándor is my fault."

"In a way," the Duke answered, then he smiled.

She looked at him in surprise because the anger had gone from his face and instead his eyes were twinkling.

"May I say, Miss Wynne, that you are not only a very formidable opponent, but also a fanatical champion of those you love."

Tamara could think of no reply and as she looked at him uncertainly he went from the Sitting-Room leaving her alone.

She ran to Sándor's room.

The Duke's valet, Watkins, was with him, a small elderly man who had always been very polite although until now they had had little to do with him.

"I've got him into bed, Miss," he said to Tamara in a conspiratorial whisper. "The poor young gentleman's going to be black and blue to-morrow, but if you ask me there's no bones broken."

"Are you sure of that?" Tamara asked. "He has a pain in his ribs and I thought one might be fractured."

"He were punched pretty hard, Miss, but I'm thinking it's his eye that'll hurt him most. I'm just a-going downstairs to get a compress. If there isn't any ice in the Castle I'll send to the ice-house down by the lake."

"It is very kind of you," Tamara said.

"It reminds me of when His Grace and Master Ronald were young. They beat up some village lads as was shooting at the deer with bows and arrows. There were two of them against half-a-dozen."

"Who won?" Tamara asked.

"They did, Miss, but His Grace had an eye as black as coal and Master Ronald had his arm in a sling for over a week!"

The old man chuckled.

"But there, Miss, boys will be boys!"

He hurried away to get the compress and Tamara went to Sándor's side.

"Are you all right, dearest?" she asked feeling the tears rise in her eyes as she looked down at his battered face.

"Uncle Howard was jolly kind," he answered. "He says I need not go back to that beastly school and he is sending me to Eton."

"I know," Tamara said, "and that is where I always wanted you to go."

"And Papa would have liked that!"

"He would, and your mother as well."

Sándor tried to smile and failed.

"Not Mama," he said. "She never wanted any of us to go away from home, but I expect I would have gone all the same."

"I am sure you would," Tamara agreed, "and Sándor, although it has been a horrible experience, you must forget about it. We all make mistakes and going to that school was one of them."

"That is what Uncle Howard said. Do you know, he sort of apologised for sending me there! That was jolly big of him, wasn't it?"

"Yes . . . I suppose it was," Tamara said slowly.

There was a silence while Sándor closed his eyes, but a minute or so later he said:

"I thought when we first came here that I hated him, but now in lots of ways I think he is rather like Papa."

When Sándor had finally been settled for the night, Tamara left a bell by his bed so that he could ring for her if he wanted anything.

She walked into the Sitting-Room and for the first time she could think of her book and what she had overheard the Duke saying to Major Melville.

She felt guilty about the cheque for £20 which she had hidden in her bed-room and thought perhaps she should return it.

But she remembered that the Duke had told Major Melville to buy up all the books which were in the shops and the Publisher's stock. That meant that neither the Publishers nor the book-sellers would suffer any financial loss.

"I will spend most of the money on the children and the rest on charity," Tamara told herself.

It would be a salve for her conscience if she did not keep anything for herself.

She thought of the terms in which the Duke had described the book and its author and felt ashamed.

It was only because she had been so incensed at the way her sister and her brother-in-law had been treated that she had tried to avenge them in the only way open to her.

When she was writing 'The Ducal Wasp', she had no idea she would ever meet the real Duke of Granchester or even see him for that matter.

It had just been a blow struck at a shadowy figure, and yet now the whole thing had come back on her in a way that was frightening.

She gave a deep sigh and told herself that whatever happened the Duke must never find out.

There was no reason why "T.S." should mean anything to him, yet Tamara wished she had used an entirely fictitious name. She had signed her first book with initials hoping that the critics would think she was a man.

But here was another pit-fall, she told herself, which might, if she was not careful, reveal her identity not only as the author of the 'most poisonous and scurrilous' novel the Duke had ever read, but also a governess.

She felt herself tremble at the thought of what would happen should she be unmasked.

It would certainly, she thought, give the Duke the excuse he needed to throw her ignominiously out of the Castle and out of the children's lives.

She felt suddenly horrified at how rude she had been to him when she told him of Sándor's disastrous ordeal.

But it was impossible to control her anger when she thought of how reprehensible it had been of the Duke to send Sándor to such a school.

He must have had some idea of how disliked he was in the neighbourhood.

"He cannot be so blind as to think everyone likes him," she said to herself.

Yet after all she supposed that, since he was a Duke and in a position of great authority in the County, there were few people with the exception of herself, who were likely to tell him the truth.

'That is as revolutionary as if I actually started a riot in the Castle,' she thought.

At the same time, even her triumph at obtaining the Duke's promise to send Sándor to Eton was offset by the fact that he was disgusted by her novel.

Other people would doubtless find it amusing, even while those who were spiteful would delight in the unpleasant picture it painted of the Duke of Granchester.

Suddenly Tamara remembered that the Duke had said that two copies had been sent to him by his relatives who had been shocked at "the family pride being dragged into the mud."

She had forgotten, that the children were part of the family.

In disparaging the Duke and attacking him in such an obvious manner as to be recognisable, she was attacking the whole Grant family, and Sándor, Kadine and Vava were all Grants.

'I have made a mess of it,' Tamara thought humbly.

When she went to bed she lay for a long time in the darkness wishing, as so many people have wished before her, that she could put back the clock and write a very different book from the one which had been published.

Because she had been so late in going to sleep Tamara, instead of being awake when Rose the housemaid came in to pull her curtains, was still dreaming.

As the sunshine came in through the windows she sat up in bed to ask:

"What time is it, Rose?"

"Eight o'clock, Miss, and Mr. Watkins said I was to tell you that Master Sándor has had a good night and is quite comfortable this morning."

"I should be attending to him."

"Don't worry, Miss," Rose answered. "Mr. Watkins loves having someone t' nurse. He often says his talents are wasted 'cause His Grace never has a day's illness."

"No, I am sure he is very strong," Tamara answered as she got out of bed.

"Mr. Watkins nursed th' late Duke afore he died," Rose went on, "and th' old gentleman couldn't bear him out o' his sight."

"I must hurry and get dressed," Tamara said. "Would you be very kind and wake Miss Kadine and Miss Vava?"

"I'll do that, Miss."

It was usually Tamara who woke the little girls and had them ready to go down to breakfast at eight-thirty in the Adam Dining-Room.

But now she was just arranging her hair when

Kadine knocked on the door and without waiting for an answer came running in.

"Sándor is awake, Miss Wynne, and says he wants an egg for breakfast. May he have one?"

"Yes, tell him he can have anything if he feels he can eat it," Tamara answered. "I will not be a minute."

She put a last pin into her hair and took down a light muslin gown from the wardrobe.

"Please, Kadine dearest, ask Rose to come and do me up," she said.

"Would you like me to do it?" Kadine enquired.

"I think Rose would be quicker," Tamara answered. "I am in a hurry because I overslept."

"I expect you were tired because you were worried about Sándor," Kadine said perceptively.

"That is true," Tamara smiled. "Now be a good girl and fetch Rose."

Kadine hurried away and Tamara put on her muslin gown, found her light slippers and was ready except for the fastening at the back of her dress when Rose came into the room.

"Will you do me up please, Rose?" she asked. "Is Miss Vava ready?"

"Miss Vava wasn't in her room when I goes in t' her," Rose answered.

"Then she must be with Miss Kadine."

"No, Miss Kadine hasn't seen her," Rose replied deftly fastening the buttons at the back of Tamara's gown.

"It is very naughty of her to run around before she is dressed," Tamara said. "I have told her about it before."

"Oh, she's dressed, Miss. I left a clean frock on a chair ready for her last night, an' it's gone, an' so have her shoes."

"I shall be very angry with her if she has gone to the stables," Tamara said. "She knows I like her to have breakfast first."

"You can't stop Miss Vava loving that pony o' hers," Rose said. "Fair dotes on it, she does!"

"I think we all want something to love," Tamara said reflectively.

"That's what my mother always used t' say, Miss. We all needs a touch of love in our lives an' without it there's only tears."

"I am sure your mother was very wise," Tamara remarked.

Then as Rose had finished doing her up she hurried from the room to see Sándor.

He was certainly better, although his eye was black and blue and his cut lip was very swollen.

"How do you feel, dearest?" Tamara asked.

"Rather sore," Sándor answered.

"If you stay quietly in your room to-day perhaps you will be able to get up to-morrow."

"If I do not have to go to school, I would much rather be riding."

"I know that," Tamara answered, "but I am afraid you would find it very uncomfortable."

"I suppose you are right," Sándor said with a sigh. "I have lots of books to read, and will you play chess with me when you have time?"

"Yes, I would rather you played games, since it is difficult to read when you have only one eye," Tamara answered. "I will play chess as soon as I have taken the girls for a walk. They can go without their lessons this morning."

"Good!" Sándor said.

Tamara put out her hand to Kadine who was hovering by the bed.

"Come along," she said, "we will go downstairs and start our breakfast. If Vava's is cold she will have no-one to blame but herself."

"Rose said Vava has gone out. It is very naughty of her, isn't it?"

"Very naughty!" Tamara agreed. "I am afraid I shall have to punish her."

"How will you do that?" Kadine asked.

"I will think of something," Tamara answered.

The most effective punishment, she knew, would be to stop Vava from riding, but this was a threat which she did not wish to put into operation unless it was absolutely necessary.

The children were usually so good and so well behaved that there was no need for any punishments.

They had obeyed their father and mother because they loved them, and Tamara knew they obeyed her for the same reason.

At the same time it was naughty of Vava to have gone out early in the morning without telling anyone what she was doing.

Tamara settled Kadine down at the breakfast-table. Then because she felt she could not eat anything herself until she had found Vava she walked through the Castle and out of a door which led almost directly to the stable-yard.

She found a number of stable-boys hurrying about but there was no sign of Vava. Then Tamara saw Abbey coming from one of the stalls.

"Good-morning, Abbey."

"Good-morning, Miss."

"Is Miss Vava here? I am afraid she has played truant and I was sure I would find her with Butterfly."

"No, Miss, her's not been here this morning."

"Are you sure?" Tamara asked.

"Quite sure, Miss. Oi've not seen a sight nor sound o' er."

One of the stable-boys passed as he spoke and he shouted:

"Hi, Bill! Have ye seen anything o' Miss Vava this morn?"

"No, Mr. Abbey."

"Ye're sure her's not been here?"

"Quite sure, Mr. Abbey. Oi've been here since six o'clock."

427

"She must be somewhere in the Castle," Tamara said and hurried back.

Kadine had finished her breakfast.

"You have been a long time," she remarked, "and I do not want any more."

"Then come and help me find Vava."

Tamara was beginning to feel worried, although she would hardly admit it to herself as they searched everywhere, in the Library, the Salon and even the kitchens.

"Have you seen *Mademoiselle* Vava, *Monsieur?*" Tamara asked the Chef.

"*Mais non, M'mselle,*" he replied. Then smiling at Kadine he said:

"If you're a good little girl I'm making you a special cake for tea."

"What sort of cake?" Kadine asked. "Is it a pink one?"

"A pink one with your name on in cherries."

Kadine clapped her hands.

"*Merci, Monsieur! Merci bien!*"

The Chef beamed at her. But Tamara, while amused and glad that he had taken such a liking to the little girls, took Kadine away.

They went up to the Sitting-Room, thinking perhaps Vava had come back but it was empty and Sándor had not seen her either.

Tamara began to get worried.

It was now nearly nine o'clock and she was certain that Vava if nothing else, would be feeling hungry for her breakfast.

She was hurrying down the front stairs when she saw the Duke come through the front door.

He had been riding as he usually did early in the morning and was just handing his riding-whip and gloves to one of the footmen when he looked up and saw her.

"Your Grace, we have lost Vava!' Tamara said.

Kadine ran ahead of her down the stairs.

"She has disappeared, Uncle Howard, and she has

not had her breakfast. We have searched everywhere. I think a goblin must have spirited her away!"

As she spoke Tamara gave a little cry.

"What is it?" the Duke asked.

"I know where Vava has gone!" she exclaimed. "She has gone to have another look at the gypsy pony! She has not stopped talking about it since she first saw it yesterday."

The Duke frowned.

"I told Melville to get rid of the gypsies."

"They had a piebald foal," Tamara explained, "and Vava was fascinated by it."

"I will go and fetch her back," the Duke said.

"Let me come with you," Tamara pleaded.

The Duke turned to the Butler.

"Order a horse for me, and one for Miss Wynne."

"It will only take me two minutes to change," Tamara said.

She picked up the front of her skirt as she spoke and ran up the stairs.

She ran to her bed-room followed by Kadine.

"You stay here with Sándor," Tamara said.

It literally took her only three minutes to put on her habit. Then she ran back down the stairs to find the Duke outside the front door with two horses.

"I have certainly never known a woman who could change her clothes so quickly!" he said, and to Tamara's surprise he helped her into the saddle.

They rode off, galloping the horses over the Park until they came to the far end of it where there was a rough, open piece of ground.

When they reached it Tamara looked at it in consternation.

There were the grey ashes where a fire had burned the night before, there were the marks on the grass of the wheels of caravans, and on one or two bramble bushes there were a few colourful rags which had obviously been discarded, but otherwise there was no sign of the gypsies.

"They have gone!" she exclaimed.

She turned to look at the Duke.

"You turned them away," she said. "Do you think they have taken Vava with them?

CHAPTER SIX

*T*here was a throb in Tamara's voice as she spoke. Then the Duke said:

"They will not have gone far and we will follow them."

He moved his horse ahead as he spoke.

They crossed the road which formed the boundary of the Park, and now stretching over the countryside there were thick almost impenetrable woods.

Tamara was suddenly afraid that once the gypsies disappeared among the dark trees it would be impossible for an outsider to find them.

She was aware that the gypsies had secret paths by which they moved from place to place, but she hardly expected the Duke would know of them.

Yet he rode confidently ahead and after twisting between the trees they came upon a narrow track which was just wide enough, Tamara realised, for a Caravan.

She saw there were deep ruts made by wheels, but at the same time they could have been made by the carts used by the wood-cutters.

The Duke went on without hesitating. Although she longed to ask him where he was going and if he was certain they were moving in the right direction, she felt as if her throat was constricted.

All she could think of was Vava being carried away by the gypsies to some unknown destination where they would never find her again.

There were always stories circulating among villagers about the gypsies. How they not only stole eggs and chickens, ducks and small lambs, but also children.

In the past Tamara had never believed such tales, thinking that the gypsies had so many children of their own that they were unlikely to want anyone else's.

But now the stories which had been repeated and repeated for generations amongst illiterate people, who were afraid of the gypsies' curse or the 'evil eye', came flooding back into her mind.

They made her feel more and more afraid with every pace her horse took.

Then unexpectedly there was a clearing deep in the wood and she saw that it must have been used as a camping-ground for years.

There were the grey ashes of a dozen fires and again fluttering, colourful rags on bushes and low branches of the trees—but there were no gypsies.

Even as Tamara parted her lips to ask the Duke what they should do now, she saw Vava.

The child came running towards them from the shadow of a fir tree.

"Vava!" Tamara exclaimed.

The Duke turned back to take her horse's bridle and she slipped from the saddle onto the ground to run towards Vava, her arms outstretched.

"Oh, Aunt Tamara! I'se frightened!" Vava cried.

Then as Tamara's arms went round her she burst into tears.

Tamara knelt down on the ground and held her close.

"It is all right, darling," she said soothingly. "We have found you and you are quite safe now."

"The gypsies left me . . . alone," Vava sobbed.

"They said I was to . . . stay here and not to . . . run away . . . but I was . . . frightened all by . . . myself."

"I am here now," Tamara said. "The Duke and I will take you home. We have been searching for you everywhere."

She wiped away Vava's tears and, picking her up in her arms, she walked back towards her horse.

"I will take her in front of my saddle," the Duke said.

As Tamara hesitated he said to Vava:

"I am sure you would like to ride on Samson."

Vava's dark eye-lashes were still wet, but now she smiled.

She held up her arms to the Duke and he took her from Tamara and set her on his saddle in front of him.

"Can you manage to mount by yourself?" he asked Tamara.

"I have managed to do so for a great number of years," she answered.

But she too was smiling. It was so wonderful to have found Vava safe and sound!

They turned their horses' heads back in the direction from which they had come.

"I went to look for the little piebald pony," Vava explained, "and the gypsy lady said I was to go with them."

"You should not have gone out alone so early in the morning," Tamara said.

But it was difficult to make her voice sound severe, she was so glad to have Vava back again.

"I wanted to see the pony," Vava said. Then looking up at the Duke she added: "The gypsies were very angry with you, Uncle Howard, because you turned them away."

There was a pause, before the Duke replied:

"I will tell you what we will do, Vava. This afternoon, if you are not too tired, or to-morrow morning, we will go to the entrance to the Park and look for the signs left by the gypsies for other gypsies who may want to camp there."

"What sort of signs?" Vava asked.

"They have one which means: 'Nice people—can camp here'," the Duke answered, "and another which says: 'These people do not like gypsies'."

Vava considered this for a moment, then she said:

"As you turned them away, that is the sign they will have left behind."

"Exactly!" the Duke agreed, "and that is why you and I will alter it. Then other gypsies will come and you will be able to see their piebald ponies if they have any."

"I would like that," Vava cried.

"But you are never to go there without me," Tamara interrupted quickly. "You know that was very naughty."

"I am . . . sorry," Vava said.

But her voice was no longer frightened as she leaned back comfortably against the Duke, putting her hands on the reins in front of his.

"I am riding Samson," she said proudly, "just like Sándor did."

"Samson is really too big for Sándor," the Duke answered, "and you will have to grow very much bigger before you can ride him."

"When I am grown up I shall take him over the jumps," Vava said confidently.

"By the time you are grown up Samson may be too old," the Duke replied with a smile.

Listening to him talk to Vava, Tamara thought she would never have imagined he could be so kind or so understanding to a child.

Now for the first time since leaving the Castle, too agitated to think of anything but Vava, she thought how handsome he was and how magnificent he looked on the big black stallion.

She found herself glancing at his clear-cut features, the way he rode as if he seemed part of the horse itself.

She thought too that the lines of cynicism at the sides of his mouth seemed lighter and there was a twinkle in his eyes she had not noticed before.

When they reached the Park Vava wished to go faster and to please her the Duke put Samson into a trot and Tamara did the same with her horse.

When they had nearly reached the Castle she said:

"Can we go straight into the stable-yard? I know how worried Abbey was at Vava's disappearance and I am sure that he will want to know we have found her."

The Duke did not reply, he merely smiled at her. Then as they rode over the cobble-stones of the stable-yard Abbey came hurrying out of a stall exclaiming in delight:

"Ye've found Miss Vava, Your Grace! It's thankful Oi am that she's safely home again."

"Quite safe, Abbey," the Duke replied.

The old groom reached up to take Vava from the saddle but she screamed:

"No! I want to ride Samson over the jumps. Please, Uncle Howard, let me ride him round the race-course."

"I am afraid you would find it difficult to keep in the saddle if I did that," the Duke answered, "but I will tell you what I will do, I will jump Samson over the five-bar gate, and you can come and watch."

"All right," Vava agreed.

She let Abbey lift her to the ground, then Tamara also dismounted and they walked hand-in-hand to the end of the stables.

The Duke took Samson back a little way, then put him at the gate and the horse went forward confidently.

It was a jump he had done dozens of times, but as he nearly reached it Tamara suddenly thought that the gate seemed higher than she remembered.

As the horse took off she thought how graceful the animal looked and how superbly the Duke was riding him.

Then there was the sound of Samson's front hoofs hitting the top bar, a sharp crack which seemed almost like the report of a pistol, and to Tamara's horror and the consternation of Abbey, who gave a hoarse cry, the gate did not give way.

Samson fell and, as he collapsed onto his knees, the Duke was shot over his head to fall heavily to the ground.

It was Tamara who reached him first and as she bent down to touch him she saw that his eyes were closed.

With a sudden fear which seemed to strike her almost like a dagger in her heart, she thought he was dead.

Tamara walked along the passage from the West Wing and as she reached the Grand Staircase she saw two men going down it, their voices low as they talked to each other.

She knew that one of them was the local doctor who had been sent for as soon as the Duke had been carried back to the Castle on an improvised stretcher. The other was the Specialist who had arrived from London a few hours ago.

Yesterday after the accident the Duke had remained unconscious and Tamara had enquired after him nearly every hour, but Watkins could tell her very little.

First thing this morning she had learnt that the Duke had regained consciousness but was in great pain.

"I've never known anything like it, Miss," Watkins said shaking his head. "It seems as if the Master's in agony, and it's not like him to complain unless it's real bad."

"Surely there is something the doctor can give him so that he need not suffer unnecessarily?" Tamara asked.

"Dr. Emmerton is waiting the arrival of Sir George Seymour from London, Miss," Watkins explained. "He's the King's doctor, you know, and one can't ask for better."

"Yes, I am sure Dr. Emmerton is right," Tamara said reflectively. "It would be a mistake to do anything of which Sir George might not approve."

At the same time it hurt her in a manner she could not understand to think that the Duke was suffering.

Watkins had said he was very ill, and she could remember all too vividly her feelings when she saw him lying on the ground and thought he was dead.

It had been agony too to watch the men lift him and carry him back to the Castle and know that he was unconscious of what was happening.

Only a little while earlier she had been thinking how magnificent he looked on Samson, and now like a great oak fallen to the ground he was helpless and still.

To look at him made her feel curiously near to tears.

She had been unable to sleep all night for thinking of him, and even the fact that Sándor was much better and, having eaten a large breakfast demanded to get up, could not erase her feeling of depression.

There was also at the back of her mind the problem of the five-bar gate.

When she had risen from the Duke's side to allow the men to lift him onto the stretcher to take him back to the Castle, she had turned to look at the gate and wondered why it had not fallen as it should have done.

Then she saw that it had in fact been nailed firmly to the posts on either side of it.

What was more she saw that her first impression had been correct and the gate was some five inches higher than it had been when it swung lightly as the Duke had designed it.

"Who could have done such a thing?" she asked.

She knew without being told that it was someone on the Estate, some employee who hated his Master and had planned to take his revenge as other labourers were trying to do all over the country.

Even while she admitted that it had perhaps been the Duke's fault, she knew that personally whatever he had done she could not bear to see him punished in such a way.

She had been waiting all the morning to hear Sir George's verdict and now as she reached the Duke's bed-room and was just about to knock, the door opened and Watkins came out.

"I came to enquire . . ." Tamara began, then her voice died away.

The old valet was crying, the tears running down his cheeks.

"What is it?" she asked in a whisper.

"It's the Master, Miss."

Tamara drew in her breath.

"He is not . . . dead?" she could hardly say the words.

Then even as she uttered them little above a whisper she knew as her heart seemed to contract that she loved him.

The knowledge was so overwhelming, at the same time so painful, that she could only stand feeling as if she was turned to stone.

Watkins, wiping his eyes with the back of his hand, said:

"No, Miss not dead, worse!"

"What could be . . . worse?" Tamara asked still in a whisper because the words could hardly pass her lips.

"Sir George says that the Master's broken his back, Miss, and he'll always be paralysed!"

As if it was too much to bear, Watkins covered his eyes with his hand.

Tamara stood staring at him, the colour fading from her cheeks leaving her very pale.

"It cannot be . . . true! Is Sir George . . . certain?"

"He's bringing another Specialist down to-morrow,

Miss, but I knows by the way he spoke and the expression on Dr. Emmerton's face they didn't think there's much hope."

There was a pause when Tamara was unable to speak before Watkins said:

"The Master'd rather be dead and gone than have to put up with such a life, I knows that!"

Tamara was sure of it too.

But because she felt the conflicting emotions within her had sapped her power of thought she could only stand staring at Watkins' wet face.

"There must be something we can do," she said frantically after some moments had passed.

"Dr. Emmerton's sending his carriage back with something to relieve His Grace's pain," Watkins said. "But he's lying there a-swearing he'll not take their damned drugs! He's never had any use for them."

Tamara did not speak and Watkins went on:

"It's terrible to see him, Miss—terrible!"

Tamara felt her fingers were clenched together. Then as she longed to do something, yearned as she had never yearned in her whole life before to be able to help, she felt as if she faced an insurmountable barrier.

She only stood immobile.

Watkins drew a crumpled handkerchief from his pocket and wiped his face with it.

"I must get back to His Grace, Miss."

He turned towards the door and as he did so a footman came along the passage.

"I was a-looking for you, Miss," he said to Tamara. "There's a man at the back-door as wishes to speak to you."

"A man?" Tamara asked, finding it difficult to concentrate on what the footman was saying.

"Yes, Miss, he says he comes from Cornwall and you'd be expecting him. He be blind."

Tamara gave a little cry.

"It is Erth! Erth Veryon! Where is he? Take me to him quickly!"

The footman glanced at her in surprise and led the way down the back stairs to the kitchen door.

Standing outside, his white hair blowing in the warm breeze was Erth Veryon and beside him stood his grandson.

"Erth! Erth!" Tamara cried putting out her hands towards him. "You have come at exactly the right moment! I need you—I need you desperately!"

"The Lord guided me here," Erth said in his deep voice with its Cornish accent. "I felt there was work for me to do."

"There is indeed," Tamara said. "Come upstairs. Come and see the Duke. He has had a fall . . . a terrible fall from his horse . . . and the doctors say that he has broken his back and will be paralysed!"

She took Erth's hand in hers as she spoke and drew him along the flagged passage which led to the kitchen door.

As she touched him she felt that strange vibration that she had felt before when he had held her hand in farewell.

They walked up the stairs.

Even as they went some part of Tamara's mind questioned whether Erth would be able to do anything for the Duke, when the King's doctor had said it was hopeless.

And yet she had seen his wonderful healing powers on her brother-in-law and on the people in the village at home.

She knew too that his reputation was so great that the fisher-folk and the villagers all over Cornwall looked on him almost as a Saint.

"Send for Erth!" was a cry that went up when anyone was injured or so ill that they had been given up by the Physicians.

Only as Tamara reached the landing outside the Duke's bed-room did she wonder what he would think if she brought him a blind healer.

She could not help feeling that he might dismiss

439

anything so controversial as such healing as being non-sense and would perhaps refuse to allow Erth to help him.

For a moment she was afraid, but as if he knew what she was thinking Erth said quietly:

"You have to trust in God, child, and His love. It never fails."

Tamara drew in her breath.

"I trust you, Erth," she said quietly and knocked on the Duke's door.

Watkins opened it and looked surprised when he saw there was a man with Tamara.

"I wish to speak to His Grace," Tamara said.

She walked forward, still leading Erth by the hand.

She had never been in the Duke's bed-room before and she had an impression of a huge high-ceilinged room that was as magnificent as its owner.

There were curtains of ruby red velvet not only at the windows but also at the sides of the great canopied bed which reached almost to the ceiling.

The family coat-of-arms was embroidered above the Duke's head and he was lying flat on his back so that he gave the impression, Tamara thought, of a stone figure on top of a tomb.

She forced the thought from her mind and went forward still drawing Erth with her until she stood beside the bed.

The Duke's eyes were closed but she could see that he was in pain by the frown on his forehead and the way his lips were pressed together as if to prevent him from crying out loud.

"Your . . . Grace!"

Tamara's voice was hardly above a whisper but he heard it and his eyes opened.

He looked at her not in surprise, she thought, but as if in a dull agony he appealed to her for help, yet knew she could not give it to him.

"Your Grace!" Tamara said again. "I have brought you a man who will heal you."

The Duke's expression did not alter and she went on:

"He healed your brother, Lord Ronald, and in Cornwall we all believed there that he has a power which is not of this world. Will you please let him help you?"

For one moment she thought the Duke was about to refuse. Then he said in a voice which was little more than a croak:

"If he can—take this damned—pain away I will— believe anything you tell me about—him."

Tamara felt a sudden lightness within her because she had been so afraid . . . so desperately afraid that the Duke would refuse to have anything to do with Erth.

Now she stood aside and the blind man went to the bed.

Tamara moved back against the wall, while Erth's grandson and Watkins stood just inside the door.

Erth stood straight and still beside the Duke and Tamara knew, for she had learnt in Cornwall how he worked, that he was seeing the patient's aura and finding out where the damage lay.

He stood without moving for nearly a minute.

Tamara held her breath waiting and praying wordlessly in her heart that the Duke could be healed.

Then at last Erth moved and very gently he slipped his hand under the Duke's body just below his shoulder.

He moved the sheets as he did so and Tamara realised that because the Duke had been examined by the doctors he was not wearing a night-shirt but was in bed naked.

Gentle though Erth was, the Duke gave a murmur of pain and the Healer spoke for the first time.

"It'll be better in a short while," he said quietly. "The pain'll go."

As he spoke he laid his other hand on the Duke's chest and this Tamara knew was the moment when the power which Erth believed came from God passed from him into the injured person's body.

Erth raised his head a little, almost as if he was looking up into the Heavens.

Tamara knew he was praying and that he spoke with God and asked Him to heal through His love the man whose body was broken.

There was complete silence in the room for several minutes. Then the Duke said:

"I can feel a strange throbbing and an intense heat. It seems to come from your hands."

Erth did not reply and after a moment the Duke said in a different tone:

"The pain is going—in fact it has gone!"

Tamara clasped her hands together.

Now for the first time the tears came into her eyes, tears of relief and happiness. As she felt them she knew how much she loved the Duke.

It seemed absurd that she should love him considering how violently she had hated him, and yet there was no mistaking the ecstasy within her heart.

She had loved him, she thought, long before she had acknowledged it herself when Watkins told her that he was paralysed.

Love had come to her so insidiously and so slowly that she had not recognised it.

She had only known it had been impossible for her not to keep thinking of the Duke. In fact even when she hated him he filled her mind to the exclusion of all else.

Then when he had been so kind to Sándor, when he had apologised to the boy for sending him to the wrong school, she had known, as Sándor had said, that he was big—big enough to acknowledge he had made a mistake.

That was something that few men in his position would have been prepared to do.

It was perhaps then, she thought, that everything she had felt about him had changed.

From that moment every minute, every hour, she had fallen deeper in love with him even though she would not admit it to herself.

The pain she had experienced when she saw him fall from Samson should have told her, but she had been too numb with shock.

It was only Watkins' announcement of what the doctors had said which had made her know the truth almost as if it had been written in letters of fire upon her heart.

'I love him!' she thought now. 'I love everything about him: his magnificence, his kindness to Vava, the way he understood what I was feeling when she was lost.'

It all flashed through her mind as she waited, tense in the quiet room to see if Erth could perform what would be a miracle.

"The throbbing and the heat are going now," the Duke said after what seemed a long time.

Erth turned his head downwards almost as if he could see. Then he said, a smile on his lips:

"Will Your Grace move your arm?"

"I—cannot do—so . . ." the Duke began.

But as he spoke he moved his left arm from his side straight out to shoulder level.

"Now your right," Erth said quietly.

The Duke did as he was told.

Then as the full significance of what had happened came to him he said in a low voice, deeply moved with emotion:

"You have healed me!"

"It is God who has done that," Erth answered, "not I."

"What can I say?" the Duke asked.

"Just give thanks to God who loves and cares for His children and allows me, His servant, if it is His will, to help them."

"I can move! I am not paralysed!" The Duke said

BARBARA CARTLAND

and the words sounded as if he could hardly believe them to be true.

He would have sat up, but Erth's hand was on his shoulder.

"Lie still, Your Grace," he said. "Your back will ache a little to-day and perhaps to-morrow, but let the power of God work slowly—slowly!"

He repeated the word with a smile. Then he turned from the bed and Tamara, knowing what he wanted, went towards him and took his hand in hers.

"How can I thank you?" she asked.

"I want no thanks," Erth answered. "I came because you needed me."

"The children will want to see you."

"Then take me to them."

"After you have seen them please do not leave," the Duke said. "I would like you to stay at least until to-morrow in case I have a relapse."

"You will not need me again, Your Grace," Erth replied, "and my grandson and I must be on our way."

"I want to offer you my hospitality for as long as you wish," the Duke said.

"I am needed to the north of where I am now," Erth said quietly, almost as if he heard someone telling him so.

"Then what can I do to express my gratitude?" the Duke asked.

Erth did not answer. He was moving across the room towards his grandson.

Tamara went to the Duke's side.

"Give him anything he wants," the Duke ordered.

"He will take no money," Tamara answered, "but I will see what I can do for him."

The Duke's eyes were looking into hers.

"Thank you," he said quietly.

Because she was afraid he would read in her face what she felt about him, she turned quickly away.

She took Erth to their Sitting-Room in the West

444

Wing and Sándor greeted him with an exclamation of surprise that was almost a shout.

"Erth! What are you doing here?"

"Erth has healed the Duke," Tamara explained.

"If you had come yesterday you could have healed me!"

"What have you been doing to yourself, Master Sándor?" Erth asked.

He put out his hand as he spoke and laid it unerringly on Sándor's bruised eye.

"It is all right, Erth," Sándor said uncomfortably.

"Stand still," Tamara ordered. "You know Erth will make it better."

"He is making it tingle," Sándor complained.

Erth paid no attention. He merely kept his hand over the bruised eye then with the other touched Sándor's split lip.

After a moment Sándor's somewhat embarrassed protests died away and he stood still.

When Erth finally took his hands from him he said:

"You are jolly good at this sort of thing, Erth! My eye feels much better already!"

The blind man put his hands on his shoulders.

"I will take away the stiffness," he said. "Your body is bruised but there is no real harm done."

"If you do that I shall be able to ride," Sándor said suddenly in a different tone.

Erth smiled.

"You'll ride to-morrow, Master Sándor, and the bruises 'll fade."

"How do you know I have bruises . . . ?" Sándor began, then looking at Tamara grinned. "He is a wizard!"

"I think that is the right word," Tamara smiled.

She was so happy about the Duke that she almost felt she could dance on air.

She longed to go back to his room to talk to him, to make quite certain that his recovery was permanent.

Instead she ordered food for Erth and his grandson.

445

When they were leaving she slipped some golden sovereigns into the boy's hand.

She offered him five, but he shook his head and took only one.

She knew she could not argue with him and he was taking only enough to take care of his grandfather on his travels.

For reasons of his own Erth would not possess any worldly goods.

Erth saw Kadine and Vava, and as they all escorted him to the front door to say good-bye he took Tamara's hand in his and said:

"The poison has gone. You no longer hate, my child, but love. That's good! Now you'll find happiness."

Tamara looked at him in a startled manner and because the children were listening she did not reply. She only bent her head and kissed Erth's hand.

Smiling as if he understood why she thanked him, he and his grandson set off down the drive and Tamara watched them until they were nearly out of sight.

They went upstairs to the Sitting room and Tamara read to Kadine and Vava until it was time for them to go to bed.

"I can dine downstairs with you to-night," Sándor said to Tamara. "You heard Erth say I will be able to ride to-morrow?"

"I heard that," Tamara answered, "and you will also be well enough to do lessons."

"That is unfair!" Sándor said. "You said I need not do any until the end of the week."

"If you are well enough to ride you are also well enough to do a certain amount of mathematics," Tamara said severely.

Sándor made a little grimace, but he did not go on protesting and after a moment he asked:

"Why did Erth come here?"

"He said he knew that we needed him."

"He really has cured Uncle Howard?"

Tamara nodded.

She had not told Sándor that the Duke had been paralysed.

Now she thought to herself how incredible it was that if Erth had not appeared he would have been obliged to lie there immobile and perhaps later only move about in a wheel-chair.

"Thank you, God, thank you," she said in her heart.

Then even as she prayed in gratitude she found a question asking itself in her mind:

"What will it mean to you?" and was afraid of the answer.

Tamara came downstairs having left Kadine and Vava in Rose's charge while they rested after luncheon.

Sándor had ridden in the morning and she had insisted on his resting in the afternoon.

Although he made a feeble protest she felt he was in fact rather tired and quite prepared without much persuasion to lie on the sofa and read a book.

Tamara was going to the Library to find a book for herself.

So much had happened in the last few days that she had felt unable to read.

Only now when she decided to sit down quietly with a book for an hour did she find she had finished the two books she had taken from the Library and must therefore change them for others.

She had learnt from Watkins that the Duke had had a good night and was thinking of getting up.

"Please persuade His Grace to rest a little longer," she said to Watkins, wishing she could say it to the Duke herself.

"You know Erth Veryon said he would feel sore for a little while."

"It's very different, Miss, feeling sore an' being unable t' move," Watkins replied.

"I know," Tamara said, "but His Grace would be wise to take things quietly for the rest of the week."

The valet chuckled.

"You'll have to talk to him, Miss. His Grace won't listen to me and he resents being 'mollycoddled' as he calls it."

"I can understand that," Tamara said, "but try and persuade him to be sensible."

She thought that perhaps she would be able to see the Duke during the evening as she had a feeling that he might come downstairs for dinner.

She was therefore surprised when she reached the Hall and was just about to go along the corridor towards the Library when a footman came from the Blue Salon to say:

"His Grace wishes to speak to you, Miss."

"He is downstairs?" Tamara queried.

"His Grace came down for luncheon, Miss."

The footman opened the door and Tamara went in.

The Duke was sitting in an arm-chair by one of the windows.

When she entered he rose to his feet.

"Please do not get up!" she begged, moving quickly across the room, her eyes on his face.

He was looking magnificent as he always did and even more handsome than she remembered.

She thought, too, that he looked happy: there were no longer the lines of pain on his face, nor were there any of cynicism.

There was a faint smile on his lips as he watched her coming towards him. When she reached his side and looked up, there was an expression in his eyes that made her heart give a sudden leap.

"I have a lot to say to you," he said quietly, "and I must begin by thanking you for saving my life."

"It was Erth who did that."

"But you brought him to me, and I gather that in some strange way which I cannot understand he knew that he would be needed here."

"He was needed," Tamara said. "He has made you well again."

"I can hardly believe it," the Duke answered, "and as I have said I have to thank you."

"You are making me feel embarrassed," Tamara protested. "We are all so grateful and so very, very happy that you are well again."

The Duke raised his eye-brows.

"We?"

"Everybody in the household."

"You are sure of that?"

"But of course!" she answered, a little embarrassed by his probing.

"I am waiting for you to tell me it was my own fault that the accident happened."

She looked at him in surprise, then he indicated a chair opposite his own.

"Suppose we sit down?" he suggested. "I think we have a lot to discuss with each other."

Tamara sat down with a look of apprehension in her eyes as she raised them to the Duke's.

"It was intended I should have that fall," the Duke said. "I have since learnt that not only was the gate firmly fixed to the posts, but it had also been raised to a height which made it impossible for almost any horse to jump it without falling."

"Who could have done such a thing?" Tamara asked.

The Duke shrugged his shoulders.

"Any number of difficult people who are dissatisfied with the conditions on this Estate."

"What are you going to do about it?"

She thought as she spoke it was perhaps presumptuous of her to ask the question.

"Change the conditions!" the Duke answered. "That surely is what you would advise me to do?"

"I gather there is unrest here, as there is in many other parts of the country," Tamara said. "I think the working people need sympathy and understanding and somebody to listen to their complaints."

"That is exactly what I intend to do," the Duke answered, "so you see, our minds are thinking along the same lines."

He smiled as he spoke and she felt as if her heart moved in her breast towards him.

"And now," the Duke said, "suppose we discuss our nephew and nieces?"

Tamara's eyes opened wide and the colour rose in her cheeks.

"You can hardly go on pretending," the Duke said quietly.

"You . . . heard Vava call me . . . Aunt Tamara."

"I had rather suspected the truth before I had that confirmation of it," the Duke answered. "I could not believe any disinterested Governess would have been quite so passionately concerned for her charges."

Tamara dropped her eyes and her eye-lashes were very dark against her white skin.

"I . . . I thought you would not . . . accept me here if you knew I was . . . Maïka's sister," she murmured a little incoherently.

"I have an explanation about that which I would wish you to listen to," the Duke said. "You see, Tamara, I want you to understand my behaviour towards my brother."

She looked up at him when he used her Christian name and her eyes were on his face as he went on:

"When my brother Ronald married I was not in this country and had no knowledge of my father's attitude until some years later."

As if he realised Tamara's surprise he explained:

"In August 1808 I landed in Portugal under the command of Sir Arthur Wellesley."

"You were with your Regiment?"

"Yes, we were fighting the French on the Peninsula, and as you are well aware it was a long-drawn-out campaign."

"So you did not know your brother had married?"

"I had not the least idea of it, for as you can imagine letters from home, if they were written, seldom arrived on the battle-field."

"I can understand that," Tamara murmured.

She was beginning, she thought, to understand other things as well.

"It was not until I returned home after the war was over that I learnt from my father what had occurred."

"Why did you not then get in touch with Lord Ronald?"

"I wanted to do so, but my father, who was still furiously angry with him for having married against his wishes, declared that he had no knowledge of his whereabouts, and although I made several enquiries no-one else seemed to have any idea where he could be."

"But his allowance . . . ?"

"I was coming to that," the Duke answered. "It was not until my father died and I inherited that I discovered that despite my father's antipathy Ronald had been paid an allowance all through the years. I continued it, but I made no further effort towards a reconciliation."

"Why not?" Tamara asked.

The Duke looked away from her out of the window.

"This is hard to explain," he said. "I do not know if Ronald ever told you what our lives were like when we were boys."

"I gathered that your father and mother did not give you very much love or understanding."

"I think they disliked us," the Duke said. "We were relegated to the care of servants. The only times I can remember my father speaking to me was when he was punishing me for some misdeed or other."

He paused as if the memories of his miserable childhood were painful to recall. Then he went on:

"We were both of us much happier at school than we were at home, and I enjoyed the Army because it gave me the companionship and I suppose a sense of purpose I had never had before."

The Duke's voice sharpened as he went on:

"But it was a hard life and a very tough one. I would want no son of mine to see the sights I saw, to endure the horrors of a battle-field or to hear the cries of the wounded and dying."

Tamara drew in her breath.

She had never expected to hear the Duke speak in such a manner or to feel so deeply about the sufferings of other people.

"I came back to England," the Duke went on in a different tone, "determined to make up for the gaiety I had missed through being continually at war. I went to London."

There was a faint, mocking smile on his lips as he said:

"You are too young to understand what London seemed like to me after being in Europe for so long."

"It . . . shocked you?" Tamara asked.

She remembered the stories she had heard of the promiscuity, the raffishness and the extravagance of the Rakes and Dandies.

"I was shocked at the indifference and callousness shown towards the men who had fought and died for the freedom of this country," the Duke replied. "I suppose you might say it made me very cynical and disillusioned."

He paused before he said:

"I was also disillusioned where women were concerned, but that is something which need not concern you."

Tamara felt a little stab of jealousy.

Women, she was quite sure, would have found him irresistible, and perhaps he had found them alluring and very desirable after spending so many years almost entirely in the company of men.

"When I inherited the title," the Duke said, "I came back here thinking that perhaps my father's way of life and his indifference to other people's feelings was better than being emotionally involved in situations one could not help."

He paused.

"I did not wish to be hurt as I had been hurt as a child by the coldness and indifference of my parents. I told myself that I did not need love, that I could manage very well without love in my life."

Then looking at Tamara he said very quietly:

"I was wrong! I cannot do without it any longer!"

Her eyes met his and for a moment she could not move, until hardly knowing what she was doing she rose to her feet and moved closer to the window.

She heard the Duke rise too. Then he was standing a little behind her and so close that she felt herself tremble.

"You know what I am trying to say to you, Tamara," he said. "I think I have loved you since the moment I saw you with your eyes blazing hatred at me, and yet I knew you were what I had been seeking all my life!"

Tamara made what tried to be a little murmur of protest, but the Duke's arms were round her.

He pulled her against him, and before she realised what was happening his lips were on hers.

For a moment she was still in surprise, then she felt a sudden rapture so wonderful, so glorious, that she knew that this too, was what she had been seeking and yet had not been aware of it.

He held her closer and still closer and the pressure of his lips deepened on hers until she felt as if he drew her heart from her body and made it his.

She had never been kissed before, she had no idea that such a sensation of wonder and ecstasy could be transmitted from one mouth to another.

Yet it was everything she had always longed for, so beautiful, so spiritual that it was part of the divine, and she felt as if her whole body became alive.

The Duke raised his head.

"I love you, my darling, I love you more than I can begin to tell you!"

"I . . . love you!" Tamara whispered.

Then he was kissing her again, wildly, frantically, as if he was afraid of losing her and must make sure she was his and she could not escape him.

Now it seemed to Tamara that his kisses awoke a flame within her, flickering at first until it seemed to grow, burning its way from her heart, through her breast to her lips, to be ignited with the flame that was burning in him.

"You are so perfect, so sweet, unspoilt and innocent," the Duke said hoarsely. "Oh, my darling, there is no-one like you."

Then even as he spoke Tamara remembered.

She felt as if an icy hand gripped at her heart and with a little cry her fingers went up to her lips.

Then wrenching herself from the Duke's arms she turned and ran away from him across the room.

She pulled open the door and still running tore up the staircase, tears gathering in her eyes and in her throat until they were choking her.

As she reached the West Wing she tore into her bedroom and shut the door behind her.

Standing in the centre of the room her hands went up to her face covering her eyes.

"Oh, God, Oh, God!" she cried. "How can I tell him?"

CHAPTER SEVEN

*T*amara stood for some moments with her hands over her eyes. Then as if she made up her mind she rushed to the cupboard in the corner of the room and pulled out a leather round-topped trunk.

She opened it and started to open the drawers of the chest, packing the first things that came to hand.

She was kneeling on the floor in front of the trunk when she heard the door open.

"I am busy!" she said, thinking it would be Rose.

The door shut and she thought whoever it was who had come to find her had gone. Then a voice asked:

"What do you think you are doing?"

She started violently, turned her head and saw it was the Duke who was standing in her room.

She only glanced at him for a moment, then she looked back again into the trunk, still kneeling, her head bent, the sunshine pouring in through the window glinting on her red hair.

"I am . . . going . . . away."

It was difficult to hear the words, and yet she had said them.

"Why?"

The monosyllable seemed to echo round the room, and as she did not answer she heard the Duke cross the carpet to stand nearer to her while she still had her back to him.

"If you go away," he asked after a moment, "what will become of the children?"

"They will be . . . all right with you . . . now," Tamara answered.

And yet at the thought of leaving them she felt the tears come into her eyes and begin to run down her face.

She thought that if she kept her head bent he would not realise she was crying and after a moment he said:

"Can you really relinquish your responsibilities so easily?"

There was silence, until he added reflectively, almost as if he was talking to himself:

"You fought so hard and so valiantly for what you believed was right for them. If you leave them now they will lack the most important thing of all—your love."

It flashed through Tamara's mind how strange it was to hear him speaking in such a way.

How could she have imagined when first she came to the Castle that the autocratic, overwhelming Duke of Granchester would ever speak to her of love?

Or even more extraordinary, that he would kiss her and she would feel as if he was lifting her up into the sky?

She would never know such rapture or wonder again, she told herself despairingly, but she could not stay and deceive him.

Worst of all she could not tell him the truth and know that what he would feel for her was contempt and disgust.

"I do not understand what has upset you," the Duke said. "Could we not talk it over together, you and I, Tamara?"

It was the hardest thing she had ever done, Tamara thought, to resist him when he talked in such a beguiling manner.

She had loved him, she thought, because he was so

magnificent and because it was impossible to compare him with any other man she had ever seen or known.

She had known when he told her how he had suffered as a boy and how disillusioned he had been when he returned from the war, that she loved him with tenderness and compassion and she longed to comfort him.

But now she found him irresistible and she loved him in yet another way.

"I thought for one magical moment that your hate for me had gone," the Duke said in a low voice. "You said you loved me, and I believed you."

"I do . . . love you!"

Tamara felt the words come between her lips without her conscious volition.

"Then why, my darling, are you leaving me?"

"I . . . have to."

"You must give me a reason."

"I cannot do that. Please . . . please let me go."

"And if I refuse?"

Tamara bent her head a little lower and now the tears were falling from her eyes into the trunk.

They splashed down onto some of the garments she had already packed, but still she made no effort to wipe them away. She only wished she could sink into the ground and be swallowed up by quicksand so that the Duke could never find her again.

She heard him walk to the window to stand looking out onto the lake. After a moment he said:

"All my life I have known there was something wrong with the Castle. It is splendid in its own way, and I am not boasting when I say that its surroundings are more beautiful than you would find anywhere else in the whole length and breadth of England."

Tamara made a little sound, which might have been an expression of agreement.

"But I always knew there was something missing," the Duke went on. "As a child I remember it being very cold, and except when Ronald was there I think I always felt lonely and out of touch with the rest of the world."

There was a note in his voice which moved Tamara deeply.

"When I inherited the title and decided to live here," he continued, "I think the Castle itself made me more reserved, more introvert, than I was already. It was almost as if my father's shadow with his oppression and inhibitions enveloped me. I began to be like him both in character and personality."

"I am sure that is . . . not true," Tamara murmured.

"I think it is," the Duke replied. "In fact I am sure that I was becoming as cold, disdainful and harsh as my father was. Then everything changed!"

A new note came into his voice as he went on:

"You appeared unexpectedly, unheralded, and when I walked into the room and saw you there something inside me which I did not even know existed came to life."

He gave a short laugh.

"I did not acknowledge it at the time. I told myself that you were far too beautiful to be trustworthy, and I suspected that you were not what you purported to be."

Tamara thought, although she did not turn her head, that he looked at her before he said with a hint of amusement in his tone:

"I was right, and let me tell you, my darling, that no woman in her senses would engage as a Governess anyone so lovely as you. It would be far too dangerous for her peace of mind."

Again there was the new note of warmth in the Duke's tone.

Tamara felt her tears falling faster and because she was afraid that she would break down all together and lie sobbing at his feet, she clenched her hands until the knuckles showed white on the leather sides of her trunk.

"Every day you seemed to creep further and further into my heart," the Duke went on. "I found myself counting the hours until I could see you. When I left the house I had to force myself to do so because I was afraid of the emotions you aroused in me."

There was no doubt he was smiling as he continued:

"You do not know how many sleepless nights I passed lying awake thinking of you, wanting you, and yet aware that you hated me."

"How . . . were you . . . sure of that?" Tamara asked as if she could not help the question.

"If I had not heard it in your voice and the way you spoke to me, I could see it in your eyes," the Duke said. "I do not think any woman could have more expressive or indeed more beautiful eyes."

He paused before he added softly:

"But when I looked at them as I lay paralysed, they told me that you were feeling something very different."

He was silent for a moment before he said again in that beguiling tone that Tamara found so hard to resist:

"I thought then that you cared for me a little, and when you came into the Blue Salon just now I was sure I saw love in your eyes."

Tamara did not speak and he said:

"Was I wrong? Oh, my darling, do not torture me— tell me I was not wrong."

There was a pregnant silence and Tamara longed to rise to her feet and run to his arms. Then she knew that because she loved him so desperately she could not at the same time deceive him.

She knew the Duke was waiting and after a moment she said, the tears making her voice almost incoherent:

"I . . . love you . . . but I have to . . . go away."

"Why?" the Duke asked as he had asked before.

"I . . . I . . . cannot tell you . . ."

"You have to tell me. Can you imagine what it would be like if you leave me here tortured with questions I

cannot answer, wondering which of my many faults
has driven you away?"

"No . . . no," Tamara cried quickly. "It is not . . .
your fault that I am . . . leaving . . . it is mine . . .
only . . . m . . . mine."

"Your fault?" The Duke asked. "What can you have
done, my precious? What possible crime can you have
committed that you will not tell me?"

She knew he was supposing she must have some
quite unimportant reason for making the decision she
had.

"Please . . . will you try to . . . understand?" she
begged after a moment. "It . . . it is best for you not
to . . . know only let me assure you that it is . . .
nothing you have said or done . . . but something
which only concerns . . . myself."

"Come here, Tamara!"

She shook her head.

"I want you to come to me."

"Please . . . leave me alone," she cried, "if you
. . . l . . . love me just make it easy for me, to . . .
go away . . . then forget m . . . me."

"Do you really believe that is possible?" he enquired.
"I am not a boy, Tamara, who can fall in and out of
love a dozen times without it being a very serious oc-
currence. I am a man, and I love you as I have never
loved a woman before in the whole of my life!"

His words made the tears flood into Tamara's eyes.

"I . . . am not . . . worthy of your . . . love."

"Is that why you are leaving me?"

She dared not speak, she merely nodded her head.

"What can you have done that makes you say anything so foolish?" the Duke asked. "Or has there been
another man in your life?"

She heard the jealousy in his voice and, because she
could not bear him to think that was her reason for
leaving him, she said quickly:

"There has . . . never been anyone else . . . and
there never . . . will be."

"Now that you have said that, do you think I could ever let you go?"

"I have to . . . go!" she said desperately.

There was silence. Then so unexpectedly that she gave a little cry she felt the Duke pick her up from the floor.

He turned her round and held her close in his arms and because there was nothing else she could do she hid her face against his shoulder.

"There is no reason why you should trust me," he said, "and yet I am begging, pleading with you, Tamara, to do so. I have to know why you wish to leave me, why you think, feeling as we do about each other, we could either of us bear to live apart."

He felt her tremble in his arms, and said very softly:

"Tell me, my darling, what you are hiding from me."

"Y . . . you will be . . . angry," Tamara whispered incoherently.

"I doubt it," he answered. "We have both been angry with each other in the past, but strangely enough it only increased my love for you."

"This is a . . . different sort of . . . anger . . . and if I . . . tell you . . . you will . . . never speak to me . . . again."

She felt the Duke's arms tighten so that she could hardly breathe.

"I am prepared to risk anything rather than lose you."

"When you . . . hear what I . . . have to say . . . you will not . . . mind losing me."

"Are you prepared to bet on that?" he enquired and now again there was that note of laughter in his voice.

Tamara drew in her breath and freed herself from the Duke's arms.

"I . . . I will . . . tell you," she said, "but you must not . . . touch me while I am . . . doing so."

"I make no promises as to what will happen afterwards," he said.

She took a glance at his face. But because she could

not bear to look at the expression in his eyes, knowing they held the love that she had longed for, she moved away from him.

She stood as he had done at the window, looking out blindly into the sunshine.

She could not see the lake or the trees in the Park because of her tears, but she forced herself to hold some control over her voice as she said softly but clearly:

"I wrote the . . . novel 'The Ducal Wasp'. I am 'T.S.', the . . . author of it!"

It seemed to her as if her voice came back to her from the walls of the room almost as if they echoed every word she said.

Then there was silence—a silence in which she could hear her heart beating. She thought that having heard what she had to say the Duke would leave.

He would walk out of the room and out of her life. She would hear the door close behind him, and that would be the end.

But he did not go and because she longed to run to him and beg him to forgive her, to go down on her knees in front of him and plead with him not to leave her, Tamara held onto the window-sill.

As she did so she forced herself to remember that she had some pride and she must let him go as he would wish.

After a moment, in a different tone from what she had expected, the Duke asked:

"You knew it was libellous?"

"Y . . . yes."

"And scurrilous?"

"Y . . . yes."

"And vitriolic?"

"Y . . . yes."

"You meant it to hurt me!"

"Not . . . exactly," Tamara answered. "I hated you because of what your father had thought about my sister and . . . I believed . . . you thought the same."

"So—it was an act of revenge?"

"Y . . . yes."

"You must have known that I and other people who read it would recognise it as a portrait of myself."

"It was half-fact, half-fancy. People talked about . . . you, and as I invented the . . . villainous Duke I thought I was . . . paying you back for what your brother had . . . suffered."

"I suppose I understand, in a way," the Duke said slowly, "but it is the sort of book I should not have expected you, or any other woman to write."

"I . . . h . . . hated you."

"As your eyes told me you did when you first came here."

"When I wrote it, I never . . . expected to . . . meet you or even . . . see you."

"But when you did . . . ?"

There was silence for a moment, before Tamara said frankly:

"I . . . thought that . . . most of what I had said was . . . justified."

"Perhaps some of it was," the Duke said unexpectedly.

Tamara did not answer.

He had not raged at her as she had expected, nor had he been icily sarcastic and caustic as he might have been.

But she thought she had lost his love, and she felt her whole being cry out because she knew that without him she would never be complete again.

'For one wonderful moment I touched Paradise,' she thought. 'Now it is gone and never again will I know such happiness.'

Then she heard the Duke say:

"I suppose you are prepared to make some reparation for the damage you have done me?"

Tamara made a little helpless gesture with her hands.

"Wh . . . what can I . . . do?"

"You could of course, pay me damages."

"You . . . know I have n . . . no money."

"Then I am afraid you will have to go to prison—and it will be a life-sentence!"

As he spoke she felt him come closer, and even as she turned her head to look at him his arms were round her and he pulled her crushingly against him.

"A life-sentence!" he repeated, "and you will be imprisoned here in the Castle and I assure you I shall be a very severe jailor. You will never escape!"

She felt as if he had suddenly lifted her back into the sky and she was floating in his arms.

"Forgive . . . me," she whispered, raising her face.

He looked at her and she saw there was a smile on his lips.

"I suppose I shall have to," he said, "and we will burn that abominable book together. Then you shall write me another."

His lips were very close to hers as he said:

"Will you write a love-story, my darling? A story of two people who love each other so much that nothing else in the world is of any consequence."

"Are you sure . . . quite sure that is the . . . truth?" Tamara asked.

"I love you!" the Duke said, "and all the books in the world could not prevent me from keeping you with me and making you mine."

His lips came down on hers as he spoke and now he was kissing her fiercely, passionately, demandingly.

The flame that had been awakened in them before rose higher and higher until it seemed part of the sun and the heat of it consumed them both.

"I love you!" Tamara wanted to tell him.

But her heart was singing and anyway it was impossible to speak but only feel that she was part of the Duke as he was part of her.

It was a long time later that the Duke looking down at Tamara's shining eyes and flushed cheeks said quietly:

"How soon will you marry me, my darling? To-morrow?"

"I want to . . . belong to you," Tamara answered. "I will do . . . whatever you tell me to."

The Duke laughed.

"I am wondering how long such submissiveness will last," he said. "I have grown used to fighting for everything I want. I shall miss my most formidable opponent."

Tamara laughed a little uncertainly, then he was kissing her eyes and her eye-lashes which were still wet, her cheeks and again her lips.

As he did so she felt his fingers pulling the pins from her hair. He released it and it fell over her shoulders in a dark red cloud.

"That is how you looked when you were playing with the children in the hay-field," he said. "I have never seen anything so lovely or so desirable."

"You rode away."

"If I had stayed I would have taken you in my arms and kissed you!"

"I felt shy and . . . embarrassed because you had seen me looking so undignified."

He kissed her again before he said:

"I realise how hard you tried to keep me from knowing how lovely your hair is. You pinned it back in that tight bun but still, my precious, you could not hide its colour. It made me long, as I have never longed for anything before, to find the fire in you."

Because of the passion in his voice Tamara once again hid her face against him.

He put his fingers under her chin and turned her face up to his.

"I think I have awakened a little flame," he said, "but my darling heart, I will teach you to burn as I do with a love which will grow day by day and year by year until we are utterly consumed by it."

He kissed her again, then taking great handfuls of her hair which hung nearly to her waist he kissed that too.

"You are so unbelievably beautiful," he said, "that each time I look at you I find you are lovelier than I remembered."

Tamara gave a little sigh of sheer happiness, then said:

"It must be time for the children to get up after their rest. I must make myself look tidy. I would also point out that it is very . . . reprehensible for His Grace the Duke of Granchester to be in the . . . bed-room of a Governess!"

"If you sleep here to-night it will be for the last time," the Duke answered. "After that, my darling, you will be with me."

She blushed at the look in his eyes. Then as she moved from the shelter of his arms she said:

"You are . . . sure you have . . . forgiven me?"

He pulled her back against him as he answered:

"I will forgive you anything in the world as long as you go on loving me. That is all I ask of life, that I should have your love, and that you will never leave me."

There was no mistaking the serious note in his tone and impulsively Tamara put both her arms round the Duke's neck.

"I love you with all my heart and soul," she said. "You fill the whole world . . . there is nothing but you."

His lips, passionate and demanding, took the last words from her lips.

Then as they clung together the door opened and they looked round to see Vava staring at them in astonishment.

For a moment no-one spoke. Then Vava said:

"You are kissing Miss Wynne!"

"No," the Duke replied, "I am kissing your Aunt Tamara."

"How do you know she is my aunt?" Vava asked. "It is a secret."

"You told me," the Duke replied, "when we found you in the wood."

Vava put her fingers up to her lips.

"Oh . . . ! That was naughty of me!"

"As a matter of fact," the Duke said picking her up in his arms. "I guessed before you told me. You see, your Aunt Tamara is far too beautiful to be a Governess."

Vava looked from one to the other and said:

"Do you love Aunt Tamara?"

"Very much!" the Duke answered.

"Does Aunt Tamara love you?"

"I think so," the Duke said. "She has promised to be my wife."

Vava put her arms round his neck.

"If you are going to be married," she said, "we shall live here for ever and ever, then I can ride all your horses."

"The whole lot!" the Duke promised, "and have dozens of ponies as well if you want them."

"Oh, really!" Tamara interposed. "You are not to spoil her! She is too greedy as it is already."

"You promised! You promised!" Vava cried, "Oh, Uncle Howard, I do love you!"

She kissed the Duke on the cheek as she spoke and the Duke's eyes were twinkling as he looked at Tamara.

Her eyes met his and she knew they were both thinking that one day they would have children of their own and he would spoil them as now, because he was so happy, he was prepared to spoil his niece.

The Duke put out his hand.

"Let us tell Kadine and Sándor," he said. "I hope they will be as pleased at the news as Vava is."

"I say, that is jolly fine!" Sándor said when they told him they were to be married. "But I am not exactly surprised."

"What do you mean by that?" Tamara asked.

"Well, I sort of felt that you liked Uncle Howard a lot," Sándor explained, "and after he was so kind to us I had a feeling he liked you too."

"You know too much," Tamara laughed, but the Duke said:

"You are quite right, Sándor, and I think your aunt will make the Castle a very happy place for us all in the future."

"You are quite certain you want us to stay here with you?" Sándor asked. "We would not want to be in the way."

"Of course you will stay," Tamara cried. "We do want them, do we not?"

She looked up at the Duke as she spoke and he smiled down at her with such an expression of love in his eyes that she felt as if her heart leapt towards him.

"I think there is plenty of room in the Castle for two families," he said.

Tamara's face lit up and she said:

"That is almost exactly what Sándor said!"

Tamara looked at the boy as she spoke and Sándor a little embarrassed explained:

"I told Aunt Tamara that I was your heir, but she said you were young and would doubtless marry and have children of your own so I must not count on it."

"I hope you will not be disappointed if I do," the Duke answered.

"No, of course not," Sándor said. "I don't want to be a Duke, all I want is one day to have my own racing-stable."

"I should think that might be possible," the Duke

answered. "In the meantime perhaps you would help me with mine."

Sándor looked at him incredulously.

"Do you really mean that, Uncle Howard?"

"You will find there is a lot to do for the race-horses when you are at home in the holidays, and as Abbey is getting old I am thinking of engaging a new trainer. I am sure he would be glad of your assistance."

Sándor gave a whoop of sheer delight. Then Kadine, who had been rather quiet, came and put her arms around Tamara.

"Aunt Tamara, I want to ask you something."

"What is it dearest?"

"If you are going to be married could I please be your bridesmaid? I have always wanted to be a bridesmaid but nobody has ever asked me to be one."

Tamara looked up at the Duke.

"We are going to be married very quietly in the Chapel here in the Castle," he said. "I am quite certain that your aunt will want not one bridesmaid but two, and Sándor of course must give her away."

The children thought this was the most exciting thing that had ever happened and they all talked at once and by the time everything had been discussed over and over again it was time for tea.

The Duke had tea with them and only when the two girls went upstairs to go to bed and Sándor went off to the stables to talk to Abbey were he and Tamara alone.

They walked out through a side-door into the garden, across the lawn and down through the rose-garden.

As they reached the water-lily pond Tamara looked at the Duke and he knew she was thinking of how she had pushed Lord Cropthorne into the water.

"Sándor told me you were laughing when you found him there," she said.

"I laughed," the Duke admitted, "at the same time I was furiously angry! How dare he try to kiss you?"

He put his arm round Tamara's waist as he spoke and drew her close to him.

"I warn you, my darling, that I shall be a very jealous husband. If any man so much as looks at you I will knock him down and if someone like Cropthorne touches you I will murder him!"

Tamara gave a little cry that was very soft and tender.

"Do you really think I would ever want any man to touch me except you?" she asked. "Oh, Howard, you are so magnificent that you make other men in comparison, seem small and insignificant. I love you so overwhelmingly that there is no need for jealousy."

The Duke held her closer still, then he asked:

"How could I have ever had one moment's happiness until you came into my life? There is so much for us to do together, my darling."

"But the first and most important thing is to make the people on the Estate happy," Tamara said. "I should never know a moment's peace if you were ever in any danger again from someone trying to avenge themselves on you."

"You must tell me what I am to do," the Duke said, "and as I have already promised there will be many changes. I have told my farm managers to raise the wages of the labourers and to improve the condition of the cottages."

"Oh, I am glad, so very glad!" Tamara cried.

"It is you who have changed everything, and you will have to help me and guide me," the Duke said.

"That will be easy," Tamara answered, "because Rose told me her mother said that what everyone needed was a touch of love. That is what we have, my wonderful, magnificent husband-to-be and nothing else is of any importance."

"Nothing," the Duke agreed, "except you!"

He looked down into her eyes and said very softly:

"You fill my whole life and you are my hope of Heaven. All I want is your love now and for eternity."

"It is yours . . . completely and . . . absolutely," Tamara tried to say.

But the words were lost against the Duke's lips for he was kissing her fiercely, possessively, passionately, so that she could think of nothing but him.

She felt an ecstasy and a rapture that was indescribable sweep through her body.

It was so vivid, so intense that it was partly a sharp pain.

She pressed herself closer to him, wanting to give him not only her body but her mind, her heart, her soul.

She was trembling and she thought he was too.

Then he carried her up into the starlit sky where there was only themselves and the Divine power which is the very essence of love.

About the Author

❧

DAME BARBARA CARTLAND, the world's best known and bestselling author of romantic fiction, is also an historian, playwright, lecturer, political speaker, and television personality. She has now written over six hundred and twenty-two books and has the distinction of holding *The Guinness Book of Records* title of the world's bestselling author, having sold over six hundred and fifty million copies of her books all over the world.

Barbara Cartland was invested by Her Majesty The Queen as a Dame of the Order of the British Empire in 1991, is a Dame of Grace of St. John of Jerusalem, and was one of the first women in one thousand years ever to be admitted to the Chapter General. She is President of the Hertfordshire Branch of The Royal College of Midwives, and is President and Founder in 1964 of the National Association for Health.

Miss Cartland lives in England at Camfield Place, Hatfield, Hertfordshire.